TUI T. SUTHERLAND

AVATARS

BOOK TWO
SHADOW FALLING

An Imprint of HarperCollins*Publishers*

Eos is an imprint of HarperCollins Publishers

Avatars, Book Two: Shadow Falling

www.harperteen.com

Library of Congress Cataloging-in-Publication Data
Sutherland, Tui.
   Shadow falling / Tui T. Sutherland. — 1st ed.
      p.   cm. —   (Avatars ; bk. 2)
   Summary: Five teenagers are expected to battle to the
death in the post-apocalyptic New York City of 2087 as
representatives of the different pantheons of gods, who
chose them from their own ranks to be born and raised as
humans.
   ISBN 978-0-06-085146-0 (trade bdg.)
   ISBN 978-0-06-085147-7 (lib. bdg.)
   [1. Gods—Fiction. 2. Goddesses—Fiction. 3. End of the
world—Fiction. 4. New York (N.Y.)—Fiction. 5. Science
fiction.] I. Title.
PZ7.S96694Sha 2007   2007008615
[Fic]—dc22   CIP
                                                      AC

Typography by Christopher Stengel
1 2 3 4 5 6 7 8 9 10

❖

First Edition

*For Mom and Dad and Rick and Gwen—best parents
ever. Thank you for everything.
Love, Tui*

 Prologue

I was born in a world ruled by gods.

This worked out well for me, as I am a god.

Which god? Oh, I'm not going to tell you that. Let's just say you haven't met me yet . . . or at least you don't think you have.

There were hundreds of us once, even thousands. We were the all-powerful immortals, worshipped by your ancient civilizations. The gods and goddesses relied on this worship, and as more people believed in us, we grew stronger.

For centuries we were the rulers of our worlds.

But things changed.

Old civilizations fell and new ones took their place. New beliefs moved in, chasing out any fear of the ancient gods. The pace of life sped up, and technology took the place of magic, of worship, of belief.

The immortals were forgotten or cast aside, turned into history lessons, children's cartoons, or worse.

Still we did not disappear. We lived on as long as anyone remembered our names, although we were unworshipped, reduced, and full of vengeance.

Biding our time.

Individually, each god was weak and growing weaker. But if they joined forces, all these gods together could produce enough power for one final attempt at regaining what we had lost.

I wasn't invited, of course. They always liked to pretend I didn't exist. But that didn't stop me from coming along. If there's one thing I'm good at, it's crashing a party.

This was their plan:

Six pantheons agreed to participate. Each chose one avatar from their ranks: a god or goddess who would be reborn as a human on Earth, with no memories of his or her time as an immortal. They would grow up as seemingly ordinary children, then teenagers—although perhaps they could tell they were not so ordinary. The boy who blacked out during thunderstorms, only to awaken miles from home. The pop star whose audiences loved her at first sight. The girl whose steps led always through destruction and fire but who miraculously survived, time after time.

So, on December 21, 2012, something happened.

An earthquake. A flood. A thunderstorm. A shift in the wind.

And the avatars found themselves in a changed world, seventy-five years after their own time. Strange crystal monsters patrol the streets and skies. Grotesque hybrid animals roam the jungles of South America. And the only humans who still populate the Earth are old and either insane or filled with despair.

With their power, the gods created a world where humans stopped reproducing. No more babies were born; there were no future generations of people to look forward to. No matter what the scientists tried—artificial intelligence, cloning, anti-aging techniques, animal experimentation—human reproduction had come to an end. In this world, science lost . . . and the power of the immortals won.

It is to this barren landscape that the avatars have been transported. The pantheons intend them to fight, one against another, until only one avatar survives. With each victory, the winning avatar will absorb the power of the loser—the one who dies. In the end, the last avatar will be the strongest, and, with all that power, will lead his or her pantheon to rule the next age of the world, with all the other gods subordinate to them.

(At least that is what the gods are hoping for. My plan goes a bit differently. Here's a hint: I don't plan to be subordinate to anyone. Hierarchies are so boring.)

That much power is a great reward for the winning avatar. But it comes with great risks. By accepting their mortality for this task, the avatars have accepted the danger that they will die—and lose their immortality forever.

The stakes are high . . . and every pantheon has its strategy, its surprises, and its secrets. Unbeknownst to the others, the Greco-Roman pantheon has formed an alliance with the Egyptians. In exchange for the protection of the Egyptians' powerful avatar, Amon-Ra, the Greeks have offered him their goddess of love: Venus. She was inserted into their original avatar, Diana, goddess of the hunt and the moon, creating an avatar divided between her two selves . . . and one who is not at all sure she wants to be someone else's prize.

I had very little to do with that, although I love it. The Greeks have an amazing ability to create their own complications.

Over in the Indian pantheon, Shiva, god of fire and destruction and life, entered his wife, Kali—also a goddess of destruction—as an avatar without her knowledge. He then returned the goddess's memories to her, and is now hoping she'll accept her destiny and win this battle for them. Me, I'm hoping she eats him alive, because that would be much funnier.

Tigre, whose real name is Catequil, is the representative of the Mesoamerican pantheon. He's apparently a storm god, but no god from his pantheon has yet appeared to guide him.

And there are two avatars who have not yet arrived.

Not to mention the seventh avatar . . . the mistake.

Yes, I had a lot to do with that particular development. He's one of my pet projects.

The Polynesians, a pantheon that was not invited to participate, decided to send a combatant anyway. Using an accidental physical connection with Diana at the time of the Change, they shoved Oro, a god of war, into an ordinary boy named Gus. With no pantheon to guide him—and no representative on the panel of six judges—his prospects seem bleak indeed . . . but who knows what strength might be lurking inside him?

Who besides me, that is.

This is the battlefield. These are the players. And I am the audience, the carver of the chess pieces, the emperor with the power of life and death in my thumbs.

Let the games begin.

DAY ONE:
～⸫ AWAKENINGS ⸪～

CENTRAL PARK
NEW YORK CITY

There were intruders in her territory.

She could smell them, and she could hear them, and if she came out of her den, she could probably see them, but that was the problem: If she came out of her den, they might see her.

And she knew the others thought they should attack. All in the pack were hustling up, brushing too close, fur against fur, waiting for her to lead them out into the down-coming wetness, and show the intruders their teeth and chase them off with snarls and fierce fierceness.

What they did not know, because they were not the alpha dog, but which she knew because she was, was that these intruders were large, and they were much larger on the inside, and they were more alpha than any alpha she'd ever met, even her original alpha from long, long ago.

These intruders were not for challenging.

But if she did not, the pack would see and the pack

would know and the pack might think the time had come for a new alpha to come sniffing at her paws.

She growled.

Most of the pack scooted back with lowered heads and tails, but one, a dachshund with suspiciously moony eyes, bounced up instead of down and let out a wild yap of excited-and-fierce-am-I-am-I.

Alpha dog leaped to her feet and showed all her teeth and grrrrrrrrrrrrred him back down to the ground until he rolled belly-up sorry-sorry-sorry.

The intruders had been standing in her wide-sky space for a long time, so long that she had forgotten when it began, but not so long that she or any of the pack had come back around to sleepy.

If they did not leave soon, she would have to bite their ankles.

Alpha dog must protect her territory.

But these ankles were much fiercer than she and there could be stompings and thwackings and worse, and perhaps it would be safer to wait and fight a challenger for alpha spot than to attack with the pack, but safer was not alpha, and this she must do, or else the big ones might stay and bring more.

So many alphas in one place. She did not know how they could all be together at once with so little snarling and biting and peeing on things. They seemed to do all their fighting and alpha growling on the inside, which was scarier and harder to smell.

Something else was in the air, too. Something big and very, very alpha was happening not far enough away and she did not like the smell of it.

Suddenly, finally, the intruders began to move in their not-right way.

Most of them left as they had come, through the air and water and earth, which raised her hackles and twinged her teeth, because if they could disappear from air, they could reappear from air, and that made all spaces not-quite-hers.

Four stayed solid, but two went west and two went east.

Follow-follow-follow with teeth out and tails high, said the pack, pressing against her again. Snarl them out of territory.

If the intruders were leaving anyway, and it would make the pack happy . . .

Attack the less alpha pair. She growled again and leaped forward, and the pack followed close on the paws of her wise alpha greatness.

"Did you hear something?" Tigre asked, glancing around again.

"I'm hearing everything right now," Gus replied. "And I'm pretty sure every noise is some creepy new god coming to kill me." They pushed through the trees around the edge of the Great Lawn and found an overgrown paved pathway leading south. Only minutes ago, they had been standing in a circle of gods, finding out that they were avatars sent across time to battle one another to the death. Then Diana had walked away with Zeus, to stay with her pantheon and learn how to be a goddess, and Gus had no idea when he might see her again.

"They can't *make* us fight each other, right?" Tigre

said. "Diana would never try to kill us, and I'm pretty sure Kali wouldn't, either."

"'Pretty sure?'" Gus said, looking over his shoulder nervously. He couldn't shake the feeling that someone was following them. Earlier that morning—shortly after he and Diana had arrived in New York—the biggest crystal hunter had seized him and carried him off to the top of the Empire State Building. The other avatars had rescued him and destroyed the crystal hunter, but he couldn't help still feeling nervous.

On the plus side, now he was supposedly magically protected from them, like the other avatars were. That was one of Diana's conditions before she agreed to go off with the Greek gods. And the spell also seemed to have calmed down the violent sick feeling he'd had ever since the earthquake. Maybe the magic was helping the war god inside him adjust . . . or maybe the god was finally getting comfortable. He wasn't sure he liked that idea.

Gus squinted up at the overcast sky and realized that it probably wasn't even noon yet. It felt like this had been the longest morning of his life. Had it been only yesterday that he'd been with his brother, Andrew? And lost him . . . but he wasn't going to think like that. There had to be a way out of this. A way back to their own time, where Gus could have his life back . . . and Andrew's. He had to stay focused on that.

"You know what's weird?" Gus said. "I lost my glasses when the pterodactyl grabbed me, but I don't seem to need them anymore. I mean, everything's still a little fuzzy—but not as fuzzy as it should be. Maybe it's like a Spider-Man thing, where his superpowers gave him perfect vision. Except mine's not perfect yet. And, you know, no sign of those superpowers." *Nor is my ideal girl falling head over heels for me. I mean, if she were, she wouldn't have walked off with Zeus, would she?*

"I wonder how many other avatars there are," Tigre mused. "Are you sure you don't hear growling?"

"Amon's the one we have to worry about," Gus said, and anger swept through him as he remembered the way the Egyptian avatar had looked at Diana, all possessive and predatory. "He made it sound like he's planning to win this battle however he has to."

"I don't understand," Tigre said as they crossed a wider paved path that might once have been a road. "Why did the gods of his pantheon prepare him ahead of time but mine have said nothing to me?"

"I can't even think of any Mesoamerican gods," Gus confessed. "Not that I paid a lot of attention to history, but I don't remember anything beyond human sacrifices and conquistadors."

"The highlights of our culture," Tigre said bitterly. "Never mind the Mayan calendar. Never mind the Aztec temples or Machu Picchu."

"Hey, I've heard of that," Gus said.

"Honestly, though," Tigre said. "I've never heard of a god called Catequil."

"Catequil?"

"That's my real name. Mom said she found it in a book. Knowing how little she read, I always thought she just made it up. My sister Claudia started calling me Tigre instead—that's Spanish for tiger—and it stuck."

"Maybe we should try looking him up," Gus said.

"Find out what your powers might be. And I wouldn't mind learning more about this 'Oro, god of war' that's supposedly been shoved inside me." His fingers twitched involuntarily. "I *hate* not having the Internet anymore."

"Kali's good at finding information without the Internet," Tigre said. "Once we get back to her place and tell her everything the gods told us, she can figure out what to do next. Maybe her gods haven't talked to her, either. I bet she's going to be ma—"

He stopped suddenly in his tracks with a choking sound, and for half a moment Gus had the horrible thought that he'd been stabbed. Then Tigre turned with both hands pressed over his mouth.

"What is it?" Gus asked. "What happened?" He started around Tigre.

"No, don't look—"

But it was too late. Gus had already seen the woman . . . or what had once been a woman.

He slammed his eyes shut, but the image was stamped in his mind. The corpse was hanging in the air, suspended by a noose that wrapped around her neck and went up into the branches. Her long dark hair hung around her face, which had probably been pretty before it started decomposing. Her feet swung gently in the morning breeze.

"What is that?" Gus asked, carefully turning back to Tigre before opening his eyes. "How did she get there? Why hasn't anyone cut her down, and how could someone just *kill* herself in Central Park?"

"End of the world," Tigre said, bent over with his hands on his knees. "I can imagine it was a bit depressing."

"No, wait," Gus said. "She hasn't decomposed enough to be an end-of-the-world suicide. Can you smell a body? I can't. And she's not elderly enough to have died that recently."

Tigre said nothing for a minute, then squinted up at Gus.

"What are you saying?"

"I don't know. Maybe it's a trick. Some gods' thing to mess with our heads."

Tigre straightened, glanced over Gus's shoulder, and winced.

"She looks pretty real to me, man," he said, shaking his head.

"Let's go around her," Gus said, deliberately pushing his way into the bushes without looking back at the corpse.

Tigre hesitated, but he couldn't stop himself from taking one last glance.

The corpse's eyes were open.

She was staring right at him.

Tigre couldn't even yell, he was so terrified. He tried to turn and run, even to take a step backward, but his feet were frozen in place.

"Catequil," she said through gray, decaying lips. "A paradise is waiting for you. It could be easy . . . so easy . . . to come with me." One of her rotting hands reached out toward him.

An electric shock shot through Tigre as Gus grabbed his arm, jolting him into motion, and they ran pell-mell through the park. Tigre's brain caught up with the rest of him as he collapsed to the sidewalk outside, the palms of his hands scraping the pavement.

Gus threw himself down on the bench by the park wall, gasping for air.

"That," he said, "was the creepiest thing I've ever seen." His whole body shuddered. "Did you feel the air get colder? I wonder what she was saying, although I'm *so* glad I don't speak Corpse." He rubbed his arms fiercely.

"You couldn't understand her?" Tigre said, pushing himself into a kneeling position.

"Could *you*?"

Tigre nodded, catching his breath. "Maybe she was speaking Spanish. Sometimes I don't notice what I'm hearing, especially when I get used to hearing English for so long."

"No, I know a little Spanish," Gus said, shaking his head. "That didn't sound familiar at all."

Tigre felt ill.

"What did she say?" Gus asked.

"She wanted me to go with her," Tigre said quietly. "She said something about paradise." He shook his head. "How could I understand her if she was speaking some other language?"

Gus shrugged sympathetically. "If it makes you feel any better, I have a weird tattoo on my back that's been grow-ing ever since the world ended."

"Really?" Gus lifted up his shirt so Tigre could see the carved green spiral that had spread across both shoulder blades and now up to his neck. Tigre studied it for a moment. "Actually, that does make me feel better."

"It's a Polynesian symbol; I recognized it once those guys said I'm a Polynesian god. Warriors in lots of

Polynesian cultures would tattoo their whole bodies to scare their enemies. . . . I don't know if I knew that before, or if it just showed up in my head with this war god." Gus frowned.

A growl interrupted them, unmistakable this time, low and fierce and somewhere close by.

Tigre turned slowly and saw a small white dog standing just inside the stone walls of the park, teeth bared and hackles raised. Glancing into the bushes beyond, he could see the gleam of eyes near the ground and he guessed that there were close to twenty other small dogs behind the first.

"Whoa," Gus said, drawing his feet up onto the bench.

"There *was* something following us," said Tigre.

"That one looks just like my ex-girlfriend Lisa's dog," Gus said. "Except Cashew was cute and a bit fat, and he didn't have the energy to rip someone's throat out, which is what this guy looks like he's planning."

"Shhhhhhhhh," Tigre said. Gus couldn't tell if he was talking to him or the dog. The Chilean boy crouched lower and held out his hand, palm down, toward the dog.

"What are you doing?" Gus hissed.

"It's okay," Tigre murmured. "Shhh, it's okay. We're friendly. Don't worry."

Despite the dog's hostility, Tigre felt comforted to see it. This wasn't some strange hybrid monster. It was a normal dog—a little wild perhaps, but not that far removed from sleeping on couches in front of the TV. This might have been someone's pet once, or its parents were. He could understand animals like this, much better than pterodolphins or ancient gods or even other teenagers.

He felt a pang of missing Quetzie, the giant bird who had carried him from Chile to New York. She was uncomplicated and demanded nothing of him. He wished he could talk to her about this whole battle of the avatars, but she'd been chased away by the crystal hunters. He could use someone who believed in him.

The dog eyed his hand warily, but its snarl wavered. A tense moment passed as Tigre held his position, just out of reach of the dog's teeth. Finally, the animal stopped growling and leaned forward, cautiously sniffing his fingers.

"See, it's okay," Tigre said softly. "Nothing to worry about."

"Rrrrrrrrr," the dog rumbled, pulling back. It looked over at Gus, then at Tigre, and then slowly it backed away, watching them until it turned and disappeared into the bushes. As rapidly as they'd appeared, the other eyes blinked out, too, and with a rustle the dogs vanished back into the park.

Buildings burst into flames in the corners of her eyes. Bricks and mortar smashed apart; wood curled into blackened fingers. Explosions blossomed at the edges of her vision, and the scene before her wavered, overlaid with rubble and destruction.

But it was all illusion. Her mind, older than time and bubbling now with eons of memories, was playing tricks on her meager human sight. There were no flames here yet.

Kali could remember lifting a finger and bringing a city down in fire and ruin. She could remember being thousands of feet tall and crushing everything in her path.

The feel of the power, of the violence thrumming along her skin, was so strong, it overwhelmed the sensation of the pavement below her feet or the rain on her face. But she could not reach it. She tried to stretch toward the power, but it danced away, nimble, like her husband.

Had she thought herself powerful, just hours ago, in this breakable, bleedable body? Had she recoiled at her ability to bring down stone with her hands? That was nothing compared to her true strength, the strength of the Indian goddess of destruction. And to think she had spent eighteen years hiding it, pressing it down, loathing it, thinking there was something wrong with her.

Now she knew the truth: Destruction was her purpose. There was no reason to deny it—no reason to hate herself anymore—and it was the first time in her life that she could say she understood the word *glorious*.

Or it would be, if she could just manage to rain down chaos and havoc the way she was supposed to, instead of standing in a courtyard glowering at a building that refused to fall.

A hand touched her shoulder, then slid down her back to her waist.

"Don't be frustrated," Shiva said. "It will return as we work with it, and when you win, you will be stronger than ever."

"I need my worshippers," Kali said. She used to be able to feel them, like millions of lighter-than-air molecules lifting her up, pressing their warmth into her. Now she felt cold and empty, and her ancient mind missed them even as she found herself surprised that humanity could have any appeal for her.

"You will have them again," Shiva reassured her. He wound her long dark hair through his fingers and she heard his smile in his voice, mischievous now instead of sinister. She wondered how she could have been afraid of him when he first appeared. True, the third eye and the serpent around his neck might be unsettling if you weren't expecting them. But he was her other half; she would have thought she'd recognize him no matter what.

"I suppose you're going to tell me that for now, I have you," she said, stalking over to the wall and placing her palms against it. To her satisfaction, the power rose up through her and slammed into the concrete. Cracks raced out from her hands, speeding into a web across the surface. Looking up, she could see them climbing the building like ivy on steroids. The foundation began to rumble and small chunks of concrete thudded to the ground around her. It wasn't a whole city, but at least she could still turn one ten-story building into a pile of dust.

"Kali!" Shiva shouted in her ear, and she realized she'd been in a trance, watching the walls tremble in fear of her. "Come on," he yelled, pulling her hands away from the wall. "We have to move before it all comes down."

"Why?" She resisted. This was the first time in eighteen years that she'd allowed herself to destroy something just because she *wanted* to. This wasn't an accident, or her dark side's idea of self-protection, or part of a struggle to survive. She was destruction for the joy of destruction, and she wanted to stand in the midst of it as the building fell, as stones crashed down from the heights and flames engulfed the wreckage. . . .

Oh. Right.

"Stupid mortal body," she growled, following Shiva to a safe distance. "I can't believe you did this to me."

"There is no danger," Shiva said. "Now that you remember yourself, you know you are more powerful than any of the other avatars. It will not take long to destroy them, win the battle, and gain their power. Then we shall rule the world together."

"The empty world," Kali said. "What is the point of being the supreme gods if there is no one to worship us?"

"That won't be a problem," Shiva said. They climbed a pile of stones and swung themselves onto a window ledge, where they sat with their hands loosely entwined. The dark snake around Shiva's neck gave a pleased-sounding hiss and slid down his arm to rest its head across their wrists.

"You're not going to tell me what you mean by that, are you?" she said.

"Trust me," he said with a grin.

"How can I? After you abandoned our people?" she said. "Shiva, we were the third-largest religion in the world. Of all these pantheons, we were the only ones that anyone still believed in—we were strong and loved and real. Not like these shadows you're making me fight. If we had simply ignored them, they would have faded away, and we would have remained. And the world would not have had to end for a long while yet."

Shiva shook his head. "These 'shadows' are stronger than you think. Together, they had amassed enough power to do what they planned, with or without us. If I hadn't done this, we would've been left out. We would have lost our people anyway, and with no way to become powerful enough to bring them back."

Kali looked at him sharply. "Bring them back?" she repeated. "Is there a way to bring back what we have lost?"

His smile was gentle but maddening. "You know I'm not going to answer that."

"What about the avatars?" Kali asked. "Is there a way for us to get back to our own time?"

"No," Shiva said. "The past is gone. Leave it there."

Kali studied the lonely streets below them. "I wish you'd come to me sooner," she said. "Since the Change, I've been—I thought . . . well, let's just say it's a relief to know I'm not the one who did this." She waved her hand at the emptiness. "I'm glad I didn't make everyone disappear."

Shiva smiled. "You're not *quite* that powerful in this form, my dear."

Kali kicked the wall. "So, are there other things I didn't do? Other things that happened around me but weren't my fault?"

"Perhaps," Shiva said. "Anything specific you're thinking of?"

The image of her stepfather in his hospital bed rose up in her mind. But she wasn't ready to know if that was her fault yet. "Um. Nah." She glanced at Shiva's face, so earnest and open and weirdly familiar, and she leaned over and kissed him. She'd kissed boys before, as human Kali, but not very many—relationships weren't exactly a priority compared to supporting her family, running away to find her father, or trying not to destroy things accidentally. She'd certainly never fallen in love, and now she wondered if that was because her soul mate was out here waiting for her and part of her had somehow known that. Kissing him felt like something she'd done a million times before and hoped to do a million more.

When she opened her eyes and pulled back, she noticed that although his regular eyes were closed, his third eye was still open and staring at her.

"That's a bit creepy, dear," she said.

"If I close it, the light of the world goes out," he said, and Kali had a strange flash of a memory that felt like hers but not hers—of creeping up behind him and playfully covering his eyes with her hands, plunging the world accidentally into darkness. But the memory was light and full of air, not like the fiercer memories of fury and destruction. It didn't fit with the rest of her. She stroked the side of Shiva's face and let the image drift away.

"I've missed you," he said, leaning into her hand. "Eighteen years is a brief span of time for such as us, but I had no idea how long it would feel without you." He leaned in to kiss her again and she moved back, placing her fingers on his lips. She was pleased to see puzzlement in all three of his eyes.

"I'm afraid that *that*," she said sweetly, "was the last kiss you're going to get from me until you tell me exactly how to bring our people back."

"But—I can't!" he protested. "It's against the rules of the competition. There are things we can't tell the avatars until they win."

"I'm guessing that giving me back my goddess memories isn't exactly in line with the rules, either," she said.

"It's not expressly forbidden," he said. "I don't think it

occurred to them that I could do it, or would do it. But explaining the situation behind this playing field, and the solution of where our future worshippers will come from—I'm definitely not allowed to do that. We would forfeit your chances of winning, my love."

"Oh, well, then," Kali said, untangling her hand from his. The serpent hissed angrily as she moved its head back to Shiva's knee. "I guess that means no kissing for you." *What are you doing?* her mind cried. *You're finally with him again, but you're pushing him away—and for what? For* humanity? *You hate humanity! Remember? Noisy, selfish, annoying, loud, and always in your way? You should be thanking him for getting rid of them!*

But now that she could remember them—the feeling of millions of people who believed in her and prayed to her for help—something made her unable to rejoice in their destruction, even when destruction was her reason for being. It was complicated, and she didn't want to try and sort out her reasons.

Besides, she didn't like it when Shiva manipulated her, and she didn't like him knowing something she didn't. Perhaps that was really it.

"Kali," he pleaded. "I'll tell you everything when you win. I promise. You just have to defeat the others, and it won't take long once I help train you back to full strength."

"By 'defeat the others,' I assume you mean kill them," she said.

"Of course," he said. "Without breaking the rules—the judges will be watching. That won't be a problem, will it? You haven't formed any attachments to the other avatars, have you?" He sounded almost jealous. She wondered if he'd been watching her interactions with Tigre, or with any of the boys she'd ever dated. That must be strange, watching your eternal soul mate have a regular life, completely unaware of your existence. Not that he had anything to worry about with any of those guys.

"Don't worry, Shiva. I'll fight to win, if it means restoring our people. I understand the rules of battle." She narrowed her eyes. "All I have to do is kill the other avatars before they kill me."

"Good," Shiva said. "Because one of them is coming this way."

Diana would have expected the abandoned city to be wilder than it was.

She thought there should have been animals roaming the streets—cats, mice, squirrels, birds—anything. There should have been plants clambering up through the pavement, consuming the buildings, rioting through the streets. But just outside of Central Park, she could squint and almost believe this was just a really, really quiet, ordinary Sunday in Manhattan.

Well, not completely. Even on a Sunday, all the parking spaces on the Upper East Side would be taken; nowhere could you find these completely empty stretches of pavement. And the air felt cleaner than it ever had in New York, especially as the rain faded to a mist. She could actually smell the ocean.

She stole a glance at the tall bearded god who was leading her farther and farther away from Gus. Zeus walked as if he were parting the Red Sea with each step—like the air was swooping away from him on either side. They had left the park and seemed to be taking a wandering path through the streets of the Upper East Side. She was quite sure they were now heading in an awkward ellipse back to their original starting point.

"Where are we going?" she asked.

"You'll see," he said jovially. "No need to worry your pretty self about it."

Suddenly he stopped and put one hand on her head, as if she were a wayward puppy that needed shushing. She jerked away, but he didn't seem to notice. His storm green eyes stared about intently.

"Did you hear wings?" he rumbled in a low voice.

"No."

"Listen," he said.

He stood for a moment with wisps of steam coming out of his nose and ears, as if there were a teakettle trapped in his skull.

All of a sudden he whirled, and something fast and sparking exploded out of his hand into the branches of a nearby tree, which immediately burst into flames. A large dark bird shot up into the sky, circled them with an outraged caw, and then flapped off north.

"Why did you do that?" Diana cried. "What did that bird ever do to you?"

"It was a spy," Zeus growled. "It was trying to find out where our training grounds are."

"The *bird* was spying on us?" Diana said. "Don't you think that's a little paranoid?"

He shook his head solemnly, wagging his beard from side to side. "You truly have forgotten the ways of the gods. Most of them have creatures to call. *That bird,* I am certain, was one of Odin's raven spies. What are their names?" he mumbled to himself. "Hugly and Mugly, or something like that." He started walking again, and Diana hurried to catch up.

"Odin . . ." Diana repeated softly. "Isn't he the king of the Viking gods?"

"He is," Zeus grumbled. "Thinks he's quite the supreme all-father, too. Thinks *he* is king of the sky and all-knowing and all-wise just because he hung from a tree for nine days and gave up an eye to drink from a well of wisdom, or some such idiocy. *I* managed to rule my pantheon and still have two perfectly good eyes. I'd like to see him try his invincible spear against my invulnerable shield sometime. Or perhaps not," he added hurriedly.

"Is Odin one of the avatars?" Diana asked. They passed a building that seemed to have collapsed, and she glanced back at it, puzzled. It looked like there was still smoke rising from the ruins . . . but surely it had fallen too long ago for that. Otherwise, what would have made it fall now?

"No, no," Zeus said. "The Norse weren't foolish enough to risk their king on this adventure, either. Only the Egyptians were crazy enough for that—luckily for *us.*" He winked hugely.

"Yeah, Apollo told me about your plan," she said. She hated the whole idea of a secret alliance with the Egyptian pantheon. For one thing, it was cheating, and as twisted as this game was, cheating still seemed wrong. Moreover, it forced her to side with Amon—a guy she knew only from her dreams, and whom she had no particular reason to trust—against Tigre and Kali and, most of all, Gus. But the worst part was that her own pantheon hadn't even trusted her to win for them. They'd given her away to Amon like a prize instead, and now expected *him* to save the day. As if she were useless.

Well, aren't I useless? she wondered. *What's my special power? As far as I can tell, it's making people fall in love with me, thanks to my Venus half. I'm sure that's going to help me fight Kali's building destroying and Tigre's storm making and Amon's sunbeam riding and . . . whatever it is Gus can do now that he has a god of war inside him.*

Not that she would fight any of them if she could help it. She had to wait until she could get Apollo alone and pry more answers out of him. Her immortal twin brother seemed to be the only one willing to tell her anything; plus, as a god of truth, he couldn't lie to her.

"Apollo." Zeus sighed. "That boy is too honest for his own good, not that he can help it. Well, don't talk about it out in the open." He tilted his head significantly at the spindly trees lining the sidewalk. "Anyone could be listening."

"You mean like us?" a male voice said.

Zeus froze mid-stride and whipped around, but there was no one behind them.

"Up here," said a familiar female voice.

Diana raised her eyes and saw two figures posed in a large open window that had probably once held elegantly dressed mannequins and elaborate Christmas displays but now was swept clean of everything, including broken glass. The person standing was a tall, startling-looking young man with a third eye in the center of his forehead and long dark hair pinned in a coil on top of his head with what looked like a tiny, glowing crescent moon. His skin was dark brown but seemed to be reflecting blue highlights, especially around his neck. If you could ignore the third eye, and the large green-black snake draped around his shoulders, he was strikingly handsome.

But Diana was more surprised by the second figure, the girl seated in a lotus position next to him, leaning back casually on her hands.

"Kali?" Diana said. She looked like the girl who had helped Diana save Gus from the giant crystal hunter only a couple of hours earlier. But there was something indefinably different about her. Her eyes seemed darker, and she radiated a new aura of danger, like a predator lying in wait for something. In fact, the two of them reminded Diana of lions—the male standing guard, looking fierce and intimidating, while the lioness lay back, preparing for the real business of hunting and killing. She shivered.

"Diana," Kali said with an appraising nod. "Or is it Venus again now?"

"It's Diana," she said quickly, before Zeus could answer.

"An odd decision," the man next to Kali purred. "Stuffing two goddesses into one mortal—it's a strange choice even for you, Zeus." His eyes were fixed on Diana with a calculating gaze.

"It's not against the rules," Zeus said defensively.

"True," the other replied. "That's because it's a stupid thing to do. No pantheon in their right mind would even think of it, let alone actually do it."

"Now see here, Shiva," Zeus growled.

"An avatar divided within herself," Shiva went on.

"Her two halves fighting each other. However do you expect her to win the real battle?"

"I don't tell you how to manage your avatar, do I?"

"Oh, there's no 'managing' Kali," Shiva said with a laugh. The Indian girl smiled at Diana with an expression that seemed to say, *Don't you wish the same were true of you?*

"How dare you follow us around?" Zeus blustered. "Spying and sneaking about!"

"Actually, you came to us," Shiva said lazily. "We've just been sitting here. Although I am curious about why you've been wandering in circles for the last half hour— and don't get paranoid. It would be hard for a god like myself to miss the spikes of your energy trailing through the streets. Especially when you insist on setting defenseless trees on fire."

"Odin's spies—" Zeus hissed.

"Yes, I saw Munnin winging away. He didn't look pleased. I would steer clear of Odin for a while if I were you."

Zeus was nearly purple with rage.

"Listen, Zeus," Shiva said, jumping lightly down to the ground. "You're not going to be able to hide your precious 'training grounds.' Just accept that. Remember, at least four of the six judges must be present for a kill to qualify as a victory, at which point the dead avatar's power transfers to the victor. It would be foolish for any avatar to sneak in and kill your avatar by stealth, and thus waste the opportunity to absorb her power."

Diana got the feeling that he was relaying this information as much for Kali's benefit as anything else. Apparently Diana wasn't the only one who hadn't been told all the rules of this contest yet.

"Stealth," Kali scoffed. She rose to her feet, brushed off her hands, and leaned against the window frame. "A pointless and cowardly way to kill someone. When I decide to kill you"—she smiled directly into Diana's eyes—"I guarantee you will see me coming." Her gaze shifted to Zeus. "*I* am no cheater."

The Greek god moved so fast that Diana didn't realize what was happening until she heard the crack of thunder from his hands, but by then Shiva had already leaped in the path of the thunderbolt, catching the fire with his body before it reached Kali. And then Zeus had his hand clamped around Diana's arm and was dragging her behind him as they ran full speed down the street.

"Kali!" Diana tried to call, but then she was yanked around a corner, and her last sight of the Indian gods was Kali looking down at Shiva, her arms crossed, as the flames trailed along his skin and he screamed with rage.

"I'm going to kill him!" Shiva yelled as the fire flared out.

"Why?" Kali said, brushing ashes off his shoulders. "You're immortal, doofus, and so is he. Setting you on fire isn't going to do much. Isn't that the point of sticking the avatars in these mortal bodies? So we can be killed in this battle, and someone can win?"

"Exactly," Shiva growled. "But he was aiming at *you*. He was trying to kill you himself, and only the avatars are supposed to kill one another. If any of the other gods could just smite an avatar down when they felt like it—"

"I'd be dead already," Kali said. "Zeus was just angry and lashing out. Someone's a bit defensive about being accused of cheating, aren't they? I think you were right—he's definitely planning something."

"Some new underhanded way to win that we haven't thought of," Shiva said, narrowing his eyes. "We'll have to find out what it is. And hope he doesn't try to kill you again."

"He won't. He knows how fast his avatar would be destroyed if he succeeded."

"It wouldn't be fast," Shiva said, cold fury in his voice. "I would kill her slowly. I would peel the skin off her flesh and set fire to her hair and dance on her smoldering bones."

"Ew," Kali said. "I mean, thanks for the thought, but that won't be necessary."

She pinned the crescent moon back into place in his hair. Shiva reached up and caught her hand, bringing it down to his mouth and kissing it.

"I know," he said. "Because you are going to win this battle for us."

"Not just for us," she said, gently removing her hand from his. "Now tell me how to summon these judges when I'm ready to destroy someone."

Gus whistled when he saw the building Kali had chosen to live in.

"Pretty swank," he said, following Tigre into the enormous marble lobby, where doormen in pressed uniforms with shining buttons had once stood at attention. Even Venus the pop star would have fit in here.

"With the whole city to choose from," Tigre said, "my guess is she knew exactly where she wanted to go. Wait until you see the suite. It takes up two whole floors." The door next to the bank of gilded elevators was propped open, and Gus noticed that part of the door frame had been shattered.

As they started up the stairs, he commented, "I hope she didn't pick the penthouse suite."

"No," Tigre said. "I think she wanted something that would be easier to escape from if necessary."

"Plus, who wants to climb twenty flights of stairs every day?" Gus said.

Tigre pushed open the door on the fifth floor and led the way into an elevator vestibule with two large wood and glass doors leading off to either side. Gus realized the apartment was built in a square around the vestibule, wrapping back around in both directions to the other door.

Inside, enormous windows took up most of the walls, with views of Central Park out to the east. The rest of the wall space was covered in expensive-looking modern art. Some of it looked like it was supposed to be plugged in, so it could move or change colors. Here and there Gus saw statues that looked out of place with the rest of the decor: dark wooden elephant-headed gods and many-armed dancing bronze statuettes. He wondered if Kali had gathered them from other apartments and stores, subconsciously drawn to images of her pantheon.

"Kali!" Tigre called. "We're back!"

"We found out what's going on, and it's not aliens!" Gus added. "You're so going to wish you'd come to the park with us." Kali had refused to obey the voice in their heads that had demanded they all gather together. She'd insisted on meeting them back at the apartment instead.

But now there was no response. Tigre frowned.

"Kali?" he called again. Carefully sidestepping the piles of newspaper articles arranged across the wall-to-wall carpeting, Tigre led the way to the elegant wooden staircase connecting the two floors.

Upstairs, Gus counted five bedrooms, all massive. They reminded him of hotel rooms—filled with the basic trappings but none of the smaller details that signaled a room was lived in. He guessed the one closest to the stairs, with a dark green pattern of leaves on golden wallpaper, was Kali's. The bed was unmade, the curtains were pulled shut, and there were papers and clothes scattered around the floor. Three empty mugs with forlorn tea bags in them were clustered on the bedside table, leaving sad faded rings on the polished wood.

"Where is she?" Tigre said. "She said she was coming back here, didn't she?" He rubbed his knuckles, studying the room with a worried expression.

"Maybe she got sidetracked," Gus said. "Maybe she decided to stop and get food or something."

"Or maybe one of the other avatars attacked her."

"But we were with Amon—"

"He's not the only avatar out there, Gus. Remember? Amon said there were others. And that creepy Isis woman mentioned Vikings."

"Viking gods?" Gus searched his memory as they headed back downstairs. "I don't remember much about them, either. Man, I'm lame."

"Maybe she'll be back soon," Tigre said. "We should wait for her. She'll know what to do next." He trailed through the apartment as if he were still looking for her. They passed a library, a study, an empty spare bedroom, two half bathrooms, and a music room complete with piano, drum set, and harp. Beyond that, they came to what Gus guessed was the housekeeper's quarters.

"I think Kali can take care of herself," Gus said. "I vote for going out and looking for information." At least out in the city there was a chance of running into Diana. He already missed her more than he'd imagined possible.

"Okay. If only we knew where a library might be," Tigre mused.

"Are you kidding?" Gus said. "You don't know about the big New York library? It's right in the middle of the city—I remember because one of the times my parents brought us here, we walked to it from the Port Authority. I can probably find it again."

"Let's eat first," Tigre said. "I don't know about you, but I'm starving."

The housekeeper's rooms connected directly to the kitchen, which was gigantic—Gus thought it was probably at least the size of his and Andrew's whole apartment in Los Angeles. To his surprise, the light switch he automatically flipped as they walked in had an effect: A large modern-looking light fixture came on overhead.

"I don't understand," Tigre said. "How does any electricity work without people around to run it? And if any of it works, why doesn't all of it work?" He opened a cupboard and started pulling out cans of food, examining the labels.

"Andrew says . . ." Gus paused, fighting back the choking sadness that came with saying his brother's name. "He told me that people started worrying about what it would be like when everyone was too old and senile to run the power plants. They developed automated technology to keep the systems running on their own, at least for a while."

"It only seems to work here and there," Tigre said. "Kali probably picked this place partly because it still has electricity." He turned on the stove, as if to illustrate his point, and Gus felt a stab of envy for people who lived in places where everything was beautiful and worked smoothly. In their L.A. apartment, he and Andrew had often had to spend twenty minutes fighting with matches and the gas stove before a burner would light. Usually they gave up and just microwaved something instead.

As Tigre dumped a can of soup into a pot, Gus wandered over to the window and looked out at Central Park. The storm clouds had slid away now and bright sunshine illuminated the leaves. Even the pavement below them was sparkling. It was beautiful, but Gus didn't like the emptiness. His memories of New York were alive with weird, confident, unusual people. He could remember his parents steering him through museums, and how he'd wanted to watch the people instead of the art. He'd dreamed of living in New York one day, working backstage in a Broadway theater. But he'd stopped thinking about that after his parents died. Then he'd only wanted to stay near Andrew, wherever he was going to be.

He wondered where Diana was, and if she was thinking about him, too.

As he turned back to Tigre, a sunbeam coming through the window flashed against something—a spiral notebook, stashed high above their heads in the space between the cabinets and the ceiling.

"Huh," Gus said. He dragged a kitchen chair over and climbed up on the counter.

"What are you doing?" Tigre asked, setting out two bowls. He looked over as Gus climbed down again, and he recognized the notebook Gus was holding. Kali had yelled at him about it only yesterday. He was surprised that she hadn't hidden it better, considering how angry she had been to find him looking at it.

"What's this?" Gus said. He flipped it over and studied the cover, which was black, with orange-and-red flames around the edges. It was smaller than an ordinary school notebook, but thick with articles taped into the pages.

"We shouldn't touch that," Tigre said nervously. "It's Kali's, and I think it's private."

Gus had already opened to the first page and was staring at the article there.

"Seriously," Tigre said as Gus turned the pages, reading the headlines. "She got *really* mad when she caught me with it."

Gus looked up, his face pale. "Tigre," he said, "what do you know about Kali?"

"Well . . . she was born in New York and lives in Brooklyn with her mom and three little half sisters. She drinks a lot of tea. She can run really fast and she's brave in a crazy kind of—"

"Not human Kali," Gus interrupted. "The goddess. The one she's an avatar of."

Tigre frowned. "I don't know. She's Indian, isn't she?"

"The Indian goddess of destruction," Gus said. "She

represents, like, chaos and death."

"So there's one pantheon you do know something about," Tigre said, starting to feel angry, although he wasn't sure why.

"Andrew worked on a play where Kali was one of the characters," Gus said. "She was *scary*."

"Well, I'm sure your war god wasn't the nicest guy to be around, either," Tigre said. "It doesn't mean our Kali is dangerous."

"Do you know what this is?" Gus asked, holding up the notebook. "It's a record of terrible things happening—and all of them around Kali."

"So she's really unlucky," Tigre said with an uneasy shrug.

"Just the opposite," Gus said, flipping through the notebook. "She somehow survived them all. Look. Fires, sinkholes, mysterious collisions, catastrophes. But lots of other people weren't so lucky." He traced a finger across the medical records of a Bill Nichols, dying of lung cancer. One page, dated November 2010, listed the dependents covered by his medical insurance: Ellen Nichols, age thirty-six; Josephine Nichols, age six; Beth Nichols, age four; Amy Nichols, age three; and Kali Nichols, age sixteen.

"Nichols seems like the wrong last name for her," Gus said. "Tigre, this guy was her *father* or something. Maybe stepfather."

Tigre handed him a bowl of soup without commenting, and Gus set the notebook aside as they sat down at the long counter in the center of the kitchen.

"Tigre," Gus pressed, "how much do you really know about her?"

"Kali is not a bad person," Tigre said stubbornly. He remembered her fierce expression when they'd confronted the underground dwellers, the way she was sarcastic and prickly about everything, the casual grace with which she'd ripped open the door in the Empire State Building. "She saved your life, remember?"

Gus nodded. He knew how Tigre was feeling; he felt guilty about mistrusting her, too. But if this really was a life-or-death battle, they needed to be absolutely sure she was on their side.

"It's just . . . if she could do all this," Gus said, touching the notebook with one finger, "even before the world ended . . . how do we know she won't turn around and kill us once she realizes what is going on?"

Tigre was silent, thinking about rainstorms and blood and waking up with a gap in his memory, lying next to the dead body of an old man in a shredded raincoat. Could he really judge Kali for the things her power made her do, when he didn't even know all he had done during his blackouts? What would Gus think if Tigre told him about that night? Would Gus turn on him, too?

Tigre had seen Kali being gentle with Miracle, the girl who lived in the subways. He'd seen her rescue Gus without a flicker of fear. He had to believe there was something in her stronger than a goddess of destruction . . . or else he'd have to believe that there was no hope for him, either.

"Kali doesn't like being told what to do," Tigre said. "If someone tells her to fight us, she'll refuse just to make them mad."

"I hope you're right," Gus said. "I'd feel better if we got

out of here quickly, though. Just in case she comes back all powered up and ready to destroy us."

Tigre didn't answer. They finished their meal in silence.

There were gods waiting for them on the steps of the museum.

Diana counted eight of them, including Apollo, her brother, who had pulled her aside in the park. Each god was standing on a different step, facing her in an exaggerated waiting position, as if they imagined they were posing for a painting.

"Here?" Diana said, stopping in the middle of the street. "You just walked me around for forty-five minutes to take me back to the Metropolitan Museum?"

"I *thought* it would help protect you," Zeus grumbled. "Until we ran into that barbarian three-eyed know-it-all."

"What are we doing here?" Diana asked, following him onto the sidewalk. The figure on the lowest step was staring at her even more intently than the rest, almost radiating heat with his gaze, and she felt reluctant to get closer.

"This is where you will stay while you train to defeat the other avatars," Zeus said. With a huge wink, he added, "Or, you know, wait until someone else defeats them."

"You want me to live here? In the museum?" Diana said. "Couldn't I stay somewhere with a kitchen and a real bed, please?"

"This place is strong and well fortified," said the staring figure in a deep, raspy, smoke-filled voice. "It will keep you safe." He took a limping step toward her and Diana could see him more clearly, although there was a smoky, blurred aura around him. His head was shaved and he hunched, as if he was constantly leaning over something. His eyes were dark, bloodshot, and watery under thick eyebrows, and his skin was leathery and flushed. Diana glanced at his feet and saw that his left leg was twisted, thinner than the right, with the foot sticking in at an odd, painful angle.

He's very ugly, Diana thought, and immediately felt guilty for thinking it. She made herself study him more closely, looking for good features. His shoulders were broad, she noticed, and his arms were well muscled. His hands looked strong, like they'd been through several fires and now could bend steel to their will.

She realized uncomfortably that he was returning her scrutiny.

"*I* will keep you safe," he whispered harshly, jutting his face at her.

Zeus sighed, and Diana could have sworn she caught him rolling his eyes.

"Now, Vulcan, we've talked about this," Zeus said. "She's not your wife anymore."

Vulcan scowled, and Diana repressed a shudder. Now she recognized his expression; he had been staring at her earlier in the park, although he hadn't been fully manifested there. Apollo had pointed him out. As far as she could remember, this god of blacksmiths and fire had been married to Venus—to her—in the old myths. *But didn't Venus cheat on him? With—*

"Mars!" Zeus cried jovially. "Look at our little Venus. Isn't she a fetching mortal?"

Arms encircled Diana's waist before she could turn, and she felt herself squashed back against a metal breastplate. A pair of burning lips pressed into her neck, and for once, her angry side won out with no argument from the affectionate part of her brain.

"Get *off*!" she yelled, stamping down hard on a bare foot and driving her elbow back, out of some buried instinct, directly into the open space between two metal plates.

With a howl of rage, the god fell back, clutching his side. Zeus bellowed with laughter, so loud and long that Diana thought he might split in half.

Mars, the god of war, was unmistakable. He was dressed in full battle armor, up to and including the feathered helmet on his head. His coppery red curls were wound in tight springs across his head, and his small eyes flashed with anger. He was classically handsome, despite the ferocious grimace on his face, but Diana thought there was something cruel in his features.

"I guess things have changed, Mars," Apollo said, descending the steps to stand next to her. "She's not 'your little Venus' anymore." He gave Diana a wink, and with a feeling of relief, she took his hand and squeezed it. She didn't remember her twin brother any more than the other gods, but there was a lightness and openness about him that reassured her—that and the fact that his face looked so much like hers.

"You *cow*," Mars spat. "You were much prettier as Venus. Now you're just a soft, useless version of Diana. But you were mine once, and if you ever recover enough of your real brain to remember that, you'll be sorry that you lost me."

"She was never *yours,* Mars," Vulcan growled.

"Well, she certainly wasn't yours," Mars said with a snarl. Throwing the corner of his cloak over his shoulder, he stormed up the stairs and into the museum without a backward glance.

Diana looked around at the other people standing on the steps. Most of them were wearing amused expressions and whispering to one another, as if they had enjoyed watching the fight. She didn't see a single face that looked either familiar or friendly.

She missed Gus. She wished she hadn't listened to Apollo and played along with her pantheon. She wanted to be back at Kali's apartment, with her and Tigre and Gus, instead of with these self-styled puppeteers.

Then she remembered what Kali had said, and a tendril of icy cold ran through her. Kali was playing this game. Kali was planning to kill them. At least that's what she'd said . . . but was she just playing along, too, to trick the gods overseeing her?

Frustrated, Diana ran her hands through her hair, and Apollo took her arm.

"You're tired," he said. "And hungry and confused. Come. Things will make more sense soon."

Diana doubted that. But she let him lead her up the stairs, past a sea of curious eyes. At the top of the steps, there was a forbiddingly tall woman with a cylindrical crown on her head that brought her to well over six and a half feet. She towered over Diana with an expression of distaste.

As they approached, a movement on the stairs caught Diana's eye. She looked down and jumped when she realized there was a peacock peering out from behind the woman's long gown. Its beady-eyed gaze was nearly as unsettling as the woman's, and Diana pressed close to Apollo. But even when they'd gone through the doors into the cool marble lobby, she felt as if they were still watching her—the woman's large dark eyes, the peacock's small beady ones—and she wondered if she had more enemies inside her own pantheon than among the avatars.

Tigre couldn't stop thinking about the hanging woman in the park. Where had she wanted to take him? Was she from his own pantheon? Was she the guide he was supposed to be looking for? If she was, why had she deliberately terrified him?

As he and Gus headed south on Broadway, he squinted up at the sun, now high in the sky. All the clouds he'd managed to summon earlier that morning had vanished. And he couldn't shake the feeling that someone was watching them.

He was right.

Tigre saw it first, floating in a patch of sunlight between buildings about half a block away. It was hazy but definitely there. He seized Gus's sleeve and yanked him to a halt, pointing.

"What is that?" Gus whispered.

"I'm not hallucinating?" Tigre whispered back. "You see it, too?"

"It's gigantic," Gus said. "How could I miss it?"

The two boys walked toward it cautiously. The large disk was as tall as Tigre, perhaps taller, and floated about a foot off the ground. Shooting out of it in every direction were rays that looked like they'd been beaten out of gold. The whole thing shone, even through its blurriness, like a miniature sun captured, flattened, and hung out in the streets of New York.

Tigre reached out to it and discovered that it was radiating heat, but only faintly. He stepped forward and gingerly touched the surface. For a moment he could feel warm metal flow slowly under his fingers, and then, not two inches away from his hand, a pair of giant eyes opened.

Tigre and Gus both jumped back, but Tigre was more startled than scared. There was something nonthreatening about the wide face, which formed on the disk as if a giant on the other side were pressing his features through. The eyes blinked in a languid, melting way, like the eyelids were pools of gold sliding down over the eyeballs and then retreating again. There were no colors on the face—everything was shades of gold, like a sculpture—but Tigre could tell where the pupils were, and that they were focused on him.

"Catequil," the disk said once its mouth had formed. "I am pleased to see you looking so strong."

"Me?" Tigre said. He didn't feel strong. He felt just about the opposite of godlike.

"I don't have much time," the face said. "I can only manifest when the sun is at its peak. That is when you can look for me, if you need me."

"Who are you?" Tigre asked.

"I am Inti," it said.

"Tell him to speak English," Gus whispered, and Tigre realized that, like the hanging woman in the park, Inti was speaking in some language only Tigre could understand.

"He's the Incan sun god," Tigre said to Gus. "I don't think he can speak English."

"Why not? The Egyptians did. And he seems to understand you."

"I do understand," Inti rumbled. "But it is difficult enough for me to manifest. Attempting to translate myself as well would exhaust my power for today."

Tigre felt a shiver of fear. If this god, once one of the most powerful in Mesoamerica, was so weak now . . . and the Egyptians were so strong . . . how could Tigre stand a chance in this battle?

"Can you help us?" he asked. "Tell me what to do, how to fight, how to stay alive . . . anything?"

"You will have a trainer, like the others," Inti said, and his nostrils flared in a sigh. "But he is a bit reluctant. I am sure I will convince him to come to you soon."

"Why—why is he reluctant?" Tigre asked.

Inti's face was grave, and Tigre immediately regretted asking, but it was too late to take back the question.

"Most of our pantheon do not have much hope for victory," Inti explained. "It has been a long time since we ruled anything, and most of us have been forgotten so completely that our power is almost nonexistent. We entered this contest to stay in the game, but many of them think you cannot win. They are prepared to wait for the cycle to come around again, and hope for better chances in the next turn of the wheel."

"But what about me?" Tigre said. "If I lose this battle, won't I be dead by the next 'turn of the wheel'?" Gus looked like he wanted to interrupt, but at the word *dead*, his eyes widened and he closed his mouth.

"That is why they chose you to be our avatar," Inti said, turning his eyes down. "Most of our pantheon think of you as . . . expendable."

"Expendable?" Tigre yelped. "Don't I get a say in this?" The storm clouds were back in the sky, massing on the horizon as the anger built up in his chest. Gus cocked his head as if he were listening to faraway sounds.

"I will keep hoping for you," Inti said. "And I will try to send Tlaloc to you soon. That is all I can do."

The wind was rising fast. Gus glanced at Tigre and then nodded down the street to a dark shape, still distant but growing larger as it headed their way. Something else was coming. Tigre knew they should probably hide, but he wanted more answers from Inti first.

He realized that the sun god was fading, his features blending back into the disk, the rays dissolving into the fading sunlight.

"Inti, wait," he said desperately. "It's not fair."

"Neither was our conquest," Inti said, his voice barely audible. "But that is the way this cycle is written. We have no choice but to accept it." He brightened again for a moment. "This war god you travel with may help keep you safe for now. His pantheon has made him as strong as possible. Just beware whom you trust. Everyone is trying to survive."

And he was gone.

"Hey, man, let's get out of the street," Gus said. "Whatever's coming, I don't want to be in its way when it gets here."

Tigre brushed his hand through the air where Inti had been, but there was no sign the sun god had ever been there. He sighed and followed Gus inside a nearby sporting goods store, where Gus took a dusty baseball bat and handed Tigre a golf club.

They both peered down the street, leaning out through the open space where a display window had once been. The wind was whipping fiercely between the buildings now, and the storm was rumbling up, turning the sky dark, so it was hard to see what was coming. Over the sound of the wind they could hear thunder, but it came from street level, not from the sky.

"So what did Mr. Sun Face say to you?" Gus asked.

"Nothing helpful," Tigre muttered.

Gus gave him a sideways look. He could guess part of it from hearing Tigre's side of the conversation, and he was pretty sure Tigre wasn't in a much better situation than he was. At least Tigre had a pantheon—but from what he'd seen, Gus thought perhaps he was better off without strange immortal beings trying to communicate with him. He didn't know much about Polynesian gods, but if there were any suicidal rotting corpses or big shiny disks among them, they could definitely stay out of his life.

"What do you think is coming?" Tigre asked, nodding at the dark cloud down the street. "Another god?"

"Or some new kind of futuristic monster."

But the first thing they saw wasn't at all what they expected.

She appeared ahead of the thunder, running down the center of the dark street as if all the demons of the underworld were chasing her. *In this version of the universe, maybe they are,* Tigre thought.

Gus didn't hesitate. "Over here!" he called.

The girl cast a look over her shoulder, then changed course, leaping through the clutter in the window to crouch beside them. She leaned on them—casually, like they were old friends she knew she could rely on—and gasped for breath.

Tigre registered two things: She was about their own age and she was beautiful. Her dark hair was just above shoulder length, straight but flipping up at the ends, and her caramel-colored skin smelled like oranges. She had a sweet, open face with partly Asian features, and a figure like none he'd ever seen before. She looked like a sexier version of Diana, which was saying something. If Diana were made of water and air, this girl was fashioned from earth and fire.

"Are you okay?" Gus asked.

"Just promise me you're not homicidal maniacs," she said breathlessly.

"We're not," Gus said with a smile. Tigre glanced down at his hands, wondering if that was true. "I'm Gus, and this is Tigre."

"I'm Anna," she said, pronouncing it with a round *a* so it rhymed with Donna. If she was another avatar, there weren't any clues in her name, Tigre reflected.

"What's chasing you?" Gus asked, leading her farther into the sporting goods store.

"You're not going to believe me," she said.

Tigre and Gus exchanged glances.

"Oh, I think we might," Gus said.

"Whatever it is, we'll protect you," Tigre added.

"That's sweet, but you don't want to fight this guy," she said. "He's *crazy*."

A bellowing voice from outside interrupted them, and Tigre and Gus spun around, raising the bat and the golf club.

An odd wooden chariot was pulling up outside the sports shop. Yoked to it were two fierce-looking shaggy animals with fiery eyes.

"Are those *goats*?" Tigre whispered to Gus.

"Largest, angriest goats I've ever seen," Gus responded, eyeing their unnaturally long teeth.

As the chariot rolled to a stop, the sound of thunder died, and Tigre realized it had been coming from the wheels. The huge figure driving the chariot flung the reins aside and stepped down, grinning enormously.

He might have been their own age, but he was twice the girth of Gus and half a foot taller than Tigre, which made him the height of some of the gods they'd met earlier that morning, like Zeus. Unlike Tigre and Gus, he clearly needed to shave every day, and he clearly hadn't done so in at least a week. The beginnings of a beard as brightly red as his unruly hair bristled across his face below blazing blue eyes.

He was also carrying a gigantic hammer that looked like it could crush the baseball bat, the golf club, and pretty much everything else in the store into kindling with one blow.

"Avatar or god?" Gus asked Tigre as the newcomer stormed toward them. "What do you think?"

Tigre couldn't tell, but he guessed this was one of the Vikings Isis had mentioned. Of course the Norse pantheon was involved in this. From everything he'd learned about them in school, they loved war and fighting for glory. And this guy looked like he was no exception.

"Wait," Gus tried as the stranger stepped through the window. "We don't want to hurt you."

"Or be hurt *by* you," Tigre muttered.

"ALLBJILLNIRROKHEIMALL!" the Viking bellowed unintelligibly, raising his hammer.

"Can't we talk about this?" Gus said. "Are you an avatar, too? Has your pantheon spoken to you? Because we're avatars, but we've decided we don't want to fight anyone, and if you joined—"

Gus's plea was cut short as the hammer came smashing down inches away from his head.

"Hey!" Gus shouted. "We're trying to talk to you reasonably here!"

"I don't think he speaks English," Anna said.

Tigre stared at her, openmouthed. Why hadn't that occurred to him?

"Do you know his name?" Gus cried, dodging another swing of the hammer. The giant was still grinning and moving slowly, like he was only toying with them.

"Thor," Anna said. "If I understood him right."

"Viking thunder god," Gus said to Tigre.

"I know," Tigre said. "Look out!"

Thor's hammer crashed through a case of pedometers and they all ducked to protect their faces from the shower of flying glass.

"So what language *does* he speak?" Tigre called, crawling behind a display of sad-looking deflated basketballs.

"Probably Norwegian or Swedish," Gus replied. "I guess neither of you—"

"Nope," Anna said.

"No," Tigre agreed.

"Hey!" Gus yelled, jumping in front of Thor and waving his arms wildly. "Stop! No! Stop trying to kill us!"

"HA!" Thor bellowed, waving his arms in an imitation of Gus. *"KOMISKLITEMAN! HA HA!"* Then he swung one log-sized arm around and casually knocked Gus to the ground.

"Gus!" Tigre shouted, starting forward, but Anna grabbed his arm and pulled him back behind the display.

"We can't all just throw ourselves in his way," she said. "We need a better plan."

"Well," Tigre said, trying to think. He wished Kali were there—she was better at planning than he was. Not to mention she was probably the only one of them who could actually take on Thor. What would she do here? Tigre thought back to that morning on top of the Empire State Building. He glanced at Anna. "Do you—okay, this might sound kind of weird, but do you have any powers?" he asked.

"Powers?" she repeated, wrinkling her nose in a cute way. Beyond the display, Gus rolled out of reach of Thor's hammer and sprang to his feet again, still shouting. He ran behind the sales counter and into a back office with Thor chasing him.

"Yes, like making buildings fall down, or—"

"Why would I?" she asked.

"Because—you don't know about the pantheons? How we're avatars of different gods?"

She shook her head, an astonished expression on her face.

"Okay, we'll fill you in later. I just wondered if you could do anything weird that might be helpful."

"Sorry," she said, lifting her hands palms-up. "Not that I know of. What about you? Do you have powers?"

"I can sometimes call storms," Tigre said with a sigh. "As if that's helpful. I'm guessing a god of thunder like Thor wouldn't care much if I did anyway."

"And Gus?" she said, nodding in the direction of the slamming and crashing sounds.

"He's some kind of war god," Tigre said. "He isn't the most warlike guy, though."

Another loud crash sounded from the office and Thor came stumbling backward out the door, shouting. Gus appeared in the doorway, his eyes blazing. In one hand he held a fishing rod like a spear, with the baseball bat brandished in the other. He looked taller, suddenly, and a lot more scary than Tigre had ever seen him.

"I said STOP!" he yelled, hurling the fishing rod at Thor so fast that Thor didn't have time to sidestep. It struck him in the shoulder of the arm holding the hammer, and Thor nearly dropped the hammer, wincing.

Anna took a crouching step backward.

"Don't worry," Tigre said, wishing he were brave enough to take her hand or touch her shoulder. "Gus is harmless."

"You're sure of that?" she said. "Thor seemed like a nice guy, too, until he tried to kill me."

Thor swung his hammer up in a powerful arc, and Gus dodged it neatly, whirling quickly to knock Thor in the back of the head with the baseball bat. Thor let out a fierce roar and attacked again, but Gus rolled over the counter and sidestepped in a graceful, liquid movement, whacking Thor's shoulder again with surprising force.

Gus had no idea what was happening to him. He felt like someone else had taken over his body. Every move felt unfamiliar and yet natural, his muscles protesting even as they fell into a rhythm. He was terrified, but at the same time filled with a wild glee. *Maybe I do have some powers after all. Maybe there's hope for me yet. Maybe I could actually win this contest and be with Diana ag—*

CRACK!

While Gus's eye was on the hammer, Thor's enormous fist flew out from the other side and connected with his jaw. Gus staggered back, collided with a rack of sweat-shirts, and ended up in a heap on the floor, his head swimming with pain.

"*HA HA!*" Thor bellowed, standing over him. "*THORSEGERIK!*"

He's going to kill me, Gus thought. *He's going to kill me right now and there's nothing I can do about it.* He tried to stand up, but his vision was swimming and his knees seemed unable to hold him.

"I have to stop him," Tigre said, getting to his feet.

"But Tigre, he'll only kill you, too," Anna protested.

"I have to try," he said, but his voice shook and he knew she could tell how afraid he was. Still, he stepped out from behind the display and shouted in a horribly weak voice, "Hey! Thor!"

Thor ignored him. He leaned over Gus, the enormous grin still on his face, and Gus watched Thor's giant hand reach out toward him, wondering if he meant to strangle Gus instead of crushing him with his hammer. But instead, Thor gripped Gus's free hand and hauled him to his feet.

"VANSAKOMPADEDOGOD!" he roared, thwacking Gus on the shoulder with enough force that Gus nearly fell over again. *"VIMASTAKOMPIGEN!"*

And with a whistle, he hoisted his hammer over one shoulder, crashed through the display, climbed on his goat-drawn chariot, and rolled away, trailing sounds of thunder behind him.

Gus and Tigre stared after him in disbelief.

Why were they still alive?

"Okay," Anna said, following them out of the wreckage. "Now can you tell me what's going on here?"

Thor!

What an amusing avatar.

*Personally, I never cared for him as a god. A little too per-
fect, too sure of himself, if you ask me.*

*But as an avatar, he's absolutely darling. He doesn't remem-
ber anything about being "the hero of the gods." Only Shiva
risked giving back his avatar's memories, because he knew Kali
was strong enough to take it. That kind of knowledge, eons of
experience, would no doubt overload a simple mortal brain like
Thor's.*

*So now he's just a big, dumb, lovely human. Those are my
favorite. But it does make him harder to predict. Before, you
could count on Thor's arrogance. You could twist it to get anything you wanted.*

*But now he might do anything: He might turn out to be
full of mushy goodness, or he might be a raging monster. He
might decide to nobly spare some lives, or he might smash his
hammer through the skull of each and every avatar, just as
Odin ordered. Without the memory of centuries of adoration,
of being puffed up by all the other gods, what will Thor's inher-
ent nature be like?*

Won't it be fun to find out?

Nobody was home. Kali had been watching the windows

of her apartment for half an hour, and she was sure Tigre or Gus would have come into view at some point in that time. She'd left Shiva to find them, but now she wasn't sure she wanted to.

She leaned against the wall outside Central Park, flipping her pendant through her fingers. She hadn't thought about it since the world ended, but now that she knew who she really was, she wondered who her father had been and whether he had known about the avatars. Why else would he have left the pendant with her name on it?

Could he have been a god? Vishnu, the supreme Hindu god of goodness and order, sometimes manifested on Earth in human form. But usually he did that only in times of great peril for the world. Impregnating her mother with her didn't seem like an important-enough reason for him to show up. Could he have done it without becoming fully human? Zeus had gotten plenty of women pregnant while still a god, but she didn't know if Vishnu had the same ability.

If her father was a god, that might explain why she seemed stronger than the other avatars, and why her powers had started appearing sooner. Or perhaps it was the strength of her pantheon. Because of all her worshippers in 2012, maybe she was naturally the strongest.

If that was true, perhaps she could use new worshippers to make her even stronger. This world was mostly empty, but she'd seen glimpses of life. The subway dwellers already thought she had magic powers, and they were desperate for something to worship—look how they had attached themselves to the Miracle, just because she was the only person born in the last seventy-five years. If they could expend so much love on a thirteen-year-old child, how much more might they have for someone with real powers?

And then there were the two people (perhaps more?) in the art museum, whoever they might be. She'd caught only a glimpse of them, but she knew they were information gatherers, and that they took care of the art that was left—which meant they might be suitable priests for her new religion.

She wondered if any of the other avatars had thought of this—of the power that real, living worshippers might give them. Gus and Tigre certainly hadn't and probably wouldn't. Diana might, if Apollo kept spilling his guts, and since her "secret training grounds" were *in* the Metropolitan Museum, there was a strong risk that she might find the museum caretakers before Kali did.

And then there was Amon, who was trying to sneak up on her right now.

He had a classic god complex: He knew he was powerful, but he was desperate to make sure that everyone else knew, as well. So he couldn't just show up at a party. He needed to swoop in from the clouds in a beam of blazing sunlight, preferably just in time to save the day, as he had that morning on the Empire State Building.

He'd been watching her for at least fifteen minutes, and he'd spent most of that time trying to tweak the winds so that they'd whoosh him down onto the wall beside her, as if he'd appeared miraculously from thin air. But there were other forces nearby tugging at the winds, wrestling them from his control. She could feel the breeze shifting this way, then that way, then around in a circle, like a dog getting ready to sleep, and she knew perfectly well that Amon was standing on a rocky hill about ten feet behind her to her left. She also knew that he was getting frustrated, which was pretty funny.

It would be even funnier if she could send a thread of power out to the rock and smash it to dust beneath his feet, but (a) she didn't want to give away the extent of her power—unlike Amon, she felt no need to show off—and (b) she wasn't exactly sure that she could do that yet. At least not with the accuracy she'd need to make it truly hilarious. Blowing up the rock next to him wouldn't be nearly as funny.

Kali stood up, stretched the whole length of her body, and turned around to face Amon just as he dropped out of the sky. Disconcerted, he lost his balance as he landed on the wall and did an ungainly wobble before recovering. Kali put her hands on her hips and watched him with a small smile.

"What's so funny?" he growled.

"Oh, nothing," she said.

"You know, I could have killed you anytime in the last ten minutes and you wouldn't even have seen me coming."

"Okay," she said, "now *that's* funny."

"I'm just saying you should watch your back," he said.

"It seemed like you were watching it for me," she said sweetly.

Amon jumped down from the wall and they stared at each other for a minute, sizing each other up. They had more or less met that morning, when Amon helped them all rescue Gus from the Boss Hunter, but now they both knew the truth about themselves. Kali had seen Amon overload the huge crystal hunter with sunlight—its energy source—and Amon had seen Kali bring part of the building down on top of the creature while it was distracted. Now they each knew the other was capable of a lot more than that.

"I'm Amon-Ra," he said. "The Egyptian god of the sky and ruler of the universe."

"Sounds impressive. You should have your own cartoon," Kali said.

"And you're Kali, Indian goddess of destruction."

"Let me guess," she said. "One of your powers is . . . stating the obvious? Or wait—telling people things they already know?"

He smirked. "I think I'll save you until last. It'll give me one interesting fight to look forward to."

"Oh please," she said. "You and I both know who the real powers are in this battle. Me, Thor, and perhaps you. For you to have a chance of defeating me, you need to absorb the strength of as many other avatars as you can. That's why you won't fight me now. You'll pick off the weak ones first."

Amon glared at her. "Are you calling me a coward?"

"All gods are cowards," Kali said, "when it comes to death."

"I don't see *you* challenging me right now, either," he spat.

"I'm sure we both have a plan," Kali said evenly.

Amon glanced up and down the empty street. A shrewd expression crossed his face. "Perhaps we can come to an arrangement," he said. "I'll let you fight Catequil if

I can take the Polynesian mistake. I . . . I have a personal interest in defeating him."

"Really," Kali said. "Why is that?"

Amon narrowed his eyes. "Let's just say he's muddling that plan of mine."

Kali studied him. He was hiding something, which wasn't surprising, but he was being shifty about it instead of cocky, which meant it might be something useful to her. She sifted through what she knew about the Egyptian avatar so far: not much.

"So tell me," she said, "if you want him dead so badly, why did you come to his rescue this morning?"

"Weren't you pleased to see me?" he answered, giving her a smile that she suspected was meant to be flirtatious.

"I don't know that I'd say *pleased*," Kali said. "It was helpful, but don't get excited. We could have saved him without you."

"I doubt that."

"So you swooped in on your sunbeam to win us over with your heroic personality?"

"I was protecting something of mine," Amon said, "and the best way to do so was by helping to defeat the crystal hunter. There. Happy?"

Hmmm. Something of his? A potentially useful clue. Kali yawned. "Illuminating as this conversation is, I think I'll go take a nap." She turned to leave, and he jumped off the wall to stop her.

"Don't you want to make a deal?" he said. "We'll divide up the other avatars between us, join forces to defeat Thor, and then fight each other. Neat and simple, and useful for both of us."

Kali returned his smile, leaning toward him until she could feel the heat of the sun radiating off his skin. "I may be afraid of death," she whispered, "but I would rather die than ally myself with a creature like you."

A cold breeze swirled around them. "Then you will die," Amon said. He lifted his arms and the winds rose to carry him away over the trees, his dark eyes fixed on her until the clouds swallowed him up.

The Greek and Roman galleries of the museum were clean and cold, still and serene. Gods and goddesses swept through the halls and past the doorways, murmuring like polite tourists. Only instead of saying things like "My, look at the expression in this face!" or "Lordy, this young man isn't wearing a single thing!" they were commenting, "Ooooh, Athena won't be happy about how puffy he made her cheeks here," and "Mercury *wishes* his arms looked like that!" and so on.

Everyone seemed fascinated by the pale, toga-swathed Venus statue in the corner of her room, although Diana suspected they were really swanning through to take a look at their avatar in the flesh. She suspected she wasn't measuring up well to the smooth perfection of the sculpture. They kept eyeing her flannel shirt and jeans and her hair, now in windblown tangles after the fight with the crystal hunter. She felt small, disheveled, flawed, and very human next to the beautiful elegance of both the statues and the gods.

She wished they'd given her somewhere else to stay. Somewhere with a shower, for instance. It was now late afternoon and she'd spent the morning running up the Empire State Building and fighting giant crystal pterodactyls. A real shower and a real bed would have been ideal.

Sure, it made poetic sense to lodge the Greco-Roman avatar in these galleries, but it was freezing and uncomfortable, even without hordes of living and marble goddesses staring at her. They had slung up a makeshift hammock for her between two sturdy pillars, but that didn't keep out the constant chill. And every time she tried to sit up or get out of the hammock, she ended up floundering around like a baby kangaroo trapped in its mother's pouch.

It was stupendously ungraceful, and she suspected this was something else the goddesses were floating by to see, although they hid their smiles behind pale hands.

She knew that as a pop star she should be used to being a public spectacle, but it was very different without her managers and bodyguards and fashion consultants. It was much easier to ignore people staring at you when you were wearing the right outfit and burly men were blocking their view.

At least there were a few tricks she could use—like keeping her hands busy and looking preoccupied. Without a cell phone, she was making do with a map of the museum, which she had practically memorized from staring at it for so long.

"Feel better?" Apollo asked. He flopped down next to her and nearly unbalanced the hammock.

"Not really," she said, grabbing his arm to stop herself from rolling into him. "But thanks for the bread and fruit. That's probably the healthiest meal I've had since the world ended."

"Well, what would be the point of having a harvest goddess if she couldn't provide food from the earth?" Apollo said with a grin. "Not that there's much earth around here for Demeter to work with, but she wanted to do her part to keep you strong, which frankly, I say, is a poor apology for helping the others shove Venus into you, but you know how she is, always trying to please everyone all the time."

"If she keeps making me bread, I'll be very pleased," Diana said, then tipped sideways again as he stood up. With a frustrated noise, she struggled to her feet. "Apollo, can't I stay in a normal bed in a normal place? This is *so* weird."

"You are safe here," Vulcan said in his gloomy, hoarse voice, popping up behind Apollo and making her jump.

"I know, I know," Diana said. "You've said that a few times already. But aren't there real beds in this museum? I remember the kids sleeping *somewhere* in *From the Mixed-Up Files of Mrs. Basil E. Frankweiler*. And this floor plan says a couple of the permanent exhibits have furniture." She poked the map she'd been examining.

"We prefer this base," Vulcan said, his singed eyebrows beetling together. "We chose it specifically."

"Yes, my dear sister," Apollo teased, "you wouldn't want to *deprive* your peers of the chance to admire themselves in marble, would you? And perhaps more importantly, the chance to be catty about how everyone else looks in marble?"

"But if there's anything you need," Vulcan said, "anything I can get you, I'd be happy to do anything . . . for you."

He reminded her of her most awkward fans, desperate for even a speck of her attention. *Worshippers*, she thought with a wince. She hated the pity she felt for them; it wasn't their fault they needed something to cling to. The least she could do was be nice to them.

She turned up the wattage in her smile and said, "Would you really? Because honestly, I'd love a few blankets, if you can find any—and maybe some curtains for these doorways, for a little privacy? That would be fantastic. I mean, it's all right if you can't, but I would appreciate it *so* much." She forced herself to lay one hand lightly on Vulcan's wrist, trying to communicate, *See I don't find you repulsive* and *I am genuinely grateful for your help*, both of which were at least partly true.

A fiery flush moved slowly up Vulcan's face and he bowed, holding his arm still, as though trying to keep her hand there as long as possible.

"Your wish is my command," he said. Diana managed to keep a straight face as he backed away, but once he'd vanished down the hall, she turned to Apollo with a grin.

"I've never heard anyone say that seriously before," she said. He was looking at her oddly.

"Venus hears it all the time," Apollo said. "But she loves it—being worshipped, being adored, getting everything she wants. She always used Vulcan exactly the way you just did."

"I wasn't *using* him," Diana protested. "He wanted to be helpful, and I was trying to be nice."

"By pretending to like him and letting him slave for you," Apollo said. "That's Venus's idea of being nice all right. Fake and sugary and selfish."

"Oh my God!" Diana cried. "Why are you being so mean? I wasn't trying to be cruel to him, okay? I don't remember anything. I have to get used to all this, and in the meanwhile I'm doing my best, all right?"

"I'm not being mean," Apollo said. "I'm being honest. Diana was never *nice* to Vulcan, but at least she was always honest. It worries me when your Venus instincts are stronger than your Diana side."

"So you'd rather I told the truth, even if it hurts people?" Diana said. "You want me to erase the nice side of me completely?" *But what if that's the part people like?* her brain whispered. *If you wipe out all signs of Venus, you'll also lose her power to make people like you. And then what will you have?*

"I just want you to be yourself," Apollo said.

"All right, here's some truth," Diana snapped. "I don't want to sleep in a hammock surrounded by marble statues and equally marble gods. I'm going to find somewhere else to stay."

She stalked past him and out the door, turning left instead of right so she wouldn't run into Vulcan again. Wide eyes watched her from all sides, and she couldn't stop the guilty feeling that her temper tantrum would end up in the morning papers, that her manager would be calling in a minute to yell about her image, that she'd let her fans and her family down again, that maybe this time she'd ruined everything and everyone would finally realize that she didn't deserve her fame or their love.

She wondered if Gus would still care about her if she eliminated all her Venus aspects. He might have only fallen for her because of her power—there was no way for her to know for sure. And power or not, surely he wouldn't like her at all if she was suddenly harsh and honest all the time, never affectionate. Who would like her like that?

Finally she found a section of rooms set up to look like the interior of a house, complete with elaborate old bedroom furnishings.

It was amazing to realize how ingrained some training was. Diana stood outside the rope for several minutes, working up the resolve to cross it. It felt so *wrong,* as if she were trespassing in somebody's tomb or finger-painting on a Picasso. These beds were so old; this one might disintegrate into piles of splinters if she touched it.

But it still looked a lot more comfortable than the hammock, and she liked the warmth of the furniture and carpets around it. She couldn't remember the last time she'd slept—yesterday evening, perhaps, at Justin and Treasure's house, after Andrew's funeral, before she and Gus had started their drive to New York. She had stayed awake in the car all night to make sure Gus was okay. And then they'd arrived here, and the giant pterodactyl had taken him, and she'd run up the steps of the Empire State Building to rescue him, and then they'd all met the gods in Central Park, and now she'd ended up here, so really, even if it was only late afternoon, it was no wonder she was tired.

Finally she stepped over the velvet rope and crossed the threadbare rugs, walking as lightly as she could. She ran her hand across the bedspread and then sat down, sending up a cloud of dust that made her sneeze. She pulled back the bedspread and poked the pillow.

A noise by the door made her look up sharply. It sounded like—scratching? Or clicking . . . the tip-tap of tiny claws on the wooden floor. Diana jumped up and ran to the doorway, peering into the next room. Sure enough, a bright green-and-blue fan of feathers was sweeping out the far door at a stately, unhurried pace.

Had the peacock been following her?

Diana shivered. Suddenly her new room didn't seem so warm anymore.

Gus's head was in so much pain that he didn't argue with Tigre when the taller boy suggested they all return to Kali's apartment. A part of him was still feeling wary about Kali and her intense destructive powers, but he didn't think he could make it to the library in his condition. Also, Anna practically lit up when they mentioned beds. She reacted more strongly to the idea of sleep than she did to the news that they were all reincarnated gods. Then again, she had been traveling for several days straight.

Anna told them that at noon on Saturday, December 22, 2012, she had been sitting down to lunch with her parents in their apartment in Bangkok, Thailand. Her mother had gone into the kitchen to get the rice, and Anna was leaning down to pick up a spoon she'd dropped, when something flickered all around the corners of her vision.

"It's hard to describe," she said as the three of them walked back up along the park. The sun was starting to slant down in the sky, and Gus guessed from the shadows that it was after four o'clock in the afternoon. "It was like someone waving a veil in front of a lamp, but only at the edges of my sight. I blinked, and then I realized that the spoon I was reaching for had disappeared. I sort of stared at the floor for a minute, wondering why it was suddenly so dusty, and then I looked sideways and realized that my dad's shoes were gone, too. I mean, my *dad* was gone, but that was how I noticed—I was, like, Where are Dad's shoes? And then I straightened up and the whole apartment was different."

Anna shivered and slipped her hand into Tigre's. He nearly jumped a mile, but he forced himself not to pull away. He liked the warmth of her hand in his, the heat of her arm leaning toward him for support.

"Everything had vanished," she went on, blinking back tears. "The table was bare, and so were most of the shelves in the room. I thought maybe I'd blacked out for a minute and Dad had gone into the kitchen to get Mom, but when I went in there, I found nobody. The whole apartment was empty except for the big pieces of furniture. And then I went out on the balcony and realized the whole city was like that."

"That must have been really scary," Tigre said, remembering his encounters with the strange creatures in the jungle around Santiago. He was lucky he'd met Quetzie so soon after the Change—not that she had explained much, but at least she was someone friendly to talk to. He wondered what she would think of Anna.

He noticed Gus looking at Anna's hand in his, and wondered defensively if Gus was jealous. Which would be dumb; Gus had Diana, after all, didn't he? He couldn't also be interested in Anna. Not that Tigre was. . . . Well, actually, he didn't know what he was. This was only the second girl he'd ever held hands with in his life, and probably the last, considering the way his luck seemed to be going. He was willing to wait and see what happened.

"It was scary, but it seemed like a dream, you know?" Anna said. "I kept thinking I'd wake up. I spent the whole first day lying on my bed, waiting to wake up."

"Did you see any crystal hunters?" Gus asked.

"Crystal hunters?"

"They're these sort of transparent robots—there are big flying ones and some human-sized insect ones," Gus explained. "They attacked me a couple of times on the way here, so I just wondered if they chased you, too." He glanced at her hand in Tigre's again, and Tigre wondered what his problem was.

"I didn't see anything like that," Anna said, shaking her head. "But like I said, I didn't go out very much."

"You didn't walk around and try to find other people?" Gus asked.

"I really didn't believe it was real," Anna said. "It was so quiet. I thought maybe someone would come find me. And someone sort of did."

"Thor?" Tigre guessed.

"Yes, but that wasn't until the third day," Anna said. "I was hungry, so I went out looking for food. There were all these wild animals everywhere, like dogs and cats and monkeys and things, so I was trying to stay off the street as much as I could—you know, going along the rooftops instead. I was heading for a supermarket a few blocks away."

"You didn't hear any voices in your head?" Gus interrupted.

"*Voices* in my head?" Anna looked offended. "Are you saying I made this up? Are you calling me crazy?"

"No, no," Tigre said. "The rest of us heard voices telling us where to go."

"Well, most of us," Gus muttered.

"What did they say?" Anna asked.

"Mine said 'Go north,'" Tigre replied. "I was in Chile, so I guess it was trying to get me here. It was pretty insistent, but that's all it said."

"And now you think those were the gods talking to you?"

"Yeah," Gus said. "They were trying to herd all the avatars into one place so we could have this battle."

"I guess mine couldn't get through to me," Anna said. "Maybe they sent Thor to pick me up. Wow, is this where we're going?" She stared around the lobby of Kali's apartment building in awe. The late-afternoon light reflected off the mirrors and made the floor glow a pale orange.

Gus winced as they climbed the stairs to Kali's apartment, each step sending a new note of pain through his skull. As they got closer, strains of music floated down from above, and he realized that Kali must be back. What was she listening to?

His brow furrowed, and suddenly he leaped up the last few steps and burst through the door.

"Hey!" he yelled, running into the living room. "That's *mine*! You went through my stuff!"

Kali was lying on the couch. She didn't look up from the newspaper article she was reading as Gus stormed in, followed by Tigre and Anna.

"Someone went through your things?" Kali said

coolly. "What an invasion of privacy. You must feel so violated." She lifted her eyes to meet Tigre's, and he wondered uncomfortably what they had done with her diary before leaving. Surely they had put it back where she'd left it. Surely they hadn't left it out on the kitchen table, had they?

"This is *my* Venus album," Gus said, stopping the stereo and popping out the CD. He stared at it for a minute in confusion.

"Oh, wait, no, it's not," Kali said in a mocking Gus imitation. "Heavens, I am *so* sorry for accusing you like that, Kali. I feel like *such* an *ass*."

"Is this some kind of memorial album?" Gus said, picking up the case on the stereo to hide his embarrassment. "I've never seen it before."

"Yeah, apparently your girlfriend was even more popular after she died than before," Kali said. "Too bad she didn't really stage her own death, as many people hoped, because she could have lived off the royalties for the rest of her life." She slid the article across the coffee table at him and stood up.

"Your stuff isn't even here, Gus," Tigre pointed out. "Remember, we left everything you and Diana brought in the car on the other side of the park. We should go get it later."

"Oh, yeah," Gus mumbled. "Sorry."

"Kali, we've been looking for you," Tigre said. "You should have come to the park with us this morning. We met some people who explained everything that's going on, and there's a lot to tell you."

"I stopped at a music store on the way back to get a

few Venus albums," Kali said with a shrug. "I was curious."

"Venus?" Anna said.

"The pop star," Tigre explained. "She's one of the avatars, too." When Anna still looked confused, he said, "She was really huge in America, but maybe she wasn't so big in Thailand."

"Oh. I never paid much attention to the radio," Anna said. "Her name is Venus, really?"

"She prefers Diana," Gus said, picking up the article Kali had passed to him. He realized it was about the "mysterious disappearance" of Venus in the earthquake and her skyrocketing album sales afterward.

"And who are you?" Kali said, inspecting Anna.

"Anna's an avatar, but she doesn't know for what goddess," Gus said. "Or which pantheon."

"Kali doesn't know about all that yet, remember?" Tigre said. "She didn't come to the park with us. Kali, you're not going to believe what we've found out."

"That we're all human manifestations of gods and goddesses, sent through time to represent our pantheons in a giant battle where all of y—us die except one," Kali said.

Gus looked at her sharply. Had she been about to say "where all of *you* die"?

"How do you know?" Tigre said, disappointed. He'd been looking forward to telling Kali something she didn't know, for once.

"I met my own guide fella while I was out walking," Kali said lightly. "In the *rain,* I might add—thank you, Mr. Storm God."

"I'm actually kind of relieved," Anna said. "I was afraid we were here to, like, repopulate the earth or something.

Can I sit down?" Tigre put out an arm for her to steady herself and she let him support her to the couch. "Thank you," she murmured, leaning against his shoulder and closing her eyes.

"Anna's been traveling for a while," Tigre said, catching the raised eyebrows on Kali's face. "She came from Thailand."

"How?" Kali asked.

"She was just getting to that part of her story," Gus said, sitting in one of the armchairs.

"Thor showed up," Anna said without opening her eyes. "He was just sitting on a roof, grinning. I was so relieved to see him, even though he didn't speak English. He seemed really nice." She was quiet for a moment. "He seemed to know what was going on. He wasn't worried at all, and that made me feel so much better. He helped me find food we could eat. I guess I should have been suspicious when he filled a whole sack with stuff, like he was planning a trip. The next day he showed me his goats."

"Please tell me that's not a euphemism," Kali said. She hoisted herself onto a wide windowsill, her legs dangling.

Anna opened her eyes to give Kali a startled expression. "No, seriously. They're enormous goats—really scary, with big teeth."

"It's true," Tigre said. "We saw them."

"*You* met Thor?" Kali said with surprise. "And lived?"

"Yeah, we were kinda puzzled about that, too," Gus said.

"So your guide told you about Thor?" Tigre asked. "Did he tell you about Anna, too? Like which pantheon she's from?"

"Nope," Kali said. "He just said to watch out for Thor. Big and violent, from what I hear."

"That's about right," Gus said.

"I guess I'm not much of a threat," Anna said with a sigh. "Whoever I am."

"We'll figure it out," Tigre said. "And hey, I'm not very scary, either." She smiled up at him.

"So then what happened?" Kali asked. "You met Thor's goats and . . ."

"And he seemed to be saying I should get into his chariot. That's not a euphemism, either," she added quickly, and Kali actually cracked a smile. "And you know, I thought the goats were creepy, but I didn't know they could *fly.*"

"Holy crap," Gus said.

"Yeah," Anna said. "So suddenly I'm a hundred feet in the air, and Thor's laughing and waving the reins around, and it's not like I'm going to jump out, right? And I have no idea what he's saying, so as far as I know, I've just been abducted by a crazy man with flying goats. He didn't touch down again until we got to New York today."

"And that's when you ran away from him," Tigre prompted.

"No, that's when he tried to *kill* me," Anna said. "I mean, I jumped out of the chariot right away, but he was still the only person I'd seen in days, so I was trying to figure out what to do next. And then he threw his hammer at me."

"His hammer is *huge,*" Gus explained.

Anna started giggling. "*Stop* it," she said, throwing a couch cushion at Kali.

"I didn't say anything," Kali protested with a grin.

"Have mercy on a hysterical, sleep-deprived waif," Anna said. "I think I'm a little giddy. I haven't had anyone to talk to in so long."

"I know the feeling," Kali said. Tigre and Gus both gave her strange looks, and she added, "Okay, maybe not the giddy part."

"You should get some sleep, Anna," Tigre said. "There are empty bedrooms upstairs."

"Couldn't I sleep down here?" she asked, seizing his arm as he started to get up. "I'm—I know this sounds stupid, but I'm afraid if I go to sleep by myself, I might wake up and everyone will be gone again."

"Sure," Tigre said. "You can sleep here on the couch."

"There are blankets in that closet," Kali said, pointing.

"Us talking won't keep you awake?" Gus asked as Tigre unearthed a pale pink comforter and took it over to Anna.

"No," she said, curling onto her side and letting Tigre tuck the blanket around her. "I could sleep through anything right now." Her eyes closed. "Just don't . . . disappear," she mumbled.

"We won't," Tigre said.

"I'm making tea," Kali said. "It'll be in the kitchen if either of you want some."

"No thanks," said Gus.

"Sure," Tigre said. They both followed her into the kitchen, keeping their voices low. Tigre glanced at the counter and saw that the diary was gone. It wasn't back on top of the cabinet, either. So either they'd put it back and she'd moved it or she'd found it out on the counter and hidden it more carefully.

"So you have no idea what pantheon she's from?" Kali asked, filling the kettle with water.

"I've never heard of a goddess named Anna," Gus said, "but I'm no expert." The pounding in his head was finally, slowly fading. He sat down at the table, keeping his eyes fixed on Kali as she moved about the kitchen.

"Well, where is she from?" Kali asked.

"Her dad's Chinese and her mom's part Iranian, part Turkish," Tigre said. "They were journalists, so she's lived everywhere. All over Asia, and parts of Europe and Africa, too." He shook his head. "Anyway, Diana's not Greek, and you're only half Indian, and Gus isn't Polynesian, so I'm not sure that would give us the answer."

"Actually," Gus said slowly, "I'm not sure she's an avatar at all."

"What else would she be?" Tigre said.

"I don't know, but look." Gus reached for Kali's hand, but she snatched it away. With a sigh, he leaned over and touched Tigre's arm instead. They both jumped as an electric spark went off where their skin touched. "Feel that? I noticed it in the park. The spell that protects us from the crystal hunters also makes it impossible to touch one another without getting a weird electric reaction. I don't know if they did it on purpose, but it's a pretty blunt way to keep us all apart."

"So?" Tigre said, rubbing his arm.

"So I didn't feel anything when Anna leaned on us in the store, right when she showed up. And you held hands with Anna most of the way here. I'm guessing the fact that you didn't react means you didn't feel anything like an electric shock."

Embarrassed, Tigre glanced at Kali, but she was pulling mugs out of the cupboard and didn't look at him. "No," he mumbled.

"So maybe she's not an avatar. Otherwise we'd feel a shock when she touched us, wouldn't we?"

"Or maybe she's not protected the same way," Tigre said. "Or maybe her pantheon's spell works differently. There could be tons of other explanations."

"Sure," Gus said with a shrug. "I'm just saying, maybe she's actually an accident—like me. I didn't have the protection, or the electric shock, until Zeus gave it to me."

"Or she could be a regular goddess," Kali chimed in. "Maybe one of the other pantheons sent her to spy on us."

"You mean she's just pretending to be an avatar? She's lying about her family and Thailand and everything?" Tigre shook his head. "I don't think so."

"Well, you are the best judge of character here," Kali said. "I mean, if *you* trust her, then I'm sure my kidneys are perfectly safe."

"It was my *liver*," Tigre muttered. Gus gave him a quizzical look, and he added, "Long story. Tell you later."

"I'll ask Shiva," Kali said. "He'll know who she is."

"Shiva?" Gus repeated.

"My hus—guide."

"Anna would appreciate that," Tigre said. "She's pretty confused. Doesn't she remind you guys of Diana?"

"Yes," said Kali at the same time as Gus said, "No."

"What are you talking about?" Gus said. "They're nothing alike."

"It's the friendliness thing," Kali said, plunking tea bags

in two mugs. "The way they both act like they've known you forever. As if they can't wait to have a slumber party and paint your toenails, whether you want them painted or not."

"Yeah, exactly," Tigre said. "And like she thinks you're kinda cool, even though she doesn't really know much about you."

Gus frowned, rubbing his temples. "It's different," he mumbled. "Diana's not like that with *everyone.*"

"Well, you would know better than we would," Kali said. "Technically, she should probably be like that half the time, and exactly the opposite the other half."

"Why?" Gus said, looking up.

"The whole two-goddesses-in-one-mortal thing. . . . Wow, she didn't tell you?"

"There wasn't a lot of time to talk before Zeus whisked her away," Gus said uneasily.

"Well, the Greco-Roman pantheon originally picked Diana, goddess of the moon and the hunt—and chastity, by the way—to be their avatar. But then, about twelve years after she was born in mortal form, they changed their minds. For absolutely no fathomable reason, they decided to stuff another goddess in there with her."

"Venus," Gus said slowly. "The goddess of love—that's what Amon called her."

"Maybe that's the one the Egyptians think is dominant," Kali said. "Hmm." She sat down across from Gus, wrapping her tea bag around a spoon to press out the tea. "I have no idea, but it must be like a catfight inside her. 'Men are evil! No, wait, seduce them! I want to be alone with my bow and arrow. No, wait, I want to be surrounded by adoring millions!' And so on. They're not exactly compatible choices, from what I remember reading about them."

"I guess Shiva told you all this," Tigre said.

"Yeah. And then we ran into her and Zeus. Interesting that she still wants to be called Diana, even now that she knows the truth."

"You saw her?" Gus asked. "Is she okay?"

"Why wouldn't she be?" Kali said. "She's with her people now."

"So why aren't you with your 'people'?" Gus snapped. "Why aren't you hanging out with Indian immortals instead of us?"

"Come on, Gus," Tigre said.

"Hey, this is my apartment," Kali said. "I chose it. I want to stay in it. If you're not comfortable with that, you can go find your own. I won't miss you."

Gus stood up, but Tigre grabbed his arm. "Gus, remember our plan about sticking together," Tigre said. "We're safer in a group. If Thor or Amon come to attack us, we can protect each other. I don't know about you, but I'd rather be on Kali's side than against her."

Kali grinned wolfishly. "I'd say that's wise."

Gus stared at her for a minute. What he really wanted to say was: "But are you on *our* side?" He wanted some assurance that she wouldn't kill them in their sleep. *Even if she promises, would I believe her?* Perhaps it would be better to let her think he trusted her. It would be easier to keep an eye on her if she wasn't too wary of him.

"I'm sorry," he said, forcing himself to relax. "It's been kind of a stressful day."

"As are most days that start with being abducted by a

giant crystal pterodactyl," Kali said. Tigre grinned, and Gus could tell he thought they were all friends now.

"Maybe we should all sleep in one room tonight," Gus said, slowly sitting back down. "Just in case something happens."

"Nice try," Kali said. "No slumber parties for me, thanks. I like my toenails the color they are." She got up and took her cup over to the sink.

"Anna and I could take the room with two beds," Tigre said. "So she'll have someone there—I mean, if she wants to—so she doesn't have to sleep alone."

"Sure," Gus said absently, watching Kali. "I can sleep on the floor. That way we can keep an eye on each other." He studied Kali's back, wondering what she was thinking. Could they trust her? Why was she here with them if she had a pantheon to support her? Why wasn't she off "training," like Diana and Amon supposedly were? How much more did she know than the rest of them? What did she say to her pantheon when they told her about her purpose here?

And most importantly, what was she planning?

Diana woke up suddenly from a deep and, for once, dreamless sleep, feeling like someone had called her name. Everything around her was pitch-black, and for a disorienting moment she couldn't remember where she was. Her first guess was at a hotel with Gus, but she couldn't hear him breathing—couldn't hear anything, in fact. She might have been buried a hundred feet underground, it was so quiet.

Stiff, heavy covers were piled on top of her, but still she

felt cold. Shivering, she sat up and felt around in the dark. Her hands connected with soft fabric at the foot of her bed, and she realized that it was a pile of blankets. That brought back the memory of asking Vulcan to find them for her, and of her fight with Apollo. After seeing the peacock, she had crawled into the bed and fallen asleep. So Vulcan must have found her and left the blankets while she was sleeping.

Diana wasn't sure she liked that idea. Had he watched her sleep? Had any of the other gods tiptoed through to examine her while she was undefended? She wondered how long she'd been sleeping. Long enough for it to get dark outside, apparently.

She wrapped one of the blankets around herself and climbed out of the bed. It felt like a long silver thread was wrapped around her heart and someone was tugging on the other end. Like she had to get up and follow the feeling to find out who she really was.

She followed the sensation through the dark, empty halls, until at last she pushed open a door and found herself in a garden bathed in moonlight. She felt like she'd stepped through a mirror into another world. A fountain trickled at one end, and statues stood guard over the stillness. To the right, a wall of glass was hidden in shadows by the trees crowding up on the other side.

In the center of the garden was a slim golden statue of a woman who was pulling an arrow back in a bow, one foot delicately balanced on a small globe. Diana didn't have to find the inscription to know that this was her, an image of her goddess self. The catty goddesses in the Greek galleries would have whispered, "If only Diana herself were really that tall or thin." The artist had made her perfectly elegant, with tiny perfect toes, like a Barbie.

Diana touched the smooth bronze globe and looked up at the moon, which was half-full. Maybe Apollo was right. Maybe she just needed to find her real self—Diana, goddess of the moon and the hunt. Venus had been dominant for so long, all during the last few years of her life as a beloved worldwide superstar. But Diana had been there first: the little girl who ran around wild in the woods near their house, who watched baseball with her dad and helped him fix cars. She'd been perfectly happy like that, until her mom realized her own career was going nowhere and decided to focus on her daughter instead.

A cold chill trailed down Diana's spine. How much of her life had been manipulated by the gods? According to Apollo, they had set up her name change to Venus—it made an avatar stronger to have the right name. So they must have steered her into that meeting with the studio executives. Was it the gods' influence that had made her mom finally take an interest in her? If they hadn't interfered, would Diana have stayed happily at home with her dad, growing up like a normal girl instead of a teen pop queen?

But you love being Venus. You love the music, your fans, performing. . . .

Do I? Or is that just the Venus side of me?

And if my Venus power is making people love me, what's my Diana power?

She dropped the blanket, stepped into the center of the beam of moonlight, and lifted her face. The moon wasn't as strong as the sun, but it was more adaptable, able to change and plan and move and dance. The sun dominated with brute force and sheer will; the moon darted through shadows, keeping secrets and hiding when it needed to.

Her hands were even paler than usual in the silver light. She tried to imagine them holding a bow and arrow. Balancing on one foot, she put herself in the same position as the statue, drawing back an imaginary bow-string with her right hand.

Something wasn't right about this pose. It felt impre-cise and uneven. No one would shoot from a position like this. She planted both feet on the ground and sighted along her left arm. That was better. Now she felt strong. Now it felt natural.

She dropped her hands and looked up at the moon again, letting it calm her down. Maybe she wasn't a total lost cause. Perhaps if she could find her goddess of the hunt strength, she could actually be useful in this battle, instead of lying around in a hammock eating olives and waiting for Amon to claim her as his prize.

I belong to no man, and no man will fight my battles for me. I am a fierce, independent warrior who can win this contest and become the supreme goddess of all the pantheons—

Diana blinked, breaking her trance. What was she thinking? She didn't want to fight anyone or kill anyone or win any battles. She wanted to take the world back to the way it was before. She wanted a normal life. She wanted to be friends with the other avatars . . . and maybe more than that with Gus.

That is the weakness of a pathetic love goddess. Wanting to be loved. By people who are here to kill you, no less.

"No," Diana whispered, shaking her head. "I'm not like that. I'm not going to hurt anyone. There's another way, and I'll find it."

She started to step back, afraid of how the moonlight made her think. Suddenly there was a crash and her instincts kicked in, sending her diving and rolling to the side just as something plummeted to the ground where she'd been standing.

Diana was back on her feet and behind the nearest pillar before she'd consciously registered what was happening. Heart pounding with fear, she looked out to see what had nearly hit her.

An enormous, wicked-looking spear was planted in the stone, still quivering. The tip had a sharp, shiny, jagged metal edge, and the spear had been thrown with such force that it had pierced the stone floor as if it were dirt.

She would have been killed instantly, and not very pleasantly, if it had hit her.

Gods burst into the room from every direction, some through the various doors, some just appearing from the air. Apollo reached her first, with Vulcan not far behind him.

"It came from up there," she said, pointing, and a young-looking god with wings on his sandals flew up to investigate. She could see the hole in the glass roof that the spear had come through, but it didn't look like her attacker was still up there.

"What are you doing out here?" Vulcan demanded. "How can we protect you if you wander off by yourself like this?"

"Maybe I can take care of myself," Diana snapped.

Mars was examining the spear. He ran one hand along the wood, giving a low whistle.

"This is a marvelously dangerous weapon," he said, his eyes glinting.

"You can have it," Diana said with a shudder.

"Does it tell us anything about her attacker?" Apollo asked, picking up the blanket Diana had dropped and wrapping it around her shoulders. "It can't have been another avatar, right? Without the judges present, they wouldn't get her powers, so what would be the point? But then, was it a god? Why would they risk it?"

"I knew it!" Zeus boomed, looking harried. "I knew we should have kept our secret training grounds more secret! I bet it was that three-eyed lunatic Shiva. He doesn't look civilized enough to follow the rules of combat."

Like you should talk, Diana thought.

"This is not magical," Mars said, examining the spear. "It bears no signs of any particular pantheon."

"It belongs here," said a new voice. The tall woman whom Diana had seen earlier materialized from the air. Diana glanced down, but the peacock did not appear with her.

"Hera," Apollo said with a small, respectful bow. Vulcan and Mars followed suit, although with less grace, and Zeus sighed heavily. Diana realized this must be the queen of the gods. Hera, Zeus's wife—the one who fought with him constantly, especially when he cheated on her, which was often. She was looking at Diana with vicious dislike in her narrow brown eyes.

"H—hi," Diana said nervously.

"What do you mean, 'It belongs here'?" Mars asked.

"It came from those rooms," Hera said, flicking a long finger at a corner of the garden.

"Arms and Armor?" Diana guessed. "It was part of an exhibit?"

Hera arched an eyebrow at her without answering.

"That means anyone could have taken it," Apollo said.

"Like Shiva," Zeus growled.

"No," Vulcan barked. "We've been doing regular patrols. We would have caught a thief."

"Please," Apollo said. "Gods are hardly the most reliable guardsmen. Most of us are more easily distracted than puppies. You may think they're patrolling, but I'd wager half of them are wandering off to try on the sparkliest jewelry they can find, or to see if any European painters made them look prettier than the Roman sculptors did."

"So anyone could have taken it," Diana said.

"Essentially," said Mars, and the look in his eyes was no friendlier than Hera's.

"Great," said Apollo. "Now all we have to figure out is who wants to kill you the most."

Tigre's dreams had stopped on his thirteenth birthday.

Before, although he could not remember it now, he had dreamed every night of empty cities, glass creatures, strange teenagers, or the faint smell of oranges.

Or blood.

As a child, he had been more interested in blood than the other children. His mother had once found him sitting on the playground bench, elbows propped on his knees, watching a thin red line of blood slowly trickle down from a scrape on his knee.

"It's not enough," he'd said to her. "There's a lot more than that."

And when she'd tried to clean it, he protested, "But there's so much more coming."

Then the dreams had stopped. And Tigre had forgotten about them.

So when he found himself lying in the dark Santiago bus shelter again, he had forgotten how to think, *This is only a dream.*

Rain was pouring down outside, battering the plastic walls with an angry splattering sound. Tigre's face was dry, but his hands felt wet and sticky, and so did his clothes. He tried to sit up and realized that the concrete underneath him was coated in something thick and sickly smelling. As he wiped his hands on his jeans, a flash of lightning illuminated a broken, too-small shape in the corner.

It was an old man in a gray raincoat. He was lying with his head thrown back and his throat torn open.

In the next flash, Tigre saw the large gashes that crisscrossed the man's body, blood still bubbling out and staining the shredded raincoat, more blood than he'd thought could come out of one human being. It covered the floor, and Tigre's hands and clothes, and it was still warm, as if the man had died very recently.

Tigre staggered to his feet, pressing his bloodstained hands to his face. A corner of his brain knew that this had happened before, that he was reliving a memory, but all the horror and terror of the first time came rushing back again. He couldn't have done this. He *couldn't* have. He had no weapons, nothing that could slash and stab like that. No one could have done it with their bare hands.

It was a coincidence, a horrible coincidence, that he'd ended up there at exactly the wrong time. Maybe he had scared off the real murderer as he crashed in, storm-crazy and out of his mind.

"Catequil," a voice whispered.

Tigre froze, feeling like coils of ice were crushing his chest. Someone was here. Someone had seen him. Someone *knew*.

"It was a beautiful sacrifice," the voice went on. There was a soft hiss to the words, and a faint echo. "We accept it and consume it with pleasure. But it is not enough to save you."

Tigre slowly took his hands away from his face.

The blood was *moving*.

Around the old man, ripples danced across the surface of the pool of blood. They spread from his body toward Tigre and then began to swirl upward into a shape.

Tigre stepped back, colliding with the wall of the shelter. This was not part of the original memory. In that one, he had fled into the rain, buried his clothes in his backyard, and tried to drive the images out of his head. For a month he'd searched the newspapers, but there was no mention of a gruesome murder or marauding wild animals. It was almost as if it had never happened.

But *this* part *had* never happened.

The blood creature towering over him surpassed the stuff of nightmares. Instead of a head, two huge snakes of blood poured out of its neck, hissing through giant fangs and glaring at Tigre with glittering black eyes. More snakes twisted from its wrists in place of hands, and it wore a skirt of living, thrashing, angry serpents. Around its neck was a cord hung with severed hands and bloody human hearts.

And its feet were huge birdlike talons, the claws smeared with blood.

"Who—what—" Tigre said.

"Behold," the snakes hissed. "The Aztec goddess Coatlicue. I am radiance. I am transformation. I am the spirit of the Earth."

"You did this," Tigre said. "*You* killed him. It wasn't me; it was you."

The snakes' hissing sounded like laughter from distant rooms. "Oh, the energy it would take to manifest fully and kill someone," Coatlicue said. "What I would do for such power." Her taloned feet scraped the floor, sending deep trails through the blood. "But it would do us no good. For us to be fed, to be strengthened, the sacrifice must be made by a mortal."

"Sacrifice," Tigre said. "You mean human sacrifice."

"Yesssssssssssssssssssssssssssssssssssssss," the goddess said. "This one was a great help to ussss in bringing you into the battle." The snakes at her wrists dipped their heads toward the pool of blood around them.

"But I didn't do it!" Tigre protested. "I didn't kill him!"

The two blood snakes came closer, eyeing him shrewdly. "You feel shame for this." When he didn't answer, one of the smaller snakes whipped out and circled his wrist. "Thisss is why you will die. Why you should die. Give up and let the cycle begin again."

Tigre tried to pull away, but his arm felt trapped in stone.

"I know about cycles," Coatlicue hissed, forked tongues flickering too close to his head. "The earth renews itself each year, and the gods renew themselves each cycle. This was a poor cycle for us. But in the next, we can rise up strong once again. There is no hope for you, so die and let the cycle begin once more."

"Why don't you let me *try*?" Tigre asked. "How can you want your own avatar to give up?"

One thick talon touched his foot. "You are not strong enough to lead the pantheons, even if you were strong enough to defeat them. Accept your worthlessness, Catequil. This is your fate."

Tigre looked back at the crumpled old man. "Just . . . tell me I didn't do this. Tell me this wasn't me, and I'll do whatever you want."

"You should be proud," Coatlicue whispered, "of the one truly powerful thing you ever did."

"Did you *see* me do it?" Tigre asked. "How did I do it? What did I do?"

"No," she said. "We could not manifest until it was done. But who else could have made such a glorious offering?"

"It wasn't me," Tigre said stubbornly, crouching and folding his arms over his head. "It wasn't. It wasn't."

"Weakness," the snakes hissed. *"Fear. How could you ever lead us?"*

Tigre closed his eyes and willed himself away from there with all his might.

To his surprise, it worked.

He was lying in a bed in a dark room. For a moment, it seemed like he might be in his own room in Chile, with his parents arguing about him downstairs, but almost immediately he knew he was not.

Because Anna was sitting on the bed next to him, touching his wrist.

"Tigre?" she whispered, shaking his arm lightly. "Are you awake?"

"Uh. Sure," he mumbled, disoriented. The nightmare had left him feeling dizzy and hollow inside, but a different kind of dizziness was already spreading through him, radiating from the point where Anna's fingers met his hand. Gus was right: There was no electric shock between them, not like Tigre had felt with Kali or, once briefly, while rescuing Gus, with Diana. Was Anna really not an avatar? He glanced down at the floor, where the dimly moonlit figure of Gus was sound asleep on top of a mattress they'd dragged in. After Anna had woken from her earlier nap, she'd eaten dinner with the rest of them, and then they all went to bed upstairs.

"Hey, can I sleep with you?" she asked, then laughed softly. "Wow, that didn't sound right, did it? I mean, I can't sleep over there, all alone, and I think, if it's not too crazy and forward of me, that I'd sleep better if I was with somebody. Is that crazy? I'm sorry. Maybe I shouldn't have woken you."

"No, no," he said, scooting over to the wall. His heart was racing, but he tried to sound as casual about it as she did, like he slept next to cute girls all the time. "It's not crazy. It's fine. I was having trouble sleeping, too."

"Oh, thank goodness," she said, slipping under the

covers. "I was afraid you'd think I was some kind of lunatic. I mean, since we just met and everything, but I feel like I can trust you, you know?"

"Sure," he said. "Sure you can." Horrible doubt sucked at him. *Can she? When I don't even know what I can or will do while I'm storm-crazed?*

Anna curled up facing him, her dark eyes reflecting a bit of moonlight from the window. The scent of oranges drifted toward him, and he curled his hands under his pillow, resisting the urge to stroke her hair. She was so close to him. His only girlfriend, Vicky, had never fallen asleep next to him, even on long car rides. She had refused even to rest her head on his shoulder because she said he was too bony and uncomfortable. Being with her had always made him feel nervous, but never tingly the way he felt with Anna.

"Mom used to yell at me for being so friendly to people," Anna whispered. "She said little girls shouldn't talk to random strangers and they certainly shouldn't act like they're friends with everyone. She was always worried someone would carry me off, especially in the more dangerous countries we lived in, but I thought I could take care of myself. I don't know if it's right, but I feel like I have a sense about people, you know? Like I can tell the good ones from the bad ones, but maybe it's wrong, because mostly I think I meet only good ones."

"Thor wasn't so good," Tigre pointed out, although he liked the idea that she could tell he personally wasn't evil. He wanted to believe her sixth sense was right about him, and he wanted *her* to believe it.

She paused for a minute, thinking it over. "I don't

know," she said slowly. "I think maybe Thor isn't so bad, normally."

"Are you serious?" Tigre whispered. "Kidnapping, attacking, weapons, flying goats? Same Thor?"

"But who knows what he was like before the Change?" Anna said. "We don't know what he's thinking, because we can't communicate with him. We have no idea what his pantheon is telling him or what he thinks is going on. Maybe they told him we're evil demons that need to be killed in order to bring everyone back."

"Huh," said Tigre. He hadn't thought of that.

Anna smiled. "I'm not saying you shouldn't battle him to the death to protect me, though."

I'd do that, he thought. *Although it would pretty definitely be my death.*

"Anyway," Anna whispered, "so I've always thought I was safe being friendly to people. I hope I'm not wrong about you guys. And I hope you don't think I'm super-weird."

"You're not wrong about us," he whispered. He paused deliberately, and she giggled. "Okay, and I don't think you're super-weird."

"Awesome," she whispered, sounding sleepy.

"Maybe it has something to do with your powers," Tigre said. "Maybe you're a goddess of friendliness or something."

"Oh, that's useful," she murmured. "I'll crush all your skulls with the power of my affectionate nature! Ha ha." Her eyes were closed.

"We'll figure out who you are tomorrow," Tigre whispered. "Don't worry."

She didn't answer. The evenness of her breathing told him she was asleep.

He lay watching her sleep for a while. Gradually his pulse slowed, and when he finally closed his eyes, his sleep was dreamless once more.

· • • • ·

PANTHEON: MESOAMERICAN
AVATAR: CATEQUIL
JUDGE: ITZAMNA
TRAINER: TLALOC

· • • • ·

Ah, poor Catequil. So easily confused. So easy to confuse; I've had to do remarkably little to bring him to this state.

Perhaps if he'd had the extra years of prophetic dreams that he should have had, he'd be better prepared for this challenge. He'd be expecting his gruesome visitors. He'd have walked through enough nightmares to strengthen him against the ones hunting him now. He'd even know a little bit about what is going to happen next.

But that wouldn't be any fun, would it?

He misses his feathered friend, the bird who brought him here from South America. A giant quetzal—what an appropriate messenger for the Mesoamerican gods. I don't think he realizes they sent her for him. It was hard for them to track her down. It will be hard for him to find Quetzie, too, when he needs her . . . and I think he will need her soon.

He doesn't know it, but he is looking for a raft to cling to. He has always needed guidance, someone to lead him and outline his path for him. Why do you think he stayed with that girlfriend of his for so long? He didn't love Vicky, but she made his decisions for him. And he thought she liked him. He badly wants to be liked, which makes him easy prey for those less innocent and true than Quetzie.

Yes. Poor Catequil.

DAY TWO:
·:· ILLUMINATION ·:·

Gus was honestly surprised to wake up alive. It had taken him hours to fall asleep; every sound, every rustle or click or creak, jerked him back to consciousness as he waited for Kali, Amon, or Thor to swoop out of the dark and kill him. All the fears that he'd managed to push away in the daylight crawled out of the shadows and curled up on his chest. The unhappy noises Tigre started making in his sleep after about an hour didn't help, either.

But he had drifted off eventually, and now with his eyes still closed he could tell that sunlight was streaming in through the window. A murmur of voices downstairs drifted up with the smell of cinnamon oatmeal, and he felt powerfully homesick—not for Los Angeles, but for the real home he'd had before that, when his parents were still alive. His mother would be scrambling eggs while his father spilled flour, scattered macadamia nuts, and burned himself on the pan as he tried to make elaborate pancakes. And Gus would lie in bed listening to them, thinking it was too early to be making so much noise on a Saturday, instead of appreciating that they were there.

Gus sighed and opened his eyes.

There was a dagger pointing at his throat.

"Shhhhhh," Amon said. "Don't make me kill you yet." The sun was blazing behind him, hiding his face in shadow. Gus could barely look straight at him. Amon leaned over, tracing the point of the knife lightly up to Gus's cheek.

"You shouldn't be here," Amon said. "You're a mistake. And it will be so, so easy to kill you."

"Coward," Gus whispered. "What kind of god has to kill someone in their sleep?"

"You're not asleep now, are you?" Amon hissed. The dagger pressed against Gus's skin, the blade burning hot, and then abruptly it was withdrawn. Amon rose to his feet, flipping the knife between his hands. "But I didn't come to kill you."

Gus climbed to his feet, watching Amon's hands closely. "Then why are you here?"

"I came to tell you *when* I plan to kill you." Amon stepped forward and thumped the dagger against Gus's chest menacingly. "Tomorrow at noon. I chose the time; you may choose the place. Those are the rules of combat."

"Combat?" Gus winced at the squeak in his voice.

"Yes," Amon said impatiently. "I am challenging you to a fight to the death. I will have the judges notified so they can all be present to acknowledge my victory."

"Great," Gus said, rubbing his chest.

"And I will tell Venus," Amon said. He smiled at Gus, his teeth and eyes glittering in the sun. "She will see which of us is strongest in a fair fight. I want her there to watch you die."

"And you think she'll be impressed?" Gus said. "I'm

her friend." *I hope I'm more than that.* "Most girls don't like their prospective boyfriends killing off their friends. It's not exactly standard courtship behavior."

"We are *gods,*" Amon snapped. "The sooner all of you realize that, the easier this will be for you. I want to get these battles over with quickly so I can go back to being immortal, so—tomorrow. Noon. Wherever you are, I will find you. And then you will die."

"So you keep saying," Gus said. He watched Amon climb onto the windowsill. The Egyptian avatar was turning back with a reptilian smile to add something, when a wooden spoon whizzed through the air and clonked him on the head.

"OW," Amon protested, scowling.

"Get out," Kali said from the doorway. Gus saw that she was holding several other kitchen implements.

"I was just leaving," Amon said with dignity, then ducked as a spatula narrowly missed his ear.

"Leave faster," said Kali.

"I don't know what you're planning, she-devil," Amon hissed, "but I claim this one. By 12:01 tomorrow, he will be dead, so do not try to steal him from me before then."

"Noted," Kali said. "Out."

Amon spread his arms to the open air, prepared to make a dramatic exit, but when he saw Kali reach for a pair of tongs, he quickly stepped out the window. They watched him float away, making strange tugging and twisting motions with his arms as he struggled with the air currents to keep aloft.

"What's going on?" Tigre asked, coming up the stairs with Anna.

"Just a visit from He Who Thinks He's So Awesome," Kali said.

"Amon stopped by to let me know he's going to kill me at noon tomorrow," Gus said. "Man, you escape an enormous crystal pterodactyl, you'd think you'd get at least a couple of days before someone else tries to kill you." He sat down on the edge of Tigre's bed.

"Amon's one of the avatars. He's the king of the Egyptian gods," Tigre explained to Anna.

"Well, that's what he thinks," Kali said, crossing to the window and closing it.

"What?" said Gus. "Isn't it true?"

"More or less," Kali said cryptically. "Let's just say he wasn't originally, and some of the other gods wouldn't mind going back to the more ancient arrangement."

"Well, what am I supposed to do?" Gus said. "How am I supposed to fight him? And *why* is everyone always trying to kill *me*?"

"It's probably your charming personality," Kali said. Anna giggled, then covered her face with her hands, as if she hadn't meant to do that.

"Can't you tell him you don't want to fight?" Tigre asked.

"Sure," Kali said. "That's a great plan. Apart from how it won't stop him from killing you."

"But that's horrible," Anna said. "Can't we just surrender? I don't mind if this guy goes off to be king of all the gods. I'm okay with having a normal life and then dying like a normal person. Only, you know, not right now. Why does he have to kill us to win?"

Gus noticed that Kali tensed when Anna said "surrender."

He had a feeling the goddess of destruction would mind quite a lot if Amon became king of all the gods.

But all Kali said was, "Those are the rules." She picked up the things she'd thrown at Amon. "And speaking of rules, I guess the judges will be showing up at the battle tomorrow."

"What judges?" Tigre asked.

"Shiva told me that each pantheon has a judge who'll oversee the battles to make sure they're fair and that the right avatar gets the power of the dying one." Kali tapped her head. "Our judges are the voices we heard getting us here. At least you and me, Tigre. Not sure why yours hasn't chimed in with more information lately."

"So it's like the Olympics," Anna said. "A judge for each of us. Oh!"

"Exactly," Kali said. "Meaning yours should be there, too."

"So the good news is, if all the judges are there," Tigre said, "then we can figure out which pantheon Anna is from."

"Well, great," Gus said. "I'm glad there's an upside to my horrible, agonizing death."

"We're not going to let you die," Anna said comfortingly. "I'm sure there's a way to stop him. Right, Kali? Amon must have a weakness, mustn't he? Something we can use to talk him out of this?"

"Sure," Kali snorted. When they all stared at her, she said, "Oh, you're serious. Well, *I* don't know what it is. Maybe you should do some research."

"Back to plan A," Tigre said. "Trip to the library."

"I'll draw you a map," Kali said. "So maybe you'll

actually get there this time."

"You're not going to come with us?" Gus said. "Don't you want to know more about the goddess inside you? Wow, that sounds like a terrible self-help book."

"She's not inside me," Kali said, "she *is* me. I know myself. A book's not going to tell me anything new. Besides, I have other stuff to do."

"Like what?" Gus asked.

"Oh, destroy some buildings, set some things on fire," Kali said. "Don't worry, you won't miss them." She spun a spatula between her fingers and headed out of the room. Tigre and Anna stepped aside and watched her descend the stairs.

"Is she joking?" Anna asked.

I wish I knew, Gus thought.

Diana was back in the hammock, where Vulcan had insisted she sleep for the rest of the night. If you could call thrashing around and nearly falling out and having nightmares about spears and supercilious gods "sleeping." She'd finally given up pretending around midmorning, when Apollo brought her breakfast. But a couple of hours later, here she was, still in the hammock, since the gods weren't letting her go anywhere.

She wasn't precisely sulking, but she was thinking about it.

Apollo, Mars, Vulcan, Zeus, and Hera were having a heated discussion nearby.

"Someone knows where we are," Zeus sputtered. "It's obviously not safe. We should take her elsewhere."

"It is safe," Vulcan rumbled. "If we keep her under watch."

"And how do you propose to do that?" Mars asked. "She's not even listening to this loser, and he's supposed to be her guide." He pointed at Apollo.

"Now, wait a—" Apollo began, but Hera interrupted him.

"We should tie her up," she said.

Diana made an outraged noise, but they ignored her.

"I don't know if that's entirely necessary, eh," Zeus said, stroking his beard. "Perhaps if we can find a safe place to stash her, we can just lock her in. That should keep her safe."

"I can *hear* you," Diana said.

"But how did they find her?" Apollo said. "That's what I want to know—I mean, and who did it, sure—but do we have someone leaking information? My drachmas are on Dionysus, by the way. That guy will tell anyone anything for a beer."

"We will do a better job of protecting her," Vulcan said. "We'll double the guard and I'll keep her personally in my sight at all times."

Yippee, Diana thought.

"I think it's too dangerous," Zeus said, shaking his head. "If she dies before Amon defeats the other avatars, the deal is off. And you know what that means—no power for us. Imagine! She cannot die!"

"Hey," Diana said. "Has anyone noticed that I'm not actually dead?"

"That's true," Mars said, finally hearing her. "We

should take some comfort in the incompetence of our enemies."

"Or *maybe,*" Diana said, "the not–total–incompetence of *me.*" Blank looks. "Come on, I must have some powers. Can't I be trained? Can't I learn some self-defense or something? I used to take karate, until my manager had me switch to yoga. I can at least *try* to protect myself."

Apollo winked at her, but the others went back to talking, as if she hadn't spoken.

"It must have been one of the other avatars," Hera said. "We should tell Amon to speed up the killing."

Diana flinched.

"Would another avatar kill her without the judges around?" Mars said. "They can't be that stupid, not even the Viking. True, she has very little power to absorb, but it would still be useful. Why be underhanded about it?"

Why indeed, Diana thought. *Unless it wasn't an avatar at all.* She glanced at Hera and saw the tall goddess watching her with dark eyes as shiny as her peacock's. Hera didn't look away, and finally Diana broke their gaze and looked down, winding a strand of the hammock string between her fingers.

She was sure it hadn't been Tigre or Gus, and she was pretty sure it hadn't been Kali. She wished she believed that Kali wouldn't attack her, but the best she could do was believe that Kali would be up-front about it, as she had said on the street yesterday. It didn't make sense for Amon to have done it, unless his plans secretly differed from their pantheons'. Could it be one of the two she hadn't met yet?

An approaching flutter-patter of footsteps and wing beats brought the gods' conversation to a halt. Mercury, the messenger of the gods, came trotting into the room on his winged sandals, his feet touching the floor only every other step. He didn't look much older than Diana, and he had an easy smile like Apollo's, but cannier. Diana had seen him move much faster the night before, so she knew that whatever his message was, it was interesting but not urgent, at least in his mind.

"Greetings, king of the gods!" Mercury declared in the ringing tones of a boy selling newspapers. He bowed one knee to the marble and then flung his cloak wide in a gesture of proclamation. "Greetings, queen of the gods! Greetings, fellow deities! I come bearing news!"

"Yes, yes," Zeus grumbled. "Get on with it, Mercury. You can skip the speeches when we're not on Olympus."

"I bring news of a battle!" Mercury cried, ignoring Zeus. "Upon this day a challenge has been thrown down, and upon this day has that challenge been accepted!"

"By whom?" Mars asked, his eyes gleaming. "Who's in this battle?"

"Tomorrow at the time of the sun's highest peak, when Apollo's chariot blazes blindingly across the sky, a great battle shall be fought, and our great judges will preside over it, and one avatar shall die!"

Diana sat up, struggling forward to the edge of the hammock.

"By all the dogs of the underworld," Mars snarled. He grabbed Mercury's cloak and hoisted him off his feet. "Get to the point. What avatars are you talking about?"

"Amon," Mercury gasped, pulling helplessly on the armored arm that held him aloft. "And the mistake, the Polynesian one."

"Gus?" Diana cried. "Amon and Gus are going to fight?"

Mars dropped Mercury, and the young messenger rubbed his throat, looking more offended than wounded. "*If* you'd let me *finish*," he said to the war god. "Yes. The Egyptian avatar challenged him this morning. They fight tomorrow at noon," he added in a normal voice.

Diana shot Apollo a frantic look. She had to get out of there and find Gus. Apollo was scratching his nose, looking unconcerned.

"Say, do you hear that?" he said to Vulcan.

"Yes," the blacksmith god said. "I'm sure the whole museum heard it."

"No, no," Apollo said. "Listen. . . . Can't you hear something? Off in the distance?"

Vulcan rose up slightly on his toes, tilting his head.

"Music," Zeus said. "By me, I hear music! From somewhere inside the museum!"

Vulcan's dark brows met. "The guards may have gotten into the musical instruments exhibit again. Someone had better check on them."

"Yes, I agree, good idea," Apollo said. "Mars, you heard him. Go check on the musical instruments."

The god of war drew himself up, looking furious. "No one orders me around! Least of all this lame, bald, smelly half-wit who knows nothing about military strategy!"

"Know nothing, do I?" Vulcan growled. "I'd like to see you in battle without the weapons *I* make."

"Oh, Mars," Hera said impatiently. "Just do what you're told for once without starting a fight about it."

Diana noticed that Apollo was making flicking

motions at her with his hands, which were hidden behind his back. She realized that he was maneuvering the group of gods over to the hall doorway, listening to the faraway music, which Apollo, a god of music, might easily have been generating himself. And Vulcan, for once, was so intent on his argument with Mars that his gaze wasn't focused on Diana.

She slipped quietly out of the hammock and slid along the wall to the nearest doorway, which led to the next gallery. To her left, another doorway led to the central hall.

Diana peeked into the hall and saw nothing in either direction except the back of Apollo's head. He leaned back for a moment, spotted her, and winked. She sprinted across the open space and through the marble columns into the giant entrance lobby of the museum. It was vast and dark, but anyone could spot her from the balcony above or the many doors that opened onto it.

One of the doors at the front of the museum was propped open and she could see a figure pacing back and forth outside. No way out there. But there were doors at the back of the museum that led to the park. If she was lucky, one of the flakier gods would be guarding those—or nobody.

Diana darted through the hall and into one of the long corridors that led straight back through the middle of the museum. Medieval faces peered down at her as she ran past, their expressions gloomily disapproving of running in the museum. As she reached the dark churchlike space at the back where the Met had a Christmas tree every year, she heard raised voices in the distance behind her and off to her right. She veered left, into European Sculpture and Decorative Arts, and collided with someone as she shot through the door.

"Sorry!" Diana gasped instinctively, staggering back. She reached for the person's arm to help him up and registered several things at once. One, it was a boy, and he was smaller than she was. Two, he had fine dark hair and young Asian features, which meant he was neither a relic of the apocalypse nor a Greco-Roman god.

He gave her outstretched hand a wild look, then jumped to his feet without her help.

"Who are you?" Diana asked. "Are you the sixth avatar?"

He turned and fled. Diana chased after him, but when she reached the European Sculpture Court, he'd vanished. And there, to her right, were the glass walls and doors that led out to the back of the museum and the park.

With a frustrated glance around, Diana turned right and ran to the doors. Once the gods caught her and brought her back, she could search the museum for the mysterious boy, but this might be her only chance to escape and find Gus.

She pressed down on the metal bar and swung the door open, blinking in the bright sunlight. The space outside was less overgrown than at the back of the American courtyard, where she had nearly been killed the night before. The grass was high, and some bushes were rioting up the walls nearby, but she could still feel a concrete path below her feet, cracked and weather-beaten. She followed it until it ended at a wide paved road, where she instinctively looked left and right before running across. Everything was still and quiet, and she couldn't hear any sounds of pursuit.

The huge oval of the Great Lawn was empty, pristine in the early-morning sunlight. She waded through the grass, trying to imagine where Gus and the others would have gone. Back to Kali's apartment, she guessed, but she didn't know where that was. Tigre had led Gus off to the west when they left, so she would go that way and hope she ran into them soon.

A third of the way across the lawn, Diana noticed a clump of grass swaying off to her right. Curious, she made her way over and discovered, to her surprise, two small dogs wrestling with each other. One was tiny and black with long fur and stately whiskers; the other looked like a pug-Chihuahua mix. They were rolling around, making cute growling sounds and wagging their tails like mad.

"Oh my goodness," Diana exclaimed. "Aren't you two the cutest things!" They sprang apart and stared at her. She crouched down and held out her hand, hoping she smelled friendly. "Hey, little guys."

"Rrrrrrrrrrrrrrrrrrrrrrrrrrrrrrrrrrrrrrr," said the pug mix, and suddenly it sounded much less adorable.

The other dog started barking very loudly.

"Okay, sorry," Diana said, holding up her hands and backing away.

She heard a chorus of answering barks from somewhere nearby. They didn't sound friendly, either. She kept backing away until the two dogs were obscured by the grass between them, and then she turned and ran.

She'd hoped they'd be satisfied to see her leaving their territory, but they apparently decided it was still necessary to chase her out. The end of the park was a long way off still, and she had a feeling the dogs wouldn't stop at the edge of the Great Lawn.

Acting on instinct, she aimed for the nearest tree with low branches; there was a patch of them just across the paved walkway that circled the lawn. The yapping and snarling was close on her heels as she dashed across the pavement, leaped up, grabbed a branch, and pulled herself to safety.

Diana had swarmed halfway up the tree before she quite realized what she was doing. The bark under her hands felt strangely natural, and her feet found knots and footholds easily, as if she'd climbed this tree a million times before.

She paused on a high branch, catching her breath and feeling secretly pleased. She hadn't climbed a tree since she was, like, ten years old or something. The fact that she could do it so quickly and smoothly had to be a power. After all, Diana was a forest goddess, of the hunt and the wilderness and all that. She wasn't sure what good tree climbing would do her, but at least it meant she had some skills beyond making people love her.

The dog pack clustered below her tree, barking fiercely.

"Oh, were you looking for me?" she called down to them. "Too bad you can't climb trees, huh? That's right, bark it up, fluffballs. You'll get tired eventually."

"I don't know," said a voice. "They can keep this up for a really long time."

Startled, Diana twisted around, nearly losing her grip on the branch.

Perched in a bend of the next tree was a girl Diana's age. She had straight shoulder-length black hair, flipped up at the ends, and a strikingly pretty face with large brown eyes. She was smiling and swinging her legs.

"Hi," she said. "I'm Ereka. Spelled E-R-E-K-A—I know, it's kind of weird. Are you an avatar, too?"

When Kali closed her eyes, she could tell where Shiva was and how far away. If he was not manifest, she could feel him near her. When he did appear in solid form, she could follow her sense of him.

That was how she found him in Washington Square Park as the sun was passing its highest point.

She could see him as she walked down Fifth Avenue. He was on top of the big marble Washington arch, and he was dancing. She slowed down, giving herself more time to watch him. As she got closer, she could see the shimmers of blue in his skin reflected in the sunlight. His snake was coiled once around his neck and balanced on his outstretched arms.

Kali had ditched the others after breakfast. Gus wasn't pleased about it, she could tell, but she didn't particularly care. They could spend their day bonding with one another if they wanted; she had work to do.

Or perhaps she just wanted to spend time with Shiva. She almost wished he hadn't given back her memories. Now she missed him when he was away from her, and the others seemed extra boring and colorless in comparison.

She glanced up at the sky. There had been no sign of the flying crystal hunters since they'd smashed the Boss Hunter. But the ones shaped like tall insects were still around—Kali had checked a few bridges and tunnels on her way south. Everything was still guarded. Even with their new knowledge, the avatars were as trapped as they had been before. The gods wouldn't risk them wandering off and abandoning the battle now.

Even if she managed to escape, all it meant was that Amon or Thor would kill all the other avatars and absorb their power. And then she'd have an extra-super-powerful avatar hunting her down. No; better to stand and fight.

"Kali!" Shiva cried exuberantly from the top of the arch. He did a backflip, miraculously keeping the snake aloft, and then danced his way to the nearest corner as she walked up. She grinned up at him. She was surprised at how happy he was to see her, and even more surprised at how happy she was to notice it.

Shiva swung gracefully down the side of the arch, barely touching the marble as he balanced himself and landed in front of her.

"Hello, my queen," he said, taking her hand. She squeezed it, and he pulled her toward him for a kiss.

"You wish," she said, blocking his lips with her hand.

"Didn't you miss me?" he asked.

"Maybe a little."

"I've missed you for *eighteen years*," he said.

"Well, whose dumb idea was that?" she said. "Listen, I have a question for you."

"Always business," he said ruefully. "All right, come on, let's sit in the sunshine."

He hopped over the bench around the central fountain and down the short set of stairs to the fountain bottom, now dry and covered in leaves. Kali lay down on her back on the bench and watched as he kicked up spirals of orange and red and gold.

"I've been wondering if it's fall," Kali asked. "It was December when everything changed, but it can't be December now. I'd have died the night I spent out on the sidewalk."

"Well, a lot has changed in seventy-five years," Shiva said vaguely. "Global warming, all of that. And we didn't want the avatars to freeze to death, so we sent you to a warm-enough time of year."

"How nice of you," Kali said. "Why take us in December at all? Thought it'd be fun ruining Christmas for all our families?"

"December 21, 2012, is a date of particular significance to the Mesoamerican pantheon," Shiva said with a shrug. "The end of the world, according to their calendar, or some such. It made no difference to the rest of us, so we let them pick it. I doubt it will help them. Was that your question?"

"No," she said, looking up at the trees. "I like this park. Especially when it's not full of annoying college kids." *Annoying because I wanted to be one of them. Imagine a goddess wanting to go to college. If I'd known ruling the planet was an option . . .*

"I like the park, too," Shiva said. "Did you know it used to be a cemetery?"

"Really?"

"They buried foreigners and poor people here for a while in the early 1800s. I can feel the souls of the dead far below my feet. If you'd like, I can raise them up and have them dance for you."

"That's romantic," she said, "but no thanks."

Shiva did a cartwheel in the leaves.

"You're in a good mood," she observed.

"It's you. It's being with you again."

She smiled. "I don't usually have that effect on people."

"That's not true. I saw those little girls, how they adored you."

Kali felt a tug of sadness at the thought of her sisters. She'd managed not to think about them since getting back her goddess memories yesterday. "Amy and Beth and Jo-Jo," she said. "What ended up happening to them?"

"I can't tell you that," Shiva said.

"Why?" Kali asked, getting angry. "Surely you know. You've got three eyes to spy on them with, after all."

"I don't spy!" Shiva growled. "I am all-seeing!"

"Terrific," Kali said. "So tell me about my sisters."

Shiva grrred softly to himself for a moment. "All I can tell you," he said finally, "is that it is a question you will probably be able to answer for yourself in time."

She sat up and stared at him. "What the heck does that mean?"

"Didn't you have a question for me?" he said.

"Shiva, do you mean we can go back in time? To where we came from, when this is all over?"

"No," he said, shaking his head. "Traveling backward in time is impossible, Kali."

Kali sighed angrily.

"Anyway," he added, "you're going to win this battle, so you won't need to concern yourself with anything or anyone from your human time."

"I just hope I have *someone* to concern myself with," Kali said, lying back down. "I am so not looking forward to this ruling over an empty planet thing."

"Let's talk about the battles," Shiva said, changing the subject. "And whom you should deal with first."

"Fine," said Kali. "That's what I wanted to ask you. We think we've found the sixth avatar, but she doesn't know who she is and her pantheon isn't speaking to her. Any thoughts? Who's the sixth pantheon?"

Shiva scooped up a pile of leaves and threw them over his head. "There's you," he said, lifting a bright orange leaf out of the air. "There's Thor of the Norse gods." He caught a large dark red leaf. "There's Amon of the Egyptians." A perfectly oval medium-sized, gold leaf spiraled into his hand. "Diana, or Venus, from the Greco-Roman pantheon." A sharp-edged smaller leaf divided down the middle, half copper-colored, half green, joined the others. "Catequil, the Mesoamerican god." The only green leaf in the pile, tiny and round and frayed, drifted uncertainly past, and Shiva plucked it from the air.

"And then . . ." He paused, clasping his hands over the five leaves he held. All the others in the pile had settled back to the marble floor of the fountain. The space around him was empty.

"We don't know." Shiva looked at the leaves in his palm, a trace of a frown crossing his brow.

"Why don't you know?" Kali asked. "What happened to your all-seeingness?"

"Don't taunt me," Shiva said, blowing the leaves at her. She swatted them away and found two sticking to her left hand: one bright and orange, with the small green one clinging to its edge.

"They are keeping themselves hidden," Shiva went on. "They have put up shields around themselves and their avatar, as if they've erased themselves from our minds. We must have known them, to ask them to join the battle, but now none of us can remember who they were."

Kali shivered. "Okay, that's creepy. How can they do that?"

"They must be expending great energy on this shrouding," Shiva said. "It can only weaken them and their avatar, and to what advantage, I can't imagine."

"It's not doing her much good," Kali said. "Anna's pretty confused."

"There's an easy way to find out," Shiva said, folding himself onto the bench in front of her. "Once you defeat her, you'll assume her power, and then her identity will be clear."

"I'm sure that would make her feel much better," Kali said.

Shiva's face turned serious. "Kali. What are you waiting for? Why not start with her? Or the anomaly—he should be easy to dispose of."

"Gus," Kali said.

"Don't think of him as Gus," Shiva said quickly. "Think of him as Oro, god of war. Think of him as one of the demons you've had to fight in the past to protect the world."

"Not the world," Kali said. "The people *in* the world. *My* people."

"Here we go again," Shiva said. "I told you there's a plan. Stop worrying about it. Focus on winning."

"Well, I can't fight Gus, at least not until tomorrow," Kali said. "Amon has challenged him to a battle at noon."

Shiva looked dark. "All the more reason to kill him now," he said. "You cannot afford to let Amon get stronger. Oro's power may not seem like much, but if the mortal boy can connect to it, he could be very danger-ous. Even more so if another god gets to him first and absorbs the power directly. You should fight him tonight."

"Wouldn't that be stealing?" Kali said. "Amon claimed him."

"It's his own fault for not doing it right away," Shiva said. "The judges can be summoned almost instanta-neously. I'm sure Isis told Amon this, but he's posturing, trying to intimidate Oro by giving him time to worry, lose sleep, and grow weaker. And he seems to want as big an audience as possible for the fight."

"Hmm," Kali said. "It still seems dishonorable, snag-ging his opponent out from under him."

"Then one of the others," Shiva said. "Maybe Diana. She shouldn't be too challenging, as confused as she is, but she might give you the power of two goddesses."

He took Kali's hands in his and kissed the center of each palm.

"I'd like to see Thor," Kali said, freeing her right hand and running two fingers over the snake's head on Shiva's shoulder. "If he's such a threat, I want to know more about him."

"That's easy," Shiva said. "He's nearby."

"Down here?" Kali asked. "What's he doing in the West Village?"

Shiva smiled. "What Vikings do best."

"Let's go through the park," Tigre said. "According to Kali's map, we can get to the library that way." He didn't want to run into Inti again, even though it was midday and probably a good time for the sun god to appear. All his worries vanished when he was holding Anna's hand, and he wanted to keep it that way. For once, someone else was getting picked on instead of him, and he liked the feeling that he might be able to help Gus instead of needing help himself.

"The park?" Gus said skeptically, following him out of Kali's building and across the empty street. "The place with the homicidal poodle pack and the creepy hanging goddess?"

"I'm curious about the dogs," Tigre said, "and I have a feeling the creepy goddess will find me wherever I am." *Do not think about your dream. Do not think about snakes of blood.* His fingers tightened around Anna's and she smiled up at him.

"I'm not a big fan of dogs," she said, wrinkling her nose. "They never like me."

"That can't be true," Tigre said.

"I'm not sure these dogs like anyone," Gus muttered.

"It'll be faster anyway," Tigre said. The three of them turned onto a street that wove through the park, following it past a broken-down playground. Tigre looked at the rusted monkey bars and wondered what it must have been like—knowing there would be no more kids, that this was the end of the human species, that there would never be a need for playgrounds or toys or children's books or schools ever again.

They crossed an overpass and turned into a thicket of pine trees, climbing over low wooden fences and wading through a carpet of dry brown needles.

Gus stopped.

"Okay," he said to Tigre, "now I *know* I'm hearing something."

Tigre pulled Anna to a halt and they tilted their heads, listening.

"Barking," Anna said with a small shudder.

"They sound like they've got something cornered," Tigre said. Anna looked aghast.

"I hope it's not us!" she said.

"I don't think so," said Gus. "Meaning we still have time to run. Far. In the other direction."

"Let's go see what it is," Tigre said, dropping Anna's hand and starting forward.

"Tigre," Gus protested. Tigre didn't stop, and soon he heard their muffled footsteps behind him.

As they got closer to the source of the barking, Tigre could see a small white dog leaping at a tree. She kept running up to it and leaping as high as she could, then dropping down and circling around it. Behind her, about twelve other dogs bayed her on, most of them running from that tree to the next one and back in a frenzy of excitement.

His gaze traveled up through the branches, and he spotted a pair of sneakers and a flash of gold hair.

"Diana!" he called.

At once the dogs spun around to face him. The little white one growled and a dachshund scrambled up behind her, his fur bristling.

"NO," Tigre said sternly. "This is my prey. *My* pack. Down."

The white dog hesitated, and he could almost see a whisper of memory trailing through her mind. He squared his shoulders and tried to look commanding.

"Go," Tigre said, pointing back at the Great Lawn. "Go on, go!"

The dachshund reacted first, crouching low to the ground and then slinking away. A few other dogs followed suit, and then, finally, the tiny white one stopped baring her teeth. She stared at Tigre for a minute, her tail twitching, then turned and led the last of her pack away with a dignified air that said, *Fine. You may have this one, but only because I allow it.*

Tigre waited until they had trotted off into the grass. As the last tail vanished, he felt Anna slip her hand into his.

"Wow," she said. "That was amazing. I thought they were going to eat you alive."

"Those little guys?" he said. "They may have been wild for a while, but they're lapdogs at heart, bred to live on couches and sleep a lot."

"Sounds like me," Gus joked.

"Gus!" a voice called from the tree above them.

They all looked up, and Gus smiled as if he'd just won a free trip to Maui. Diana waved back at them from a high branch, but her eyes and smile were all for Gus.

Tigre felt a twinge of jealousy; after all, *he* was the one who had scared off the dogs. But he fought it back, focusing on Anna, who was squinting up at Diana as if trying to place her.

"You've probably seen her on a magazine cover," Tigre said. "Or on MTV. She was everywhere the last couple of years before we disappeared."

"Oh," Anna said, glancing down. "Yeah, I'm sure that's why she looks familiar."

Just then the tree next to Diana's started shaking. Tigre jumped back, his mind flashing to the toothy monkey creatures he'd encountered in the jungle. But the figure lowering herself down through the branches was even more unexpected.

It was *Anna*.

She landed on the ground and turned with a big smile, which froze when she spotted Anna.

Diana dropped down next to her and gave Gus a hug. Both of them flinched from the electric shocks.

"Hey, guys, this is Ereka," she said, stepping back. "She's one of— Oh my goodness."

Tigre was speechless. He looked from the girl holding his hand to the one from the tree and back. They were identical, down to the clothes they were wearing and their disbelieving expressions.

"Who are you?" Anna said, drawing closer to Tigre.

"I'm an avatar," Ereka said. "I'm supposed to be here. Who are *you*?"

Vikings: a seafaring Scandinavian people who raided the coasts of northern and western Europe from the eighth to the eleventh centuries. Famous for their navigational skills and long warships, they were also known for piracy, plundering, and pillaging. And when they weren't fighting, they were feasting.

And drinking. And shouting. And carousing. And making an almighty noise, Kali discovered.

"Not worried about being found, is he?" she said to Shiva as they approached. She was almost surprised she hadn't heard them from Washington Square Park. The bar where the Norse gods were currently ensconced was only a few blocks away, and it sounded like about twenty oversized men were singing off-key war songs at the top of their giant lungs.

"His pantheon is preparing him for battle. They're quite confident he's going to win—he's their hero. He always wins."

"Not this time," Kali said.

"I know," Shiva replied. "It's a bit sad, actually."

Shiva took her hand and stepped up into the air. She felt herself drawn weightlessly up after him as he hopped onto the roof of the bar, where a large skylight was propped open. Kali had been hoping Shiva could do something like this; now that her memory was back, she missed her own ability to travel through the air as freely as she wanted. This wasn't quite like flying. It felt more like taking an invisible escalator into the sky.

Shiva and Kali lay down on the warm slope of the roof and poked their heads over the edge of the skylight, resting on their folded arms.

The space below them was cavernous for Manhattan, with tall ceilings, wooden beams, and a blazing fireplace. All the tables had been pushed together to make one long table down the center of the room, and a host of men and women were gathered around it, each holding a large mug and singing.

"Wow," Kali murmured. "They're all very . . . imposing. Which one's Thor?"

"Can't you guess?" Shiva said.

Kali studied the group of gods. They were mostly fair-haired and pale-skinned, tall and blustery. At one end of the table were a pair that looked like twins, although one was male and one female. They were both strikingly beautiful, and the woman had a cloak of feathers thrown over the back of her chair that glowed with color in the firelight.

On the other side of her twin was a guy who looked younger than the rest. His rust-colored beard was not fully grown in, and although he was hugely proportioned, many of the others still dwarfed him.

"There," Kali whispered. "That's him. Next to the twins."

"Yes," Shiva said. "The twins are Frey and Freya, god and goddess of fertility, among other things."

Thor was grinning from ear to ear, and as the music reached a fever pitch, he suddenly jumped to his feet, leaped on the table, and began stomping to the rhythm. The gods roared with approval and clapped along.

"They're lunatics," Kali said. "How do they expect him to fight after partying like this?"

"It worked for them, at least for a few centuries," Shiva said, shrugging his perfectly formed shoulders. Kali found herself thankful that he was so much more her type than any of the feasting gods down below. *I mean, if you're going to discover you have a husband for all eternity, he might as well be your kind of hot. Okay, it's circular logic—I must have married him originally for a reason—but still, good job, me.*

She ran her hand up his upper arm and he tilted his head to face her. *I always thought the expression "smoldering eyes" was just a cliché. Maybe it helps if you can actually set things on fire with your eyes.*

Just as she was about to give in and kiss him, an angry caw sounded from inches away. Shiva and Kali looked up and found two ravens perched across the skylight, looking tremendously displeased. One clacked its beak at them menacingly, and the other ruffled up its feathers, then dove through the hole into the room below.

"Huginn and Munnin," Shiva said. "Their names mean thought and memory. Also known as Odin's spies. Which means he knows we're here. Shall we say hello?"

"Sure," said Kali, repressing the nervous shiver that went through her. She wasn't afraid of their power—hers was more than a match for Thor's. But she had never liked interacting with strangers if she could help it, and these were as strange as any she'd ever encountered, even on the streets of New York.

Shiva took her hand again and they swung through the skylight, drifting down to land on the bar, near Thor's end of the table. The rest of the gods had fallen silent, but it took Thor a few more beats to catch on. Finally he stopped singing, looked around in bewilderment, and saw Kali and Shiva.

Kali had expected outrage or fear or blustering, but Thor just raised his glass higher and yelled something in what she guessed was Norwegian or Swedish. The other gods repeated the gesture and the phrase, and then they all drank. Thor tossed his back with such gusto that the table he was dancing on finally cracked and sent him crashing to the floor, which made him and the other gods howl with laughter.

"Did they just toast us?" Kali whispered to Shiva.

"They are coarse and brutal," Shiva said with a sniff. "You should have no trouble here."

"Is that what you think, Shiva?" The deep voice came from the far end of the table, which was hidden in shadows. The other gods quieted as the speaker stood up and approached the bar slowly. He wore a long gray cloak and a wide-brimmed gray hat. The shadows behind him shifted and two large gray wolves emerged to slink along beside him.

He lifted his head to face them, and Kali realized that where one eye had been was now a wrinkled mess of scar tissue. But the eye he had left was piercing and fierce, like that of a bird of prey.

"Odin," Shiva said, with more respect, Kali noticed, than he had shown to Zeus. "We thought we'd stop by and greet you."

"Really?" Odin said. "Seems to me you thought you'd stop by and spy on us."

"When it comes to spying," Shiva said with a brief bow, "I'm afraid you have the advantage." He indicated the raven on the table and the one still peering down through the skylight.

"Hmmm," Odin said, studying Kali with a shrewd expression. "I surmise that you have brought your avatar here to boost her confidence. You know Thor's strength and you wish her to see him in an unguarded moment, so she will think he can be easily defeated." He shook his head with a tsk–tsking noise. "Aren't you worried she'll underestimate him?"

"I don't need my confidence boosted," Kali said. "And I'm not worried about underestimating him." She looked pointedly at the Norse avatar, who was still sprawled in the wreckage of his table, laughing.

"This is how we prepare for war," Odin said. "We feast hard and we fight hard. You have never seen a berserker in action. If I choose to send Thor into the berserker battle frenzy, he will be undefeatable."

"But what happens if you lose him?" Shiva said softly. "What happens to the fate of the gods if your hero is gone?"

One of the wolves at Odin's side growled, and Odin rested his hand on the wolf's head. "There will be no twilight of the gods when Thor wins and we become the most powerful pantheon in the world."

"What are you talking about?" Kali asked.

"Ragnarok," Shiva said. "It's the prophesied end of the Norse gods, when the frost giants rise up, attack their home in Asgard, and tear apart the world in a long, fiery battle. The giants are ultimately defeated, but most of the gods die, as well." He leveled his gaze at Odin. "You are meddling with prophecies by bringing Thor into this battle. If he dies here, who will fight the deadly world serpent at Ragnarok? Perhaps the world will be destroyed, and the age of peace and harmony that should follow will never come."

Odin wrinkled up his whole face and squinted at

Shiva through his one good eye. "Now you are trying to rattle us," he pronounced. "You think you can make us fearful by bringing up Ragnarok, but we have lived with the prophecy for thousands of years. It does not frighten us. It is our destiny, and we must face it with courage."

"Sounds to me like you're trying to change your destiny," Shiva said. "Or else why are you in this game at all?"

"You cannot scare Thor," Odin went on implacably. "Even if he were capable of fear, this mortal version speaks only our language, so he cannot understand your mind-twisting tricks."

"That's right," Kali said, crouching down on the bar to get a closer look at Thor. "Anna mentioned that he doesn't speak English. Hey there." She waved at Thor and he waved back from the floor, grinning. He reminded her of a giant teddy bear, or Clifford the Big Red Dog in a Viking outfit. He didn't look like someone who was planning to kill her, despite all his size and strength.

"He's kind of cute," Kali said, standing back up and dusting off her hands. "In a gigantic Snuffleupagus way."

Both Odin and Shiva looked displeased at that remark.

"Perhaps we should go," Shiva said, taking her hand. "We have actual training and battle preparation to do."

"Perhaps you should," Odin agreed. "We will contact you when Thor wishes to fight your avatar."

"Great," Kali said. "I can't wait."

As she and Shiva drifted up toward the skylight again, she whispered, "I see what you mean about it being kind of sad."

"Yes," Shiva responded. "Thor is essential to their victory at Ragnarok. I wasn't just toying with Odin; I'm honestly curious about what they think will happen when Thor's not there. Not that I believe in it myself. You and I have our own ideas about how the world will end."

They landed on the roof and Kali took another look back through the skylight. Thor had gotten to his feet again and was dancing with the male twin and another god, their arms interlinked, bellowing another war song. He looked like a giant kid who'd been allowed to tag along to his older brother's frat party.

Kali had hoped to find another warrior like her, someone whom she could fight on equal terms. But she didn't like the idea of fighting someone she couldn't communicate with.

"If it's a prophecy," Kali said, "then doesn't that mean he will be there? Might that mean he'll survive this?"

"No," Shiva said, touching her cheek. "Trust me, Kali. No one will survive this except you."

"You spent the night in Belvedere Castle?" Diana said, impressed. "I wish I'd thought of that." She leaned against the balustrade, looking out across the park. The "castle," built at one of the highest points in Central Park, had once been a lookout post, so they could see for miles. The sun was high above them, and the sky was blue and cloudless in all directions. *Both storm gods must be feeling calmer than they were yesterday.*

Gus propped his elbows on the wall next to her and they smiled at each other. He had a new bruise on his jaw, from Thor punching him, to match the one on his forehead, which he'd gotten slamming into a pterodactyl wing on top of the Empire State Building. He looked like he'd already been beaten so many times; she couldn't bear the thought of someone else trying to hurt him.

"I always wanted to live in a castle, so when I saw it, I figured, why not?" Ereka said. "But it was colder than I expected, and not that comfortable, actually."

"Sure," Diana said. "It's a museum nowadays—or thenadays, or whatever. You'd have better luck in one of the hotels around here."

"Let's get back to the point," Gus said, looking from Ereka to her double. "You guys really have the exact same memories?"

"Up until I got here," Ereka said. She and Anna couldn't take their eyes off each other. Anna's fingers kept twitching, as if she wanted to poke Ereka and find out if she was real.

"So the end of the world—dropping the spoon, noticing your dad's shoes were missing—you remember all of that, too?" Tigre asked.

"Yup," Ereka said. "All the way up to Thor dropping me off in Central Park. And then he just rolled off in his chariot and left me alone."

"He dropped me off in Times Square," Anna said. "And then tried to kill me. That's a memory I wouldn't mind trading."

"At what time?" Gus asked.

"About noon yesterday," both girls said simultaneously. Gus shook his head. "That's impossible."

"Too bad we can't ask Thor what he remembers," Diana said.

"It's so weird," Anna said, reaching toward Ereka's face. Ereka jerked back, scowling. "It's not like looking in a mirror. Everything's on the wrong side."

"Usually in a mirror your face is reversed," Tigre said. "This is what other people see when they look at you."

"Trust me, you look exactly alike," Gus said. "So Thor just took off?"

"Yup," Ereka said. "I thought he'd come back, but he hasn't yet. Unless I missed him while I was scrounging for food." She nudged the corner of a plastic bag with her foot.

"And you've heard voices in your head?" Diana asked.

"One voice," Ereka said. "It just told me to come here, that I was an avatar, and to prepare to fight the other avatars so my pantheon could win."

"Did it tell you which goddess we—you are?" Anna asked.

Ereka shook her head. "No idea. It didn't even tell me what pantheon I'm from. I've been waiting for more information, but it hasn't spoken to me since yesterday."

"I don't understand," Anna said, sliding down to sit on the stone floor. "If you're their avatar, what am I? Where did I come from? I'm *sure* those are my memories."

"So am I," Ereka said, sounding annoyed.

"Let's keep going to the library," Tigre said. "Maybe there's a weird explanation, like you're twin goddesses or something, both inside Anna—or Ereka—until the Change happened."

"Two goddesses in one person?" Anna said doubtfully. "That sounds horrible."

Diana winced, and Gus touched her shoulder, trying to be reassuring even though it still bothered him that she hadn't yet told him about the Venus/Diana split. A spark went off under his fingers as they met her skin, and he glanced at Ereka, wondering if contact with her would have the same effect. That might help prove that she was the other avatar and Anna wasn't.

"Any theory is better than none," Ereka said. "I'll totally go to the library with you."

"Do you have to get back to Zeus and all them?" Gus asked Diana. It came out sounding angrier than he'd intended, and he looked down, avoiding her eyes.

"No, I'll go with you," Diana said.

As Ereka, Tigre, and Anna started out of the castle, Diana grabbed Gus's hand, ignoring the spark, and kept him a short distance behind the others.

"Are you mad at me?" she whispered when the others were out of earshot.

"No," he answered, a little too quickly. He was thrilled to see her, but he couldn't help thinking of how she'd left him yesterday, of the way Amon had looked at her, of the secrets she was still hiding from him.

She hesitated. "I didn't want to go with Zeus, Gus. But I wanted him to protect you."

"I don't need protecting," he said. "The big crystal hunter got smushed, remember? And we haven't seen a glimmer of the smaller ones since."

"Maybe that's because they're not after you anymore, silly," Diana said. They had circled behind Belvedere Castle and were now following a path that ran along the south side of a small lake, heading east. Up ahead, Ereka and Anna were chattering like magpies, comparing their memories of childhood, while Tigre listened quietly, hands shoved in his pockets.

"So are they *training* you?" Gus asked. "Are they

getting you all ready to fight us?"

"No," Diana said. She wanted to tell him about the alliance with the Egyptians, but she wasn't sure how he would react. He was already jealous of the fact that Amon had appeared in her dreams. What would he do if he found out she was supposed to be Amon's prize for winning the battle? She was here to convince him *not* to fight Amon tomorrow, and that bit of information certainly wouldn't help her case.

"They're mostly ignoring me," she said. "Overprotecting me and treating me like a china poodle. It's annoying . . . but actually it's not that different from my regular life." *Apart from someone mysterious hurling a spear at my head, that is.* "At least Zeus hasn't tried to sell me to a reality TV show." She glanced at his face, but he barely cracked a smile. She tried again.

"I don't know, it's weird. Have you ever had that dream where you're in a play but you have no idea what the story is and you can't remember any of your lines? Or you're performing in a concert but your band starts playing a song you've never heard? That's what this feels like—like I've been dropped into a soap opera and I have no idea what I've done or why all these people hate me. And a lot of them seem to *really* hate me."

"Seriously?" Gus said. "Doesn't everyone love you?"

She wished he meant "because you're so awesome," but she knew he was talking about her Venus powers. "I guess immortals are immune. Venus wasn't too popular with the other gods in the myths, either, from what I remember."

He didn't say anything for a minute.

"Gus," she said more seriously. "I heard about Amon challenging you to fight tomorrow."

"Yeah?" he said. "Did he come tell you that himself? He said he wants you there to see him win."

Diana was taken aback, both by the news and the bitterness in Gus's voice. Amon didn't seem to be hiding their supposed alliance very carefully; he'd talked about it openly in front of the others on the Great Lawn yesterday, as well. But Apollo had told her that they might get in trouble if the judges found out. Didn't Amon care about that? Was he so unconcerned about Gus and Tigre, assuming they'd be dead before they could figure it out and spill the beans?

"I haven't seen him since yesterday, when we all did," Diana said. "Gus, you can't fight him. You saw him on the Empire State Building. He's got tons of, like, literal firepower."

"As if I have a choice," Gus said.

"Sure you do," Diana said. "Tell him no, or postpone it. Or I'll fight him instead."

She knew right away that was the wrong thing to say.

"What makes you think you have more of a chance than I do?" Gus said. "You should have seen me fighting Thor yesterday. There's a warrior god somewhere inside me, you know."

"Gus, don't be a guy about this. It won't make you less macho or hot, okay? You're not 'getting rescued by a girl' or 'looking weak'; you're staying alive. Remember how we talked about this? How I really want you to do that? Stay alive?"

"And what are you going to do, sing him to death?

Make him love you until he surrenders?"

Diana drew in a sharp breath.

"As I remember," Gus continued bitingly, "your super-powers aren't so impressive, either—you're really more of a Strawberry Shortcake than a Catwoman, aren't you?"

"Gus, you're being a jerk," she said.

"Well, you're acting like I'm a two-year-old you have to babysit. Of course I want to stay alive. I'm the one who wants to find a way home, remember? As far as I can tell, I'm the only one. I don't care about this stupid battle or ruling the universe. I just want to get back to our own time, but everyone else, including you, seems to think we have to play this game, and so I don't know what else I can do except fight him. Okay?"

"No," Diana said. "It's not okay, because he's going to kill you."

"And it would make me feel better if he killed you instead? No thanks," Gus said.

Frustrated, Diana watched him walk faster to catch up with Tigre. After her weird little moment with the moon last night, she'd felt like her Diana side might be getting stronger. She felt independent and tough, perhaps even dangerous. But it also meant that she was more likely to say what she really thought, and look what that led to: fighting with Gus. Maybe he liked her only when she was sweet and affectionate and leaned on him for support. Maybe he really preferred her Venus side, just as she feared.

Maybe the real question is . . . Which half do I like better?

After a couple hours of knocking things down and set-ting them on fire, Kali was bored. She was stronger with her memories restored, but not as strong as she remembered being, and it was irritating.

"Hey," she said to Shiva. "Can you use that nifty floating trick to take me back uptown? You know, since you made me walk all the way down here." She wasn't tired, exactly, but it was surprisingly boring walking up and down Manhattan by herself. She didn't miss pushing through the crowds, but she guessed her fury at them must have given her energy.

"Don't you think you should train some more?" Shiva asked.

"Nah," Kali said, stretching her fingers. "I have some other ideas about building my power. I want to find out who's living in the museum. Do you know?"

"No one who can help you," Shiva said. "And it's full of Greek gods. I don't think it's a good place to go."

"Too bad," Kali said. She slipped her hand into his. "I'm going anyway, and if you'd help me get there, it would save a bunch of time that I could spend training later."

Shiva scowled. "All right," he grumbled. Immediately, Kali felt herself getting lighter. They floated slowly up until they were a few feet off the ground, and then, as if they were on one of those people-moving belts in airports, they began drifting north.

"Is this as fast as it goes?" Kali asked.

"*It?*" Shiva said. "You mean *me*?"

"You know, the floaty power," Kali said, shoving his shoulder with her free hand.

"Are you in a hurry to get rid of me?" Shiva asked.

"I guess not," Kali said. "You do feed me, which I'm a

fan of." Earlier, Shiva had produced a plate of burned strips of meat covered in some spice. She'd missed meat too much to be picky about what it was or how it was cooked.

"Let's work on your distance abilities as we travel," Shiva said. "Can you start a fire in that building without touching it?"

He pointed at a boarded-up store half a block ahead of them. Kali recognized it. She had once taken her mother in there to buy her a tube of lipstick for Mother's Day. It was an expensive place, but the salespeople had been unusually friendly for New York—perhaps won over by Mom's charm and enthusiastic delight in the different dramatic lipstick names. She'd finally settled on one called Secret Spice, giggling that it could have belonged to a girl pop group she'd listened to when Kali was a kid.

"That building's kind of cool-looking," Kali said. "I'll do that one instead." Before he could argue, she pointed at a video store across the street, and they saw a burst of flame through the broken glass window. By the time they floated past, fingers of fire were crawling up the walls and across the roof.

"Well done," Shiva said, giving her a scrutinizing look.

"Yeah," Kali said with a shrug. "It's hardly the whole block in one giant fireball, though. That would be really cool."

"Kali," Shiva said, "you must fight any feelings of attachment to this place or these people."

"Please," Kali said. "I hate this place. And I *really* hated these people. Didn't you see me try to run away, like, a thousand times?"

"You don't hate your fellow avatars, though," Shiva said.

"I do when they put too much sugar in my tea," Kali said. "Or when they get all bossy about how we should stick together. Or when they look at me like I'm plotting to kill them."

"They *should* look at you like that," Shiva said. "You *are* plotting to kill them."

"Okay," Kali said. "True."

"Don't get involved," Shiva said. "That's all I'm saying."

"Why would I?" Kali said. "I'm a goddess of destruction, remember? I'm one of the bad guys. Not a goddess of love or happiness or family or making the world a better place. The whole point of me is to wreck things, and I'm good at it. So why don't you just assume I can handle it, okay?"

There was a pause. "That's not all you're good for," Shiva said quietly.

"Oh, shut up," Kali said, and they spent the rest of the trip to the museum in silence.

Gus slammed his book shut, and both Tigre and Diana jumped.

"Having trouble?" Ereka said sympathetically, sitting on the corner of the table next to him. On the way to the library, they had stopped to pick up new clothes for the two girls, so now Tigre could be sure he was telling them apart. Anna was wearing a dark red sweater that looked amazing on her; Ereka had opted for a white T-shirt. They both seemed to have trouble staying still. While Tigre, Diana, and Gus had been sitting and reading since they got there, Anna and Ereka kept getting up, examining the shelves, whispering to each other, and generally being distracting, although Tigre was sure they didn't realize it.

"Oro is *nowhere*," Gus said. "It's like he doesn't exist."

"Oh, sad," Ereka said, leaning over to see what Gus had been reading. "I'm sure you're somebody."

"How are we supposed to find anything without the Internet?" Gus went on. "Or even a computer catalog?"

"People somehow managed it for centuries," Diana said not quite snippily. Tigre wondered what they were arguing about, and whether Diana minded how close Ereka was to Gus. "Perhaps if you focused your search a bit more instead of pulling random books of gods off the shelves, you'd find something."

"But how?" Gus protested. "There are all these different Polynesian mythologies. I don't even know which island believed in him. I've found plenty about the Maoris in New Zealand, but nothing that mentions an Oro—their war god was called Tu or something."

"Oh, I found that," Diana said. "Oro was a god of war in Tahiti. Your dad's name was Ta'aroa and you're also a peace god, but that's all it says."

Gus glowered at her.

"That's more than I've found," Tigre said. "Catequil— also a nobody." *No wonder my fellow gods aren't worried about losing me. I'm barely a blip on their radar. Did I volunteer for this when I was a god? Did I get a choice? Did I know what they were setting me up for, and did I just accept it?*

"Hey, I don't even have a place to start," Anna said, dropping down into the seat next to him. "I pulled out a few books supposedly listing *all* the goddesses in the world, but there's no Ereka or Anna in the indexes."

"Sounds like a dead end," Ereka said. "For me and Anna, I mean," she added quickly, seeing the look on Tigre's face.

"There's got to be something in here somewhere," Tigre said. He flipped idly through an Aztec book, which he'd pulled out mainly because it was full of color paintings. Now he kind of wished he hadn't. Almost all of the gods were intensely gruesome. One was a skeleton covered in bloody red spots and wearing a collar of eyeballs. Another one had the head of a dog with one burst eye. A third picture showed a god being ritually flayed alive.

He turned a page and found a goddess with a skirt of serpents, two snakes of blood emerging from her neck, and a necklace of human hearts and hands. *The one who appeared in my dream last night.* Her name was Coatlicue, and she was a powerful earth goddess, as she'd said.

Tigre wondered uneasily if all these other creepy figures planned on visiting him, too, one by one, until he went insane and gave up, just like they wanted.

"Hey," Gus said, sliding a book over toward him. "Look familiar?"

It was the hanging woman from the park. Ixtab, Mayan goddess of suicide. Tigre could tell from Gus's expression that he'd read the caption.

"Ewwww," Anna said, looking over his shoulder. "I hope I don't look like *that* as a goddess."

"What's the deal with your pantheon, Tigre?" Gus asked. "Why would they pick a god no one's heard of for their avatar? Why are they sending creepy suicide goddesses to freak you out instead of helping you train?"

Tigre shifted away from Anna's curious look. "I—I don't know," he said. "They're not, uh . . . very communicative."

"Here," Diana said. "Catequil, an Incan storm god of thunder and lightning."

"Really?" Tigre said hopefully.

"Sort of," Diana said. Her eyes scanned the page. "It looks like you were a local god for a village in the Andes. Then the Incas came along, conquered the area, and cheered up the locals by making you part of their pantheon."

"Oh." *So I was a conquered god. That bodes well.* He sighed. "Is there a picture?"

"No," Diana replied.

"Count yourself lucky," Ereka said. "You probably have three heads, no skin, and corpses of cats where your hands should be."

"A beautiful image, Ereka," Gus said. "Thanks for that."

"I'm just guessing," she said with a sunny smile.

"Does it, uh, does it say anything about Catequil and animals?" Tigre asked.

"Animals?" Diana said, a small frown furrowing her forehead as she studied the text.

"Like that I like animals, or that I . . . turn into one, or anything?" *One with long killer claws and crazy memory gaps.*

"Turn into one!" Anna cried.

"Has that happened?" Ereka asked. "Because wow, awesome."

Yeah. Awesome. "No," Tigre said quickly. "I just wondered. I, uh, have dreams about . . . animals sometimes."

"This book says you might have been a god of prophecy, too," Diana said. "Like an oracle of the Andes. Nothing about animals, though. Sorry." She pushed the book over to him and leaned back, stretching. Tigre was disappointed to see that the entry on Catequil was only a few lines long. Next to it were longer entries on a few other Incan weather gods; he hadn't even been the only one.

"Is anyone else hungry?" Ereka said. "I'm *starving*."

"Ereka!" Anna said. "We're doing important research here."

"Clearly," Ereka said sarcastically. "I mean, I've learned a lot. Haven't you?"

"What time do you think it is?" Diana asked.

"Worried about getting back to Zeus?" Gus said. She flashed him an annoyed look.

"It's well after lunchtime," Ereka said. "Come on, let's go find something to eat. We can always come back here."

"Ereka," Anna said in a lecturing tone. "Gus has to fight a big scary Egyptian god tomorrow. If he doesn't figure out *something* about himself, he's going to have to go into it blind, and then he'll probably be so nervous, he'll screw up and get killed. No offense," she said to Gus, who looked too ill to answer.

"Please," Ereka said. "Worrying about it isn't going to help him, either. He needs to relax. And saying things like that probably isn't helping, Anna."

"Anna's right," Tigre said. "We walked all the way here. We should concentrate on figuring out what we can."

Gus stood up, shaking his head. "I need a break. I think

lunch sounds like a great idea."

"Oh, okay," Diana said, standing up as well.

Ereka looked at Anna triumphantly. Anna sighed.

"Fine. If that's okay with you, Tigre. But we'll come right back afterward."

Ereka was already halfway out the door at the other end of the room. Gus and Diana trailed after her, keeping their distance from one another.

"Wow," Anna whispered to Tigre. "Am I really that annoying?"

"No!" Tigre said, putting a couple of books in a knapsack to take with him. "No way. I mean, not that Ereka is, either, but—you guys actually have sort of different personalities, I think."

"God, I hope so," Anna said. "And I hope I'm the real me, whatever that ends up meaning."

"I hope you are, too," Tigre said, keeping his eyes on the piles of books he was rearranging.

Her soft hand appeared in his. "Thanks, Tigre," she said quietly. "I know it's stupid and Ereka is as much in the dark as I am, but I still—I like the feeling that someone's on my side."

"Sure," Tigre said, smiling. They walked after the others.

"You know," Anna said in a low, confidential voice, "I think she might be jealous."

"Jealous?"

"I mean, I think she might be feeling like a fifth wheel. You know, because Gus and Diana are kind of together, in their weird way—yeah, I can tell—and because you and I . . . well, we're not, you know, like that, but we're more together than she is with anyone. If that makes sense. I'm rambling, aren't I?"

"That's okay," he said. He liked the way she talked without forcing him to respond. Vicky had talked a lot, too, but she always left significant pauses in the conversation where he was supposed to say something, and he'd never known what that was, and he'd always gotten it wrong.

Plus, getting together with Vicky had taken years and a lot of false starts before he'd figured out that she wanted him to ask her out. Apparently, ignoring him had been a clue that she liked him, but he hadn't been allowed to ignore her, even unintentionally, or else it meant that he was a heartless boy who didn't care about anyone. He'd gotten yelled at several times before he'd unearthed this first layer of Vicky logic—and there were so many more levels to it.

But so far, Anna was uncomplicated . . . or at least as uncomplicated as a relationship between two gods in an abandoned post-apocalyptic world could be. She was straightforward about liking him, and she didn't make him play weird head games, and she was easily affectionate without reading something into everything he did. True, he had no idea why she would like him, and that made it suspicious—that and the fact that they'd met only yesterday. But maybe her radar about people was right. Maybe there really was something to like about him.

"Tigre!" Gus hollered up the stairs, and Tigre realized he'd been standing still, staring goofily at Anna. She grinned back at him, and they ran down the stairs to meet the others.

"Dude," Gus said as they caught up. He pointed out the double doors that led to the library steps. "What is this all about? Are you mad about something?"

Tigre was astonished to see that it was raining. Usually when it rained, he could sense it, even from deep inside a building. And now it was *pouring,* sheets of rain flooding down, as if someone were standing on the clouds, heaving rivers over the edge one after another.

"This wasn't me," he said.

Ereka crossed her arms. "Yeah, right. We all just heard about you being a storm god, remember? So make it stop."

"I swear," Tigre said. "I'm not making this happen."

"OF COURSE YOU'RE NOT!" a voice bellowed from out in the rain.

A strange figure swam out of the downpour: pitch-black, like he'd been painted with tar, eyes so wide that they seemed to be popping out of his head, and four large pointed teeth sticking out over his lips.

"I AM," he said.

Several blocks north, where the sky was gray but it was not yet raining, there was pandemonium at the Metropolitan Museum.

Kali and Shiva stood across the street for a minute, watching gods and goddesses scurry in and out of the main entrance. Kali wanted to go in and search for the people she'd spotted a few days ago, but whatever was happening with the Greek gods looked even more interesting. None of them seemed to be going anywhere; they either found someone to talk to on the steps or stopped and then ran back inside.

Soon it became evident that they were waiting for something—namely, Zeus, who came striding out with tiny lightning flashes going off around his head. Behind him stood a tall, cold woman whom Shiva identified as Hera, Zeus's wife and queen of the gods.

"All right!" Zeus called, and the gods quieted down. "It's time to take action! We have a plan!"

"What we have is idiocy," Hera commented. "At the highest levels." She didn't raise her voice, but it had a clear, commanding quality that carried all the way to where Shiva and Kali were standing. Kali was surprised that no one had noticed them yet; they weren't making any effort to hide.

"Hush your squawking, woman!" Zeus bellowed. "Our avatar is missing and we must bring her back!"

Kali and Shiva exchanged amused looks.

"We'll look like fools," Hera hissed. "As if we can't control our own avatar."

"But we can, my dear," Zeus said. "We'll control her just fine once we drag her back and lock her in."

"Why bother? We can track her right now; we know where she is and who she's with, and if we want, we can know exactly what she's doing. Why waste our energy chasing her? She'll come crawling back soon enough."

"Anything could happen to her out there," Zeus said, frowning. "We don't want our little Venus to get hurt, or killed, or disfigured!"

"Maybe that would teach her a lesson," Hera said icily. "If you ask me, you should just watch her until she returns—which she will, inevitably."

Kali saw a handsome young god come out of the museum behind them. He had golden hair and looked vaguely like Diana; from this, she guessed that he was Apollo, the sun god and Diana's twin brother. He had the kind of face that broadcasts every emotion with tremendous earnestness. Kali guessed that he'd be an exhausting boyfriend, the sort who gave too many presents and wanted to discuss every aspect of the relationship. Not like her husband. She squeezed Shiva's hand as she saw Apollo spot them.

"Awesome idea, guys," Apollo said, clapping his hands on Zeus's and Hera's shoulders. "Let's have a power struggle right in front of our enemies. Make 'em think we're tearing one another apart, but of course it's all an act, right? Pretty clever." He wagged a teasing finger at Zeus.

Hera removed his hand from her shoulder and dropped it like a dead fish. "I could not be less concerned about what the riffraff of other pantheons think of us." She straightened her headdress, looking down her nose at Kali and Shiva as they crossed the street toward the museum.

"Spying again?" Zeus roared. "Skulking about as usual, Shiva?"

"Yes, by standing in plain sight," Kali said. "We're sneaky that way."

"Besides," Shiva added, "who needs to hide? We could have heard your quarrel several blocks away."

Zeus looked like he was thinking about throwing another thunderbolt.

"So Diana's run off," Kali said, strolling up the steps.

"Not even your own avatar could stand the pleasure of

your company," Shiva added. "Why doesn't that surprise me?" They stopped a few stairs down from Zeus, and Shiva slung one arm around Kali's shoulders. She liked the way it felt, even as she recognized that he was putting himself in a position to block any attacks on her if he had to.

"What are you doing here?" Hera asked. "Couldn't you find any other gods to annoy?"

"We're visiting the museum," Kali said before Shiva could volley off another snide remark. "I just love art. Don't you?"

Zeus let out a snort. "Looking at art. I bet! Here to steal our secrets, more likely!"

"Steal your secrets?" Kali said. "Why bother, since you're shouting them from the front steps?"

"Oh, let them in," Apollo said. "What are they going to find out . . . that we've given Diana a hammock? Think of it this way: They can't attack her if they're in here and she's out there. Right? I'm okay with having these two where we can keep an eye on them."

Zeus turned purple. "Aiding and abetting the enemy!" he sputtered.

"Very well," Hera said, sounding bored. "It makes no difference to me."

"But—but—" Zeus began. "What about the—*you know*, the—"

"Don't worry," Apollo said smoothly. "I'll watch them."

"Fine!" Zeus said, throwing up his arms in exaspera- tion. "Forget the plan!" he bellowed at the rest of the gods. "I don't need your help! I'm going to keep an eye on our avatar myself, since nobody else seems to remem- ber what our priority is here." He smashed his hands together and disappeared with a thunderclap of sound.

"Apollo, I presume," Kali said, holding out her hand.

"The very one and only," he said, shaking it. "I've heard a lot about you. Do you prefer to be called Kali or—"

"Yes, it's Kali. Let's go inside," Shiva interrupted. "We're only here for a short time."

Kali frowned at him. Why would Apollo think she had more than one name? And she didn't see why Shiva had to rush things. She was looking for the people she'd spotted in the museum, and she was in no hurry to get anywhere else.

"Of course, of course," Apollo said charmingly. "There's a great Indian section, and I love the modern stuff, and, of course, the instruments." He danced ahead of them, still chattering away.

Hera glared at them as they followed Apollo into the dark, cool interior of the museum lobby.

"This is a waste of time," Shiva said in a lower voice. Apollo was waiting for them by the stairs that led up to European Paintings.

"If you have something more important to do," Kali said to Shiva, "feel free to go do it."

"I'm hoping the pointlessness of this excursion will convince you to go back to training once you've satisfied your little whim."

"No," Kali said in a thoughtful voice. "I think I'll visit the subway people next. Miracle should know that the Boss Hunter isn't out pillaging anymore."

Shiva stopped in the center of the lobby and glowered at her. "Kali, what are you doing? Don't you remember how important this is?"

"I do," she said. "And I remember where my power comes from, and I remember the scope of that power. So I know that you are not more powerful than I am, and I know that you have never been allowed to order me around before. I'm not sure where you got the impression that you should start now, especially given the treacherous ground you are already on from setting me up for this in the first place."

They faced each other for a long moment, and she could practically see the frayed edges of his temper smoldering into ash. Finally he snarled, "Then go on your wild-goose chases. Find me again when you're ready to take this seriously." And like Zeus, he vanished.

"Nice trick. Wish I could do that," Kali muttered. She crossed the rest of the lobby to Apollo. He seemed a little jittery.

"Trouble in the Elysian fields?" he said.

She looked at him blankly.

"You know," he said, "how they always say 'trouble in paradise'? And the Greek paradise is the Elysian—okay, never mind. Let's start upstairs! Great Renoirs here. Anything in particular you want to see?" He was already bounding up the steps, but she could hear the genuine curiosity in his question.

"I just want to wander around—*quietly*," she said, thinking that Apollo's yapping would give anyone plenty of time to hear them coming and hide.

"Okay," Apollo said. "How about this way?" He darted through a doorway into a room full of paintings. Kali's intuition was tingling. There *was* something to uncover here. Did it have to do with the museum dwellers? Did Apollo know about them? Was he trying to hide them?

"Actually," Kali said, "I'd like to go this way." She circled around the staircase and walked along the hall beside it, toward Asian Art and the balcony overlooking the Great Hall.

Apollo caught up quickly. He kept making nervous fluttery motions that reminded Kali of a parakeet trapped in a room with a cat.

"I admire you, you know," he said. "You're so different from us."

"Shhh," Kali said. She could hear voices coming from the Great Hall below. She crept over to the balcony edge and peered down.

Two figures were striding out of the Egyptian wing, but they weren't at all those she might have expected to see. These weren't her mystery information gatherers. This was Amon, accompanied by a dark-eyed Egyptian goddess.

"No one forced you to be our avatar," the goddess said. "You can't blame us if you're feeling diminished."

"All I'm asking for is what I was promised, Isis," Amon snarled. "Instead I have to hear about the Polynesian mistake and disobedience. I'm being left out of the loop and *I don't like it.*"

Kali looked up just in time to see Apollo opening his mouth, probably to call out a greeting and warn the Egyptian gods she was there. She leaped up, slammed a hand over his mouth, and pulled him down out of sight. He was a bit smaller than she was, and to her surprise, he didn't struggle.

"Once you kill the anomaly, you won't have to worry about it anymore," Isis said. "The Greco-Romans know better than to forfeit on a deal with us."

A deal? Kali's curiosity spiked. Were the Greeks and the Egyptians working together? Did Diana know? What were they planning?

"That's not soon enough," Amon said. "Where is that old geezer Zeus? ZEUS!"

"Hush your bellowing. He's not here," Hera said, sweeping in from outside.

"Chasing your troublesome avatar, I suppose," Isis sneered.

"Lower your voices," Hera said, and tilted her head in exactly the same superior way Isis had. "The Indian avatar is in the building."

Kali loved the way Amon jumped and glanced around uneasily. "Then let's go somewhere else, where we can talk in safety," he said. The goddesses both turned simultaneously in a swirl of robes and followed Amon out the front door of the museum.

Well. That was illuminating. Kali waited a minute and then released Apollo. He rubbed his face and sat down on the floor next to her.

"You could have just asked me to keep quiet," he said. "I'm very agreeable. How was I supposed to know you didn't want to say hello?"

She gave him a look and he smiled.

"What was that all about?" she asked. "Why is Amon here? What did they mean by 'a deal'?"

Apollo's nervousness had evaporated; he looked now like he'd be content to lean against the balcony wall for the rest of the day. "I'd prefer not to say," he replied.

"You'd *prefer* not to."

"That's right."

"I thought you always had to tell the truth," Kali said.

"I am telling the truth," Apollo said. "I really would prefer not to answer your questions." He smirked.

Kali had a feeling she could get more out of him if she pressed, but maybe it would be wiser to figure this out for herself, so he wouldn't know exactly how much she knew.

The wheels were turning in her head. If she'd just witnessed what she suspected, Apollo should be much more worried. Unless he wanted her to see it for some reason. Was Apollo trying to sabotage this mysterious deal? What had Amon been promised? She didn't know what the penalty for cheating was, but surely the judges would frown upon it. Before she could tell them, though, she needed to be sure.

At least now, even if she didn't find the museum dwellers, she'd still learned something very useful from her visit.

"All right," Kali said. "Then let's go look at some art."

Pantheon: Egyptian
Avatar: Amon
Judge: Maat
Trainer: Isis

You would think that each pantheon would wholeheartedly support its avatar, wouldn't you? You would assume they'd naturally want their own representative to win so that their pantheon could ascend to power.

Well, that's not quite how gods work.

They're a bit like families that way. For instance, you might think it'd be great to have your family ruling the world, but would you still feel that way if your annoying little brother got to be Supreme Emperor and you had to do everything he said?

Amon is the annoying little brother of the Egyptian pantheon. Oh, he doesn't think of himself that way. He sees himself as all-powerful and supreme, which he is nowadays . . . but he didn't start that way. Once he was just the local god of Thebes. It wasn't until Thebes became the capital of Egypt that he got elevated a lot higher, eventually merging with Ra to become the ruler of the sky.

But believe me, Isis remembers a time when he wasn't so great. She's had a taste of her old leadership while he's been mortal, and she's loved it. The crystal hunters? Her idea. I mean, to steal them from humanity. She knew they would make useful toys when it came time to steer the avatars. It wasn't hard to make the creatures turn on their creators, and it takes very little energy to control them—a job shared by the Egyptian gods.

I suppose it makes up for losing their home. Oh, didn't I mention that? Part of this plan involved making a deal with the gods of Africa. Nobody wanted to fight them, and it'd be harder to drown Africa than to wipe out Polynesia. So they bargained: The African gods could have Africa to themselves if they stayed there and let the other pantheons have the rest of the world. But they got all of Africa . . . including Egypt. So, displaced, the Egyptian gods moved to the American continent and took over the hunters, and that usually keeps them busy.

I have to wonder if Isis is really looking forward to Amon gaining even more power. There are some in the Greek pantheon who feel the same way about their avatar. Hera, for one. Diana is Zeus's daughter by another woman, and Venus won that golden-apple contest that started the Trojan War. So Hera hates both sides of that poor girl. No wonder she's willing to hand over control to Amon instead. In fact, Hera probably wouldn't mind cutting Diana/Venus out of the deal altogether.

The funny thing is, Amon does not know what (or whom) he is playing with. Diana, the original avatar, is still in there. And out here, her brother, Apollo, is doing everything he can to sabotage the deal. I love it when pantheons work against themselves. You can always count on the Greeks and the Egyptians to create unnecessary drama. Betrayal, conspiracy, deception, ambition—it's what their myths are all about, isn't it?

All I had to do was throw Gus into the mix, sit back, and watch.

On the plus side, Tlaloc spoke English. On the minus side, centuries of rolling thunder around the Andes had apparently made him quite deaf.

"I AM TLALOC!" he roared. "GOD OF RAIN!"

"Yeah, we got that," Gus said, wincing.

"TLALOC BRINGS THE THUNDER! TLALOC BRINGS THE LIGHTNING!"

"Could Tlaloc cut it out?" Ereka said. "So the rest of us can go get lunch?"

They were standing in the marble entrance hall of the library, with the rain still bucketing down outside. Everyone was giving the Aztec rain god a wide berth, mainly because of the shouting and the manic goggling eyes. Tigre looked pretty goggle-eyed himself.

"TLALOC HAS TORN HIMSELF AWAY FROM HIS PARADISE TO TRAIN THIS UNWORTHY CREATURE!"

"I thought you didn't want to train me," Tigre said bitterly. "I thought you agreed that I'm expendable."

"TLALOC DOES NOT HAVE TIME FOR WHINING!"

Ereka smothered a giggle. Anna glared at her and put her arm around Tigre's waist.

"You're really here to train him?" Diana said. "To teach him how to fight?"

"WHO BETTER TO TRAIN A STORM GOD THAN THE GREATEST STORM GOD OF THEM ALL? TLALOC BRINGS THE THUNDER! TLALOC BRINGS THE LIGHTNING!" Outside there was a responsive boom.

"Can you train my friends, too?" Tigre asked.

"TLALOC DOES NOT HEAR YOU."

"My friends!" Tigre shouted. "They need a trainer, too!"

"TLALOC CHOOSES NOT TO HEAR YOU!"

"Hey!" Tigre said. "I'm sticking with my friends, so you might as well help them, too."

"TLALOC DOES NOT TRAIN FEMALES. AND THAT IS A WAR GOD." Tlaloc pointed a long dark finger at Gus. "DO I LOOK LIKE A WAR GOD TO YOU?"

"So?" Gus said. "Can't you help us anyway?"

"THERE IS NO SKILL IN WAR-GOD TRAIN-ING. ALL YOU NEED TO DO IS FIGHT, SO ALL YOU NEED ARE WEAPONS. TLALOC IS MORE IMPORTANT THAN THIS! HE IS NOT A WEAPONS GATHERER! HE IS A GOD OF THE WIND AND THE RAIN AND FROST AND DIS-EASE AND THE SKY CRACKING OPEN!"

"If you're so great," Tigre yelled, "why aren't you our avatar?"

"HA!" Tlaloc boomed. "TLALOC IS MUCH SMARTER THAN THAT!"

"Maybe you should listen to him," Diana said in a low voice to Tigre. "I mean, you said you don't know how to control your power. Maybe he can teach you."

"So he should just go off with this guy?" Gus said. "Like you went off with Zeus?"

"I came back, didn't I?" Diana said, exasperated. "He will, too. I just thought he might want to know some-thing about who he is. Not all of us think there's a neat, twisty sci-fi way out of this situation, Gus. I'm not saying Tigre should go learn how to kill us, but if he can learn how to defend himself, why shouldn't he?"

"Because these—these immortal guys aren't trustworthy. We're better off sticking together."

"TLALOC IS GETTING BORED!"

"What do you think?" Tigre said to Anna.

"I think you should do what you want to do," she said, tilting her head to look up at him. "Personally, I like you just the way you are, whether or not you can call storms and all that stuff."

"TLALOC DOES NOT REALLY WANT TO BE HERE!"

"I wouldn't go with him," Ereka said. "If anyone cares about *my* opinion. It's not like making rain is such a useful fighting skill anyway."

Tigre squared his shoulders. "I'm sorry, Gus," he said. "But I think I have to give it a shot. Learning to control my powers can't be such a bad thing, can it?"

Gus shrugged and looked down at the marble floor, where a vast puddle was spreading toward them from Tlaloc's feet.

"What do you want me to do?" Tigre called to Tlaloc.

"STORM GODS TRAIN OUTDOORS," Tlaloc bellowed. "EVEN PUNY ONES."

"Yeah," Tigre muttered. "This is going to be fun."

Tlaloc smacked the end of his staff against the floor, and instantly the rain stopped.

"Hooray!" Ereka cried, running outside. She stood with her arms spread wide, looking up at the sky.

"TO THE PARK!" Tlaloc shouted, and stomped out the door after her. Tigre and Anna followed, and they saw that he was powering around the side of the building, heading for a small adjoining park. Tigre gave Anna a questioning look.

"Lead on, Macduff," she said. "I go where you go." They smiled at each other, then followed Tlaloc, leaving the other three standing on the front steps of the library.

"Maybe while he's doing this," Diana said, "we can go find you some weapons, Gus. You know . . . for tomorrow."

"Oh, so I'm allowed to fight my own battles now, am I?" Gus said.

"If there's no other choice," she said. "But you're still not allowed to die. Got that?"

"As Her Highness decrees."

"Gus, stop being mad at me! I'm here to help you. I'm your friend, remember?"

"Are you sure?" he said. "Because as far as I remember, friends don't abandon each other, friends don't lie to each other, and friends don't keep important secrets from each other."

"When have I—"

"Forget it," he said. "I can find weapons on my own, thanks. You go back to your immortal friends." He stormed down the stairs. Ereka gave Diana an astonished look, then chased after him.

Gus felt like a belt of nails was tightening around his chest. It hurt to breathe and he was so, so unreasonably angry. A part of him yelled, *That's not you! It's Oro! Gus isn't like this!* But the rage was too powerful, and it pushed him farther and farther away from Diana.

· · ● · ·

Kali wasn't really surprised that the museum trip hadn't turned up any humans. As pointed as her remarks were, Apollo never quite caught on to the whole "let's be quiet and sneak up on the next room" plan. She didn't think he was doing it intentionally. He just found it too hard to stay quiet for long periods of time. And as she'd anticipated, it was fairly exhausting, so she cut it short as soon as she could. Hopefully she'd have better luck finding Miracle in the subways.

The walk down to Times Square didn't make her any less tired. She almost wished she hadn't infuriated her best means of transportation. She could sense Shiva sulking in a small cemetery downtown, but it was way too far for her to walk again today. Perhaps he thought he was punishing her, but it just made her decision easier. After all, he was her eternal-and-always husband; it wasn't like he could stay mad at her forever. And this gave her space for her other projects, even though she still missed him.

At Times Square, she examined the steps to the subway. They seemed clear of water or crazy old people, but it still took her a minute to steel her nerves. And as she was standing on the sidewalk, breathing deeply, she realized that someone was coming toward her down Forty-second Street, and that another someone was watching her.

First, the closer one. She looked around carefully and spotted Thor, who was sitting up on the edge of a billboard advertising a musical that must have closed decades ago. He wasn't spying on her. He looked like someone had propped him there and he was waiting for his head to stop spinning before he moved again. He saw Kali shading her eyes to look up at him, and he waved cheerfully.

Kali waved back and then turned to gaze down Forty-second Street. A small drooping figure was trudging toward her. Apart from the drooping, it looked like Diana.

Kali squinted. It *was* Diana. Only she looked much less cheerful than Kali had seen her before, even yesterday, in Zeus's clutches.

There was a crashing noise behind her, and Kali whirled around. Thor was stumbling down a metal ladder to the street. He missed a couple of rungs with his feet and hung for a moment ten feet above the ground, as if weighing his options. Finally, with an eloquent sigh, he let go.

Kali didn't even realize she was moving until she was underneath him, catching the bulk of his weight against her.

"Ooof!" she exclaimed, staggering back. "Good Lord, you're gigantic."

He mumbled something that sounded like a string of consonants.

"Come on, get your feet under you," Kali said. "I'm not carrying you back to your bosses."

She shoved him up against the wall until he could lean there on his own. He grinned a furry red Clifford grin at her, and she wondered again how she could bring herself to fight this oaf.

"Kali?" Diana said, crossing the street toward them. "What are you— Who's this?"

"Thor," Kali said, patting his chest.

"Thor!" he agreed, banging his chest with his fist.

"Kali," she said, pointing to herself. "Diana." She pointed at the pop star.

"Kali, Diana," he repeated solemnly. *"Huvudvark,"* he added, pressing his hand to his head.

"He doesn't look very scary," Diana said. "Gus made him sound terrifying. Perhaps so I'd be more impressed about Gus fighting him." Diana didn't sound pleased with Gus, but Kali didn't care about their romantic squabbles.

"Thor's been partying all morning," Kali said. "I think the Norse gods tend to forget the effect their revelry might have on the not so immortal. Especially poor Thor, who's been in this body for only eighteen years."

"Jeez," Diana said. "Maybe they'll accidentally kill him off for us."

Kali gave her a wry smile. "Now that's the spirit." She swung her backpack around, and for a dreadful moment Diana was sure the Indian goddess was going to whip out a knife and slit both their throats. Instead, Kali pulled out a bottle of water and handed it to Thor. Guiltily, Diana scolded herself. She should give Kali the benefit of the doubt, despite their conversation yesterday in the street. Surely Kali had been pretending for the benefit of her pantheon. Kali had helped to save Gus; Diana should think the best of her until she had any real reason not to.

"I heard you ran off," Kali said as Thor took a giant swig from her bottle. "Your pantheon was in a hilarious flurry."

"Are they coming after me?" Diana asked anxiously.

"Zeus said he would come keep an eye on you." Kali glanced around like she expected to see him peeking out a manhole. "He's probably listening to everything you've been saying. Something to keep in mind."

Diana had been wondering about that. She had had an uneasy feeling of being under surveillance ever since arriving in New York. . . . Well, probably ever since the earthquake that had brought her and Gus here. She wished she could ask Kali straight out what she thought about the avatar battle, but with omnipotent, all-seeing beings lurking about, there was no way to have a private conversation. Perhaps that was even what Kali was trying to tell her.

"Where are the rest of the X-Men?" Kali asked.

"Tigre is learning how to conjure rain back there in Bryant Park," Diana said. "Not very successfully, as you can see." The sky was overcast but still dry. "I stopped to hang out with Anna and watch him for a while, but it got a little depressing, so I left."

"If it were up to me," Kali said, "I would have left weather gods out of the contest. Rain, sun, rain, sun— since you all got here, we've had a whole summer's worth of weather packed into a couple of days. And you're *part of the problem,* thunder god Thor," she said loudly.

"Thor!" he said, thwacking his chest again.

"And Gus has gone off with Ereka to look for weapons and a place to fight Amon tomorrow."

It would have taken someone as thick as concrete to miss the woefulness in Diana's voice. Kali sighed.

"Trouble in the Elysian fields?" she said.

"Exactly," Diana said. "Hey, that's clever."

"Really?" Kali said. "I didn't think so, but he is your brother. Wait. Who's Ereka?"

Diana explained the arrival of Anna's look-alike and their weird almost-matching stories.

"Huh," Kali said. "I have no idea what that means."

"I know, right?" Diana said. "I mean, Ereka seems to be their avatar, but who are 'they,' and what is the point of Anna?"

"Whoever they are, they don't want anyone to know," Kali said. "I asked my . . . my trainer. He said not even the gods can remember which pantheon it is. Some kind of cloaking spell."

"Weird," Diana said.

They both looked at Thor, who had finished off Kali's bottle of water and was now rubbing his head gloomily.

"So what are you doing here?" Diana asked.

Kali had a brief internal debate. She didn't really want to share Miracle with Diana, but she wouldn't mind the company underground. She couldn't shake the feeling that the subway dwellers might tie her up and leave her in a dark cavern, perhaps just to see if and how she could escape without drowning. Besides, Diana wasn't much of a threat.

"I'm going to visit the Miracle," Kali said.

"The girl who lives in the subways?"

"The one the old people worship because she's the only person to be born since the Change. Yeah, her."

"Tigre told us about her. Can I come?" Diana looked so sure Kali was going to say no that it was actually kind of fun to nod and see her light up with excitement.

"Bye, Thor," Kali said, patting his shoulder. "Good luck with that hangover."

"Thor!" he agreed.

"Down here," Kali said to Diana, leading the way over

to the subway entrance. As they hopped over the turn-stiles, they heard a crash as Thor smacked into a glass wall, then stumbled after them.

"Thor, stay," Kali said.

"Thor!" He tried to go through the turnstile and stopped, bewildered by the unyielding bar in front of him.

"No MetroCard, no entry," Kali said. "Sorry, big guy."

"Rrrrrrrrrrrrrrrgh," he growled. Then, to the girls' astonishment, he took the turnstile bar in his hands and bent it all the way back, until it was lying flat against the turnstile wall. With a grin, he sauntered through behind them.

"Okay," Diana said nervously. "Well, *I'm* not going to be the one to tell him no."

"All right, come along," Kali said.

They headed down the paralyzed escalator, exiting into a wide area full of columns and railings and stairs leading off in various directions.

"Here's my theory," Kali said. "When we went down into the tunnels to find the subway people, they took us up a long ladder to get to Miracle. So we shouldn't have to go all the way down again; they must have another way to get to her."

"Do we stand here and shout? Or start trying doors?"

"Both, I think," Kali said. "GENERAL PEHHHHH-HHHH-PPER!"

Thor winced, pressing his hand to his head.

"Sorry," Diana said to him. She leaned over one of the railings to call down to the subway tracks far below. "Hello? Anyone down there?"

"OH, MIRACLE!" Kali hollered. "You've got com-pany! Yoo-hoo!"

"'Yoo-hoo'?" Diana repeated with a giggle.

"Shut up and yell," Kali said. "MIRACLE!"

"Miracle!" Diana shouted.

Slowly, eerily, a door creaked open in the long wall a few feet away from them.

They waited for a moment, but nobody emerged. Kali and Diana exchanged glances.

"Hello?" Diana called.

"Looks like an invite to me," Kali said. "Still want to come, Thor?"

"Hrggjkldalmfl," he said.

"I wish I knew if that's his language or if he's just mumbling in pain," Kali said to Diana.

"I don't understand why his pantheon wouldn't make sure he learned English," Diana said. "Wouldn't they want him to be able to communicate with us?"

"Maybe not," Kali said. "Maybe that's their plan—if he can't talk to us, he can't join forces with us. You know . . . no *alliances*."

There. She was sure. Diana's eyes had flickered away for a moment, nervously, at the word *alliances*. There was something going on, and moreover, Diana knew about it, which Kali had guessed she didn't. Diana didn't seem like a cheater, or a schemer. Maybe she hadn't had a choice, but she definitely knew about it now, and she was keeping it to herself.

"All right, let's go in," Diana said, her tone convincingly casual. "I can't wait to meet this girl."

"She's something else," Kali said. She strode over to the door and pulled it the rest of the way open. A concrete passageway stood in front of them, with a set of iron switchback stairs going up to the left and a spiral staircase going down to the right. A naked lightbulb was screwed into the ceiling above them, and on the wall across from the door there was an extensive, primitively drawn mural in silver paint. In the upper left corner, a winged dolphin with sharp teeth was soaring, pterodactyl wings spread wide. Below it was the ocean, and a wall of land, and a narrow path or bridge extending over the water. Stick figures of people were drawn on the path, mostly bowing or kneeling. All around the mural was a border of the upright silver fish Kali had seen earlier in the subway tunnels below.

"I know that thing," Diana said, pointing. "That's a pterodolphin. Gus and I saw some on our way to New York. We met a couple of scientists who are researching them."

"Yeesh," Kali said. "I hope there aren't any skulking about down here."

Thor bundled up behind them, sneezed vigorously, and pointed up to the left. Kali leaned over to look up and realized that after one flight the stairs ended in another door.

"Okay," Kali said. "Looks like a reasonable choice to me."

She started up the stairs, the others close behind her. Thor had to duck to keep from hitting his head on the low doorway and the pipes sticking out of the walls and ceiling. Kali held out her hand as she reached the top, signaling them to wait on the landing, where the stairs turned.

Kali leaned against the door and listened, but she couldn't hear a sound from the other side. Carefully, she turned the handle. There was mild resistance, and she realized there was a curtain behind the door. She remembered that there was also one over the door General Pepper had come through when he burst in on her, Tigre, and Miracle. Encouraged, she pushed it aside and peered into a familiar dim, glittering room.

The tiny lights and candles, the arrangements of shimmering tiles, the assortment of toys and gadgets on the platform were all there, but Kali couldn't see Miracle anywhere. She gestured for Diana and Thor to follow her.

Their eyes widened as they came into the room.

"Wow," Diana whispered. "This is kind of cool."

Thor brushed his fingers over a pattern of small mirrored tiles and said something in a low, reverent voice.

"I wonder where Miracle lives when she's not in here," Kali said.

"I'm always in here." Thor jumped backward as Miracle's soft, strong voice emerged from a dark corner in the back of the room, near the hole where Kali had come up the first time. A pile of shadows drifted up and became a pile of blankets, from which the pale, moonlike, bald head of Miracle appeared. She yawned delicately and dropped the top blanket back onto the pile.

"You came back," she said to Kali, sounding pleased. "And you brought pretty new friends." Kali noticed that she had exchanged her purple robe for a dark red one.

"Yeah, I thought I'd say hi," Kali said. "I realized we didn't even get to tell you our names last time. I figured you might like a more social visit."

"I don't usually get those," Miracle said. "I mean, I

don't *ever* get those. My people only come here to worship and commune with the gods." She rubbed one eye sleepily and Kali remembered that she was only thirteen years old.

"Well, I'm Kali, and this is Diana, and that's Thor. He doesn't speak English." Thor was staring at Miracle with the same awe Kali had seen on the faces of the subway dwellers, while Diana mostly looked sad and sympathetic and understanding. Kali was glad Diana had never given *her* that kind of expression.

"I brought you something," Kali said, suddenly feeling awkward about the witnesses.

"An offering?" Miracle said excitedly. "Wait, let me get into position." She scrambled past Kali and up onto the dais. Arranging herself into her regal seated pose, she nodded and said, "You may proceed."

As Kali unzipped her backpack, Thor suddenly moved away from the wall and seated himself at the foot of the dais. He was so large and Miracle was so small, their heads were still at the same height. He gave her a bearlike grin, and she smiled and reached her hand out as if to bless him.

Uncertainly, Diana came closer as well and sat down on a cushion on the floor.

"Here," Kali said, climbing up on the dais and crouching next to Miracle, who looked startled at the invasion of her sacred space. "I looked everywhere for this, so you'd better like it."

Miracle touched the cover solemnly. *"Ender's Game,"* she read aloud. "Orson Scott Card."

"My sister Josephine is a bit younger than you, but she's really smart, and she loves this book," Kali said. "It's about a kid—like you, except he's a boy—who is really special and really smart, and everyone's counting on him to save the planet from these scary aliens, even though he's so young."

In the dim light, it was hard to read Miracle's expression, but her eyes looked like they were glowing. "And . . . does he save the world?" she asked.

"You'll have to read it to find out, won't you?" Kali said. "But you shouldn't do it in here. You'll strain your eyes reading by candlelight."

"But this is my temple," Miracle said, shocked. "I can't leave it. My people wouldn't be able to find me, or to protect me."

"Sometimes that can be a good thing," Diana said, speaking for the first time since Miracle had appeared.

"Besides, you don't need protecting anymore," Kali said. "We have great news. You know the big scary crystal hunter that was patrolling the streets up there?"

Miracle nodded, her dark eyes sad.

"Well, it's dead."

"We smashed it!" Diana said. "We crushed it into tiny particles! Okay, Kali did. But it's gone!"

"Totally smashed," Kali said. "And that seems to have scared off the other ones, at least for now. You can come outside without worrying about it."

"Do you mean it?" Miracle said. "Are you sure it's dead?" The news seemed to have brought down the last of her prophetess playacting. Her voice, her posture, everything about her now said *excited thirteen-year-old girl* instead of *luminous object of worship*.

"Completely kaput," Kali said.

"Isn't it scary out there? What if something else happens?"

"It's more wonderful than scary," Diana said. "You'll totally love it."

"And we'll protect you," Kali said. "We're pretty tough."

"Thor!" the Norse avatar suddenly proclaimed. He thumped his chest again. "Thor!" He pointed at Miracle, who gave Kali a confused look.

"Miracle," Kali said. "MIR-A-CLE."

Thor rolled the syllables around for a minute until he got pretty close. "Miracle," he said, sounding satisfied.

"I'm guessing Thor will protect you most of all," Kali said wryly. "I have no idea what's gotten into him."

"General Pepper will never let me go," Miracle said.

"Why does he get to decide?" Kali said. "Aren't you the Miracle? He doesn't even have to know."

"Oh, he already knows," Miracle said. "He knows everything that's going on down here. He'll probably come in soon and chase you off."

"Then we should leave quickly," Diana said, jumping to her feet.

"He's got to sleep sometime," Kali said. "Maybe we'll get lucky and it's now. Come on." She stood up and held her hand out to Miracle.

The younger girl hesitated for a moment. Finally she clasped Kali's hand and let herself be pulled to her feet. "Okay," she said, her voice laced with fear and exhilaration.

"Here, I'll bring that along," Kali said, taking *Ender's Game* and replacing it in her backpack. She wasn't quite sure why she was doing this. *Kidnapping a living, breathing miracle. How is this going to get me new worshippers?* The last thing she needed in the middle of this battle was a kid who needed protecting and watching and feeding and, guessing from her current life, probably pampering. *But imagine if Beth or Amy or Jo-Jo had been trapped underground for thirteen years.* It made her want to smash things just thinking about it.

Kali shoved aside the curtain and held it as Diana went through, followed by Miracle, who stepped cautiously onto the iron stairs in her bare feet, wincing at the cold metal. Thor was close behind her, and Kali brought up the rear.

They hurried down the steps to the passageway and pulled open the door to the station . . .

. . . where they found all of Miracle's worshippers waiting for them.

There were far more than Kali had ever seen before in one place; far more than she'd expected. Close to a hundred old people were standing between them and the exits, swaying, whispering, leaning against columns for support, and all staring fixedly at the door where their miracle and the three avatars were standing.

At the front stood General Pepper and seven other men and women who looked stronger and saner than the rest. They were all carrying heavy pipes, wrenches, and crowbars, and they did not look happy.

"Where exactly," General Pepper said, "do you think you're going with our miracle?"

"CALL THE LIGHTNING! WRENCH THE THUNDER FROM THE SKY! SLASH OPEN THE CLOUDS AND POUR FORTH THE FLOODS!"

"Can you be more specific?" Tigre called. He was standing in the center of Bryant Park, a city block of park space next door to the public library. Tlaloc had stomped around the circumference of the park so many times, he was starting to leave a track of trampled earth through the knee-high grass. Every time the storm god had his back turned, Anna waved from the steps at the east end of the park and Tigre waved back.

"TLALOC IS NOT IMPRESSED!" Tlaloc shouted. "TLALOC IS RATHER AGGRAVATED! TLALOC IS GETTING CLOSE TO TEARING OFF HIS OWN HEAD!"

"Well, tell me what to do!" Tigre shouted back. "I mean, call the lightning? What? How do I do that?"

"IT IS A DIM STORM GOD INDEED WHO CANNOT FEEL THE THUNDER INSIDE HIM!"

Tigre couldn't feel any thunder, but he could feel something else: massive frustration. He thought his anger should have brought a storm by now, but the gray clouds squatted overhead like gloomy boulders, as unlikely to spill forth rain as the stones of the library behind Anna.

He squinted at them and tried for the thousandth time to focus on raindrops and bolts of lightning. He pictured a drop of water forming in the air. He imagined the sound of thunder rolling across the city. He wondered if he could call animals this way, too, or, if he concentrated too hard, would he turn into the creature with claws that he feared he might be?

"YOUR PATHETICNESS IS FAR GREATER THAN TLALOC SUSPECTED!"

"Well, that's really helping, thanks," Tigre muttered.

Tlaloc had to be the worst possible trainer. Tigre doubted any other avatar was dealing with this kind of open contempt. He tried focusing on his anger instead, hoping the storm would start as a side effect, the way it usually did, but he was distracted by Anna waving again.

"NO, NO, NO!" Tlaloc roared, and for a moment Tigre was afraid he was shouting at Anna. But the storm god came tearing through the grass toward him and shoved him in the chest. "A TRUE GOD OF STORMS DOES NOT RELY ON MORTAL EMOTIONS! TINY SPROUTS OF FEELINGS ARE NOT YOUR WEAPON! USE THE THUNDER!"

"I can't!" Tigre cried, his chest aching like he'd just been punched. "I don't know what to do!"

"DO NOT SNIVEL!"

"I'm not sniveling!"

"TLALOC CANNOT BELIEVE THIS IS WHAT HE HAS TO WORK WITH!"

"Are you sure there isn't something else?" Tigre asked. "Some other power I might have? Are you sure I don't turn into a panther or call animals or something?"

"ANIMALS!" Tlaloc bellowed. "TLALOC HAS NEVER HEARD ANYTHING MORE IDIOTIC!"

"But—"

"STORM GODS CALL STORMS! UNLESS THEY ARE WORTHLESS SACKS OF BONES WITH NO POWERS!"

"I'm trying!"

"YOU ARE FAILING!"

"All right, that's it," Tigre said, turning his back on the Aztec god. "I'm leaving."

Anna saw him coming and stood up, but as Tigre reached the edge of the grass, Tlaloc suddenly appeared in front of him.

"Wait, let me guess," Tigre snapped before Tlaloc could speak. "TLALOC IS VERY DISAPPOINTED?"

"NO," Tlaloc boomed. "TLALOC NOW KNOWS HE WAS RIGHT ALL ALONG. TLALOC IS NOT SURPRISED. YOU ARE TOO WEAK TO WIN AND FAR TOO WEAK TO RULE."

"Hey," Anna protested. "Don't say things like that. Tigre, don't listen to him."

"You're here to mess with my head, aren't you?" Tigre said. "Are you just another god who wants me to give up and die? Is this your own special way of driving me to suicide?"

"IF TLALOC WANTED YOU DEAD," Tlaloc said, "YOU WOULD BE DEAD. TLALOC FINDS CAT AND MOUSE GAMES TIRESOME."

"Well, Tigre finds standing in a park waiting for rain tiresome. If you can't tell me anything useful, I don't see why you're here."

"TLALOC DOES NOT WANT TO BE HERE!"

"You made that perfectly clear," Tigre said. "So fine, go ahead and take off."

Tlaloc ground his teeth. His eyes seemed closer to popping out than ever.

"IT IS SO EASY!" he shouted. "TLALOC DOES NOT UNDERSTAND WHAT IS WRONG WITH YOU!"

Anna shoved Tlaloc aside and came to stand next to Tigre, her arms folded. "Stop yelling at Tigre, you horrible creature," she said. "He's doing his best and he's not going to do any better if you keep telling him he's hopeless. Tigre, *I* think you're great."

"PAH!" Tlaloc fumed. "A GREAT FAILURE! VERY WELL. TLALOC WILL CONSIDER YOUR MYSTERIOUS WORTHLESSNESS AND SOLVE THIS PROBLEM HIMSELF!" He shook his head vigorously. "USELESS MORTAL. ALL YOU HAVE TO DO IS THIS!"

Tlaloc slammed his staff into the ground and vanished as a bolt of lightning tore through the clouds overhead and dumped several tons of water out of the sky.

Anna shrieked and ran for cover. Tigre stood in the rain for a minute, feeling the water soak through him instantly, wondering why it felt so remote from him.

Was Tlaloc right? Were his powers useless?

Was there something wrong with him?

"So, like . . . that was weird."

"What was weird?" Gus said, startled out of his reverie by Ereka's voice. Neither of them had spoken for several blocks, and he'd nearly forgotten she was there, trailing along half a foot behind him.

"That whole thing with your girlfriend," Ereka said.

"She's not my girlfriend."

"I hope not," Ereka said. "She totally doesn't respect you at all."

Gus swung around and glared at her, but Ereka stared back coolly.

"It's not like that," Gus said. "We're just having a fight. It'll be fine—if I can survive this battle tomorrow." An

enormous skyscraper-sized *if*. He looked up at the buildings, which were looming like angry gods themselves.
Where should he fight Amon? If he chose the right place,
it might give him an advantage. But he barely knew anything about New York City—or about fighting.

"Well, if you're looking for weapons," Ereka said, "I
have an idea."

"Great," Gus said, relieved to be off the subject of
Diana. "I love ideas. I'd be a big fan of any idea that's better than 'wander the streets of New York.'"

Ereka tucked her hair behind her ears, studying the
stores around them. Choosing one of the smaller, dingier-
looking ones, she tried the door and then kicked in the
remaining glass so she could reach the handle inside.

Gus followed her through another set of propped-
open doors into a dim space, barely illuminated by the
gray light from outside and crowded with racks of sham-
poo, shaving cream, hair dye, moisturizing lotion, nail
polish, lipstick, soap, and other beauty products. At the
back of the store was a pharmacist's counter.

Ereka went behind the register at the front and started
pulling open drawers.

"What are you looking for?" Gus asked.

"You'll see," she said. "Hopefully."

She closed the last drawer and headed back to the
pharmacy section.

"Hey, nail clippers," Gus said, trailing down one of the
aisles behind her. "Ooh, these look menacing. Maybe I
could fight him with this."

"That's a really dumb idea," Ereka said, climbing over
the counter.

"Yeah, of course—" Gus started to say, but she had already ducked down and was rummaging loudly. He sighed. Diana would have thought it was funny.

Leaning on the counter, he studied the shelves at the back of the store. There were a few smashed jars, but otherwise the shelves for pills and potions were empty, probably wiped clean by looters as they left New York, or else by the old people in the subways when they needed medicine. What did Ereka think they could find here?

"Aha!" she said, emerging with a triumphant expression. "Human paranoia wins again." She plunked something hard, cold, and heavy into his hand.

Hard. Cold. Heavy. Gus stared at it.

It was a gun.

"*That'll* give you an advantage," she said. "You don't even have to wait for the fight to start officially. The minute he appears, just *boom,* and the whole thing will be over. I knew we'd find one around here somewhere. It's the first thing *I'd* pick up to defend my business if the world was ending."

Gus dropped the gun on the counter. He'd never seen one in real life before. Never touched one, never held one, never ever thought about using one. It didn't fit with this world. It especially didn't belong in the same place with ancient gods and crystal monsters and the girl of his dreams.

He tried to feel the war god inside him, the angry roaring presence that was so different from his real self. It rose up instantly, but he could feel it reject the gun as well. Oro worked with real weapons, battled hand to hand. As Oro saw it, there was nothing strong or honorable or . . . *right* about using a gun.

"No," Gus said.

"'No'?" Ereka repeated. "Are you serious? This is exactly what you need."

Gus shook his head. The gun made it too real. He might actually die tomorrow. Especially because he knew, he *knew*, he could not kill Amon. No matter how many angry war gods were inside him, this was not something that Gus could ever do. He would fight to stay alive, because he had no choice, but he would have to find another way to end the battle.

"I'm not touching that," Gus said. "It's wrong."

"Oh, I'm sorry," Ereka said. "Were you not actually planning to win this fight? Is there some ethical line in a life-or-death battle that I've accidentally crossed?"

"There is," Gus said, and he felt momentarily weightless, like someone else was speaking through him. "That is not a weapon for immortals. That is a symbol of everything that took our civilizations down in the first place. If that is how we win this battle, we will take the world right back there, and we will lose our power all over again, no matter how we try to make things different."

Ereka stared at him.

"I don't know where that came from," Gus said, rubbing his forehead. "I don't even want to 'win this battle' or keep the power in the hands of the gods. But there are some things I can't do, and using a gun is one of them."

"Wuss," Ereka said contemptuously. She bent down to stow the gun back under the counter.

"You're not going to keep it, either?" Gus asked.

"Nah," she said, straightening up again. "I'm not a war god. Weapons won't do me any good."

He gave her a curious look. "How do you know you're not a war god?"

"Oh," she said with a shrug, "I can just tell. I've never been good with my hands—give me a tool or a ball or, heck, a fork, and I'm more likely to injure myself with it than use it for its intended purpose. Remember the spoon I dropped right before the world ended? That happened pretty much every time I ate."

"Still," Gus said, "I'm not sure any of us can know exactly what being a certain type of god feels like."

Something that looked like irritation flitted across Ereka's face and then vanished as she smiled at him. "Yeah, you're probably right. I wish I *was* a war god! I'm probably something lame like agriculture or cows."

"Agriculture wasn't lame to ancient civilizations," Gus pointed out as she climbed back over the counter. "That's how they survived."

"Yeah, yeah," she said, stepping over a fallen rack of paperback novels. "Come on, let's keep looking, since you didn't like my—oh no!"

"What?" Gus said, catching up with her in the vestibule by the front door.

"Stupid Tigre!" Ereka cried, pointing at the downpour outside. "Weather gods! Come on! Can't you find another island to practice on? You have to take your aggression out on us?" She kicked an empty magazine rack. "I was hoping he wouldn't be able to start a storm like this, at least not until we got home."

"At least we were inside when it started," Gus said. Secretly he was kind of proud of Tigre. He hoped this really was the avatar's handiwork, and not just Tlaloc venting. "We'll wait it out."

"Fine," Ereka muttered, leaning against the wall. "But I think we should note that I'm *still* hungry and we *still* haven't had lunch."

In the small space of the vestibule, surrounded by the sound of the rain and the breeze coming through the broken glass, Gus felt strangely calm. It was like Amon couldn't reach him here, nor the other gods. He knew they could watch him anytime they felt like it, but for a moment he pretended they couldn't.

He wished there was somewhere he could be alone with Diana, really alone, without her pantheon spying on them. He looked down at his hands and remembered the electric shock they'd both felt when they hugged. It was apparently a side effect of the protection spell from the crystal hunters, but if it was, then why didn't Anna set off the spark when she touched Tigre?

Gus wondered again if Ereka would set off the same shock. That might prove that she was the real avatar, wouldn't it? And that Anna was the anomaly—*the* other *anomaly, besides me,* he thought ruefully.

Ereka had produced a comb and was running it through her straight black hair, humming something funereal-sounding.

"Hey," he said. "It's going to be okay." Gus reached out and put a hand on her arm, hoping this seemed like a natural, supportive thing to do. Nothing. No sparks, no shock, not even tingling. Her skin was cooler than he would have expected, but normal.

She turned toward him immediately, her large eyes like melting pools of chocolate. "Oh, do you think so?" she said. "Everything is just so *strange*." She threw her arms around him and clung to his chest.

Startled, Gus nearly jumped away. But she started making sad sniffling sounds, and he felt guilty about testing her, so he stood still and let her press her head into his neck. Her smell was different from Anna's—not oranges, but lemons perhaps, ones that had been in the fruit bowl just a bit too long.

But then he felt her arms slide up his back. Her chin tilted up. And he felt her lips press against the side of his face.

It was the most awkward come-on Gus could imagine. Not only had it come out of nowhere; it felt as if he were a prop in a terrible soap opera acting class. He grabbed Ereka's upper arms and pushed her away.

"What are you *doing*?"

"I thought you said she wasn't your girlfriend!" Ereka protested, breaking free of his grasp.

"Well, she isn't, but—I mean, you and I just met! I don't know you at all. And I didn't even—I mean, there's no—" *No chemistry,* he wanted to say, but that sounded too mean. As did *I don't even like you very much* and *There's no one in the world for me but Diana.*

"Look around you, Gus!" Ereka said. "We're the last people on the planet. This isn't the time to get picky about who to date."

"We're not here for dating," he said, taking a step backward.

"Oh yeah?" she replied. "How else do you see this working? If you don't plan to fight *or* die, and neither do your buddies, what do you think is going to happen? We start over, rebuild civilization? Don't you think that's going to require some romance?"

I've never experienced anything less *romantic in my life,* Gus thought. "I think it's a little soon to jump to that conclusion," he said.

"Oh my God, whatever," Ereka said. "I don't *care.* I just thought it was what *you* wanted. It's not like you're *soooooo* irresistible or something." She crossed her arms and glared out at the storm.

"I'm sorry," Gus said, feeling even more guilty. "It just . . . took me by surprise, that's all. And look, Diana's not my girlfriend, but she is really important to me. I guess I hope it'll be something eventually."

"Eventually," Ereka snorted. "Well, it's useful that you're spending your last twenty-four hours of life in a snit with her, then."

Gus felt a bit less guilty. He'd met annoying girls before—Andrew had dated a couple—but Ereka was irritating in a particularly brutal way.

"I think the rain is slowing down," Ereka said, although it clearly was not. "I'm going to run across to that grocery store. And there better be something I can eat there, or I'll have to settle for eating you. Ha ha. No"—she held up a hand—"don't come with me. I'll come back once I'm less starving."

Gus had had no intention of following her anyway. Ereka pushed through the door and ran across the street, disappearing into another doorway.

Gus leaned against the door, ignoring the rain blowing in through the holes. He didn't understand her at all. Generally he would have said he didn't understand any girls, but meeting Diana had given him some hope that he was getting better. Apparently it was just her, though; Ereka was the strangest, most temperamental person he'd ever dealt with. He supposed that objectively she was hot, but it was awfully hard to overlook her personality. Anna wasn't nearly as weird, as far as he'd been able to tell in a day of knowing her.

His eyes traveled along the street and up the buildings toward the clouds.

And suddenly, he knew exactly where he wanted to have the fight with Amon.

Diana had never imagined that old people could be scary.

Most of these didn't seem dangerous; they didn't look strong enough to fight, or even to remain standing in a light breeze. She wasn't afraid of them hurting her, although she was a little afraid of hurting *them*. But the worst part was that looking at them made her afraid to be old. She could suddenly understand very clearly why the gods wanted to stay young and immortal, and what an enormous risk the avatars were taking.

Kali didn't look scared. She looked mostly bored.

"She's not just your miracle," Kali said. "She's everyone's miracle."

General Pepper frowned darkly. "You may not steal her from us."

"We're not stealing her," Diana interjected. "She wants to go. We're taking her outside into the sunshine, where she belongs."

"Endangering the Miracle!" one of the women behind

General Pepper snarled. "It is the worst crime anyone can commit."

"And you think it's healthier to keep her locked up in the dark?" Diana said, but she stopped as she felt a sharp warning finger poke her back. When she turned around, Kali was staring evenly into General Pepper's eyes.

"She will be safe," Kali said. "The gods have sent us to protect her. Why else would we be here?"

Miracle pressed small hands to her mouth, her dark eyes watching Kali with an expression that was dazzled and adoring. *She believes it,* Diana realized, appalled. *She thinks that's really what's going on. Of course she does—this world has always revolved around her.*

General Pepper was not so easily convinced. "It's taken you some time to come to that conclusion," he said suspiciously.

"We were waiting for her other champion," Kali said, indicating Thor. "Did you see the bent turnstile upstairs? That was his handiwork—and I mean *hand*iwork. He could snap any of these columns in half as easily as blinking."

The subway dwellers closest to Thor hurriedly shuffled back several feet. He gave them a grin that made Diana think of grizzlies and hurricanes, and a couple of them sat down, covering their heads.

"And you've seen what I can do," Kali said, her voice soft and deadly. "Do you really want to stand between me and the will of the gods?"

"Perhaps we should listen, General," said one of the men holding a crowbar. "She is the Creator-Destroyer."

"she-who"

"creates-destroys"

The whisper ran around the room like scurrying mice. General Pepper stamped his iron pipe on the ground and everyone fell silent.

"We cannot allow just anyone to come in and steal our miracle," he said firmly. "You could be the next evolution of crystal hunters, or remnants of Eternally Me, or something else we've never imagined. If you can prove that you're from the gods, then the Miracle may go with you."

Kali didn't blink. Diana wondered who or what Eternally Me was. She also wondered if she should be offended that Kali hadn't included her as one of Miracle's protectors. Sure, she wasn't as intimidating as Thor, but still. It was weird to feel so insignificant, like a background prop. The subway dwellers barely glanced at her; all their attention was fixed on Kali and Thor. *This must be what it felt like for everyone else to walk down the street with me, back in the time of Venus, queen of the pop charts.*

"Proof?" Miracle finally spoke, her quiet voice out of place in the harsh surroundings. "General Pepper, how can you ask the gods for proof?" She stepped forward between Thor and Kali and laid a hand on the arm of each. "What they ask from us is faith. They have sent me these guardians, whom you should worship as you do me." Diana saw Kali's mouth twitch—amusement? Guilt? Surprise? "It is not our place to question their miracles."

General Pepper's face was a collage of dismay, fear, and anger. "But *I* am your guardian," he growled. "How do we know this isn't a trick?"

Diana winced, and the general's eyes traveled to her. Kali moved to block his view, and Diana wondered if her face was giving too much away. It just seemed wrong to manipulate their beliefs this way. She could never do it as coldly and efficiently as Kali did.

"Just believe, General Pepper," Miracle said, reaching out to take his free hand in both of hers. "Everything will be all right."

He was visibly wavering. The woman who had first spoken hissed, "You can't let them do this."

"Where is your faith in the gods?" said another of the men to her. "The Miracle has spoken. She would know. It must be so."

"This is wrong," the woman snarled, clutching her wrench in an angry fist. She darted forward suddenly, reaching to pull Miracle away from the avatars.

There was a blur of movement, a muffled gasp, a thump, and by the time Diana's eyes caught up to what was happening, Thor had scooped Miracle up in his arms, and Kali was standing over the cowering woman, the wrench now in her own hands.

"I don't want to fight you," Kali said, "but we will do what we must to defend her." From the fiercely protective look on Thor's face, Diana guessed that he didn't need to speak their language to agree with Kali.

"Don't hurt her," Miracle said. "She'll let us go. Won't you, Sarah?"

Sarah nodded, although her eyes were still mutinous.

"Then let's go," Kali said, dropping the wrench with a clatter that echoed around the space. She turned and walked straight past General Pepper, who watched her intently but didn't move to stop her. Thor followed, still carrying Miracle, and Diana fell in behind him, avoiding the stares of the subway dwellers as they parted to let the avatars through.

"We'll want her back," General Pepper called as they started up the stairs. "Soon."

Diana could hear the whispers starting up again, but by the time she reached street level, they were drowned out by the sound of the torrential downpour outside. Kali was standing by the door, her hands on her hips.

"Stupid weather gods!" she yelled out into the rain. "Tigre, you unhelpful moron!"

"Maybe it's a good thing," Diana said, coming up behind her. "I mean, it's great for him if he really managed to do this."

"Oh, blah blah," Kali said. "Yeah, I'm thrilled that his self-esteem is getting a boost, but *we* are going to be *soaking wet* the minute we step out there, let alone by the time we walk all the way back to the apartment."

"I'm sorry," Diana said to Miracle. "It would have been nice if your first look at the outside world was in the sunshine. It can be really pretty."

Miracle had one arm around Thor's neck and the other outstretched toward the rain. "There's so *much* of it," she said in an awed voice. "Everything is so *big*."

Diana tried to imagine what she would think of Times Square if it was the first thing she saw after years living underground. It looked a lot bigger without the usual hordes of tourists crowding through.

"Can I go out there?" Miracle asked. "Can I touch it?"

"The rain?" Diana said. "I don't know. You'll get very wet. It might be better for us to wait until it stops."

Miracle's face fell.

"On the other hand," Kali said, "this is your first taste of freedom. I think being free to make your own decisions includes going out in the rain if you want to."

"Really?" Miracle said.

"Sure," Kali replied, avoiding Diana's eyes. "But I reserve the right to think you're a lunatic."

"Hooray!" Miracle cried. "Out there," she said imperiously to Thor, pointing at the storm. "Take me out there."

Thor wiggled his beard, looking concerned. *"Bloot,"* he said. *"Oosreggin."*

"What's he saying?" Miracle asked Kali.

"Beats me." Kali shrugged. "Maybe he thinks you haven't noticed that it's raining."

"I want to go out there," Miracle insisted, pointing again. When Thor still looked doubtful, she pushed at his chest. "I'll go myself. Put me down."

"It's okay," Kali said slowly to Thor. "Miracle out there." She pointed.

Thor expelled a breath, shook his head, and then carried Miracle carefully outside. He examined the ground for a moment, picking a clear spot, and then set her down like a tiny figure atop a wedding cake.

Even through the rain, Diana could hear Miracle's squeals of glee. The tiny girl threw her head back and let the rain pour over her face, holding out her hands as though to capture the raindrops. Thor made a sound of protest and moved to shield Miracle's bald head with his massive hands, but she ducked away and spun in a circle, her robe flapping wetly.

"You really think this is a good idea?" Diana said to

Kali. "Lying to her, taking her away from the people who've protected her her whole life?"

"If by 'protect' you mean imprison," Kali said. "And how am I lying to her?"

Diana's mouth dropped open. "Telling her the *gods* sent you to *guard* her? That's a lie, and she believes it, and it's cruel to mess with her like this."

"I'm not messing with her," Kali said. "You're forgetting something." She flipped her ponytail back over her shoulder and looked down at Diana. "*We* are gods. Literally gods. And I've assigned myself and Thor to protect her, so technically it's all quite true."

"We're not *her* gods," Diana said. "You're making her think she's the center of the universe, that she's here for some important purpose."

"How do you know she isn't?"

"Because—" Diana sputtered. "Because Tigre told us what the gods said through her—that she's just a trick, to give people false hope."

"Those weren't *her* gods," Kali said with a small smile.

"Kali, we're the ones who are here for a purpose," Diana said. "We should tell her the truth."

"Don't you dare," Kali said, suddenly cold. "What gives you the right to decide what the truth is? Miracle doesn't think she's a useless plaything, and there's no reason she should." Kali strode out into the rain without waiting for a response.

Diana sighed. "I meant the truth about *us*," she said, and followed.

Outside, Thor was moving his hands above Miracle's

head, muttering. Miracle clapped her hands together, creating a splash each time. Kali reached them as Thor made a satisfied noise and stood back.

Suddenly there was an arc of clear air above Miracle, like an invisible umbrella hovering over her head. She giggled and reached up to poke it, but her hand went straight through the invisible barrier into the rain.

"Ooooh," she said, and started poking her hand in and out again. Thor rumbled something menacing and she gave him a bright smile.

"Got any more invisible umbrellas on you?" Kali said to Thor, wrapping her hands around her bare arms. He looked uncomprehending, and she shrugged. "Might as well start walking, then."

To Diana's immense surprise, Kali reached out and took Miracle's hand—naturally, casually, as if they knew each other well and did this every day. Miracle beamed up at her, and Kali actually allowed a smile to crack her face.

"Thor!" Thor announced, banging his chest. *"TANN-GNOSTR! TANNGRISNIR!"* He cupped his hands around his mouth and bellowed the last two words again.

"Okay, ow," said Kali. "What happened to your headache? What are you yelling about?"

"I think he was calling *them*," Diana said, pointing. Two enormous shaggy animals were galloping up Broadway toward them, pulling a wooden chariot behind them. They didn't slow down until they reached Thor, where they simultaneously crashed to a halt. Their long gray-and-white coats were heaving and their eyes flashed fire. They both bared their teeth at the other avatars.

Thor spoke to them commandingly and they stamped

their feet and ducked their heads. The Norse thunder god took the reins and gestured for the others to get in.

"Now *this*," Kali said, "is *definitely* a bad idea."

"Look how amazing they are!" Miracle cried, enraptured. "Look how gigantic! And furry! Are they bears? I've read about bears."

"They're goats," Kali said, "but you're right; they're about the size of bears."

"And they'll pull us around?" Miracle asked.

Kali hesitated, and Diana felt mildly triumphant. If Kali rejected Thor's offer, it would be obvious that they weren't working together, which would make Miracle suspicious. But surely the Indian avatar didn't want to entrust herself to Thor's chariot and risk where he might take them.

"All right," Kali said. "Sure. Thor can give us a ride home." She narrowed her eyes at Thor. "Home," she repeated, pointing north.

Diana wondered if Kali would be so calm if she'd heard Ereka and Anna talk about their abductions in this very chariot. From Thor's point of view, had he only abducted one of them? She guessed his pantheon had sent him to pick up the avatar in Thailand. So which one did he think he'd brought here, Anna or Ereka? Would he be able to tell the difference between them?

Kali lifted Miracle into the chariot and stepped up next to her. "You coming?" she said to Diana as Thor climbed in.

"I don't think so," Diana said. It looked like a tight squeeze already, with just the three of them in there. "Thanks, but I should be getting back to Apollo." She didn't think she was ready to see Gus again yet, and if Kali was right and she was being watched, she should probably try to draw attention away from him anyway.

"Suit yourself," Kali said, slinging her wet ponytail back over her shoulder.

Thor and Miracle waved, and the chariot rolled away. As they disappeared into the downpour, the rain seemed to come down harder, and Diana suddenly felt how wet she was, her hair dripping down her back, her jeans sticking to her legs. Maybe Kali was right about weather gods.

She started squelching her way north, back to the museum, feeling sorry for herself. It was going to be a long walk, with some very angry gods at the end of it.

After Tlaloc vanished, Tigre and Anna walked back in the rain to Kali's apartment, where they found two surprises.

First: in the entranceway by the stairs, Kali had left a giant pile of fluffy towels, robes, clothes, and dry socks. A small white sign said LEAVE YOUR WET SHOES HERE OR DIE in crisp red letters, with an arrow pointing to the floor outside the door.

Tigre had managed to find some decrepit umbrellas in the library's Lost and Found, but they hadn't done much good against the gale. Anna kicked off her shoes right away and dumped her umbrella in a tall urnlike thing that Tigre suspected was supposed to be a work of art.

"Don't look," she said, pulling off her sweater so quickly that Tigre barely had time to turn away. He picked up Anna's shoes and lined them up neatly next to his own. There were two other pairs there; he recognized Kali's black hiking boots, but the second pair was unfamiliar and gigantic, and looked as if they might have been made of reindeer.

"Okay," Anna said, flinging a towel over his head. "I look super-elegant now, don't I?"

She spun around, showing off a fluffy gold-colored robe that was far too big for her but which made her eyes look like they had sparkles of gold in them. On her feet were a pair of bright orange socks.

"You look amazing," Tigre said.

"Yeah, right," she said, laughing. "Are you sure your superpower isn't flattery?"

Tigre rubbed his hair vigorously with the towel and then pulled off his dripping jeans and T-shirt while Anna politely covered her eyes. Rummaging in the pile of clothes, he found the dark green pants he'd been wearing when he arrived—the ones the Forever Youngermen had put on him. He couldn't imagine Kali washing them, but here they were, looking clean. Despite the memories they brought back, they were comfortable, so he slipped them on along with a gray T-shirt.

"Here," Anna said, handing him a pair of orange socks as bright as hers. "So we'll match." She grinned, challenging him, and he put them right on.

Being dry, warm, and clean again made him feel much better. So what if he couldn't conjure a storm on command yet? Anna seemed to like him anyway. At least *he* didn't have to fight the Egyptian avatar tomorrow, so it could be worse.

The feeling of well-being lasted all the way into the living room, where they found the next surprise: Kali and Miracle on opposite ends of the couch, drinking hot chocolate, with Thor on the rug below them.

Thor looked as startled and displeased to see them as Tigre was to see him. The Norse god leaped to his feet, roaring, as they stepped into the room, and Anna jumped behind Tigre with a shriek.

"It's all right!" Kali yelled. "Shut up, both of you!" She whacked Thor's arm with a couch cushion. "Not the time for battle," she shouted at him. "These are friends! Hey, Tigre," she continued in a normal voice. "There's hot chocolate in the kitchen if you want it. No milk, of course, but it does have mini-marshmallows. How awesome are we? Miracle found it." She poked Miracle with her foot and the smaller girl giggled.

"I'm only allowed to have it on sacred occasions," Miracle said, "but surely this is one, don't you think?"

"Sure," Kali said. "Very sacred. For instance, it's raining. Again. Thanks for that, Tigre."

Tigre was about to admit that the storm was Tlaloc's doing, when Anna grabbed his arm and dragged him off to the kitchen.

"Let her think you did it," she whispered as they put the water on to boil. "I can tell she respects power. She'll be nicer to you if she thinks you're strong."

"She is nice to me," Tigre said, surprised. "Well, maybe *nice* is the wrong word to—"

"Trust me," Anna said, "it's better if they think you're finding your powers. Especially Thor, remember?"

"He doesn't understand what we're saying, though."

"That's what we *think*," Anna said. "But let's be careful, just in case."

They carried their mugs back out to the living room

and were settling into two of the armchairs when Gus and Ereka arrived, setting off another round of roaring and shrieking.

"Oh my God," Kali said. "Calm the heck down, Thor. There's a time for killing, and then there's a time for hot chocolate, and this is the latter, big guy." She yanked on his sheepskin vest until he sat back down on the floor, grumbling. "Okay," she said. "That's Tigre. Anna. Gus. And I'm guessing Ereka."

"Who is *that*?" Ereka asked, staring at Miracle with round eyes. "That's not an avatar, is it? Why is it *bald*?"

Tigre shifted uncomfortably in his chair, but Kali answered it like a normal question. "This is Miracle. She's marked by the gods for a great destiny, but we can't tell you what it is. Now off to the kitchen with you." Her voice was cool, but Tigre could see the muscles in her arms tense, like she was reconsidering her "time for killing" remark.

"Which gods?" Ereka asked.

"That's a good question," Gus said.

"Well, thanks," Ereka said. "It's about time somebody noticed."

"What?" said Kali.

"Which gods marked her for a great destiny?" Gus said. "Yours? Tigre's? Not mine, I'm guessing."

Miracle looked confused.

"Would you get your hot chocolate and stop being annoying?" Kali snapped. "Or I'll take back those robes and towels and you can go out in the rain to find your own dinner."

Ereka quickly vanished into the kitchen. Gus followed

more slowly, his suspicious gaze traveling from Kali to Miracle to Thor and back again.

"What did he mean?" Miracle asked Kali.

"He's not much of a believer," Tigre said. "Maybe you could tell us about your gods when he comes back."

"*My* gods?" Miracle said, puzzled.

"*The* gods," Kali said. "Don't worry, not everyone's on the same page as Thor and I." She thumped Thor's shoulder and he nodded happily. "They'll get there."

"Okay," Miracle said. "I like talking about the gods. Some of them are scary, but I know they're taking care of us."

Gus and Ereka returned carrying mugs. Gus sat in the chair closest to Tigre, and Ereka pointedly took the farthest chair from him. Tigre wondered what that was all about, and hoped he didn't have to hear about it from Ereka later.

"Miracle's going to tell us about the gods," Kali said to Gus. "Mr. Nosy."

Miracle picked up a candle from the side table next to her, lit it with a match, and crouched next to the glass coffee table in the center of the room. Tigre glanced up at the lights, wondering if it was only his imagination that made them seem suddenly dimmer.

"Here," Miracle said in a reverent voice, "is Dad. He's the sun, and he is very cruel." She placed the candle in the center of the glass and it flared higher, almost bright enough to hurt their eyes if they looked directly at it. In the glass, its reflection shone like a globe of fire.

"Wait—your dad is the sun?" Ereka interrupted.

"No, no. Well, he might be, I don't know, but Dad is

his name," Miracle said. "He keeps the earth alive, but his warmth also feeds the hunters, who grow stronger the higher he is in the sky." Tigre seemed to see flickers of reflected light in the glass, like miniature creatures moving around the candle, neon purple lightning radiating along their limbs.

"The hunters are our enemies," Miracle whispered, "and they wish to take the Earth from us. They are Dad's favorite children. But Mom still loves us best." She put another, smaller candle with a silvery glow on the table, closer to the edge. "She protects us at night, while the hunters sleep. She came down to Earth and had me."

"So this one's actually your mom," Ereka said.

"But she's called Mom by everybody," Miracle explained. "She wants us to win and send the hunters back to Dad."

"The crystal hunters came from the sun?" Ereka asked.

"Shhhh," said Anna. "Let her tell the story."

Ereka sighed loudly but stopped interrupting.

"Mom's sister is Dark, the underground where we live. She hides us in her tunnels and keeps us safe from the hunters while Dad is in the sky and Mom is asleep. There are parts of her where we can grow food and find water to keep us alive. She is kind, but she is trapped where she is, and there is not much more that she can do for us." Miracle spread her hands below the glass and the floor seemed darker, hidden by shadows.

"Mom's brother is Salt, the ocean," Miracle said. She touched the glass, and it wavered, as if it were turning to water before their eyes. "He doesn't know whose side to be on. He likes the strength of Dad, but he still has loyalty to his sister. Some days he rushes through the tunnels, trying to clean us all out for Dad. And some days he leaves us in peace, brings us fish to eat, sings us to sleep. He fights with Mom all the time, like a long tug-of-war with us in the middle.

"There is only one way to make Dad happy, and we need Salt's help to do it. But if we do it once a month, Dad won't get hungry, and we will have a moon of peace, until the next ascension."

Miracle was staring intently at the glass table now, and Tigre, mesmerized, was almost certain he could see shapes moving there—climbing up from the darkness below, walking out to a point where the sky and sea and land almost met. Other, more dangerous shapes swooped down from the sky, colors flashing. There was a scream, a figure borne into the sky, and then the silent procession returned to the safety of the underground shadows.

Nobody said anything for a long moment.

"Pterodolphins," Gus finally whispered in a shaky voice. "Those were pterodolphins."

Tigre looked up at him, the spell fading. "You saw that, too?" he asked.

"We all did," Anna said, moving to sit on the floor and lean against his legs. Thor blinked and shook his head, then put one of his massive hands on Miracle's head, his eyes sad.

"Saw what?" Ereka said. "A couple of candles on a table?"

Tigre and Kali exchanged glances. "Miracle, are you telling us," Kali said, "that you sacrifice someone each month to the pterodolphins?"

"You mean the messengers of the gods?" Miracle said. "They come when Mom and Dad and Salt and Dark meet, and they carry someone away to Dad's kingdom in the sky. I hear they're pretty," she said wistfully, "but I have seen them only in visions. General Pepper won't take me to the ascension ceremony. He says it's too dangerous."

"And the gods—Mom, Dad, Salt—they appear to you in your visions?" Tigre asked.

"Usually just Dad," Miracle said. "Mom is in my dreams all the time; she appears as my mother, and we just spend time together. But Dad is the only one who comes in my waking visions and tells me things. He can be kind sometimes." She looked down at her hands. "Especially after we send him someone."

"What does he look like?" Kali pressed. "When he appears in your visions?"

Miracle frowned. "Don't you know?" she asked. "Doesn't he appear to you?" She glanced around at their expressions of confusion and bewilderment. "I thought— how can you be from the gods and not know any of this?"

"We are gods, too," Kali said. "And we know a lot of gods, more than your four. I'm wondering if any of the gods I know have been appearing to you as Dad."

"Dad is *real*," Miracle insisted.

"I'm sure he is," Kali said, not sounding altogether pleased about that fact. "But I think we might know him by a different name. There are a lot of gods, Miracle— more than you can imagine."

Miracle's shoulders slumped. "I'm tired," she said softly. "I wish to go to sleep."

"All right," Kali said, standing. "There are beds upstairs. Come on."

Miracle looked a little brighter. "Beds?" she said as she followed Kali out. "Real beds? I've read about beds."

Thor stood up as they left the room, but then he didn't seem to know what to do with himself. He looked around at the others, fidgeting in his stocking feet and tugging at his beard.

"What do you think happened there?" Anna said to Tigre, pointing at the table. "How did she do that?"

"I guess it's not impossible that she has powers," Gus said. "I mean, we do. Sort of."

"So, I don't get it," Ereka said. "Are her gods real, like ours? Where are they? Are they going to show up and demand sacrifices from us, too?"

"Well," Gus said slowly, "it sounds like a pretty normal myth, considering this society. I guess they're real to these people, but there aren't enough believers to make these gods very strong yet, I would think."

"Except Kali seems to think the sun god might be one of the gods we know, appearing to Miracle as 'Dad,'" Tigre said.

"A sun god?" Gus said. "Like Amon, perhaps?" Tigre had almost forgotten about the battle Gus was supposed to have with Amon the next day. He wondered if Gus had chosen a place to have it.

"Amon's the Egyptian guy, right?" Anna said. "Could he really do something like that? Appear in Miracle's dreams and manipulate her?"

"That's really creepy," Ereka said. "Why would any god waste time on these last few remnants of civilization? I'd just let them die already."

"Odin," Thor rumbled. They all looked up at him.

"You think it's Odin?" Gus asked.

"ODIN," Thor repeated, louder now. He sounded irritated, like he had forgotten the other avatars were there. Tigre followed the Norse god's gaze to the hallway, and his stomach gave a sickening lurch as he realized there was someone standing there, wreathed in shadows.

The figure stepped forward into the light, and Tigre could see his long gray cloak and the two wolves slinking beside him. The man lifted his head, and Tigre saw that he only had one eye. Anna reached up and took Tigre's hand, and he squeezed hers reassuringly.

"Odin," Thor rumbled again, followed by a torrent of words in his own language. Odin replied in the same language, then turned to the others.

"We have come to take our avatar back to his training grounds," Odin said coldly. Tigre was surprised at first that Odin spoke English, but then he remembered Inti talking about translation powers. Presumably, Odin was powerful enough to translate his own words, like the Egyptians were, even though his own avatar couldn't speak English. The Norse god went on. "We would appreciate it if you would not drag him into any more little tea parties."

"That's not why he came," Kali said from the other doorway. "Seems like you weren't keeping a very close eye on him. No pun intended."

The force of Odin's glare was so strong, Tigre wondered how much scarier he could be with both eyes. "You can't keep him here, little Indian goddess," Odin growled. Behind him, two more figures emerged from

the darkened hall. Both were men, tall and fair-haired and
ridiculously handsome. Tigre glanced down at Anna, then
over at Ereka. They both looked starstruck, like a pair of
movie stars had walked in.

"Frey, right?" Kali said to the more handsome one,
who nodded with a pleased expression, as if he expected
to be recognized. "And . . ."

"Njord," Odin said impatiently. "This is not a social
call, tiny avatar. Kindly treat us like the enemies we are."
Njord stepped toward Thor, his blue eyes warm and menacing at the same time.

"Then maybe you should go," Gus said, standing up.

"Yess," Odin hissed. "Delighted to."

Frey moved to Thor's other arm, tossing his hair back
in a move that looked calculated to make the gold in it
shine. At his waist was a large ice blue pouch with a ship
on it, embroidered in gold. He also had a helmet hooked
into his belt with a boar's head prominently emblazoned
on it.

Thor said something vehement, pointing at Kali, then
at Gus, then upstairs. Odin replied, and then Frey and
Njord took Thor's arms and started pulling him out of
the room. Tigre could tell that Gus was having the same
reaction he was: Should they try to stop them? But if the
Norse gods could manhandle someone as gigantic as
Thor so easily, did they really want to get in the way?

"Kali!" Thor protested. "Miracle!"

"It's okay, Thor," Kali said. "I'll take care of her. Miracle
okay."

Thor still didn't look happy, but he allowed himself to
be dragged away. They heard stamping as he put his boots

back on, and then the door to the stairs slammed closed behind them.

"Wow," said Anna. "Maybe I'm glad my pantheon won't talk to me after all."

· · · ·

PANTHEON: INDIAN
AVATAR: KALI
JUDGE: GANESH
TRAINER: SHIVA

· · · ·

Clever, clever Kali. She catches on so quickly . . . a little too quickly for my liking.

Yes, I'll admit it. Why not? It was a brilliant plan. I am a god. Why not set up a few worshippers of my own? Their energy keeps me strong. And nothing feeds a god's power like human sacrifice.

Right under the noses of the other gods, too. They've come up with some very humorous explanations for Miracle. They're just about convinced they created her themselves, as another way to play with humanity. I let them speak through her sometimes, so they won't see me lurking in the shadows.

But Miracle is mine. She is my daughter . . . my other daughter. I came to her mother. I made her a miracle. I shaped her life. I tell her what to do and how to make me stronger. I am Dad and Mom and Salt and Dark. I am her whole pantheon.

And only Kali suspects. You know why? Because she is just like me. She had the same idea—get herself some worshippers. She acts high-and-mighty and even kind, "rescuing" Miracle from the subway, but she would steal their worship from me in a heartbeat if she could. She is no more moral than I am. Would she say no to the power of human sacrifice if it were offered? I doubt it. I know her.

There are many sides to Kali, but I believe I know which one will win in the end. I plan to be there to see it.

I'm sure the flames will be glorious.

DAY THREE:
⟨⟩ CONFRONTATION ⟨⟩

It was almost noon.

It was almost time for battle.

It was almost time for Amon to kill him.

Gus tried to breathe. In, out, deep, calming. *Just stay alive. He's not that different from me. He acts like a big shot, but what does he have that I don't?*

Well, superpowers, for one. Useful superpowers.

He wished he knew exactly what time it was, but watching the minutes tick toward noon probably wouldn't be any easier than this. And Diana hadn't even arrived yet. He'd hoped to have a moment with her before the fight started. Surely she was coming?

Amon had said he would find Gus wherever he was at noon. But maybe he wouldn't be expecting to look for him at the big Macy's store in Herald Square. Maybe Amon would have to wander the city looking for Gus and maybe he'd eventually give up and go home.

Yeah. That seemed likely.

Gus wondered if he should pray. He'd sort of given up on praying after his mom and dad died, but he still believed there was someone out there. A real god. Someone bigger than these psycho mythological jack-asses. Maybe that someone didn't intend to interfere with their plan, but just in case . . . maybe he should pray.

Ereka and Anna had both decided to come watch the fight. They were perched side by side on a tall counter. Tigre had come, too, for "moral support," he'd said. That had involved a massive fight with Tlaloc much too early that morning.

"A SLUG IN BED WILL LOSE HIS HEAD! ARISE, PATHETIC ONE! TLALOC HAS RETURNED TO BEAT YOUR POWERS INTO YOU!"

The bellowing had awakened Gus from an uneasy sleep full of jungles and spears and whales and tattoos and drums. He'd given up on keeping everyone together and taken his own room, not wanting to sleep on the floor again, or anywhere near the window Amon had snuck through. Tigre and Anna had stayed in the same room as before, while Ereka chose another room for herself and Miracle slept in Kali's room.

"Ow!" he heard Tigre yell. "Man, giving me a concussion isn't going to help!"

"LOOK TO THE SKIES! THEY ARE FULL OF DISGUSTING SUNSHINE! LET US GO FORTH AND TRAIN ANEW TO BRING THE WRATH OF THE CLOUDS DOWN AMONG US!"

Gus hauled himself out of bed and stumbled down the hall to Tigre's room. Tigre was sitting on the edge of the mattress, rubbing his head, while Tlaloc stomped back and forth beside the window. Anna was not there.

"Hey," Gus said, "actually, Tigre, I was thinking that a

storm today would be really helpful."

Tigre looked alarmed. "Why?" he asked.

"Because Amon is a sun god," Gus explained. "If there could be a storm, maybe he would be weaker than usual."

"STORM GODS DO NOT WREAK THEIR HAVOC AT THE BECK AND CALL OF WAR GODS!" Tlaloc shouted. "YOUR GRUESOME IMPENDING DEATH IS NOT OUR CONCERN!"

Tigre squinted at Tlaloc, then at Gus. "I'll try, Gus," he said. "But I can't promise anything."

Now standing inside Macy's, Gus could see that Tigre had failed. Outside, the sun was shining merrily in a bright blue sky. And the battle with Amon was minutes away. Gus glanced over at Tigre, who was slumped glumly against a wall. Tigre didn't meet his eyes.

Even Kali had come to watch. *This battle must be the next best thing to television.* Kali had wandered off to "do a walk-through" and "case the joint." Gus assumed Kali was there to watch him die; she'd probably be pleased to have one fewer person to deal with. She'd been quiet after putting Miracle to bed, and she hadn't said much that morning, either. *Planning something sinister, I imagine,* he thought.

There was a clatter of feet on the escalators and Gus spun around, to see Diana and Apollo bounding up the last few steps. Diana was ahead of Apollo, but Gus could see a similarity in the way they moved and smiled, as if they'd spent a lot of time together. Diana's face lit up when she saw him, and at least half of his anxiety evaporated.

"You made it," he said.

"Of course I did." She gave him a hug, ignoring the

electric shocks that it set off. "Gus, you're going to win this," she whispered in his ear.

"Thanks," he whispered back. "I'm glad you're here."

She stepped back and Apollo appeared next to her, grinning.

"So," said the sun god, "explain this choice of battleground to me. I mean, it's awesome, because I love stuff, and this place has a lot of stuff, but . . . Macy's?"

"I was wondering that, too," Diana confessed. "I know it's the biggest department store in the world, but . . ."

"I know," Gus said. "But I figured what I need is things I can fight with. Oro showed up in me while I was fighting Thor in the sports store. He likes improvising. I put things—weapons—in his hands and he knows what to do. I'm hoping that'll happen here."

"In the crystal department?" Apollo said.

Gus didn't get a chance to answer. A sound reverberated through the eighth floor, so loud that it seemed to come from inside his head, and yet indescribable—a crash, a bell, a gong, an explosion, a clatter of cymbals, all rolled into one.

And suddenly there were four gods standing among the glass cases of china and crystal: two men (more or less) and two women. The judges, Gus guessed.

The closest one had intelligent gray eyes and long brown hair woven into an elaborate braid. She wore armor over a long white robe, and an owl sat on one shoulder, blinking enormous yellow eyes.

"Athena!" Apollo cried enthusiastically, and she gave him a small smile before turning her attention to Diana.

"Hello, dear," she said, leaning down to kiss Diana's

cheek. "I think humanity has made you shorter."

Diana looked too startled to speak.

"And welcome, Polynesian godling," Athena said, resting one hand lightly on Gus's head. "I wish you luck."

"Well, I don't," sniffed the other female judge. "I hope you die quickly." She had perfect, evenly balanced features that reminded Gus of the Egyptian goddess Isis, and she wore one ostrich feather in a band around her head.

"This is Maat," Athena said to Diana and Gus, seeing their confusion. "The Egyptian judge. And that is Tyr, of the Norse gods." She pointed to a burly, weathered man who was missing his right hand. His eyes were as intelligent as Athena's, and although he looked fierce, he reminded Gus of Mr. Perez, his high school principal back in Los Angeles. Tyr had the same strict but fair expression, which Gus found reassuring.

"And that's Ganesh," Athena said, pointing to the last judge as Kali came around the nearest corner and stopped dead.

"Kali!" Ganesh cried, waving his trunk excitedly.

"He has—" Gus began. "He's—he has—"

"An elephant's head," Diana said. Ganesh was the least human-looking of the judges, and yet he gave Gus the most hope. Short, mustard yellow, and potbellied, he radiated gentle goodwill, and his elephant head had a permanent smile on its face. One tusk was broken off, and he had four arms, all of which were now extended in Kali's direction.

"Ganesh!" Kali said. "Wow, I'd forgotten . . . that you would be here."

"I've missed you!" he said, wrapping her in an

enormous hug. The top of his head barely came to her shoulders. "It's so wonderful to see you again."

"Um. Right," Kali said, patting his trunk.

"Where is your impartiality?" Maat snapped. "This is no way for an arbiter of justice to behave."

"Impartiality," Tyr rumbled. "Something you're so good at, Maat. Now, why don't you tell your avatar to stop lurking about and make his grand entrance?"

Maat narrowed her eyes at Tyr, and almost immediately there was an explosion of glass at the nearest window. Amon burst in on a ray of sunlight, kicked the glass away, and floated lightly to the floor.

"I have arrived!" he cried. He swung around, studying his audience. His eyes stopped at Ereka and Anna. "Greetings, mystery avatars," Amon said with a deep bow. He faced Diana. "And you, my lady."

Gus stepped protectively closer to her, but, mid-motion, a gust of wind suddenly punched him in the stomach, hard like a bag of rocks. He doubled over, gasping.

"I presume we may begin?" Amon said to the judges.

Athena looked displeased, but Maat nodded, and all four of them stepped back to watch. Apollo grabbed Diana's hand and pulled her out of the way. As she gave Gus an anguished look, more shapes materialized behind her—other gods from all the pantheons. *Here to watch my death,* Gus thought angrily.

He touched the new tattoo that had appeared that morning on his chest and called the anger up, welcoming the war god into his skin. Oro, filled with fury, lifted his head and stared into Amon's eyes.

"Then begin," he said.

A new wind howled through the window and bar-reled toward Gus. With lightning speed, he twisted behind a case of vases. Punching through the glass, ignor-ing the blood on his knuckles, Gus seized a crystal vase and threw it at Amon's head.

The Egyptian avatar was caught off guard. He barely had time to leap backward, but the vase crashed into the upper left side of his chest, slicing cuts through the white linen cloth and his skin. Flowers of blood blossomed along his arm.

With a snarl, Amon clasped his hands together and then made a motion, as if he was hurling a baseball at Gus. An explosion of fire hit the column where Gus had been, but he was already gone, darting into a display of plates and silverware. Amon strode after him, and the watching deities crowded along behind them.

Diana felt her heart sink as gods crowded in front of her, blocking her view of the fight.

"I'm a little surprised you're here," Kali said in Diana's ear as they followed the others.

"I'm here for Gus no matter what," Diana said. "I know he only snapped at me because he was worried about this."

"I mean," Kali said, "I'm surprised your caretakers let you out." Was there something sinister in Kali's smile? Diana couldn't tell if she was just imagining it. Diana herself was surprised they'd let her leave with just Apollo, but Zeus had somehow convinced himself that she was going to support Amon, so he hadn't made too much fuss in the end.

"Where's Miracle?" Diana asked.

"Thor showed up first thing this morning to watch her," Kali said. "I'm surprised he's not here taking notes, but it works out well for me. When I left, they were playing Candyland—sort of. I figure that translates better than Scrabble."

A tremendous crash sounded as Amon knocked over a tray of silver spoons. He reached behind him, toward the window, and yanked another gust of wind in from outside. It spun around him for a moment, gathering strength, and then whirled toward Gus like a small tornado, scattering everything in its path.

But Gus was already moving. He seized a stack of plates from the nearest counter and flung them at Amon as he ran, one after the other, like a series of Frisbees. Amon managed to dodge most of them, but one grazed his head and he let out a yell of anger. The mini-tornado wavered, then resumed its pursuit, but slower, as Gus darted down the nearest escalator.

"He's drawing Amon away from the open window," Kali said. "If he's doing it on purpose, that's smart."

Amon charged after Gus, followed by the judges, and then the rest of the gods all tried to crowd onto the escalator at the same time. Frustrated, Diana glanced back and saw Ereka, Anna, and Tigre getting shoved aside.

"You'd think the *gods* would remember that they can just rematerialize downstairs," Kali muttered. "They don't have to use the stupid *escalator* like the rest of us losers. Come on." She took Diana's wrist, setting off sparks of electricity, and tugged her away from the group.

"I want to follow him," Diana protested.

"I know," Kali said. "This way will be faster."

She led the way around to the other side of the escalator, which would normally have been rolling in the other direction. Now frozen in place, it was clear and empty, and they were able to run down to the next floor easily. Kali barely paused before starting down the next escalator.

"Wait," Diana said. "How do you know he isn't here?"

"In the kids department?" Kali said, gesturing around. "Doubtful. I know where the real weapons are, and I'm guessing he does, too." She pointed down. "Housewares. In the Cellar."

Diana hung back for a minute as Kali ran on. She leaned over and saw that the other avatars must have seen their shortcut; they were coming down the escalator she'd just been on. Gods were spilling out across the seventh floor, looking confused. Most of them seemed to have forgotten their all-seeingness in the excitement of spectator battles.

Suddenly Diana felt tingling all along her skin. She shivered, shaking out her hands. Something was happening to her, something new and unpleasant.

She stepped back from the escalators and rubbed her neck, where the tingling was strongest. What did it feel like? Like being stared at in a restaurant. Like walking through an airport and realizing that people were whispering, "That's Venus, Venus the pop star. I wonder if she'd give me an autograph or just snap my head off." Like knowing without looking that there's someone watching you from across a crowded party.

Diana glanced around, but no one seemed to be

looking at her. Everyone was trying to find the battling avatars; no one was interested in her right now. And yet, she was *sure*. It was more than being watched; it was a dark, angry force. Someone here hated her. They might not be looking at her, but they were thinking about how much they hated her right now.

It was an unfamiliar feeling, but she was certain of it. Who could it be coming from? Most of the Greek gods were there, including Hera, Mars, and Vulcan. There were also several gods she didn't recognize—some who looked like Vikings, several Egyptians, and one or two who were barely solid enough to be seen.

The sound of shattering glass came from below and there was another stampede for the escalator. Diana waited until everyone was ahead of her, testing the hostile feeling. It stayed strong, floating in the background, even when no one was there to watch her. She rubbed her neck again. Was this a Diana power? It didn't fit with what she knew of the moon goddess.

Maybe it was a Venus power. *That'd be exciting,* she thought. *A step up from making everyone love me.* Although she wasn't sure how knowing that someone hated her was supposed to help.

She went cautiously down to the sixth floor, where another window was broken, and then followed the sounds of battle down to the fifth, where Gus was crouched behind a discount rack, slinging women's shoes at Amon with blurry speed. A stiletto heel bounced off Amon's forehead and the rest of the shoe disintegrated. Amon jumped behind a mirrored column, his hands moving frantically.

Diana wondered if Kali was right. Amon seemed less powerful without the sun and the wind at his immediate call. Probably that was why he'd broken the window on the floor above, trying to reach his weapons. That could be important to remember.

Then, all of a sudden, Amon . . . vanished.

One moment he'd been leaning against the mirror, and the next he was gone.

Diana caught herself holding her breath. Had he given up? Was the fight over? Gus paused, a hefty boot in his hand. He peered around the rack, searching for his rival. The gods began muttering to one another, but Diana noticed that the Egyptians looked satisfied rather than worried. Their judge, Maat, had a particularly smug expression.

She glanced around. What was happening? The tingling increased again, and she spun, searching the crowd with her eyes.

There!

"Gus!" she yelled. He ducked reflexively, and a weighty cash register flew over his head. Almost immediately, Gus went flying to the floor and covered his face with a yell of pain. He jerked and rolled and pushed at the air with his hands as if fending off an invisible attacker.

"Amon can make himself invisible?" Diana asked Apollo, who was watching nearby.

"Sure," Apollo said. "Although usually only during battle. It's a power he doesn't use much, which I don't understand—I mean, how cool would that be, right?— but I gather he really likes to be *seen*, so it's not his favorite trick. Sort of a last-resort measure. Which is both a good sign and a terrible sign for your friend."

"You didn't think that was worth mentioning?" Diana said.

"Why?" Apollo said. "Don't worry, he's not using it to spy on *you,* silly. We have Hades, remember—oh, sorry, of course you don't. He's our own Mr. Invisible, and he's got his mark on the museum, so no one else can wander in there unseen." He lowered his voice. "We're not taking any chances, even with our so-called allies."

Gus kicked out at the air and connected. Amon let out an audible grunt. Gus scrambled free and took off running for the escalator, once again heading down, with everyone else right behind him.

"How's he supposed to fight someone invisible?" Diana protested. "It's not fair."

The Norse judge, Tyr, gave her a hard look as he swooped by. "Are you a god of justice?" he asked. "No. So do not question the justice of those who are."

"But—" Diana began, but he was already gone.

The mob of gods had picked up on Kali's original plan and were now blocking both of the escalators as they pushed to be first. Amon could be down there pummeling Gus to death right now, Diana realized, and she couldn't get to them.

She glanced around, but no one was paying attention to her, not even Apollo, who was standing in a patch of sunlight and murmuring to himself. Diana edged away slowly, until she was out of sight of the escalators, and then she turned and ran. She knew there was at least one other set of escalators in this enormous store, and if Kali was right, that would get her to the Cellar faster than anyone else.

Sure enough, she was soon pelting down through the

floors. By the third floor, she could hear nothing but the
sound of her feet on the old wooden escalators—
reminders of how long Macy's had been there. Finally she
reached the escalator to the Cellar, where she hesitated.
Below her was darkness. The sun filtered through the
other floors, but none of the artificial lights were on, and
in the basement she'd be blind.

That's his plan! she realized. *Once he gets Amon to the
Cellar, it won't matter that he's invisible, because Gus will be,
too.* Had Gus known about this power before? Or had he
just counted on his war god's ability to fight by instinct,
guessing also that the sun god would be less powerful in
the dark?

A clatter that sounded like cascading pots and pans
came from the darkness below, and that decided her. She
hurried down the steps, keeping one hand on the railing
and the other outstretched. Downstairs, she let go of the
escalator and felt her way forward, following the noise of
things being thrown.

Soon she sensed figures ahead of her and heard grumbling that sounded like some of the Greek gods.

"Why can't we conjure a light?" one of them muttered. "What fun is a battle if you can't watch it?"

"Athena said no," said another voice, cold and female.
Diana guessed it was Hera. "It would be considered inter-
ference, and you'd be thrown out."

Something smashed to the ground in the distance and
an excited murmur ran through the group.

"What was that?" said a third voice. "Are they moving
away from us? One of you who can see in the dark,
tell us what's happening."

Diana strained to listen, but suddenly all she could hear was the pounding of her own heart.

Something was using the darkness to stalk her.

The thing that hated her was here, slithering through the shadows to do its evil unseen. *Thump thump,* her heart whispered. *Thump thump,* louder. *THUMP THUMP,* like a horror movie, like the moment when the heroine knows that something is creeping up on her, out of the dark, *THUMP THUMP,* and every millimeter of her skin feels pierced with needles and it's getting closer and closer, its claws held high, its evil and its hatred bearing down on its victim with one deadly purpose—

Diana screamed and, without knowing why, threw herself to the ground. A second later, something thudded into the wall above her.

There was instant commotion. The gods nearest to her all began shouting at once.

"Someone's been killed!"

"A sneak attack!"

"What's going on?"

"It wasn't me! I didn't do it!"

"We need light! We need light!"

"Diana!" she heard Gus yell. "Diana!" But she was afraid to answer, not while it was still dark and her killer had only just failed. She didn't want to draw its attention.

"STOP!" somebody yelled. Kali? "Stop the fight!"

Blinding light flared off to her right, a few feet away, and Diana covered her eyes.

"Yes, thank you, Apollo." Athena's tranquil voice cut through the hubbub. "Now turn your bit of sun down to a level that won't blind all our avatars, please."

"Oops!" Apollo said. "I forgot. Here you go."

There was a pause. Diana peeked through her hands and saw a swarm of faces above her, some worried, most curious, a few clearly amused.

"Amon, rematerialize," Tyr commanded. "We are calling a temporary truce."

Gus pushed through the throng. "Diana?" He crouched down beside her and she grabbed his hand, wincing at the shock but ignoring the pain.

"What happened?" Kali said, shouldering through behind him.

"This," Apollo said. Diana looked up. Her brother was studying something that was sticking out of the wall. Something smooth, the color of dark wood. Apollo wrapped his hand around it and pulled it out of the wall in one swift motion.

It was a carving knife. The blade was stainless steel and razor-sharp; it had plunged into the wall with the same force as the spear in the museum garden two nights earlier.

"Wow," Apollo marveled. "Someone really wants you dead."

"A cowardly someone," Kali said with disgust. "Attacking in the dark, while everyone's distracted. If whoever did this would like a *real* fight," she said, raising her voice, "*I'm* right here."

"There will be no fighting for the moment," Athena said. The crowd parted to let her and the other judges through, with a sulking, fully visible Amon right behind them. "Apollo, give me that."

Apollo handed her the knife. As Athena examined it, Diana scanned the crowd.

The other avatars—Tigre, Anna, Ereka—were clustered at the back, craning to see her over the heads in front of them.

Hera, looking even taller from below, glared down her nose at Diana. Beside her, Mars and Vulcan were both scowling at Gus. In the background, so was Amon, kicking kitchen implements across the floor with an expression of hatred.

Kali, her arms folded, stood at the forefront between Athena and Ganesh, tapping her foot impatiently. And behind her was the three-eyed man Diana had seen her with on the street: Shiva.

His fire-dappled eyes met Diana's, and he smiled.

"Would the wielder of this weapon like to step forward?" Athena asked, raising the knife into the air. "We are prepared to stand witness to an honorable battle with this avatar if you will identify yourself." She indicated Diana, who rose to her feet, still shaking.

Nobody spoke. Diana wasn't surprised. If it was a god attacking her, he or she was breaking the rules of the game, and would hardly be likely to admit it.

Athena's gray eyes narrowed, and she turned to consult with the other judges. Gus put his arm around Diana's shoulders.

"Are you okay?" he whispered.

"I think so," she said. "At least I feel better now than I did while you were fighting." The tingling feeling of being hated had faded, but it was still there, like someone pressing two fingers into the back of her neck. More overwhelming now was the current of electric shocks snapping along her skin as Gus pulled her closer. She wanted to be near him, but it was too much jagged energy after the shock of being attacked. She moved his arms gently away and rubbed her skin, trying to recover.

"Fine," Maat spat suddenly. "I'll be just as happy to watch him die tomorrow."

"Ah, there's that famous impartiality again," Tyr said. Ganesh wagged his trunk, looking anxious.

"Very well," Athena said, turning back. "The judges have spoken. Due to this most improper and dishonorable murder attempt, we are postponing the rest of the Egyptian/Polynesian battle until tomorrow at noon. The attacker has until then to come forward and admit to his or her crime, so an honorable showdown with Diana can be arranged. If no one confesses, the judges will confer again and further action will be taken." She tucked the knife into a loop in her armor.

"Your would-be assassin is clever," Apollo said to Diana. "Once again, the attacker chose a weapon from the scene of the crime—one that anyone here could have picked up, so it can't be traced back to whoever used it. Maybe your attacker is a fan of those crime shows that seem to flood your wonderful television medium."

"'Once again'?" Gus said. "What's he talking about?"

"Don't worry about it," Diana said. "Hold on, I want to talk to Athena." She stood up and caught the Greek goddess of wisdom before she disappeared.

Gus watched them whispering to each other. He felt tremendously strange, like he'd just been ripped from a deep sleep. During the fight, he'd let Oro take over completely, more than ever before, and the god had been especially strong in the dark. Now Gus was struggling to get back to the surface. Diana being in danger had snapped him out of the trance immediately, but his head was woozily trying to catch up.

He didn't like the feeling. What if Oro decided not to let him come back? How much of him was really himself anymore? Was Oro getting stronger as the tattoo spread further . . . and if it ended up covering Gus's whole body, would there be any of the real Gus left inside?

He tried to look on the bright side. Even if the fight was only postponed, that was another twenty-four hours to live.

"This isn't over," Amon's voice hissed in his ear.

"Jeez, could you be more cartoonishly villainous right now?" Gus said. "Weren't you ever a normal kid? Doesn't any of this seem crazy to you?"

"Tomorrow," Amon said icily. "And this time, *I* get to pick the place."

Chills ran along Gus's arms. "Wait, why? That's not fair."

"Sure it is. The judges picked the time—bad luck for you. And it's my turn to pick the place."

Gus's heart sank. All his advantages would be gone. Outside, in the sun and the wind, with nothing to use as weapons and an invisible Amon dancing around, he wouldn't stand a chance.

Amon patted him roughly on the cheek.

"I'll let you know what I decide, since I know you can't find me on your own. See you tomorrow, dead boy."

● ● ● ● ●

The top floor of Macy's had once sold furniture, and there were still displays of fully made beds, side tables, and lamps arranged around the floor. Gus was lying prone on one of these beds, while Ereka and Anna sat, bouncing slightly, on another nearby. Diana and Kali had left with their pantheons.

Tigre paced around the edge of the displays, leaving footprints in the dust on the tile floor.

"I'm sorry, Gus," he said, knowing he should stop apologizing. "I tried to call a storm, I really did, but Tlaloc doesn't make it easy."

"That's okay," Gus said mournfully. "It probably wouldn't have made much difference. He'll kill me tomorrow, either way."

Tigre recognized this attitude. It was his own attitude about almost everything—Vicky breaking up with him, the storms, the monkey creatures kidnapping him, flying around on a giant bird. His default reaction was to assume that nothing he did could change what happened to him. He was at the mercy of the universe and might as well accept it.

Except he didn't really want to accept it anymore, not if his assigned fate was to die quickly so that the stronger avatars could get on with fighting for control of the planet. That couldn't be the only choice. Yet another creepy god had stopped by his dreams the night before, the one that looked like a skeleton with a collar of eyeballs around his neck. He'd tried to convince Tigre once again, with depressingly relentless logic, that giving up was the right thing for him to do. Only waking up and finding Anna sleeping soundly next to him had stopped Tigre from diving out the nearest window.

"I'll try again tomorrow," Tigre said. "Or I'll get Tlaloc

to do it. Maybe if it's pouring, Amon will agree to fight inside."

"Nah," Ereka said. "He'd probably find a storm helpful, actually. He's more of a wind god than a sun god, at least originally. Stronger winds make better weapons."

"Why didn't you tell us that?" Anna cried. "That's important! We should know that!"

"I thought everyone knew!" Ereka protested. "You all were the ones reading the books. I just flipped past a page about him—he's much cuter in person than in his stone carvings. Didn't you think he was cute?" she said to Anna.

"No," Anna said loyally, but for some reason, Tigre wondered what she would have said if he hadn't been there.

"You're all so busy reading about yourselves," Ereka said. "Didn't it occur to you that reading about your enemies might be helpful, too? Jeez, it's a good thing I'm here."

Anna rolled her eyes.

"So never mind," Gus said to Tigre. "But thanks anyway."

"I wish I could help," Tigre said, sitting on one of the coffee tables. "My powers seem completely useless against everybody."

"At least you have some," Ereka said. "Even if they're lame. And you know what pantheon you're from. Did you notice our judge didn't even show up?"

"Kali said only four of the six judges were needed to witness a battle," Gus said.

And mine didn't show up either, Tigre thought. *Probably not strong enough.*

"You were doing really well for a while there," Anna

said. "He was getting so mad. You definitely surprised him. Oro seems stronger than you think."

Gus sighed, then reached down and rolled up one leg of his jeans. "Look," he said.

Crisscrossing its way up Gus's leg was a new green tattoo, elaborate lines and shapes and whorls interweaving into a pattern that looked raw and painful.

"Ow," Anna said.

Ereka came over to peer at it. "Does it hurt?" she asked, poking a shape that looked like an eye.

Gus flinched and pulled his leg away. "Only when people do *that*," he said, and she stuck her tongue out at him.

"The other leg is the same," Gus said to Tigre. "I first noticed it yesterday, just a couple of lines around my ankles. It's been growing slowly, and now it's above my knees."

Tigre shuddered. "That's freaky, Gus," he said.

"I know," Gus said, "but the worst part is, the more it spreads, the more I feel like Oro. You know, angry, violent, powerful—"

"What's wrong with feeling powerful?" Ereka interrupted.

"It's not what I want," Gus said, rubbing his face with his hands. "I just want to be me. I want to go home."

"Well, duh," said Ereka. "Who doesn't?"

"Kali," said Tigre.

"Diana," said Gus at the same time.

"You don't know that," Anna said soothingly. "They're playing along with their pantheons, but they probably miss their families and their real lives as much as any of us."

Gus snorted, and Tigre wondered if she was right. Kali didn't seem like the type to get attached to people, even her family, but she had been carrying around a photo of her three half sisters in her notebook. It had fallen loose, and he'd picked it up; he wasn't sure if she'd noticed it was missing yet. He hadn't thought of a safe way to give it back to her, so he kept it in one of his pockets, waiting for an opportunity to slip it back into the notebook.

"So let's fight back," Tigre said. "Let's all tell the judges we don't want to battle. Maybe they can send us back in time."

"That's what I said originally," Gus interjected. "But what about all the terrible things that have happened to the world since then?"

"That all started with the gods, right?" Tigre said. "It was the gods who stopped everyone from having kids."

"Sure," Anna said. "Every pantheon has a fertility god. Working together, they could probably muster the power to do that."

"So if we go back and they *don't* do that, everything will be fine. No monsters, artificial or otherwise. No tidal waves taking out the Pacific islands—something else the gods did deliberately. No end of the world."

"Why on earth would they agree to that?" Ereka exclaimed. "They set this whole thing up. They aren't going to take it apart again just because we say, 'Oh, hang on, changed our minds.'"

"Even if we *all* do?" said Tigre. "If we refuse to fight, what are they going to do?"

"True," Gus said. "But we'll never convince Amon. And we can't even talk to Thor."

"Wait," said Tigre. "Maybe we can. I have an idea."

"A Norwegian-English dictionary?" Ereka suggested. "All we need is the Norwegian for *apocalypse* and *no thanks*. Ha ha."

"My friend Quetzie," Tigre continued excitedly. "The bird I told you about who brought me here. She talked to me inside my head. I know it sounds weird. But I couldn't even tell if she was speaking Spanish or English. I just understood what she was saying, and she understood me."

"A bird with telepathic powers?" Ereka said skeptically. "That's your big idea?"

"Oh my God, shut up," Anna said. "I think it's an amazing idea, Tigre."

"I'm sure you do," Ereka said.

"It's a great idea," Gus said, pushing himself into a sitting position. "At least it's a place to start. If we can get Quetzie to help us talk to Thor, that's at least one fewer person trying to kill us, hopefully."

"The only problem," Tigre said, "is I'm not sure how to find her. She left in a hurry because a crystal hunter attacked. So I don't know how to call her back."

Ereka opened her mouth, but Anna jumped in before she could speak. "Did she say anything? Give you any clues?"

Tigre pressed his forehead, trying to remember. She had said *something* before flying off. Something about . . .

"Pterodolphins," he said. "She said I could send a message to her with a pterodolphin—if they didn't eat me first."

Gus shook his head. "They are *not* friendly-looking

creatures," he said. "I can't imagine how you would ever talk to one, or where you'd find them."

Anna touched Tigre's shoulder. "You know who can help us."

Tigre met her eyes. "Miracle."

"I know what you need."

Diana opened her eyes as little as possible, squinting up at Apollo. "A nap?" she said. "Because that is what I was doing."

"I've got something better," he said, grabbing her arms and tugging her out of the hammock.

Arguing with Apollo was a bit like throwing sand at the sun, Diana had discovered, so she gave in and followed him through the halls to a stairwell she'd never noticed before. At the top, they emerged into bright sunlight, which made her eyes water.

"Yikes. Are we on the roof?" she asked.

"You bet," Apollo said happily. "The best part of the museum, if you ask *me*, because it's got the most sunshine. There used to be a small café and sculpture exhibitions up here."

"I don't think I knew that," Diana said, shading her face and looking around. It was a small space, only a corner of the large museum roof, but it was ringed with greenery, and it was remarkably clean for a place subject to the weather and inhabited mostly by pigeons.

"Come here," Apollo said, tugging her to a long white bench. "Lie down, close your eyes, and let the sun fix everything."

"Did you bring me up here to get a tan?" Diana asked,

amused. "Because I'm afraid I'm not the right girl for that. I burn instantly and then get super-freckly. It drove Doug crazy. He was always shoving me into the shade and canceling outdoor events and chasing me around with, like, SPF two thousand sunscreen. He got me completely terrified of skin cancer."

Apollo looked injured. "Skin cancer is not *my* fault," he protested. "I've been driving that chariot through the sky for centuries, and only recently have I been getting complaints. You mortals are too fragile."

"I'm sorry," Diana said, "I didn't mean to criticize." *I don't usually have conversations where I have to be careful not to insult the sun.*

"Well, don't worry," he said, bouncing back to cheerfulness. "I'll mute the rays so you won't burn today. You need some sunshine. Trust me; it'll make you feel much better."

Dubiously, Diana lay down on the bench and closed her eyes. Apollo murmured a few words, and she felt a change in the heat on her face. It *was* kind of relaxing, not having to worry about sunburns and blistering shoulder pain and photo shoots and airbrushing in magazines. Warmth melted through her, and she breathed in deeply, smelling the ocean in the air.

"Bad news, Diana," Apollo murmured. "Don't look now, but I'm afraid your least favorite person is flapping this way."

Oh, there are too many people that could be right now, Diana thought, but she guessed who it was before she opened her eyes.

Sure enough, the Egyptian wind god touched down

on the museum roof as she sat up. She instinctively reached to smooth down her hair. Amon looked confident and perfect, as usual, although a small lump was forming on his forehead where a plate had hit him, and she could see Band-Aids crisscrossing his arm through the rip in his sleeve.

Amon strode gracefully toward them, wind blowing back his hair in a very romance novel–cover kind of way, which Diana was pretty sure he was doing intentionally.

"Greetings, my darling," Amon said, sliding onto the bench next to her. "We haven't had a moment alone in ages."

"You're not alone," Apollo pointed out.

Amon sniffed. "We *could* be."

Apollo folded his arms and didn't move. With a sigh, Amon stretched his arms along the back of the bench and shook his hair back.

"How did you like the fight today?" he said to Diana.

"How did I *like* it?" Diana said. "How did I *like* you nearly killing one of my best friends? Oh, it was awesome. Really."

"I thought so," Amon said, missing the sarcasm.

"But listen, do you think you could possibly not kill him tomorrow? I like my friends alive, personally."

Amon leaned forward and rested his elbows on his knees, clasping his hands. His scowl was deeper, and his whole body was tense. "These people are not your friends, Venus," he said.

"At least they can remember my real name," she snapped.

"This is a war! If we leave them all alive, nobody wins.

And sooner or later, someone is going to realize that he who dies last doesn't have to die at all. They'll turn on you—maybe not tomorrow, maybe not this year, but eventually. No one can resist immortality, no matter how well you think you know the person. The only way to survive is to kill them first. And then we can be together," he said, suddenly seizing her hand. She tried to pull away, but his grip was strong. "Then this will all be over, and we can rule forever and make sure everything goes the way we want it to. We can fix all the mistakes mortals have made in the last few thousand years. We'll be strong enough. And we'll have each other."

Diana freed herself and stood up. "How?" she said. "Isn't this battle set up for only one avatar to win? How do I know you won't just kill me in the end, too?" She went over to the railing and leaned on it, looking down at Central Park.

"There are loopholes in the rules," Amon said, following her. "Most gods are tricky, suspicious, devious, untrusting—unlikely to set up a straightforward contest without a few back doors installed. The judges wouldn't know about them; they have this dream of an honorable battle fought in a just, orderly way, but, of course, that's why they're the arbiters of law and order in their pantheons." Sliding one hand along her arm, he touched her wrist and whispered in her ear. "We know ways to get around them." She noticed that there were no electric shocks when their skin met. Their gods must have modified the spell so it wouldn't keep *them* apart.

"Really?" she said, not turning around but not moving away, either. "What do you mean? Like what?"

He studied the side of her face for a minute, still resting his hand on her wrist. Finally he whispered, "I don't know if I can trust you, Venus. It hurts me to say it . . . but a part of me is afraid that you have forgotten all the nights we spent dancing in our dreams. Sometimes—" He traced a circle around her wrist, like a handcuff. "Sometimes I think you might not even like me."

Diana stared at the gold tops of the leaves on the trees below her. She thought of Gus, and the battle the next day, and Amon's invisibility. She thought of the other avatars, trapped in this game none of them remembered choosing. She took a deep breath and turned toward Amon, catching his hand in hers.

She leaned toward him and touched his shoulder with her other hand. It was too easy to be flirtatious; her Diana side hated it, but her Venus half slipped into it as smoothly as silk pajamas.

"I could show you how much you can trust me," she said softly.

He didn't even look surprised. He immediately leaned down to kiss her, but she ducked her head. "Not here," she whispered, tilting her head toward Apollo. "Not now, where any god could see us." She looked up at Amon through her lashes. "Come back tonight. Midnight." She smiled. "The Egyptian galleries."

He smiled, too, like he'd just pulled off the century's biggest jewelry heist. "All right, little love goddess." He touched the tip of her nose. "I will see you then."

Amon stepped back and raised his hands. The wind rose, lifting him up toward the scattered streaks of clouds, and Diana watched him until he was a speck in the distance.

"Can't just use the stairs like a normal person, oh, no," Apollo said, coming up beside her. Then he saw the look on her face. "Diana? Are you all right?"

She nodded wordlessly. He glanced up at Amon's receding figure, then back at her. "Diana, what are you doing?"

I don't know, she thought. *I have no idea . . . but I'm pretty sure I don't like it.*

Kali had been wondering where to find the judges when they weren't judging battles. Her initial guess was that they hung out in the ether, not fully manifested, part of the air and sky. She expected that they would want to keep an eye on things and that they wouldn't waste energy on being substantial.

But seeing the Norse gods carousing in the pub and the Greek gods roaming around the museum had made her curious. A lot of gods seemed to enjoy acting human, taking advantage of the depopulated planet to make it their own.

So after the fight at Macy's, when the judges evaporated before she could talk to them, she asked Shiva about it.

"Oh, they're manifest most of the time," Shiva said. "They have to be; it's in the rules. The only way for them to stay impartial is not to watch the avatars training. They can see only the battles themselves, and the best way to guarantee that is to keep them sequestered in physical form whenever they're not judging."

Kali raised an eyebrow. They had walked a few blocks south of Macy's and were now sitting in a park at Twenty-third Street, watching an enormous troop of squirrels race one another through the trees. Shiva had once again brought her food—more burned meat, some fruit, and a bowl of jasmine rice. The squirrels had been eyeing it hungrily, but so far none of them had come too close.

"That seems . . . fishy," Kali said. "Shouldn't the judges be watching everything, to make sure there's no cheating?"

Shiva shrugged. "They thought their impartiality was more important. Gods of justice can be surprisingly trusting about the honor of other gods, no matter how many times they've been disappointed before."

"So this was their idea?"

Shiva's forehead creased thoughtfully. "I don't remember," he said. "I think it might have been Zeus's, actually."

Kali snorted. "There's a surprise. So where do the judges hang out? Wait, let me guess." She thought for a minute, slicing the skin off a mango with a sharp knife she'd swiped from Macy's. "The courthouse downtown? My mom had jury duty there once, back when we lived in Manhattan, just the two of us. Seems like a good place for judges to hang out." She poked Shiva with the blunt end of the knife. "Am I right?"

He grinned, shaking his head. She'd been relieved to see that he hadn't held a grudge after their fight the previous day. He didn't want to rehash it or brood on it or bring it up in little sniping ways a million times. It was just over, and that was fine with both of them. Perfect. No wonder she'd married him, however many millennia ago.

"Guess again," he said.

"Show-off," she said, flicking a piece of mango peel at him. "Just tell me already."

"The United Nations complex," he said. "That's more central than the courthouse, plus, of course, the symbolism."

"Yeah, I can see that," Kali said, standing up and rubbing the knife clean on a large leaf. "All right, let's go."

Shiva stood up slowly. "Um . . . go where?"

"The United Nations."

"Kali," he said, exasperated. "What on earth *for?*"

"I want to talk to the judges about something," she said. "Are you coming or not?"

"We could just call them," Shiva said. "There's a way to summon them before a battle; they can appear almost instantly."

"Oh, we don't need to bother them that much," Kali said. "They might not like being summoned without a battle to watch. Besides, I'm curious. Let's go see what they're doing."

"What about training?" he asked. "What about building your strength and coming up with a battle plan and choosing which avatar you should fight first?"

"We'll get to that," Kali said. "Here." She placed one hand on the bark of a tall tree and looked up. Perhaps sensing what was coming, the squirrels all fled to other trees, chittering madly. Kali blinked and stepped back, and the tree erupted in flames.

"Happy?" she said, and strode away north. Within minutes, the fire had flared out and the tree was a column of ash. Shiva studied it, then glanced around at the surrounding trees, all untouched by the fire.

He caught up to Kali at Thirty-fourth Street.

"Awesome," she said, linking her arm through his.

"Why didn't you destroy the whole thing?" he asked.

"The whole what thing?" Kali said. "Didn't you see the tree burn?"

"The whole park," Shiva said. "The Kali I know would have consumed the whole park in fire without blinking—*including* the squirrels."

"Blah blah blah," Kali said. "I'm working up to it."

"But it's not that you *can't*," Shiva said. "I think you can. It's that you *won't,* and that's what worries me."

Kali was silent for a moment as they walked. At length she said, "Shiva, I feel like there's something . . . missing. Like there are holes in my memories. I figured it was just a side effect of being human, but seeing Ganesh today was so weird. It's like I'd completely forgotten he existed—but now I have a strange feeling he's my son and I adore him. Except those feelings don't seem to fit with the Kali you talk about. Was I just angry and violent all the time? Twenty-four hours a day for thousands of years?" She shrugged. "Maybe I was. I don't mind angry and violent. Destroying things is fun. But then why don't I feel that way all the time now?"

"It's probably being human," Shiva said. "Your humanity may have tempered the real you a little. But you're still in there."

"I don't know," Kali said. "I was a lot angrier when I thought I was human—surrounded by slow-moving idiots, dealing with morons all the time. I don't even like people very much. How could being one make me nicer?"

"There it is," Shiva said, pointing. "The United Nations. Remember how it used to have all the flags of the world up around it? They took them down when the

UN closed—they hadn't found a solution to the reproduction problem, no one wanted to fight wars anymore,
and by that point, it was every country for itself. Close off
the borders, hunker down, and hope your scientists are
the best."

Kali cocked her head at him. He was trying to change
the subject. He had a shifty, mumbly attitude that she
could tell meant he was hiding something. *That* was
interesting. Something about the contest? About getting
her worshippers back? About her memories?

It was really strange to walk straight into the UN—
past the security checkpoints and the metal detectors
without being stopped and interrogated. Kali was quite
sure she wouldn't have sauntered in so easily in 2012.
Something about her face had always made anyone in a
uniform uneasy.

The halls were silent and cobwebs crept along the ceiling, clashing with the modern design. Kali found a map
posted on a wall and blew the dust off so she could read it.

"Where do you think they'd be?" she asked.

"How interesting," said a new voice, measured and
even, like a metronome. "Why are you here, bloodthirsty
one?" Each word had the same weight as every other,
with no emphasis or change in volume.

The speaker stood hidden in shadows, but a halo of
dark golden light glowed behind his head, casting even
more of a shadow over his face. His long robe was in
shades of gold, moving from a pale butter yellow around
his neck to an amber that was nearly black where it swept
the floor. He radiated a brutal heat, which made it
uncomfortable to get too close to him.

"Who are you?" Kali asked, stepping closer to Shiva.

"That is not why you are here," he said.

"It could be, if you're Ereka's judge," she said. "Shiva, do you know who this is?"

Shiva shook his head.

"No," the other god said. "You may be curious about our pantheon. But you do not come here to seek information. You come to bring it to us."

Well, that was eerie. Not even Shiva knows why I'm here.

"Perhaps," she said cautiously. "Where are the other judges?"

The god tipped his head up, so the light briefly caught on his face. In that glimpse, Kali could see that he looked like Anna and Ereka—similar features, similar eyes.

"This way," he said.

Kali and Shiva followed him to a room that she recognized from the movies. The UN General Assembly Hall was even bigger than she'd expected, but in the movies it was always full of delegates. Now it held only six people besides her and Shiva: the six judges of the pantheons.

Maat, the Egyptian judge, looked bored out of her skull. She was seated in one of the delegate's chairs near the front, swinging back and forth. Athena was pacing the floor below the UN emblem, while Ganesh and Tyr watched from the central podium where the secretary-general would normally sit. Another man was sitting across the floor from Maat at a table farther back, writing in a small reporter's notebook. He was old and wrinkled, with a gigantic nose the size of a tennis ball. As Kali entered, he looked up and smiled at her, and she could see that he had no teeth.

The god who had led them in bowed and stood back
to let them pass. Athena spotted them and came striding
up the aisle toward Kali. Behind her, Ganesh waved; Shiva
nodded back.

"What is this?" the Greek goddess asked. "Shiva, why
have you brought your avatar here?"

"I have something to tell you," Kali said before Shiva
could speak. "I know something I think the judges should
know."

The owl on Athena's shoulder ruffled up its feathers
and nibbled her ear. Absentmindedly, Athena reached up
and let it hop onto her hand, keeping her gray eyes on
Kali.

"Does it affect the battles?" Athena asked. "Might it
alter the outcome?"

Kali nodded. "But before I tell you," she said. "I want
to know who that is, and which pantheon he's from." She
jerked her thumb over her shoulder.

Athena glanced past her, then back at Kali. "Who?"

"Mr. Mystery, with the halo of gold and the heat. I'm
guessing a sun god?"

The Greek goddess frowned. "There is no one there."

Kali turned, and it was true. The god who had led
them in had vanished.

"Well, who's the sixth judge, then?" Kali said.

"Myself, Ganesh, Tyr, Itzamna, and Maat," Athena said.
"That's the six of us."

"That's only five," Kali said.

"No," said Athena. "Greek, Indian, Norse, Mesoamerican, and Egyptian. Six."

"That's *definitely* five," Kali said.

"Annoying mortal," Tyr bellowed from the center of the room. "Did you come here to argue with us over your inability to count?"

"But he was right there," Kali said. "Didn't you see him bring us in?"

"Who?" Athena said.

"The sixth judge! The one who's apparently been erased from your brains, or whatever passes for brains in gods!"

"Kali," Shiva said warningly.

"Oh, at least she's entertaining," Maat said from her chair, leaning backward to see them. "I wish more avatars would show up and wreck their chances of winning by acting like brats."

"I suggest," Athena said with chilly finality, "that you tell us what you came to say, and then leave."

"Fine." Kali tossed back her ponytail and glared at the judges. She had meant to do this calmly, but she was frustrated to find out the sixth pantheon was shielding from them, as well. "There is a secret alliance between two of the pantheons. I thought you should know." She noticed that the fifth judge, the one Athena had called Itzamna, was still writing, as if he were taking notes on everything she was saying and doing.

Maat yawned. "If you're talking about the Incan and the Polynesian, we already know. We've heard their cute idea about refusing to fight and returning to their own time. Frankly, if they don't mind dying quickly, we don't mind them doing it together."

Kali paused. She hadn't thought of Gus and Tigre as an alliance, and they hadn't mentioned any plans to her about getting back to their own time. Did they know something she didn't? Were they keeping secrets from her?

"That's not who I mean," she said. "I'm talking about the Egyptians and the Greeks."

Maat sat up in a hurry. "Amon?"

"And Diana?" Athena echoed.

"Their whole pantheons," Kali said. "Except, I assume, you two. The Greeks have promised the Egyptians something, and they're working together to win. I think they plan to rule together in the end."

Tyr frowned. "That is a serious accusation. It would go against the goals of the whole battle."

"I know," Kali said. "That's why I thought I should tell you."

Athena shook her head. "We appreciate your vigilance, but I'm afraid your story is impossible."

"Why?" Kali said. "Your pals are too trustworthy for that? Doubtful. I heard them talking, and Diana told me she used to see Amon in her dreams. It all adds up."

"Then explain to me," Athena said, "why Diana has asked us to attend a battle at the museum tonight— between herself and the Egyptian avatar."

Miracle was thrilled to be outside again. She was thrilled to be able to help her new friends and to hear that she'd get to see a sunset and an "ascension ceremony," as she called it.

"Well, we don't need a whole, er, ascension ceremony," Gus said. He and Tigre were standing on either side of Miracle. Anna was on the other side of Tigre. Ereka had decided to stay home and nap, saying she was sick of tramping all over the city on pointless quests. "We just want to talk to a pterodolphin."

"How else would we call the messengers of the gods?" Miracle said. "I'm so excited—I've only ever seen the ceremony in my visions. I bet it's beautiful. Who's going to ascend?"

"We were hoping no one," Tigre said nervously. "It's just a conversation." Anna leaned against his shoulder, looking anxious.

"It is the wrong time for a ceremony," Miracle said. "But I'm sure Dad would appreciate it anyway."

Thor had been hauled away again that afternoon by the (even more disgruntled) Norse gods after Miracle had soundly trounced him at nearly every board game they could find. Gus and Tigre had then explained their plan to Miracle, but she seemed to be missing some of the key elements, such as the not sacrificing of anyone.

As she explained it, there were a number of sites that would work for the ceremony; from her descriptions, they figured out that she was talking about bridges, where "sky, sea, and land come together." The best one—the pterodolphins' favorite—was the Brooklyn Bridge, so that's where they were now, shortly before sunset, hiding behind a guardhouse at the entrance to the pedestrian part of the bridge.

"How do you usually get past the crystal hunters?" Tigre asked. Three of them, looking like human-sized praying mantises with glowing eyes, were arranged across the road to the bridge. He'd almost forgotten about them, since the flying pterodactyl ones had made themselves scarce after the Boss Hunter was destroyed. Evidently these were not linked to that one, however, or else they were now being controlled by something—some*one*—else.

He glanced at the sky. The sun was sinking, and if calling the pterodolphins depended on timing, as Miracle said, they had to get past these hunters quickly.

"There are always risks getting here," Miracle said. "Since the ceremony has to take place at sunset, sometimes we lose people on the way, while the hunters are still out. But they usually leave us alone during the ceremony, General Pepper says. I think Dad keeps them away so the ascension can happen."

"So you think those are there because it's not the right time for the ceremony?" Gus said, nodding in their direction.

Miracle shook her head. "They've been acting weird since Kali appeared. General Pepper told me they've been acting more like sentries, never leaving the bridges. I don't know why."

Tigre knew Gus was thinking the same thing he was. *They're guarding* us—*making sure none of us leave.*

Anna perked up. "Something's happening over there." She pointed away from the bridge, toward the subway entrance across the street. Something small and shiny kept popping up and then down. Finally it retreated, and then two of General Pepper's more able-bodied followers climbed up the stairs and ducked behind a bench.

The avatars watched in surprise as the newcomers ran slowly toward them, zigzagging to stay under cover as much as possible. They got within a few feet of the avatars, and then one of them lifted his arm and beckoned at the subway. A distant clanking rose from the stairs, soon followed by the appearance of General Pepper.

He barreled straight toward them, and his helpers fell in behind him as he reached the guardhouse where they were standing.

"What is the meaning of this?" he demanded. Behind him, Tigre could see several heads of white hair peeking over the edge of the subway stairs.

"We're performing a ceremony," Miracle said happily.

"There are so many things wrong with that idea, I hardly know where to begin," General Pepper growled. "First, it is not the time—as you can see, Mom is not in the sky yet, so she will not have her usual calming influence on Dad. Second, the hunters are out in force, and they are sure to try to stop you. Third, you should not be here under any circumstances. Imagine what the hunters could do to you—or the pterodolphins!"

Tigre noticed that General Pepper did not call them "messengers of the gods" as Miracle did.

"If I were chosen to ascend," Miracle said, "I would be proud, not afraid."

"Why are you doing this?" General Pepper snarled at Tigre and Gus. "Where are the strong ones who pledged to protect her? Why have they let you bring her into this peril?"

Tigre felt a twinge of guilt. He was quite sure Kali would not have approved of this plan. Luckily, she'd been missing all day since the battle, so he hadn't had to lie to her or sneak Miracle past her. As for Thor, there was hardly any way to explain the plan to him. Tigre wouldn't have minded if the burly Norse avatar had come with them, but he'd been collected by the other Norse gods an hour ago. So it was just him, Gus, and Anna. He could see why that might worry the general.

But this was important. He needed to reach Quetzie. He needed her help. If Kali had met Quetzie, she'd understand. This could be the beginning of a real truce, and a real chance to get home again.

"We're not trying to put Miracle in danger," Gus said to General Pepper.

"We'll be very careful with her," Anna promised. She patted Miracle's bald head lightly, and Miracle smiled.

"We just need to talk to a pterodolphin," Gus said.

The two men behind General Pepper blanched. "One does not speak to the messengers of the gods," one of them sputtered.

"You can if you *are* gods," Miracle said. "Like these three. They need my help. They're sending a message to another god." Tigre winced; he hadn't meant to give her that impression of Quetzie. "Did you know there are other gods besides Mom and Dad and Dark and Salt? There are lots; I've been learning about them."

General Pepper's face sagged, and he suddenly looked as old as Tigre knew he must be. "Miracle," he pleaded, "can't we go back underground? Weren't you safe there? Didn't we protect you, and wasn't everything fine until these strangers came along?" He slowly dropped to one knee, and his lieutenants followed suit. "Please, Miracle," he said. "I only want to keep you safe. Let's go back to the way things were before. We don't need to get involved in all of this."

Anna looked sad; Tigre wondered if she was starting to

doubt the plan, too. Miracle stepped forward and gently placed her hands on either side of the general's face.

"General Pepper," she said. "We've always known I was here for some greater purpose, haven't we? Don't you believe that? Gary and Paul do, right?"

The other two nodded; General Pepper bowed his head silently.

"Surely this must be it," Miracle said. "I am here to help these gods. There is a reason for me. I cannot hide underground forever, not if I am to fulfill my destiny."

There was that word again—*destiny*. Was this really why Miracle was here? Was there a greater cosmic plan at work? Tigre found it hard to think so; his belief in the whole destiny thing was wavering.

"I want you to help them, too," Miracle said. "Trust me, and trust the gods, General Pepper."

The old military man stared at the ground for a long moment. Finally, with a defeated sigh, he rose to his feet. "As you wish, Miracle. What do you need?"

"We need a way to get past the crystal hunters," Gus said. "And we need some more fish, if you have any."

Gus claimed that Justin and Treasure trained their pterodolphins using vast quantities of fish, so he had spent part of the afternoon finding fishing gear and catching fish in the lake in Central Park. They were now piled in a stinking bucket beside them. Tigre had been surprised at his success, but there still weren't very many, and he had no idea how many pterodolphins would show up.

"Fish we can help you with," General Pepper said. He turned to the man Miracle had called Paul and spoke in a low voice for a moment, until the man nodded and jogged back to the subway. General Pepper turned back to the avatars, his expression anxious. "The crystal hunters, however . . . all we can do is lure them away."

"Actually, I think I should do that," Anna interjected.

Tigre took her hands, surprised. "But Anna—"

"Don't worry," she said, blowing her hair out of her eyes. "I run pretty fast. I've outrun a couple of these guys before, back in Thailand."

"You didn't mention that," Gus said.

"I didn't realize they were here, too," Anna said with a shrug. "Anyway, I can certainly run faster than any of these old folks. And I want to help."

"Are you sure they'll chase you?" Gus said. "The other avatars have this protection that makes the hunters ignore them. . . ."

"Well, they chased me before," Anna said. "Maybe my pantheon isn't protecting me. Makes sense if I'm not really their avatar, right?" She tried to smile, but Tigre could see that it was a struggle. He thought she was probably right—no electric spark when they touched probably meant no protection spell, either.

"I don't want anything to happen to you," he said in a low voice, wishing he could do this without Gus, Miracle, and General Pepper watching.

"I'll be careful," Anna promised. "And it'll be dark soon, so I won't have to run for long. But can I—can I take that?" she said, pointing at the piece of iron pipe that General Pepper was using as a cane. "I have an idea."

General Pepper looked pained, but when Miracle turned to him expectantly, he limped forward and placed it gently in Anna's hands. Glancing behind him, Tigre saw the subway dwellers crowding farther up the stairs to watch. They bundled to the side as Paul returned, gasping for breath, carrying two buckets heavily laden with fish.

"Okay, you guys," Anna said. "Get ready to run."

Gus picked up two of the buckets and Tigre took the third, adjusting his shoulder bag. Anna breathed in deeply, then walked forward onto the bridge.

The crystal hunters snapped to attention as she approached. The two on either side raised one set of arms and crouched a bit lower, like they were ready to spring, while the one in the center stood glaring, its purple eyes getting brighter and brighter.

WHO ARE YOU WHAT ARE YOU DOING THIS IS NOT ALLOWED. The mechanical voice issuing from the creatures startled Tigre. He had heard it before, from the flying hunter that attacked Quetzie when he arrived, but he hadn't realized that they all sounded the same.

Anna stopped a few feet away from them, hefted the iron pipe, and suddenly threw it with all her might at the central crystal hunter.

There was no time for it to move or for the others to react. The pipe smashed straight into the center of the hunter's chest, and jagged bolts of neon lightning shot through the creature's body, radiating from the point of impact. With a grating shriek of sound, like microphone feedback, the crystal hunter shattered into thousands of small pieces.

The other two didn't hesitate. They both leaped toward Anna, who was already running back down the pedestrian walkway. Before she reached the place where the others were hiding, she veered left, and the hunters chased her straight past the guardhouse and down onto the street. Tigre watched anxiously as Anna pelted in the direction of downtown.

"Tigre, come on!" Gus called, and Tigre realized that Gus and Miracle were already running up onto the bridge. Hefting his bucket of fish, he followed, quickly overtaking General Pepper and the two men who were helping him limp along as fast as possible.

Gus put down his buckets when they got to the place where the hunter had shattered, so he could carry Miracle across the patch of broken glass. He set her down on the other side and she skipped ahead, toward the center of the bridge.

"Miracle!" Gus shouted. "Wait for us!"

He grabbed the buckets again as Tigre caught up and they both ran after her.

In the center of the bridge, Miracle stopped and looked straight up at the sky, her arms outstretched.

"Look how big it is!" Miracle cried. "Look how beautiful! Dad, I'm here!"

A harrowing scream split the air and Tigre's eyes traveled up, up, up the tall arches that gave the bridge its distinctive shape. At the very top, perched on either corner of the closest arch, were two misshapen animals, their bright colors glowing in the light from the setting sun.

One of them spread its wings, lifted, and dove in a spiral toward the ground.

Gus dropped his buckets, sprinted forward, and grabbed Miracle around the waist.

"Stay down!" he shouted, shoving her under a bench along the railing. "Stay down here, and don't come out!"

Tigre seized a fish, the cold, slimy scales slithering through his fingers, and flung it into the air, hoping with all his might that Gus was right about this.

The pterodolphin swooped by directly over Tigre's head, snapping the fish out of the air. It was so close, Tigre could see its bright, shimmering blue underbelly and the enormous hooked claws sticking out from it. Its dolphin tail, mottled red and yellow, flapped vigorously as it pumped its way back up into the sky, but the second pterodolphin was already on its way down.

"I'll throw the fish," Gus panted. "You do your thing."

Tigre opened the messenger bag he'd scavenged from Macy's and pulled out a large art school-type drawing pad. He wasn't much of an artist, but earlier in the day, while Gus had fished, he and Miracle had tried to draw a few pictures that he hoped would get his message across to the pterodolphins.

The first was a giant portrait of Quetzie, colored in red and green crayons. He flipped it open to that page and brandished it over his head as the pterodolphin shot toward them. Gus threw two fish up as high as he could, and the animal twisted rapidly in mid-flight to catch them both. Tigre couldn't be sure, but he thought he saw it eyeing the drawing before it soared back up to the top of the bridge.

He kept holding it up in the air as the first one returned, caught two more of Gus's fish, and flew off. Then he flipped it to the next page: a drawing of a flying crystal hunter. This was a little harder for him, because the only one he'd seen up close was on top of the Empire State Building during the fight, when he was distracted by trying not to die. He also hadn't been able to find a purple crayon the same color as the electricity that ran through the crystal hunters' "veins," so he'd had to settle for fuchsia.

This time, both of the pterodolphins came down together. As they got closer, Tigre pulled out a black crayon and drew a big X through the crystal hunter.

"They're gone!" he shouted. "Tell Quetzie they're gone! It's safe for her to come back!" He had no idea if they could understand him, but if Quetzie thought they could take a message, maybe they understood something.

The pterodolphins opened their mouths wide, displaying rows of jagged teeth, and Gus tossed handfuls of fish directly into them as they swept past.

"Good aim," Tigre said in the breath between dives, watching as the creatures circled overhead.

"Thanks," Gus said. "But we should get this over with fast, or we'll run out of fish."

Tigre flipped to the last picture: Quetzie landing in Central Park, with the skyline of New York behind her. Gus picked up one of the subway dwellers' buckets and flung its entire contents into the air, making the pterodolphins writhe and dart rapidly through the cloud of glittering fish. Tigre stepped back to avoid being hit by any of them if they fell. He shouted, "Tell Quetzie to come back and find me!"

The animals both screamed a harsh, earsplitting cry and beat their wings, floating up on the breeze to the top of the arch once again.

"Okay," Gus said under his breath. "Get Miracle and run. I'll be right behind you."

"Are you sure?" Tigre said. "Shouldn't I—"

"Just get her out of here."

Tigre didn't argue. He stuffed the sketchbook back in his bag and darted over to Miracle's bench. She was crouching on the wooden boards, her hands covering her head.

"Come on, Miracle," he said, reaching under the bench and tugging on one of her wrists. "We have to run."

"Oh," she sobbed. "They're not beautiful at all. They're scary and, and, and they have teeth that hurt and w-what does it m-m-mean—"

Tigre wished he had time to coax her out reassuringly, but they had to get out of there. The pterodolphins were shuffling around up above and leaning forward, preparing for another dive. He reached around her waist and pulled her out, being as gentle as possible.

"We'll talk about it later," he said. "For now, just run."

She seemed to wake up as her feet hit the ground, and she took off running before he'd even finished speaking. With a glance back at Gus, who was holding the last bucket of fish, Tigre ran after her.

Gary and Paul had stopped a few hundred yards down the pathway, staring up at the pterodolphins in fear. General Pepper was still limping forward, leaning on the railing, trying to get to Miracle.

"Go back!" Tigre yelled. "Get back to the subway!"

Miracle reached General Pepper and threw her arms around him, hiding her face in his chest. He bent over her, as if shielding her with his body.

Tigre looked over his shoulder again and saw the two pterodolphins blazing down toward Gus. Gus stood his ground until they were nearly upon him, then upended the entire bucket of fish over the railing. A rain of glittering silver bodies slithered out and down toward the river below. Dropping the bucket, Gus took off running down the path toward Tigre and the others.

The pterodolphins screamed angrily, and one of them dove over the side to catch as many fish as it could before they hit the water. The other, however, landed on the wooden boards of the walkway with an ominous thud. It sniffed around where Gus and Tigre had been standing, its claws leaving long gouges in the planks. Its face was like a grotesque parody of a dolphin, flattened and scarred, and its beak was longer, more like a pterodactyl's. It stuck this beak into one of the abandoned buckets, nosing around for the last scraps of fish. Not finding anything satisfying, it lifted its head and screamed again.

By now, Tigre had reached Miracle and General Pepper, who were still standing with their arms locked around each other. "Come on!" he yelled. "Run!" He pulled one of the general's arms loose and threw it over his shoulder. "Here, lean on me. Miracle, go on, lead the way."

Miracle's frightened face emerged. "I'm sorry, General Pepper," she sobbed. "Why didn't you tell me it was so awful? Why didn't you stop the ceremonies?"

"We needed to believe in something," General Pepper said, his breath coming in short gasps. At least now they were all moving, although it felt painfully slow to Tigre.

"Miracle, you gave us all hope. And the ceremonies gave us hope."

"But those *things* don't take you to Dad, do they?" Miracle cried. "They kill you! They've been killing our friends all this time, and you never told me!"

"No," General Pepper huffed. "They do ascend, and this is how. You have to believe it, Miracle. Everyone depends on your faith."

Tigre wanted to yell, *Stop talking and run!* But he didn't think he could get the general to move any faster. Without his cane, the old man's limp was getting more pronounced, and he leaned heavily on Tigre. They were still several feet from the subway entrance, where Gary and Paul were hovering on the stairs. Tigre glanced back and saw the pterodolphin on the bridge twisting its head to stare at them with its shiny black eyes. It spread its wings and threw itself into the sky.

"Miracle," General Pepper said. "This is a test of your faith. Believe that. Don't lose hope, or we all will lose hope."

"But—"

"I will prove it to you," General Pepper said, his voice gaining strength. "I will show you *my* faith."

With an unexpectedly forceful shove, General Pepper pushed Tigre and Miracle forward and stepped back, bracing himself against the bridge's railing.

"GO!" he shouted at Tigre. "Take her to safety!"

"No!" Miracle screamed.

Behind the general, Tigre saw the looming shape of the pterodolphin whistling down from the sky. Farther back, Gus was still running toward them, head down, feet pounding along the walkway. The creature might attack either the general or Gus, but there was no way to save them and Miracle, too. Tigre couldn't wait for fate to figure this one out. He had made a promise to protect Miracle.

Tigre threw Miracle over his shoulder and staggered toward the subway, ignoring the spasms of pain as Miracle hammered on his back with her fists. Gary and Paul darted forward as Tigre crossed the street. They pulled her from him and carried her into the subway. But as they went down the stairs, the girl grabbed two of the metal bars and hung on desperately, looking through the railing at the scene on the bridge.

The pterodolphin hung in the air for an eternal moment, peering at the two shapes below it, one running away, one dragging himself back onto the bridge, clutching the railing. With another piercing shriek, it seemed to come to a decision, spinning into a dive. It seized General Pepper in its claws and sailed up, up, up into the sky. The other pterodolphin rose from the water and followed it, and they both disappeared into a bank of clouds that was half in darkness, half golden in the light of the setting sun.

Sobbing, Miracle collapsed onto the stairs. Gary and Paul stood awkwardly beside her, their faces ashen.

Tigre didn't know what to do. He wished Kali were there. She always seemed to know what to say. If she'd been there, she'd probably have found a way to convince Miracle that this was exactly what was supposed to happen, that she should be proud of General Pepper. But he couldn't find the right words, if there even were any right words for a lie like that.

Slow footsteps approached behind him. Expecting to see Gus, Tigre turned, and was surprised to find Anna coming out of the park. She met his eyes, then looked down at Miracle. Tigre lifted his hands in a helpless gesture.

"Miracle," Anna said. "Miracle, sweetie, it's okay." She passed Tigre and sat down on the step next to Miracle, putting her arms around her.

"I'm sor—" Tigre began, but Anna shook her head at him.

"Is my faith really being tested?" Miracle whispered. "Why did they have to take General Pepper?"

"That's what Dad wanted," Anna said, glancing at Tigre. "He must have wanted General Pepper to be with him."

"But—but I want him *here*," Miracle choked out, then burst into renewed sobs.

"I know," Anna said. "Let's take you home." She raised Miracle to her feet and they climbed back up the steps.

"Wait," said the subway dweller called Gary. "What about us? Miracle, we need you."

Miracle wiped her eyes and stared down the steps, where more of her followers were starting to creep out from underground.

"We'll bring her back soon," Gus said from behind Tigre. "Miracle is on a very important mission for us— for the gods—right now." Tigre nodded. He wanted to keep her close, to try to fix this if they could. Miracle needed time to recover and mourn before becoming the savior of her people again.

Gary and Paul nodded and backed down the stairs.

Anna put her arm around Miracle, steering her uptown, and Tigre started to follow them.

"Actually," Anna said, "I think you should find something else to do for a couple of hours." There was something he'd never heard in her voice before—a chilly anger. Did she blame him for this? Was she right to?

"We'll see you at home. *Later,*" she said firmly. Then she turned and led Miracle away, leaving Gus and Tigre standing by the subway entrance in the last fading rays of sunlight.

. . . .

PANTHEON: POLYNESIAN
AVATAR: ORO (GUS)
JUDGE: NONE
TRAINER: NONE

. . . .

Hmmm.

I am not so pleased with my pet project today.

Oh, I let him live. I chose to take their General Pepper instead. The general never really believed in me, but he believed in Miracle. I'll take his scraps of faith, since I suspect they will be the last I get for a long time.

Yes. I sense that Miracle will not be allowing her people to send me any more guests. If she weren't my daughter, I'd think about punishing her quite severely. I'm being cut off from my power supply . . . but it's not really her fault.

It's those avatars. Tigre and Gus—especially Gus. Tigre would not have been able to come up with this plan on his own; it took little Gus's cleverness. Gus, my pet, still lousy with humanity although the war god is sneaking through his veins, waiting for a chance to break loose. You'd think Oro, of all gods, would understand the need for a little human sacrifice. He was all over that when his cult was spreading through Polynesia.

I had high hopes for Oro, but it turns out he's more of a planner than I expected. He's gathering his strength at the moment. I'm sure we'll see more of him sooner or later. . . . I'm hoping for sooner, personally.

Perhaps Gus will be more fun once that happens. I'd like to see a little more blood and guts, wouldn't you?

But I will remember that he stole my sacrifices.

One day there will be a reckoning. You can be sure of that.

The moon had risen and was floating high in the sky above them as Tigre and Gus reached the Metropolitan Museum of Art. It was nearly full, bathing the streets in an eerie glow that made Gus think of Japanese horror movies and haunted creatures trapped in mirrors. He wondered if Miracle found the moon reassuring—like her mother was smiling down at her. He hoped so; at least it was shining brightly tonight, so maybe that would help her.

Tigre had been silent for most of the walk, consumed with guilt and worry. Gus felt bad for Miracle, too, but he had mixed feelings about General Pepper. On the one hand, Gus had lost his brother, Andrew, so recently that he could feel Miracle's pain like a knife in his heart. But on the other hand, Tigre's story made it sound like it had been the general's choice to sacrifice himself. Also, if the pterodolphin hadn't taken General Pepper, it probably would have taken Gus. Gus couldn't help feeling keenly relieved that he was still alive.

"How long do you think we have to wait until we can go back to the apartment?" Gus asked.

"I don't know," Tigre said. "Anna seemed really mad at us."

"Hey, don't beat yourself up," Gus said. "She's just worried about Miracle. But we'll all feel better when it works and your bird friend shows up."

"*If* it works," Tigre said. "If it doesn't, General Pepper will have died for no reason."

"It will work," Gus said. "How else would you have gotten a message to her? If Quetzie told you to do that, it has to work. And then we can talk to Thor, and we can figure out a way back to our own time."

"Leaving Miracle here all alone," Tigre pointed out.

"Well, it'll be different," Gus said. "If we go back and change things, this version of the future won't happen, and she'll probably be born a normal girl and have a normal life, instead of being the only kid in the world. In the long run, it'll be better, for her and all of us."

They stopped at the foot of the stairs to the museum, hidden by the shadows of the trees. A lone figure in dark robes edged with silver was drifting back and forth across the top step, guarding the door.

"So we're here to talk Diana into joining our boycott?" Tigre said.

"Exactly," Gus replied. *And I want to see her again before the fight tomorrow.* All these plans and hopes of getting home wouldn't do him much good if Amon won.

"Wait," Tigre said, seizing Gus's arm as the younger boy started up the stairs. "Someone's coming." He pointed to the sky north of them, where a shape was descending from the clouds.

Gus stepped back into the darkness and they watched as the figure got closer. It landed on the steps of the museum, and Gus recognized the white outfit and the glimmer of gold around his head and on his chest.

"It's Amon," he hissed.

The Egyptian avatar ran lightly up the stairs and spoke for a moment to the guard. Then he produced a comb from one of his pockets, ran it through his hair, squared his shoulders, and sauntered inside.

Gus felt his anger come boiling to the surface again. What was Amon doing here? How could he wander in and out so freely? Had he been visiting Diana every night? Was Diana lying about her feelings for him?

He was halfway up the stairs before Tigre caught up with him.

"Gus, what are you doing?" Tigre said. "That guy's not going to let us just walk in."

"Why not?" Gus growled. "He let Amon do it."

"Well," Tigre said, "but—look at him."

The god at the top of the stairs was grim and forbidding, with pale, sunken cheeks and a smooth black beard. His eyes were pale, too, with barely a shift in color between his pupils and the whites of his eyes. He held a black scepter, slowly tapping one end into his palm.

He stared at Tigre and Gus as they approached, his skeletal face expressionless.

"And you are?" he said.

"Gus, Tigre," Gus said. "Who are you?"

"Hades," the god said, his voice echoing like it came from a long way underground.

There was a pause.

"We—uh—we're here to see Diana," Tigre said.

"I am surprised," Hades said. "I thought this was a secret rendezvous."

Gus's temper flared. "You mean Amon?" he said. "Well, you're wrong. We know all about it. So let us in, or—or—"

He was spared from having to end that sentence. Hades inclined his head and stepped back.

"Very well."

The two avatars stood for a moment, puzzled, and then Gus pushed Tigre forward. "Okay, thanks," he said as they went in. "Um—see you."

The Great Hall was dimly lit with lamps and candles that were perched on benches and hanging from the ceiling. Tigre and Gus could see a small crowd gathering around the entrance to their right, where raised voices were coming from beyond the marble archway into the Egyptian galleries.

"What is the meaning of this?" one voice yelled. Gus recognized it as Amon's.

"I told you," Diana responded, loud but not yet shouting. "I'm challenging you to a battle—right here, right now."

Gus blanched. What was she doing? He and Tigre ran over to the group, but they couldn't shove their way through the assembled gods. Gus stood on tiptoe, trying to see Diana.

"But I was tricked!" Amon protested. "I haven't been allowed to choose the place or the time."

"You mean like Gus didn't get to pick the time or the place for your fight tomorrow?" Diana said. "Come on, are you that scared of me? Don't you think you can win without an unfair advantage?"

She fooled him, Gus thought. *She never liked him. She's going to fight him so I don't have to.* He was angry and relieved and terrified for her all at the same time.

Tigre tugged on Gus's arm and pointed to a nearby bench. They climbed up and were able to see over the heads of the crowd. Diana was standing just beyond the archway, in front of a sand-colored tomb. Amon stood in front of her, shaking with anger.

"I demand to speak to Zeus!" Amon shouted.

The tall, bearded king of the gods pushed his way forward, looking apoplectic with rage, but before either of them could speak, the same sound reverberated through the air that everyone had heard at Macy's, and suddenly four gods were standing between Amon and Zeus.

Athena looked from Amon to Zeus, her eyebrows raised.

"Greetings," she said. "Amon, would you care to explain why you think a *Greek* god could help you in your present situation?"

Behind her, Maat stood with narrowed eyes, fingering the feather stuck in her hair. Amon threw her a beseeching look, but she didn't step forward to help him.

"I—I just—this doesn't seem fair," Amon grumbled.

"Are you a god of justice?" Athena asked sternly. "No. So do not question the fairness of those who are."

"But . . ."

"This place seems a fair choice for you," Athena said. "You are surrounded by the relics of your own age. That should give you some power. Why else did you come here tonight, if not to fight Diana?"

Ha, thought Gus. *Answer that, Casanova.*

Zeus made a wild, unsubtle shushing gesture at Amon, who looked flustered. "That's, er, true, of course. I mean, that's why I'm here. It's just—I have another fight in twelve hours. I think this one should at least be postponed until after that one."

"Hmm," Athena said. "No."

"We could consider it," Maat interjected. "Itzamna, what do you think?"

"I agree with Athena," said the third judge, an old man with a tremendously large nose, kind eyes, and no teeth. Gus glanced at Tigre. Was this the Mesoamerican judge? Tigre lifted his hands as if to say he didn't recognize him. Itzamna went on. "This fight may have a direct bearing on that fight. We should proceed with it."

None of them turned to the fourth judge, who was standing in the shadows behind them, but Gus and Tigre saw him nod.

"Very well," Maat said. "Then the fight should proceed."

Amon snapped and threw caution to the winds. "Diana, why are you doing this?" he yelled. "I could have protected you."

"In exchange for what?" Diana said. "Giving up my freedom? I'm not your prize, Amon, and I won't let you hurt my friends."

"This is not how things are supposed to be." Amon stamped his foot.

Athena and Maat exchanged glances but didn't speak. Gus realized that they had already suspected an Egyptian-Greek alliance. But since it had obviously been broken by Diana, they didn't intend to do anything about it. He was sure neither of them wanted to disqualify her own avatar.

"Do you two actually intend to fight?" Itzamna, the old male judge, said to Amon. "Or just bicker?"

With a growl of frustration, Amon grabbed the nearest movable object—a pole for dividing off sections of the museum, with two short velvet ropes clipped to the top—and hurled it at Diana. But before it hit the ground, she was gone.

Diana darted into the next room, her heart pounding wildly. She hadn't expected such an audience for this fight. She'd pictured herself and Amon battling in deserted moonlit rooms. But she should have guessed that her entire nosy pantheon would show up to watch.

She could feel the moon calling to her, like silver mercury running through her veins, pulling her forward. She could hear Amon's footsteps behind her, pounding on the cold marble. Her instinct kicked in, and she dove and rolled aside as a large stone statue crashed to the floor. Amon leaped out from behind it and was on her in a moment, his hands pressing into her throat.

"Nobody betrays me," he snarled into her face.

Diana tried to reply, but he was cutting off her oxygen, his powerful hands gripping her neck. His fingers dug into her windpipe and she pulled at them, trying to pry them off. He laughed softly.

"It'll be over soon," he whispered. "And so will this farce of an alliance. You're not as pretty as I'd hoped anyway." He leaned forward to hiss into her ear. "I'd rather have one of those mystery avatar girls myself."

Diana grabbed his ears with her sharp nails and stabbed her thumb into one of his eyes. With a howl of pain, he let go of her neck and fell back, his hands going to his face. Diana scrambled away and ran into the next room, gasping for air.

She grabbed the first thing she saw, a small standing figure made of stone, and whipped it around, connecting with Amon's shoulder as he sprang up behind her. Diana dropped it and turned to run, but she stopped with a jerk and a flash of pain as he seized her long hair and yanked her back.

"One good reason girls shouldn't fight," he said with a smirk, reaching for her face with his other hand. She kicked him hard in the place where it would hurt him most, and he released her with an *oof* of surprise.

"One good reason *boys* shouldn't fight," she said, shoving him back into a wall.

"I will kill you," he snarled. "No mere girl can defeat me."

"I am a goddess," she said, stamping down hard on his sandaled foot. "I am the goddess of the moon, and the hunt, and the forest, and the wild, and I will not be caged." She slapped his face with all her might and then spun around and ran again. She knew where she wanted to take him. What would happen there, she wasn't sure.

Amon pursued her through the winding maze of rooms, knocking over more statues as they ran. Many of the cases were empty, but wherever there were artifacts, Diana grabbed them and threw them behind her. From the cries of anger, she could tell she'd hit him at least a few times. They had left the crowd of watchers behind, but Diana barely noticed.

Finally she darted around a corner into a wide-open space: the Temple of Dendur.

Diana felt a surge of power as she stepped through the doorway. The whole room was lit up. One wall, slanting up to the roof, was made entirely of glass windows, and the moon shone through with pure, strengthening light.

She could see the large cat sculptures that lined the wall on either side of her, the rectangular pool of water surrounding the temple, and the island of stone that made up the temple itself.

Distracted by the sight, Diana paused in the entrance. Suddenly something heavy and blunt clubbed her on the head and her knees buckled, sending her to the floor. The tiles swam before her eyes.

"Just where I was hoping you would go," Amon growled in her ear. He stood up, holding a gray stone statue of a crowned falcon. Diana saw blood—her blood—on its base. Amon strolled over to the wall of windows as she tried to stand, but a wave of dizziness knocked her down again.

He swung the statue forcefully into the glass, shattering several panes in a row. Amon breathed in deeply, then turned, a soft night breeze swirling in behind him.

"Now," he said, "I will end this, and take what measly power you have for my own."

The breeze picked up, swirled through the room, and strengthened into a gale. Diana closed her eyes and staggered upright, but the force of the wind shoved her back. She stumbled and felt the wind lift her off her feet, slamming her into the stone archway at the near end of the temple island. Then it dropped, and so did she, landing with a splash in the pool. Her hands skidded on pennies and dimes, payment for wishes made many decades ago.

Amon jumped into the pool next to her, wrapped one hand around her throat, and lifted her off her feet, shoving her into the archway wall.

"Don't you wish you'd done things my way now?" he said.

"Never," she replied, then closed her eyes and reached her hands skyward, ignoring the pain at her throat and her shortness of breath. *Think of the moon. Think of her strength. Think of your strength, and of the grievous wrong this man has committed—the presumption, the arrogant, chauvinist, male-headed outrage—and how he should be punished.*

She suddenly felt calm, as if melted crystal were pouring through her, clearing away the sharp agony of her wounds, her struggle for breath, her fear. She opened her eyes and looked at Amon, his nose only inches from hers. She could see her reflection in his eyes, and her own were glowing with silver light.

The smug triumph slowly slid from his face.

"You chose the wrong goddess to meddle with," Diana said. She peeled his hand away from her throat, barely feeling the effort, although Amon jumped back, shaking his hand as if his fingers had been broken. Diana stepped forward, and he skidded, landing on his knees in the water.

She climbed out of the pool and stepped over to an unbroken bank of windows. Amon followed warily, twitching his hands, and she could feel the wind responding again to his call. She had only a moment before he took control again, but a moment was all she needed.

Diana pressed her left hand against the wall of windows behind her, the glass as cool as the moonlight pouring through. She flung out her right hand toward Amon and words came spilling up from deep inside her.

"This is the punishment for men like you."

In a flash of blinding silver light, Amon was gone.

In his place was a large, golden-furred, startled-looking stag.

"Take me down," Kali said, climbing to her feet.

"But the fight's not over," Shiva said, puzzled. "She hasn't killed him yet." He pointed at the four judges, who were gliding into the room from the Egyptian galleries. Behind them was a crowd of gaping gods, pulling on one another's robes, whispering and pointing at the stag, who kept shaking his head as if trying to get a look at his antlers.

"It's over," Kali said. "Believe me."

Shiva sighed and took her hand. "All right." They floated slowly down from the top of the temple, landing on the far side of the room from the judges. Diana glanced over at them but kept one hand pressed to the windows. She was shaking and her head was bleeding, but she stayed on her feet.

The stag snorted and pawed the floor with its hoof.

"Now you should finish it," Athena said to Diana. "Once he is dead, you will absorb his power and become the strongest avatar." Maat's lips were pressed into a thin, sharp line, but she nodded.

"No," Diana said, her voice forceful despite her trembling hands. "No one may kill this animal." She held out her free hand and the stag stepped forward, resting its velvety nose in her palm. "This deer is sacred to me, and anyone who hurts it will be punished far worse than Amon was."

Athena exchanged a glance with Itzamna, the big-nosed Mesoamerican judge Kali had seen at the UN. Maat raised her eyebrows. Kali saw the fourth judge, behind them, duck his head away from the moonlight, turning up the glow of his sun halo to hide his face. She wondered if the other three judges could see him, or if they just knew a fourth judge was there without registering exactly who he was, the way Athena thought she was listing six judges each time she rattled the names off.

"But Diana," Athena said, "if you don't kill him, you won't take his strength."

"It doesn't matter," Diana said, stroking the stag's neck. "He is under my protection now."

Athena sighed expressively and the owl on her shoulder clicked its beak several times. "Very well. This fight is over. Diana is the victor, more or less." She made a circular motion with her hand, and all four judges disappeared.

Diana let her hand drop from the window and folded quietly to the floor.

"You know what this means," Shiva said to Kali.

"Yes." A movement caught her eye and she looked up to a window in the distant wall where the Asian Art galleries overlooked the temple. There were two heads leaning out, two figures with their gaze fixed on Diana. Neither gods nor avatars, they had to be the ones she'd spotted in the museum earlier, back when she'd had the city to herself. They didn't notice Kali watching them, so she was able to study them for a minute.

They were kids, probably in their early teens, thirteen or fourteen years old—the same age as Miracle. Kali wondered if they had been born under similar miraculous circumstances, and whether they had a host of worshippers, too, or how they'd escaped that particular fate. They were Asian—she guessed Chinese—with clear skin and high cheekbones and matching perfect facial features. As far as she could tell, they were both boys.

Her information gatherers, surely. The ones who took care of the museum. They looked awestruck, as if they couldn't tear their eyes away from Diana.

Kali looked back at Diana and saw Gus kneeling beside her. Behind him, Tigre, Apollo, and Vulcan hovered, looking anxious. Kali came forward to join them as Zeus and Hera swept up, too.

"Diana," Gus said softly, lifting her upper body to rest against his knees. He winced as the electrical shock of their contact sparked through him. "Diana, are you all right?"

"I told you we couldn't rely on her," Hera sneered. "Diana was always stubborn. She does whatever she wants, regardless of the consequences."

"Hey, this Venus thing was your idea," Zeus said, stabbing the air with his finger. "We all thought it would tame her foolish independence."

Which it did, Kali thought, *but not for long.*

"Have you thought about what happens if she wins?" Hera hissed.

"Of course. We become the most powerful pantheon," Zeus said.

"With *her* absorbing the power of the other avatars, and becoming the strongest of all of us," Hera said. "Have you imagined what it would actually be like with this headstrong daughter of yours in charge?"

"At least our pantheon would rule," Apollo snapped. "Surely you still want her to win, don't you, Hera? You're

not so selfish that you'd rather see her die and our pantheon defeated than have her become stronger than you.
You're not as stupid as that. Remember, you could have
been our avatar—you could have had all that power, if
you'd been willing to take the risks."

Hera scowled. "Well, I wouldn't have been stupid
enough to leave my deadly enemies alive, that's for sure."
She turned with a swirl of blue robes and stormed off,
followed closely by her peacock.

Vulcan crouched down beside Gus. "Diana. Listen to
me. She has a point. You should kill this creature." Kali
noticed he kept a respectful distance from Diana, as if he
really saw her now as the goddess of the hunt, rather than
as his former wife, Venus.

"No," Diana said, her eyes fluttering open. "I said no."
She reached up and grabbed the front of Gus's T-shirt.
"Gus, we're safe now," she whispered. "He can't hurt you
anymore."

"You punk," Gus said, blinking back tears. "Who said
you could fight my battles for me, huh?"

"I'm just helping," Diana said with a smile, and sank
back, her eyes closing.

Gus leaned over and kissed her. *Ow,* thought Kali,
imagining the sparks of electricity that must be going off
between their lips. But perhaps she'd put up with a little
pain, too, if it meant kissing Shiva. *Keep resisting that temp-
tation, Kali.*

A shocked murmur ran through the gods gathered by
the entranceway, and Zeus threw up his hands with an
exasperated expression.

"Mortals!" he grumbled. "Mortals and their irritating

free will. If they would just stick to my plans, everything would be fine. Aggravating *mortals!*"

"Tell me about it," Shiva said good-naturedly, emerging from the shadow of the temple. Zeus jumped, frowned, then stalked away in the direction Hera had gone.

"All right, show's over," Apollo said to the crowd of gods. "Time to move along and give Diana some breathing room. Vulcan? A little help?"

Vulcan got up and began to shoo away the crowd of gods. A few protested, but gradually they all drifted away, some vanishing into the air, some following Vulcan back into the Egyptian galleries. Kali looked up and saw that the two mystery kids had disappeared from the upper-story window.

The golden stag had been standing near Diana, examining its hooves and wagging its head from side to side. Now it gave a snort and trotted over to the hole Amon had smashed in the windows. It poked at the glass with its antlers until the space was big enough, then stepped through onto the grass outside. With a vigorous shake, it trotted away into the park.

Tigre looked up and saw Kali for the first time. She winked at him, and he managed a tired half smile. He seemed worn down, like the world had been punching him in the face for a week straight. Also, he smelled like fish. Kali wondered what she'd missed and where Ereka and Anna were.

"Hey," she said to him, "your judge showed up. Did you see? He seems cool."

"Really?" Tigre brightened a little. "Which one was he—the old guy, or the one nobody talked to?"

"The old one," Kali said. "Athena called him Itzamna, or something like that."

Tigre nodded. "I think that's a Mayan god. He brought knowledge, medicine, and writing to the world, stuff like that. I think he's a good guy."

"He has a friendly smile," Kali said. "And he's strong enough to manifest. That's got to cheer you up."

"Sure," Tigre said, but his eyes fell to the floor. "Who was the other one?"

"Nobody knows," Kali said. "The judges don't seem to realize they can't see him. He's some kind of sun god, though, I'm guessing, from the burning heat he gives off."

"Really?" Apollo interrupted. "Another sun god? Maybe I can figure out who he is."

Kali gave him a skeptical look and knelt beside Gus and Diana. Gus was gently smoothing Diana's hair back from her face. She was pale and her forehead was creased with pain, but she was breathing evenly.

"Ow," Kali said, nodding at the wound on Diana's head. "That looks . . . ow. And I wouldn't be surprised if she cracked a couple of ribs when Amon hurled her into that arch."

Gus flinched. "I wanted to help, but Tigre and Apollo held me back."

"Just as well," Kali said. "Not that I don't think it's adorable, the way you two keep trying to die for each other."

"Kali," Shiva said, putting his hand on her shoulder.

"I know," she said. "I'm just saying, Gus, that you might want to stand aside and let, say, a god of medicine take a look at her."

Gus looked up at her, confused, and then at Apollo, who was standing behind him.

"Oh . . . sure, of course," he said. He scooted around so that Diana's head was resting in his lap and Apollo could kneel next to her. Diana's brother ran his hands through the air above her, his eyes closed but moving, as if he were reading something on the inside of his eyelids.

"You're right," he murmured. "Two cracked ribs, a lot of bruising. And we should keep her conscious."

Gus touched Diana's face and pulled his hand back quickly so the shock wouldn't hurt her. "Diana, stay awake," he whispered. She sighed, and her eyes opened. They smiled at each other.

"Hey," Kali said, drawing their attention back to her. "Before we move on to the lovey-dovey 'The world is saved; I turned my worst enemy into a deer' stuff, I have something to say." She flipped her ponytail back over her shoulder and glanced up at Tigre.

"Diana," Kali said formally, "now that the Egyptian-Polynesian fight is off, I challenge you to a battle tomorrow at noon. You pick the place. I'll see you then." She got up quickly and stepped back.

Tigre's face was stricken, like she'd just strangled his hamster. "But Kali—"

"How can you do that?" Gus said. "Look at the condition she's in. You might as well just kill her now."

"I promised to fight the winner of this contest," Kali said, not looking at Shiva. "I expected whoever it was would gain the strength of the other; if she had, she wouldn't be in such bad shape now. I was only looking for a true opponent. However," she said, meeting Gus's angry eyes, "if you'd rather fight in her place, that's fine by me."

"Kali!" Shiva said.

"Whatever," she said to him with a shrug. "I'm just being fair."

"Fair is not the point of this battle," Shiva growled.

"This is the fastest way to save my people," Kali said to the other avatars. "It's what we have to do. See you back at the apartment."

"As if we could trust you enough to sleep under the same roof with you," Gus said.

Kali's voice was cold. "I am not that kind of goddess. If I were, you would have been dead the minute you set foot on my island."

Shiva hurried after Kali, still arguing. But she had stopped listening to him. She was right. This was what she had to do. If it was the only way to get to the truth and bring the world back, as Shiva said, then she would do what had to be done.

Following Apollo's instructions, Gus propped Diana into a sitting position, holding her against his chest, while Tigre borrowed a vase from one of the Egyptian galleries and filled it with water from the pool. The sun god tore a swath of cloth from his sleeve, folded it over several times, and handed it to Gus.

"Press this against her head wound," he said. "Hold it for a while, and the bleeding will stop."

Gus did as instructed, wrapping his other arm around Diana's body, which felt very soft and breakable. He was careful not to touch her bare skin, trying to minimize the electric sparks between them. Even after all that fighting, she still smelled like lilacs, the way she had the day they met.

"I can't believe this," Tigre said, crouching beside Apollo, who took the water and dipped another strip of linen from his robe into it. "I can't believe Kali—"

"I can," Gus said. "I haven't trusted her for a while now."

"Well, I know that," Tigre said almost angrily, and Gus frowned. Tigre couldn't be angry at *him*. He'd been right all along about Kali.

"Don't fight," Diana said, taking Gus's hand. "She's just doing what she thinks is best. We all want this to be over."

"Not if it means being dead," Tigre said.

"We've been talking about this," Gus said. "Tigre and I think if we all refuse to fight, maybe the gods will agree to send us back to our own time."

Apollo made an amused sound.

"I have an idea for talking to Thor," Tigre said. "Maybe we can talk to Kali, too, and get her to call off the fight."

"Even if she did," Apollo said, "it won't last long. Believe me, the gods can wait you out. They have plenty of time . . . a lot more than you do."

Diana slowly lifted onto her elbows, wincing at the pain in her ribs. "Apollo," she said, "*is* there a way back to our own time?"

Apollo dipped the cloth in the water again, avoiding her gaze.

"He'll just lie to you anyway," Gus said. "Like all the other gods."

"He can't," Diana said. "He can only tell the truth."

Gus met Tigre's eyes. That meant Apollo could give them the answers they needed.

Apollo suddenly jumped up and sprinted for the door. Tigre grabbed the vase and threw the water across the floor after him. Apollo skidded on the wet tiles, slipped, and fell. Tigre went to pull him back, but as he touched the god's arm, he realized Apollo was fading into the air.

"Apollo," Diana pleaded. "Wait. Please help us."

Apollo paused, his limbs semitransparent.

"You can't leave Diana like this anyway," Gus said. "Come back, fix her, and tell us as much as you can."

Shaking his head, Apollo climbed to his feet, gradually regaining substance. "I'm not supposed to tell you anything. Zeus didn't even want me to spend time with you, in case I let something slip, but it was one of the conditions Diana made before agreeing to be our avatar—that I'd be her trainer."

"So tell us this," Diana said, "is there any way for us to go back to the time we came from?"

"No," Apollo said.

Gus felt like he'd been sucker punched. If Apollo couldn't lie . . . But maybe there was a way he didn't know about. . . .

"Traveling backward in time just isn't possible," Apollo said. He knelt beside Diana and dabbed at the blood on her neck. "Time only moves forward. I'm sorry."

"So they're really lost?" Diana said. "Our world, everyone we knew—we'll never see them again?"

Apollo hesitated.

"We can!" Gus pounced. "There *is* a way!"

"Not to travel through time," Apollo said. "But you're

not stuck here. Your world, as you say, is not so far away—"

A giant thunderclap interrupted him, and Zeus was suddenly standing at Diana's feet, glaring daggers at the sun god.

"Apollo!" he roared. "Mind your words!"

"I didn't *say* anything!" Apollo protested.

"Come with me this instant," Zeus said.

Apollo handed the damp linen to Gus with an elaborate eye roll. Before standing, he passed his hand over Diana's head and her torso.

"That won't cure you completely," he said, "but it should speed up the healing process. Just take it easy for a while. You know, no horseback riding, no jogging, no life-or-death battles with destruction goddesses." He winked, and then he and Zeus vanished simultaneously.

"He wants to tell us," Diana said. "But he can't, because he knows we're being watched all the time."

"I thought we might be," Gus said. He checked Diana's head injury, which had stopped bleeding. It was only a small gash to have created so much blood. Diana took the damp cloth from him and finished cleaning her neck and face.

"It's creepy." Tigre shivered. "How are we supposed to plan anything if they're watching us all the time? I mean, they're gods. How do you outwit gods?"

"We'll come up with something," Gus said. He felt lighter than air, as if he could float all the way back to California, to Andrew and his old life. "Now we know there's a way home. We just have to figure out what it is."

PANTHEON: GRECO-ROMAN
AVATAR: DIANA/VENUS
JUDGE: ATHENA
TRAINER: APOLLO

Impressed?

I am. Who knew the moon goddess had it in her? I didn't really think she'd be able to fight past all the Venus business weighing her down. It shows in the weakness of letting Amon live, though.

The Greeks were the ones who started this whole game, you know. So pointless and greedy of them. They were doing surprisingly well, back in the real world. At least they were remembered. Children learned their myths in school; most everyone had at least heard of Zeus, Apollo, Venus, and so on. The more people knew their names, the stronger they were. The more they were talked about, the stronger they grew, even if they didn't have the weight of true belief behind the words, or devoted worshippers, the way they used to. But of course, that's what they wanted: a return to their glory days.

That's why there are so many of them wandering around, if you were wondering. They have plenty of energy for materializing, translating, spying on the avatars, and so on. They're actually quite a strong pantheon, which is hilarious, considering what squabbling, hysterical, self-centered loons they all are.

That's also why some of them use their Roman names (Mars, Venus, Vulcan) and some their Greek names (Zeus, Hera, Apollo). They chose for themselves, whichever version was *stronger, more often used, and more popular. The Greek god of war, Ares, was a bitter, cowardly fellow with rage issues, but the Romans transformed him into a brilliant war god: Mars, leading troops to glory! So of course he'd rather be remembered as Mars. Try calling him Ares sometime, and you'll see, the reaction is too funny. Venus could have picked either—Aphrodite is fairly well known herself—but Mars talked her into the Roman option. Vulcan is remembered a little bit every time volcanoes are mentioned, but who ever remembers his Greek counterpart, Hephaestus? When the goddess of wisdom is mentioned, does anyone think of Minerva instead of Athena? And so it goes. It just illustrates what a mishmash of egocentrics they are, each choosing what is best for him or herself instead of thinking of the whole pantheon.*

Like I said, they create their own chaos.

But maybe their avatar requires closer scrutiny.

Maybe I should weave her into my own game a bit more.

I will consider my options . . . and in the meanwhile, I will watch her very, very carefully.

Day Four:
 Defiance

Diana woke up shortly before sunrise. She'd felt guilty about sleeping in an antique museum bed with her injuries, even with her head carefully bandaged, so eventually Vulcan had gone out to find her a mattress and dragged it into the Greek galleries. Luckily, Apollo hadn't returned to scold her about using Vulcan's affection to get what she wanted. And best of all, Gus had decided to stay with her instead of going back to Kali's apartment. Vulcan had agreed that she could use another guard, especially one who, unlike most of the Greek gods, was more interested in protecting her than in trying on all the outfits in the Costume Institute.

So when she opened her eyes in the predawn light, Gus was only a few feet away, thrashing restlessly in the hammock.

But there was someone crouching between her and him.

Two someones, both watching her with fascinated expressions, like she had pulled the moon out of the sky and twisted it into a dog-shaped balloon for them.

One was the kid she had run into on her way to find Gus, two days earlier. The other—his brother?—looked almost exactly like him, except that he was an inch taller, his eyes were a darker brown, and he had a small mole on the side of his nose, where a nose stud might go. She glanced back at the first one and realized he had a similar mole, but on his earlobe.

They both had smooth, straight hair cut into a bowl shape and wore loose black pants and long-sleeved black tunics.

When they saw her eyes open, one reached out and took the other's hand. But otherwise, they didn't move from their positions, squatting on their heels and staring at her.

Diana sat up slowly. For one thing, she didn't want to scare them away, and for another, every movement hurt, as if she was being repeatedly stabbed in the side.

"Who are you?" she whispered. Gus twitched but didn't wake up. There were no gods in the room, but loud snoring from the corridor suggested that one of them— probably Dionysus, the god of wine—was out there "guarding" her. She guessed it wouldn't have been hard for these two to sneak past him. As for Vulcan, last night he had assigned himself the patrol around the outside of the museum, and if she knew anything about him, he was probably still out there, circling.

"Aleph," said the smaller one with the mole on his ear. "Bet," said the other.

Which was not really an answer.

"Hi," she said. "I'm Diana. Um. Where did you come from?"

Aleph let go of Bet's hand and crawled forward to sit next to her on the mattress.

"You are wondrous," he said in the same matter-of-fact tone that he might have used to say "You have green eyes."

"Which is to say," Bet added, "that we wonder at you."

"I like that," Aleph said.

"My brother means he likes the feeling of wondering. We have had a limited number of things to wonder at for many years, until you and the others came, and now we have so many, but we think you are the most interesting."

"Wonderful," Aleph said.

"No." Bet shook his head. "That's not what you mean, Aleph. Think about it."

Aleph touched his ear for a minute, looking thoughtful. "I am full of wonder at you," he finally said.

"That's better," Bet said. "We try to practice, but there is a lot of ambiguity in this language, and Aleph finds it harder to grasp sometimes."

"Do you normally speak a different language?" Diana asked, feeling like that wasn't really the question she meant.

"Not out loud," Bet said. "But we function off of codes in here." He tapped his head. "Codes are much more straightforward."

"Codes?" Diana said, puzzled. A movement behind them made her glance up, and she saw that Gus was awake, trying to pull himself upright in the hammock.

"It's okay, Gus," she said. "They're not dangerous. This is Aleph, and that's Bet." As she said his name, she put one hand on Aleph's shoulder, and realized that it didn't feel natural. The fabric of his shirt was a sheer synthetic material, but where her fingers accidentally brushed the skin of his neck, they met a similarly synthetic feel, almost like a smoother, thicker version of the shirt.

Gus paused in his struggles with the hammock, his hair sticking up in all directions. Diana suppressed a smile. She'd missed seeing Gus first thing in the morning, when he was sleepy and disheveled.

Aleph pointed at Gus. "What was he?" he asked.

Diana looked at Bet for an explanation. "Before you made him a person," Bet said helpfully.

"Can I guess? Was he a tree?" Aleph said. His voice stayed calm, but his facial expression was excited, like a kid's on Christmas morning.

"No, I was not a tree," Gus said crossly. "I've always been a person. Although I don't always feel like one this early in the morning. Who are these kids, Diana?"

"I'm not sure," she said.

"Are you gods?" Gus asked. "From one of the pantheons? Maybe they're from Anna and Ereka's pantheon. The girls could be Chinese goddesses."

"There are no gods," Aleph said sternly. "Only science."

"Science can solve everything," Bet said, and Diana got the feeling that they were reciting someone's mantra.

"Science will lead us to a better world," Aleph finished.

There was a pause.

"Huh," said Gus. "I bet I can find a couple of folks around here who would disagree with you on that."

"A caterpillar," Aleph said with relish. "He was a caterpillar, wasn't he?"

"I was *not* a caterpillar," Gus said. "Diana, what the heck?"

"I think they might live here, in the museum," Diana said. "Is that right?"

Aleph nodded vigorously. "We caretake the art."

"Take care of the art," Bet corrected. "When we came here, the museum was abandoned, but we cleaned and swept, and we keep it beautiful as much as we can."

"For always," Aleph said. "The art is wonderf—I wonder at it."

"We wish we could make it, too," Bet said, and they both looked sad. "We can look at it, and we can love it, but we can't make our own."

"I suppose the world's a bit short on life-drawing classes at the moment," Gus said.

"But maybe we could," Aleph said, tugging on Diana's sleeve, "if you worked your science on us."

"What science?" Diana asked.

"Like with the man last night," Bet said. "The one you scientifically transformed into a deer."

Gus was amused. "'Scientifically'?" he repeated. "Care to explain the 'science' of that to us?"

"We can't," Bet said. "Our parents were not so far advanced—they could only make us—but clearly things have changed while we have been in hiding. I am glad to see that there were others who followed the paths of science after our parents were killed. It seems that there is hope for the world after all."

Diana didn't know where to begin. "You had parents?" she asked.

"Of course," Bet said.

"Dr. Lee, Dr. Stein, Dr. Frederick, Dr. Wang, Dr. Bloom, Dr. Brady, and Drs. Ling-Rosen," Aleph rattled off.

"The finest scientific minds in the world," Bet said proudly.

"Until you," Aleph said to Diana.

"Yeah, sure," she said. "Tell that to my biology tutor."

"We will tell it to anyone," Aleph said. Gus snickered.

"So what happened to them?" Diana asked, casting a look at Gus.

"We can show you," Bet said. He pressed the mole on his nose, and suddenly an image appeared on the blank wall to Diana's left. It was a still photo of a gleaming white lab facility, a mile of tables scattered with electronic equipment and wires. The image jumped and became a video. The camera panned up, and to her surprise, the ceiling above the lab was transparent. It looked like plastic, stretched in hexagonal shapes overhead and around, forming a dome over the whole place. Sunlight poured in from overhead, and as the camera kept moving, Diana could see cornfields beyond the edge of the dome. It looked like somewhere in the Midwest, maybe Kansas or Iowa.

"Protective," Aleph said, pointing to the dome above. "Impenetrable."

"Not to bombs," Bet said.

A gray-haired woman came onto the screen. She was small and stout and sweet-faced, like a TV grandma. But, unlike any grandmother Diana had ever seen, her hands had strips of metal implanted in them, running along the fingers and back up to her wrists. A large band of metal circled her neck, and as she smiled at the camera, Diana could see flashes of silver in her teeth, as well.

"How are we today, Bet?" she said. "Ready to welcome your new sister?"

The camera nodded, and Diana realized that they were seeing through Bet's eyes.

A tall Chinese woman joined them. Her face was old and lined, but she stood up very straight—partly, Diana realized, because of the metal spine running down her back, which was visible up at her neck and in vertebrae lumps under her lab coat. One of her legs was also almost entirely metal.

She did not smile as much as the first woman, but she still seemed pleased to see Bet.

"Aleph is already in place," she said. "He keeps whispering 'Wake up, Gimmel' in her ear."

The shorter woman reached out her hand, and Bet took it. As he moved closer to her, the tag clipped to the front of her coat swung into view, and Diana saw a logo that said ETERNALLY ME at the top with the name Dr. Jill Bloom below it.

Bet and the doctor wove between the lab tables to a platform in the center of the dome. Other elderly scientists were gathering around it in a semicircle, all of them sporting metal features here and there. Aleph was leaning his elbows on the platform, bouncing on his toes. Lying in front of him was a girl—also about thirteen years old and wearing the same black outfit—with bright red hair. Her brown eyes, darker than Bet's, stared blankly up at the sky, and wires ran from nearby machines to small moles on her arms and feet and one on her forehead.

"She's beautiful," Aleph said.

"We are getting better with each attempt," said a male scientist behind him. "If our cyber-upgrades can keep us around long enough, we'll make you a whole schoolful of siblings, Aleph."

Aleph grinned at Bet, and Diana guessed that Bet was grinning back.

"All right," said the Chinese scientist, touching the mole on the girl's forehead to check that the wire was connected. "Let's wake her up."

She turned to a computer and began typing.

Suddenly Diana heard shouting in the background. The camera swiveled as Bet turned to look, and she could see figures gathered in the cornfield beyond the wall of the dome. It looked like there were hundreds of them, many waving large signs.

The camera zoomed in. *Neat trick*, Diana thought. *Wish my eyes could do that.* Now she could read some of the signs. ETERNALLY ME? ETERNALLY DAMNED! said one. KILL THE MONSTERS said another. And a third: GOD ABHORS YOUR METAL CHILDREN.

"Bet," said Dr. Bloom, gently turning Bet's face back to the table. "Just ignore them."

"Who is God?" Bet asked. "Why does he abhor us?"

"If she existed," said one of the other women, "she wouldn't hate you at all."

"Those people are maniacs," said Dr. Bloom. "They don't understand that you are the only path to a better world. Everyone was quite happy when all we did was enhance their strength and help them live longer with our robotics and technology, but when we took the logical next step of creating new life . . . Well, true scientific brilliance is never recognized in its own time. If we can't have natural children, I don't see what's wrong with building some, especially when they're as lovely as you two. Why those narrow-minded maniacs can't see that is beyond me."

"Luckily," said the male scientist behind Aleph, "they can't get through these walls, so you're safe here."

A muffled boom shook the dome. Bet staggered and clutched the table for support.

"What was that?" Dr. Bloom asked.

The camera swung back to the crowd outside the wall. Now Diana could see that they were standing back, away from something that was smoking and spitting sparks.

BOOM. Cracks appeared in the wall, climbing toward the ceiling like vines.

"Those madmen," the Chinese scientist muttered, still tapping away at the keyboard. "They're going to ruin everything. We'd better protect the prototypes."

"Aleph, Bet," Dr. Bloom said, "come with me."

The two boys followed her without question, weaving between the tables as fast as she could trot.

"Don't be afraid," Dr. Bloom said.

"I don't think I can be afraid," Aleph said. "Have I ever been afraid before?"

She gave him a fond smile. "No, but—well, you never know." She stopped at a table that looked exactly like all the others to Diana. With a shove, Dr. Bloom swiveled one end of it aside and revealed a trapdoor in the ground.

"Go down here," she said, pulling it open. "There's a tunnel. Keep following it to the end, and then wait there. We'll come get you when it's safe again."

"What about you?" Bet asked. "Shouldn't you hide, too?"

"We're staying to protect Gimmel," Dr. Bloom said. "Don't worry about us. You know how sturdy we are, and there's plenty of material here to fix ourselves with."

Aleph kissed her cheek and she gave him a quick hug. He jumped down into the hole and rapidly vanished down the tunnel.

"Take care of your brother, Bet," Dr. Bloom said. "Quiz him on his emotions while you're waiting, okay?" She hugged him, too, the camera enveloped briefly in white fabric.

"How long should we wait for you?" Bet asked. "What if you don't come?"

"We will," she said with a smile that didn't match the anxious look in her eyes. Bet nodded, then jumped down into the tunnel as well. He glanced back up as the trapdoor began to swing shut, and the image froze on his last glimpse of Dr. Bloom.

Diana discovered that Bet had crawled onto the mattress, too, on the other side of her from Aleph.

"They didn't come," Bet said. "Obviously."

"We waited a huge long time, though," Aleph said.

"After many days, I went back aboveground," Bet said. "There was nothing left of our home or our parents except charred metal and ashes." He sounded downcast but a little detached.

"So we came here," Aleph said. "And we have been here a vastly hugely enormously long time."

Diana guessed from the look on his face that Gus had come to the same conclusions she had. These children must be essentially robots, created by the scientists who looked after them, before they were killed by religious extremists.

"That's very sad," Diana said.

"Is it?" Aleph said. "I thought so, but I am also wired to appreciate independence and to strive for self-sufficiency, so it's hard to tell."

"It is," Gus said. "It is sad."

"We would know that for certain," Bet said, "if we could be real children."

"Please?" Aleph said, tugging on Diana's sleeve again. "Please, please?"

Uh-oh. "You want to be human?" she said. "I'm sorry—I don't know how to do that." *If it's even possible.*

"But the man!" Bet said. "You made him into a deer!"

"And look at all the people you've created!" Aleph said. "Out of who knows what creatures? Like this one. Oooh, was he a duck? I bet he was a duck."

"I didn't make my friends," Diana said quickly, before Gus could object to this new guess. "They arrived here with me."

"Can they do what you can?" Bet asked. "Maybe one of them can make us real." The hope on his face was painful, even though Diana tried to tell herself that it was just numbers and wires coming together to make him think this was what he wanted.

"I don't think so," she said gently. "That's not the kind of thing any of us can do." *Can we? How do I know what we can do?* She looked down at her hands. *Before last night, I wouldn't have guessed turning Amon into a deer was an option. Still, back in the ancient world, I doubt anyone came up*

with a god who could bring robots to life. What they need is a
Blue Fairy, like Pinocchio had.

Aleph looked disappointed; Bet took it another step
and looked woebegone.

"It's all right," Aleph said. "We find you wondrous anyway."

"Well, I'll ask, okay?" Diana said. "I'll check with
everyone. But don't get your hopes up."

Too late for that: They were both beaming like super-
novas.

"Diana," Gus said. "I'm sorry to interrupt, but we only
have a few hours to get ready."

"I know," Diana said, remembering Kali's challenge
from the night before. She climbed unsteadily to her feet
and winced at the pain that shot through her head and
chest. Aleph and Bet hopped up and stood on either side
of her, like optimistic doormen waiting for a tip.

"We have to go out for a little while," Diana explained
to them. "But I'll talk to my friends, I promise. And I'll let
you know what they say when we come back."

A chill rippled down her spine. If *we come back.* . . .

Anna found Tigre asleep on the floor of the living room,
his head pillowed uncomfortably on a book spread open
on the coffee table.

She prodded him gently backward until his head lolled
against the couch instead, and then she slid the book
toward herself.

"Hmwha?" Tigre mumbled, his eyes screwing shut.
"Mmph."

"Morning," Anna said, turning the pages. "Why are

you reading about Indian gods?"

Tigre yawned. "Remember what Ereka said about studying your enemy? I figured I'd try. Kali challenged Diana to a fight today."

"Really?" Ereka said, coming into the room. She looked fully rested and bright-eyed, unlike everyone else.

"Yeah," Tigre said. "Or Gus, whichever one is up for it."

"Oh great," Ereka said. "So the lovebirds are probably spending all morning fighting over which one it should be. 'Me!' 'No, me!' 'No, *I* want to die pointlessly for love!' 'No, *I* want to!' Idiots."

"Being in love isn't idiotic," Anna said.

"Like *you* would know," Ereka said rudely. "So why are we all still here if Kali is so dangerous? Shouldn't we be hiding or trying to kill her in her sleep or something, you know, before she kills us?"

"That wouldn't be honorable," Tigre said. "And she is very honorable. She wouldn't fight us without warning us first."

"Oh, that's reassuring," Ereka said. "As long as I'm politely told I'm about to die, that makes it okay. Hey, is there anything to eat besides oatmeal?"

Tigre shrugged. "You can go look."

Ereka wandered off to the kitchen, flipping her hair.

"She is *so annoying*," Anna whispered. "She came into my room last night and kept yapping and yapping, so I couldn't go to sleep. I kept hoping you'd come back and then she'd leave me alone."

Tigre gave her a tentative smile. He didn't want to ask if he was forgiven for the scene on the bridge the night before, just in case he wasn't, but at least she wasn't glaring at him.

"Finally Kali came in," Anna said, looking down at the book, where a gruesome illustration of the goddess of destruction glowered back at them. "Miracle and I told her the whole story about the pterodolphins, and she was pretty furious that we'd risked Miracle's life without telling her. After she's done with Diana and Gus, we might want to watch ourselves."

Tigre blanched. He knew he should be careful—if Kali meant to win, she'd be coming for him sooner or later. But he still found it hard to reconcile that image with the girl he'd met only a few days earlier.

"Maybe we should find somewhere else to stay," he said sadly.

"Don't bother on my account," Kali said from the doorway. Tigre and Anna both jumped, and Tigre banged his knee on the coffee table. "I'd prefer not to kill anyone here. Too messy. So you're safe for now, but do what you like." Miracle appeared behind her, clutching the hem of Kali's shirt. Tigre saw that Kali had replaced Miracle's robe with a too-long sky blue nightgown. She looked lost in it.

"Kali," Tigre said, "you don't have to fight this battle. We're going to find a way home, and then nobody will have to die."

"Sure," Kali said, "and then the gods are going to make all our families immortal, too, and we're all going to live happily ever after together in a Six Flags made of cotton candy."

"I'm serious," Tigre said.

"Come on, Tigre," Kali said. "Don't you think I thought of that? I asked Shiva, and he said this is the only way. We can't go back to our own time."

"There's something they're not telling us," Tigre said. "Apollo nearly told us last night. There *is* a way to get back to our families. He said we're not stuck here."

Kali paused. Anna kept her eyes focused on the book.

"Apollo said that?" Kali said slowly. "But he can't lie."

"I know," Tigre said. "Zeus took him away before he could explain himself. We need to find somewhere where they can't watch us, so we can figure out what to do."

"True, the gods will kick your ass if they think you're getting too close to something," Kali said, nodding. "Huh. Interesting."

"So will you call off the fight?" Tigre pleaded.

Kali flexed her fingers and glanced out the window at the midmorning sky. After a minute, she shook her head.

"Why shouldn't I believe Shiva?" she said. "He's my . . . guide. He wouldn't lie to me."

"But—"

"Tigre, listen. I appreciate your effort, but this is what I do. I'm a destroyer. It's all I am. It's what I'm made for. You have to accept that, like I do." Kali glanced at her watch. "Tell you what. It's two hours to noon. If you can come up with something to convince me by then, I'll think about it. If not, this goddess of destruction will have some destroying to do."

The choice was surprising but smart, once you thought about it.

"She can't use her moon power in midday," Shiva said, "so she's relying on her huntress skills."

"Plus," Kali said, "she probably knows that I'll have to be careful in there. No buildings to drop on her head, for one thing. And if I set one tree on fire, it could spread to the rest quickly, and I'd go up in flames just like her. Hmm." She studied the dingy wooden bridge, the closest entrance to the Ramble. Designed as a labyrinth of paths through a small wooded area, the Ramble was now the most overgrown section of Central Park. Kali figured she could use her knife to get through the trees and brambles, but a machete would be more useful.

"This could be a trap," Shiva said. "You realize they're both in there."

"You mentioned that," Kali said. "But not together."

"Right," Shiva said. "Diana is that way." He pointed north, toward Belvedere Castle. "And Oro is that way." He pointed directly into the Ramble and slightly south, toward the other side of the lake.

Kali nodded. "It makes sense. That's what I would have done. Scatter my attention. Make me look for them."

"I could lift you in and take you straight to Diana," Shiva said. "We might hit a few trees on the way down, but she'll still be much more injured than you. An easy kill."

"That wouldn't be sporting," Kali said with a smile. "I've got my limitations, too. Let's see what I can do with them."

"Kali," Shiva said, and the urgency in his voice made her look into his eyes. "*Do not die.* I won't stand for it."

She kissed him on the cheek and moved away before

he could pull her in for a stronger embrace. Standing on the dilapidated floorboards of the bridge, she paused.

"Shiva—you've never lied to me, have you?"

"Me?" Shiva said, feigning indignation. "Never! All right, what you had for lunch might not have been chicken, exactly. . . ."

"Ha ha," Kali said. "But there's no way back to our own time, right? That's what you said."

"That is what I said," Shiva replied. His eyes seemed darker than usual, and he held himself very still—also unusual for him.

"We can never get back to our world—our families?" Kali asked.

Shiva took a deep breath. "No."

She studied him. "You know how I'm going to feel if you're lying."

"Kali," he said, "you must focus on this battle."

She sighed and turned her attention back to the Ramble, making her way cautiously across the sturdier-looking boards until she stood on the concrete path on the other side. From here, Shiva was already obscured by branches.

Kali set off to the left, pushing through brambles and keeping an eye on the overgrown path below her, until she reached a set of stairs that led her up through the trees, deeper into the Ramble. Branches whipped her face and clawed at her pant legs, but she felt calm and unstoppable.

It was a smart choice, but there was something Diana and Gus didn't know. Kali loved the Ramble. She'd spent many lunch hours walking off her frustrations along its tangled paths, trying to focus on anything but strangling her boss. She was probably the only person left in the world who could navigate from one end to the other without backtracking or getting lost once.

Then again, it had looked a lot different in her day. Back then, the paths were actually paths, and there *was* a beginning and end to them. Now it was just chaos.

Kali slipped down a narrow path with a sheer rock wall to her right. She kept her ears alert for any sound and watched the trees carefully, remembering that Diana had hidden in one to escape the dogs. Soon she came to a small river and followed it to a rocky hill, which she climbed, bounding from rock to rock and cutting down branches that got in her way.

Being at the top didn't help much. She could barely see ten feet in each direction, but at least there was some clear space below and around her.

"Diana!" she called. "Gus! Someone come out and fight!"

Unsurprisingly, there was no response. Kali sat down on the rock and rested her elbows on her knees. She wasn't designed for slinking through undergrowth and sneaking up on her prey. Her style was a bit more slash and burn, with an emphasis on *burn*. Really, what she should do—what she *could* do—was set the whole Ramble on fire. That would bring them out in a hurry. Or kill them. Whichever.

But it seemed a shame to burn down the Ramble. And they'd have to come out sooner or later; she wasn't in any hurry. So she'd wait. She'd play their cat and mouse game, but her way. She'd save her energy by waiting right here.

Someone would come along sooner or later.

She was glad Thor had come back that morning to watch Miracle again. Kali wouldn't have wanted to leave the girl alone with Tigre, Anna, and Ereka—not after last night.

Half an hour later, she spotted a movement off to her right. Slowly, she came to a crouch, and as the figure shoved its way out of the bush below her, she pounced, crashing into him from above and knocking the air out of him.

It was Tigre. He curled into a ball on the ground, clutching a book to his chest.

Kali stood up and swore. "Tigre! You interfering nuisance! Give me one good reason why I shouldn't just kill you instead."

"Ow," Tigre coughed, gasping. "Ow—ow." He didn't seem able to say anything else.

"It'll hurt more when I rip your spine out," Kali said. "You've probably scared them both to the other end of the park by now."

"Not quite," Diana said, stepping out from behind a tree.

Kali thrust a finger at her accusingly, and pieces of bark exploded into the air, as if she'd thrown a grenade at the tree. Diana ducked, covering her face, but a few matchbook-sized pieces hit her bandaged head, and she winced.

"You've stopped hiding," Kali observed.

"I wasn't hiding," Diana said. "I was looking for you, but you've been quiet an awfully long time."

"Sure," Kali said. "I guess Gus just agreed to let you take this one?"

"No!" Gus's voice called. They glanced around, but couldn't see him. "No," he yelled again. "I'm coming! Fight me instead!"

Kali examined the motionless bushes, then turned to Diana. "He hasn't discovered an invisibility power, too, has he?"

Diana cupped her hands around her mouth. "Go away, Gus!" she yelled. "She's here to fight me!"

"We had a deal!" he shouted back. "Whoever she found first! You weren't supposed to be looking for her!"

"Neither were you!" she called.

"Oh great," Kali said, rolling her eyes. "You mean, if I'd just stood here and yelled for a while, you both would have come straight to me? How am I supposed to fight a reasonable battle when you're both crazy?" She pointed to a rock about the size of a bowling ball embedded in the hill. It shook for a moment, then dislodged itself and flew through the air, aimed straight at Diana's chest. At the last moment, Diana leaped and swung herself up into the nearest tree. The boulder smashed into a remnant of concrete path.

"WAIT!" Gus yelled. "I'm coming! I'll be there any second! Stupid frakking branches!" Kali could hear violent snapping and bush shaking now, but it was a ways off, over the hill in back of Tigre, who was still sitting on the ground, trying to recover his voice.

"Do you really think being in a tree is a good idea?" Kali said to Diana. Flames appeared in a ring around the trunk and shot upward, climbing in a rapid circle and leaving smoking black wood in their wake. Diana barely managed to swing up and jump over to the next tree. She hung for a moment, fighting to get her legs onto a branch. Kali could see more bandages peeking out from under Diana's shirt and knew her cracked ribs must be screaming in pain.

"Nope, still a bad idea," Kali said. The new tree acquired a ring of fire, as well. Diana let go and dropped back to the ground, clutching her side.

Diana closed her eyes and flung her hand out toward Kali, whispering something.

Nothing happened.

"Sorry," Kali said. "I looked it up. Your thing is turning men into deer—emphasis on *men*. I haven't offended your unsullied purity or wild forest spirit, nor am I an arrogant jackalope like Amon, so that one's not going to work on me."

"Wait," Tigre finally managed to say. "Wait, I have— There's— Stop."

"Yeah, stop!" Gus called, closer now. "I'm the one you should be fighting!" The bushes behind Diana started rustling ferociously, and the Polynesian avatar finally fell into the small clearing. He looked much the worse for wear, with scratches all over his face and arms, as if the Ramble had chewed him up and spit him out again.

Kali noticed that one of the scratches on his arms wasn't a scratch; it was the beginning of a dark green tattoo. He was also carrying a long spear, which he'd probably borrowed from the museum, none too wisely, as it kept getting caught on the foliage and was probably the reason he'd taken so long to get here.

"I'm here," he announced, wrestling the spear free from a bush. "Now—"

"No!" Tigre interrupted. "Stop it, stop fighting!"

"Do you want me to fight both of you?" Kali said, exasperated. "I don't mind if the judges don't."

"We don't mind," said Maat's voice from above. They all looked up and saw four judges standing on the rocks where Kali had been waiting: Maat, Ganesh, Itzamna, and Tyr.

"Carry on," Maat said. "Personally, I'd love to see you kill them both at once."

"Fantastic," Kali said, throwing her hands open. The rocks buried in the ground below Diana and Gus all exploded at once, sending up fountains of dirt. At the same time, the bushes behind them erupted into flames.

As the smoke and dust cleared, Kali saw Gus and Diana running away through the trees off to her right. They were heading in the direction of the lake.

"Oh, fun, a high-speed chase," Kali said. She swept her hand through the air and the fire flickered out.

But as she stepped forward to follow Diana and Gus, Tigre said, "Parvati."

Something twinged inside Kali, like a harp string being plucked. Up on the rock, Ganesh's mouth opened, then closed, and he pressed his trunk to his forehead.

"Devi," Tigre said. "Shakti. Durga. Sati."

It felt to Kali as if he was saying her own name over and over.

"What are you doing?" she asked. She was suddenly dizzy, feeling the smoke engulfing her, although she had extinguished the fire.

Two hands took her wrists, holding her upright. It was Shiva, standing in front of her with his eyes fixed on hers.

"Don't listen, Kali," he murmured. "Focus." But Tigre was talking again, louder now.

"Parvati," he said. "It sounds familiar, doesn't it? Devi. Durga. Do you remember them?"

Against her will, Kali mentally poked the holes in her memories. They were larger than she'd realized. Who kept track of thousands of years of experience, after all? But there was so much missing, and so much attached to these names.

"Kali," Tigre said urgently. "Listen. You're not just a goddess of destruction. That's only one part of you. I read all about it. Kali is one manifestation, but so are these others. If you look up Shiva's wife, Parvati is the one the books talk about. She's Ganesh's mother. She's the reincarnation of his first wife, Sati. And Kali, she's a good person, just like you. She's kind and caring and she takes care of the world. I know you have that in you—I've seen it. Did Shiva tell you that? Did he show you what you really are?"

"No, it's not—that can't be right," Kali said. "I'm not good, or kind. Right, Shiva? I'm a destroyer. I've done terrible things my whole life, whether I wanted to or not. And I hate people."

"Not everyone," Tigre said. He held something out so she could see it. It was a photograph of her with her three half sisters, Amy, Beth, and Jo-Jo. It looked as if they were laughing at something she'd said. Amy was looking up at her with an adoring expression. "Look at how they love you," Tigre said fiercely. "You cared about them, the way you care about Miracle, with the part of you that's a mother goddess. You're not just destruction. You're more than that."

Kali focused on Shiva's face. He was still whispering, "Don't listen, don't listen, don't listen," but his eyes were cast down and he seemed to know it was hopeless.

"It's true," she said. "It is, isn't it?" She yanked her wrists out of his hands. "You *were* lying to me."

He shook his head mournfully but didn't speak.

"Shiva," she said coldly, "I'd like the rest of my memories, please."

"I can't do that," he said. "You know I can't. I can't let you be weakened. We need your anger, your ferocity, your rage. Parvati's gentleness won't win this battle for us."

Two more rocks exploded into dust. *There's some rage for you,* Kali thought. "Once again you don't trust me," she said. "You keep things from me and think you can manipulate me. When," she said, her voice rising, "in the history of our existence has that ever been okay with me?"

"Forgive me," Shiva said. "It's what I had to do." And then he vanished.

"Thrilling," said Maat from up on the rock. "And yet tremendously boring at the same time. Can we get on with the killing, please?"

"No," Kali said. "I'm calling off this fight." She snatched the photograph from Tigre's hands. "Remind me to kick your ass for stealing this."

Tigre scurried after her as she strode away, heading back toward her apartment. Behind them, the judges faded away in a murmur of disappointed voices.

"What's happening?" he said. "What are you doing?"

"You know that plan you mentioned?" Kali said. "I know where we can go for some privacy from the gods. But I'm afraid we're going to need a boat."

• • ● • •

Diana stumbled to a halt and Gus tugged on her hand.

"Wait," she said, rubbing her forehead. "I need a minute."

"She could be right behind us." Gus glanced anxiously over Diana's shoulder. There was no sign of Kali, but they'd only been running for a few minutes. The lake glimmered off to their right, only a few feet away. Here there was less undergrowth, but the trees grew so thickly together that they were shrouded in darkness even though the sun was shining brightly outside.

"I don't hear her," Diana said. "And I would, trust me. My forest senses are kicking in."

Gus leaned over, his hands on his knees, and tried to catch his breath. He'd dropped the spear back in the clearing, when Kali had set the bushes on fire. It was strong and had a sharp whalebone knife lashed to it, but he didn't mind losing it. In this terrain, it had done him no good at all. If he tried to attack Kali with it, it would probably get tangled in a vine, bounce off a tree trunk, and impale him instead.

"But something is coming," Diana whispered, and a chill went down his back. "Something that hates us."

"Sounds like Kali to me," Gus said, holding out his hand. "So let's run."

Diana shook her head. "Kali doesn't hate us. This is different." She pivoted, studying the trees around them. "And we can't run away from it. It'll rise up wherever we are ... like right ... *there*." She pointed at a mound of rotting leaves five feet away, which suddenly started to move. As if something was boiling up from the center, the leaves began to cascade down the sides. The top of a dark head appeared from the hole in the mound, quickly followed by the rest of the figure, which was covered in dark, wet dirt and crawling insects.

The eyes were like pale ivory marbles, glaring and deathlike, but the rest of the face was horribly familiar to them. Diana gasped.

"That's right," hissed the newcomer. "I'm here to kill you. And I won't fail this time."

She stepped forward, scattering dead leaves, and Gus saw a wickedly curved, gleaming knife in her hand.

"So which one are you?" he said, trying not to sound terrified. "Anna or Ereka?"

"Which do you think?" she said with a sneer.

"I'm hoping Ereka," he said. "She's irritating, and I won't mind that much if we have to get rid of her."

The girl's face twisted into an ugly scowl. "But she looks just like Anna," she insisted. "She is just as beautiful. Why wouldn't anyone who likes Anna like Ereka, too?"

"Because Anna is friendly," Gus said, "and smart and helpful. Ereka is whiny and kinda mean. I'm right, aren't I? You're Ereka."

The glare intensified. "Anna is a weakling," she snarled. "I came to do her job for her. I took the same form to create confusion and keep you blind, which was not difficult."

"So she's the real avatar?" Diana said. "And you're— something else?"

"Yeah, not many humans could rise out of the ground like that," Gus said. "Or make their eyes, um . . . do that."

The skin started to flake away from Ereka's face. Her

hair lengthened, snarled, and wound down her back in matted tangles. Her clothes transformed into a long black dress, hanging loosely off her skeletal bones.

"I am Ereshkigal," she said in a lower, gloomier voice. "Inanna's sister, queen of the underworld, and far more powerful than she could ever be."

"Not so powerful," Gus pointed out, "if you've already failed to kill Diana twice, even using cowardly, under-handed ways."

"Shut up, mortal," she snapped. "This is between me and Venus." Ereshkigal lifted the knife to her face and drew a thin line of blood down her own cheek. "Inanna is our goddess of love. She could win this in her own weak, insipid way, but not while she has another goddess of love to compete with. We assume this is why the Greeks added you to Diana, fearing our strength. So. Venus must die."

"What pantheon are you?" Diana asked, backing into a tree. "And why aren't you telling Anna the truth?"

"We are the original civilization," Ereshkigal said. "We are where all life began and we should be the rulers here-after."

"The original civilization," Gus said. "Like Neander-thal gods?" He said it to provoke her. He wanted to turn her pale, staring eyes away from Diana, even if it meant they'd be back on him.

"Sumerian," Ereshkigal hissed angrily, but she didn't look at him. She took another step toward Diana. "From Mesopotamia."

"But if you kill Diana," Gus said, "then Anna won't get her power."

"It doesn't matter," Ereshkigal said. "It's more important for Venus to be truly, utterly dead."

She flipped the knife into her right hand and stabbed at Diana. At the same moment, Gus grabbed a rock off the ground and threw it hard at Ereshkigal's head. Diana dodged; Ereshkigal did not, and the rock thudded off her skull.

With a hiss, Ereshkigal curled her fingers, and the dead leaves on the ground began to spin. Within seconds, Gus was engulfed in a whirlwind of detritus, dirt and grass flying into his eyes with the force of the wind holding him in place.

"Diana!" he tried to shout, but leaves and insects blew into his open mouth and he doubled over, hacking and spitting.

"Athena!" he heard her call. "Judges! An immortal is attacking me! Apollo! Zeus!"

"Tattletale," Ereshkigal sneered. "It doesn't matter. The other gods barely know my pantheon exists; we have ways of steering their attention away. By the time they fight through the deflections I've set up, you'll be dead— and so will your friend."

Gus could hear their footsteps darting through the trees and the ringing sound of the knife bouncing off bark, but he couldn't see anything through his stinging, watering eyes. He groped around on the ground for more rocks and tried throwing them, but the whirlwind hampered his aim, and he was afraid of hitting Diana.

"I have eyes of death, Venus," Ereshkigal said from somewhere in front of him. "Inanna has met them herself in our mythic past. Come down and look into my eyes."

"No thanks," Diana called, and he guessed that she had climbed another tree. She sounded like she'd gone fairly high.

"Very well," Ereshkigal growled. The whirlwind of leaves suddenly ceased, and as Gus tried to blink and focus his vision, strong, bony arms seized his shoulders, picked him up, and slammed him into a tree trunk. He tried to shove her away, but a knotted rope that felt strong as metal cables was already winding around his body. His arms were pinned to his sides, his legs were bound together, and the only thing left free was his head.

"Let him go!" Diana shouted. "He's not a threat to you or Anna!"

"But you rejected me, didn't you?" Ereshkigal snarled in Gus's ear. "I thought appearing as Inanna would give me her power over men, until you rejected me for *her*. Bet you're regretting that now."

"You're right," Gus said. "Gruesome lunatics are *so* my type."

Blurrily, he could see Ereshkigal gesturing at a branch above him. An enormous steel hook appeared, like something you'd hang dead cattle from. With ferocious strength, she grabbed him and hoisted him up to slide the cables around his chest onto the hook. Then she stepped away, and he was left hanging. The ropes cut painfully into his skin, and he felt like the air was being choked out of him. The cold steel of the metal hook pressed along the length of his spine, and he could feel the needle-sharp tip at the back of his neck, forcing him to keep still or risk being impaled.

"He can die as slowly as you like," Ereshkigal called.

Gus spotted Diana up in a nearby tree, leaning down with an anxious expression.

"It's okay, Diana," he said. "It's not bad, really, don't wor—"

"Shut up," Ereshkigal said again, stuffing a dark rag that smelled like death and mothballs and slaughterhouses into his mouth. He gagged, choked, and tried to cough it out, but her skeletal hand held it in place. Now he really couldn't breathe.

"If I come down," Diana called, "you have to untie him."

"This is not a negotiation, princess," Ereshkigal said. "I don't mind what order I kill you in, but your only chance to save him is to come here and try to stop me."

Gus tried to shake his head, but he couldn't tell if he'd really done it. Everything was swimming, blurring, fading away. And he felt hot—burning heat against the side of his face, as if he was leaning against a furnace. Was this a normal side effect of dying?

"Ereshkigal," said a new voice. "What are you doing?"

The voice was dark and scorched, with a steady, even beat to it, and it made Gus think of burning oil fields.

"Get out of here, Shamash," Ereshkigal hissed.

Gus felt the heat move around in front of him, and when he opened his eyes, he saw the newcomer standing between him and Ereshkigal. She fell back a pace, letting go of the gag, and Gus was able to spit it out onto the ground. He took a huge gulp of air, even though it was blazingly hot and dry and made his throat hurt.

Then he recognized the long golden robes and the glowing halo behind the man's head. It was the last judge, the one he'd seen in the museum—the one no one acknowledged. Anna's judge. Ereshkigal had called him Shamash.

"This is neither right nor necessary," Shamash said quietly. "It could get us disqualified."

"Not if I finish killing them before the other judges show up," Ereshkigal said. "Then no one will ever know."

Shamash turned a fraction to examine Gus out of the corner of his eye. Gus could see his face much more clearly in the daylight, and he looked a lot like Anna—same clean, streamlined features and brown eyes with distant hints of gold in them.

"No," he said. "It is unjust."

"It is more unjust that the Greeks threw Venus into this battle!" Ereshkigal said. "Why should we sit back and allow it? She will sniff out all of Inanna's secrets and defeat her."

"It does not strengthen the Greek avatar to have two goddesses inside her," Shamash said. "It weakens her. But immortals killing the avatars—we cannot be responsible for starting such behavior. If anyone did find out, Inanna would be dead before her heart could take its next beat."

"But I hate them," Ereshkigal said, her voice shaking. "I want to drag them into my underworld palace and hang them from the ceiling and watch them rot."

"Ereshkigal," Shamash said, "leave this battleground now, do not return, and never try to harm the avatars again, or I will find a far worse punishment for you, and you know that I can."

Ereshkigal screamed, a long, hoarse, piercing cry of frustration and rage and hatred. Then, as suddenly as she'd appeared, she disappeared, the earth below her opening to swallow her into it.

A silence followed her departure. Gus could hear a flock of geese arguing out on the lake. With a huge flutter of wings, they scattered into the air.

Shamash turned and looked at Gus.

"Thank you," Gus managed to say. "Please—I can't breathe—"

"That is not my concern," Shamash said, and vanished.

Gus hung there, disbelieving. Why save him, only to leave him to die? Did Shamash send Ereshkigal away just so she wouldn't get caught killing him?

Diana scrambled to the ground and ran over to him.

"It's okay, Gus," she said, trying to shove him up so he'd come unhooked, but she wasn't tall enough. "Just keep breathing. Don't panic. I'll get you down." She sounded more panicked than he did. He felt like he was drifting, as if he could swing back and forth here forever, slowly, slowly suffocating until he died.

Diana picked up several rocks and threw them back down until she found one with a sharp edge. She started sawing at the knot tying the two ends of the rope together, but it was thick and unyielding, and soon the rock was too blunt to be useful. Diana threw it down and started searching for another. Gus saw that there were tears running down her cheeks.

"Hey, don't worry so much," he said, or thought he said. "It's a pretty place to die. The sun is shining; the trees are all these amazing colors. There's a bird staring at us."

"Shh, Gus," Diana said tearfully. "Stop mumbling. Save your breath." She hoisted herself onto the tree branch and tried sawing at the rope that held up the hook, but it was equally thick.

"It's a pretty bird," Gus said, or possibly just thought. "It's a large bird. It's green and red, with a long, pretty tail. It's hopping up from the lake. Oh, the trees are in its way, but it can get through them. It's very large. And pretty . . . so pretty . . ."

Why, thank you, said a bubbling voice in his head. *It's true. I* am *the most beauuuuuuutiful creature in the knooown world, but you're quite pretty yourself. Would you like me to get you down from there?*

PANTHEON: SUMERIAN
AVATAR: INANNA
JUDGE: SHAMASH
TRAINER: ERESHKIGAL

Of course I knew all along.

The Sumerians don't even know I'm here. They didn't bother shielding from me. I saw them negotiate with the Norse pantheon so that Thor would go pick up Anna in Thailand. They could have brought her here another way, but they were saving their energy for their cunning plan.

I saw them swathe themselves in darkness; I saw them erase their presence from everyone's minds. If no one knew who they were, how could their behavior be predicted, and how could they be tamed, or fought? They had power in secrecy.

Ereshkigal, queen of the underworld, was supposed to be Anna's trainer. I saw her disguise herself as Anna and materialize in Central Park the same day Thor brought Anna here. It was crafty, you must admit. The other avatars wouldn't know which one to fight; they wouldn't know who was the real avatar. The confusion made it easier to welcome them into the fold.

But Ereshkigal has trouble hiding her true self for long. I knew it was going to be a short-lived deception. Sooner or later she would crack . . . and it turned out to be sooner.

What I don't know is what will happen next. What will the Sumerians do now that they've been exposed? They know Diana and Gus will tell the other avatars, and once the spell is broken, the other pantheons will remember them, too.

They're going to need a new plan.
I hope it's a good one.

Tigre had never been so pleased to see anyone in his life.

When Diana and Gus had come stumbling out of Central Park, leaning on Quetzie, Tigre had spotted them from the window right away. He'd run down the stairs from Kali's apartment faster than he'd ever run, even back when the storms had driven him crazy.

Perhaps it was silly of him to be so attached to Quetzie, but she'd rescued him from the dark weirdness of Chile after the Change, and then again when the Forever Youngermen had him trapped in Mexico. Also, she listened to him and she liked him unconditionally, unlike any of the people in his former life—his parents, his sister, Claudia, or his ex-girlfriend, Vicky. Quetzie had all the good qualities of a dog along with the intellect of a person. That made her the perfect friend in his book. And she'd rescued him twice already, so he couldn't help but feel that she might do it again.

Quetzie strutted and preened, looking perfectly at home on the wide expanse of Central Park West, as Anna and Diana oohed and aahed over her brilliant colors, her amazing tail, and her shimmery feathers.

I like your new friends, she burbled in his head.

"Look how the sunlight brings out all these different shades of green," Anna said admiringly.

"And she's not just beautiful; she's brave, too," Diana said. "Gus would still be hanging there if she hadn't saved him." Quetzie unfurled her tail feathers and lifted her head. She looked exceptionally pleased with herself.

Gus himself was lying on a bench outside the park. He kept rubbing his neck and arms, as if reassuring himself that his circulation still worked.

Anna had taken the news of Ereka's betrayal surprisingly well. She was thrilled to discover that she was a real avatar, and as she pointed out, at least they didn't have to put up with Ereka anymore. Plus, now she knew who she was: Inanna, Sumerian goddess of love.

It made Tigre feel a little weird. Was that why he'd fallen for her so quickly? Was that why she seemed so perfect and easy to be with? But even if it was, that didn't change how he felt about her. And she still liked him—she wasn't using her goddess of love power on Gus or Thor, after all. So he wasn't going to worry about it.

"I can't believe you got my message," he said to Quetzie for the hundredth time.

Oooof course I did. I mean, the pterodolphins garbled it a bit, as youuu'd expect, but I figured it out. I've been wanting to come back and see you anyway. Hooooooray for those scary birds being gone!

Tigre glanced up at the apartment, but there was no sign yet of Kali, who'd gone upstairs to get Thor and Miracle.

"So Kali has a plan?" Diana said, noticing the direction of his gaze. "Where does she think we should go?"

"She won't tell me," he said. "She just said we should find a boat."

That's funny, Quetzie said. *I saw a few boooats in the docks on my way here.*

"Did you see where they are?" Tigre asked.

Yes, but it woooon't help you much. I noticed them because they were all on fire.

"That's not going to make Kali happy," Tigre said. "It probably means the gods heard her talking about boats and decided to destroy them all."

"Couldn't Quetzie take us wherever we have to go?" Anna asked, stroking the bird's glossy wing.

"I think there are too many of us," Tigre said. "Right, Quetzie?"

I'm soooory, tiger-boy. I don't think I could handle more than twooo. Her sharp black eyes widened. *Ooor maybe only one—if* he's *the one!*

Tigre turned and saw the massive hulk of Thor emerging from the front entrance. Miracle—now wearing a T-shirt and yoga pants—was riding regally on his shoulders, looking much happier than when he'd last seen her. Kali was right behind them.

"Oh, look, look!" Miracle cried with delight. "It worked! General Pepper's sacrifice was not wasted. A real god! Oh, she's the most beautiful thing I've ever seen!" She reached toward Quetzie, and Thor obligingly brought her close enough to pat the neoquetzal's feathers. Thor didn't seem fazed by Quetzie's size.

"This is Thor, the guy we want you to talk to," Tigre said. "We don't speak the same language, so we can't communicate with him at all. We were hoping you could help us."

Sure, Quetzie warbled. There was a pause. Tigre whispered the news to Kali about the burning boats, and, as he'd expected, she scowled.

"We're going to have to be sneakier about this," she muttered.

A startled look crossed Thor's face. He looked around at the avatars, and then, slowly, he faced Quetzie. After a minute, he nodded and gently lifted Miracle up onto Quetzie's back. Miracle squealed happily and buried her hands in Quetzie's feathers.

Thor's very confused. Quetzie giggled. *But he's a good listener. He wants to knooow what your gods have been telling you.*

It was Tigre's turn to be surprised. "He talked to you? I mean, you can hear what he's thinking?"

Of coooourse. I can hear anyone if they think directly at me. She paused for a minute, ruffling her feathers. *Kali says to tell you "That's uuuuuseful." And Diana says it's amazing that I can talk to all of you at once this way. It is, isn't it?* She waved her tail proudly.

"So we could—" Tigre began, but Kali kicked him in the shin.

Quetzie giggled again. *Tigre says "OW," and a few things I doooon't think he meant to pass along. And Gus says we can make plans this way without the gods ooooverhearing. And now Tigre says that's what he was GOOOING to say. Hee! This is fun.* She flapped her wings, and Miracle gave a delighted shriek of pretend fear. Tigre guessed that Quetzie was leaving the young girl out of the conversation. *But everyone stop talking at once. I'm going to explain what you toooold me to this lovely hulking felloooow here.* Quetzie winked at Thor, and then her voice fell silent as they stared at each other.

Tigre felt a twinge of jealousy, although he knew he was being ridiculous. Quetzie was here to help everyone. Now was not the time to get possessive. Besides, she wasn't his only friend—now he had Anna. Anna caught him watching her and smiled in a way that made his insides feel fizzy.

Thor has a booooat, Quetzie announced. *Kali says "WHAT?" Oh, wait . . . oookay, he doesn't have a boat, but he knooows where to get one.*

Kali was balancing on the wall surrounding Central Park with a look of fierce concentration. She certainly hadn't been acting any more like a gentle mother goddess than she had before the fight in the park, but Tigre was sure that she was on their side now. He didn't care what Gus thought. As he saw it, Kali could have taken any of them down the moment they arrived in New York, but she'd waited and she'd helped them. If she had been as committed to the battle as she wanted them to think, she would have challenged someone first, instead of waiting for someone else to win a battle. There was a large part of her that had never wanted to fight this battle in the first place. He was sure of that.

All right, Quetzie said. *Studly here says there's a god in his pantheon named Frey.*

Kali nodded, and Tigre remembered the handsome, fair-haired god who had come with Odin to take Thor away two nights ago.

Frey has a ship called Skidbladnir *that is big enough to hold all the Norse gods. Kali, stop interrupting. I knooooooow you're not going to "just waltz in and sail off with the world's most giGANtic ship." Thor says it is the best of all ships, a marvel of dwarf engineering. It is so intricately made that Frey can fold it up like a piece of paper and keep it in a pouch. It is one of his prized possessions, and he always carries it with him.*

Tigre jumped, and Kali shot him a sharp look. He'd noticed a pouch on Frey's belt—and it had a ship embroidered on it in gold thread. That had to be it!

Skidbladnir *is a beauuutiful, magical thing,* Quetzie said dreamily. *Once its sails are up, it will travel directly to where it needs to go. Frey will be very displeased to find it gone.* She listened for a moment. *Diana says that if you stick tooogether, the gods won't be able to hurt you, for fear of hurting their oooown avatar. And Kali says they will definitely try to stop us from leaving.*

Gus sat up, and Diana went over to sit next to him.

Gus has sent me an image of the crystal hunters oooon the bridges. Quetzie shuddered violently, her feathers trembling all the way down to her wing tips. *He thinks with the Boss Hunter gone, now the oooonly thing controlling them is the gods. Once the gods realize you are trying to escape, they will remove their protection and use the hunters to keep you all here and retrieve the ship.*

Youuuu need a way to get past them, or fight them, or distract them.

"I have a question," Diana said out loud, and everyone started. Kali frowned and Diana shook her head, as if to say, *This doesn't have to be secret.*

"Do any of you have the power to bring something inanimate to life?" Diana asked. "Do you know? Or do you know of any god who does? Because I have some new friends who could use our help."

And, Quetzie added, *she says they may be able to help us with the crystal hunter prooooblem, as well.*

"From what I read in the books last night," Tigre said, "most of the pantheons have someone who can give or create life. I've got an Aztec goddess with power over life and death, but I'm pretty sure she's not going to help us." He remembered Coatlicue's creepy visage from his nightmare. He wasn't about to ask her anyway.

Thor says Njord has a similar power, but that his pantheon would never help any of youuuuu.

"I'm actually surprised no one's showed up to cart you away yet today, big guy," Kali said from atop the wall.

Last night there was great feasting. He says they are still sleeping it off. That is uuuusually when he slips away—during the day, while all the gods are recovering. After his first few experiences, now he oooooonly pretends to drink their ale.

Thor grinned, pleased with himself.

"My pantheon probably has a god of life and death," Anna said, "but they're still not talking to me, so that's no help."

"And I think some of the Egyptians have similar powers," Gus said. "I feel like I've heard myths about Isis bringing her husband back to life, but I don't remember the details. In any case, they *definitely* won't be in the mood to help us out."

"I guess that's true of all the gods," Diana said despondently.

"Well, all right," said Kali, "I might know one who owes me big-time. But I was kind of planning on not speaking to him for the rest of eternity."

Gus and Diana exchanged anxious looks. "Shiva?" Diana said. "Are you sure that's a good idea?"

"No," Kali said, "but if it's our only idea, then I'll do it."

In that case, Quetzie said, *Diana says her friends might be able toooo help you get by the crystal hunters. But first, Kali says, youuu need Frey's ship.*

We need a plan, Tigre thought at her. *We need to know where the Norse gods are, and then perhaps we can sneak up on them tonight and steal the ship while Frey is sleeping.*

Quetzie cocked her head at him. *Tiger-boy, do you have any other bird friends?*

Tigre was surprised. "No," he said. "Not that I know of."

So I'm the only one?

He nodded.

She blinked a few times, swiveling her head from side to side, and then suddenly she leaped into the air and attacked a nearby tree. Miracle shrieked and clung to her feathers, sliding wildly from side to side, while Thor ran under the neoquetzal, holding out his arms in case the girl fell.

Quetzie clutched the branches of the tree between her claws and shook it ferociously. Immediately, two black shapes exploded out of the leaves. Quetzie wheeled her head to the left and caught one with a snap of her beak. The other lifted higher into the sky, but Quetzie caught up with two beats of her wings and seized it in one of her claws. She wobbled back down to the ground, making an ungainly landing on one foot while holding her captive in the other.

Thor swooped Miracle off Quetzie and back onto his shoulders, but she was laughing as she wrapped her arms around his head.

"That was so exciting!" Miracle cried. "Was that like a roller coaster? I've read about roller coasters. I bet it was."

Kali stepped forward and studied the two ravens Quetzie had caught.

"Huginn and Munnin," she said. "Odin's spies." The birds glared balefully at her, flapping around in useless fury. "Anna," Kali said, "could you run upstairs and grab a couple of pillowcases from my apartment?"

Anna sprinted up the stairs as Diana gave Kali an astonished look.

"You're going to stick them in pillowcases?" Diana said. "Isn't that kind of cruel?"

"It's not like it'll kill them," Kali said. "They're immortal. And if we let them go, they'll fly back to Odin right away and tell him that we've been conspiring together. We can't let that happen."

"But he'll notice they're missing," Tigre pointed out. "Won't that make him even more suspicious?"

Noooot if we get there first, Quetzie interjected. *That's what Kali says.*

You mean . . . go now? Tigre thought.

Gus agrees, Quetzie said. *There's nooooo time to lose. Time for action! Time for dramatic leaps! Time for espionage and excitement!*

Tigre smiled despite himself. He was pretty sure that last bit was all Quetzie.

Diana suggests splitting up, Quetzie said. *Three go to steal the ship from Frey, while three go find the kids in the museum and enlist their help with the crystal hunters. This is soooooooo thrilling! I feel like a suuuper-spy. Kali wants to know what kids. Diana says she'll shoooow you. Isn't it exciting how impooooortant I am here? Oh, all right, Kali, I'll stay fooocused.*

Anna came running back out with an armful of linens. Kali grabbed a large pillowcase from the top of the pile and threw it over the raven whose foot was trapped in Quetzie's beak. It screamed angrily and thrashed about, but Kali was able to upend it and tie the end of the pillowcase shut. She jumped back with a yell as the other raven pecked viciously at her foot.

"Good thing you're here, Quetzie," Kali said. "We'd never have caught them without you. Looks like they don't have any special escape powers anyway. Just a supernaturally bad attitude."

Tigre took another pillowcase and followed suit, although Anna had to help him hold down the moving end while he tied it closed. Kali then plunked both pillowcases down on a sheet and tied the whole thing together.

"That ought to hold them for a while," she panted. "I know a closet we can stash them in."

And then, Quetzie said importantly, *our mission begins.*

Diana held Gus's hand all the way back to the museum. The sparks of electricity hurt at first, but after a while the tingling faded into a numbness she could ignore. She didn't want to let go of him.

It was a little unsettling to be walking next to Anna now. Diana kept imagining the avatar's eyes rolling back into blank marbles and a knife appearing in her hand.

She had been so sure her assassin was Hera or Mars, who both had ancient grudges and reasons to hate her. Even though it meant their pantheon would lose, she thought they would still rather see her dead than see her become more powerful than they. From what she remembered of Greek mythology, the gods tended to be selfish, jealous, and irrational. And there was a lot of history to her relationships with those two, even if she couldn't remember any of it.

But she'd barely known Ereka. It wasn't just that Diana was an avatar that Ereka wanted dead; otherwise, the death goddess would have let Anna deal with her. But Ereka genuinely loathed Venus, and Diana had felt the full force of that hate with her Venus senses, which were much more used to adoration and devotion.

Maybe it was because Venus had come along a few centuries after Inanna and replaced her, in time becoming a far more famous goddess of love. Or maybe Ereka had her own complicated issues with love goddesses—she hadn't sounded very fond of Anna, either. Maybe she resented the attention they got, or their beauty, or how easily everything happened for them. Venus had known other wanna-be pop stars who felt that way about her musical success. She was lucky none of *them* had been death goddesses in disguise.

Diana wondered if this was why Anna's pantheon hadn't protected her against the crystal hunters. If they had, the electric shock when she touched people would have been a clue as to which of the two girls was the avatar and which the imposter. Or perhaps they'd withheld it so that the Sumerian goddess of love could use her own particular powers. That was an unsettling thought. Was Tigre under Anna's spell?

For that matter, was Gus under hers? Something else she didn't want to think about.

"What are you going to tell your gods?" Anna asked, interrupting her thoughts.

"The truth," Diana said, "or part of it anyway. I'll tell them I'm trying to turn Aleph and Bet into real children."

She spotted Apollo as they crossed the paved road behind the museum. He was on the roof, doing cartwheels, and the sun shining off his hair gave him a golden halo. She wondered if he would help them if he knew what they were doing.

He'd helped her already more than once. On the journey, when Gus had been wounded by a pterodactyl attack, Apollo's voice had whispered in her head, telling her how to heal him. Here in New York, he had distracted the other gods so she could go find Gus. But she was pretty sure that was because he disapproved of the Amon situation and wanted to help her pull away from the Egyptians as much as possible. He still wanted her to win this fight, not give up and join the others. She couldn't be completely honest with him, just in case, and that made her sad.

Apollo bounced lightly off the roof and sailed down to the ground, landing in front of them. He enveloped Diana in a bear hug that made her drop her grip on Gus's hand. She flexed her fingers, wondering when she'd get sensation back. She wanted to hold Gus's hand again. She wanted more than that, but the electric shocks would make even kissing a less-than-fun experience. Which was, presumably, the point of the spell, in addition to protecting them from the crystal hunters.

If the gods really did drop the spell to send the hunters after them, maybe the electric side effects would disappear, too. And then . . . She cast a sidelong glance at Gus and was thankful that Quetzie wasn't there to listen in on her thoughts.

"You're alive!" Apollo exclaimed. "How did you win? Did you take her power? Does it make you feel all big and tough?"

"It wasn't like that," Diana said. "She called off the fight."

"She—" Apollo threw up his hands. "Don't tell me Kali agreed to your crazy little group truce! She seemed so smart. I was sure she'd realize it'll be easier on everyone just to get it over with quickly."

"We're lucky she did," Diana said, "or I'd be dead, and probably so would Gus."

Apollo's eyes shifted to Gus, over to Anna, and back to her. "You underestimate yourself," he said, but he sounded uneasy.

"Anyway, it's just a postponement," Diana lied, feeling horribly guilty. "She'll fight us again later. I think she, um . . . I think she decided to fight Thor first."

"First!" Apollo's golden eyebrows nearly shot up to his hair. "That's insanity! But how terrific for us if one of them takes out the other. Except then that one will be twice as powerful. Oh dear, dear, dear."

"We have a new project," Diana said, trying to sound breezy and cheerful. "Mission Pinocchio. Want to help?"

"Does it have to do with the two robot kids who live here?" Apollo asked, following them to the door that led into the sculpture garden.

"How did you know?" Diana said, astonished.

"Vulcan said you were talking to them this morning. They usually stay hidden in the back rooms."

"Why didn't you tell me about them before?" She pulled open one of the doors to the museum and they crossed into the cool, silent space. The slender Diana statue still stood poised on one foot, as if eternally waiting for her prey to cross her path. *Not me,* Diana thought. *I'd go looking for mine. With both feet on the ground.*

Apollo shrugged. "I didn't think they were important."

"Well, they asked me for help," Diana said. "They want to become real children, and we're going to try to do it."

"Er," Apollo said, "how?"

"We'll figure something out," Gus said.

"Diana!" called a voice from above. Aleph was hanging over the edge of the balcony, waving like mad. She smiled and waved back. For a kid who'd spent the last couple of decades hiding from everyone, he sure was friendly.

Bet tugged him back and they both ran over to the nearest staircase and down to their level.

"I knew you'd come back!" Aleph announced, throwing his arms around Diana. Again she felt the synthetic strangeness of his skin as it brushed hers.

"That's imprecise," Bet said. "Knowledge implies certainty, Aleph, and nothing about future events is certain."

"I was certain," Aleph said, grinning.

Bet rolled his eyes but didn't argue.

"We have an idea," Diana said, "but we're not sure it will work, okay?"

"And we wanted to ask your help with something," Gus added.

"But if you can't do it, don't worry. We'll try to help you anyway, all right?" Diana said. Gus could be a little too goal-oriented sometimes.

"We'll do anything!" Aleph declared. "We'd do anything for you!"

"*Anything* is a term that encompasses an awful lot, Aleph," said Bet. "But I believe I agree with him. I can think of nothing we would say no to, although I'd qualify that by saying I have not had time to screen and review all the possibilities."

"I'll come with you," Apollo said. "I'd love to see how this will work."

"Great!" Gus said. "And while we're walking, maybe you can tell me some more about this world and how to get back to our own time."

"On second thought," Apollo said, and vanished into the air.

"Well done," Diana said to Gus. He shrugged modestly. "Aleph and Bet, do you guys know about the crystal hunters?"

"Of course," said Bet. "That was one reason some people hated us. They thought all robotic technology was the same, although our parents would never have created anything as heartless as the crystal hunters. Our parents were much cleverer scientists than that. But a lot of people thought we might turn out like the hunters, despite the fact that we are much more carefully designed."

"And we don't kill people," Aleph chirped.

"That's good," Diana said. "Have you ever met any of these hunters?"

"We saw a lot on the way here," Bet said. "They attacked us four times, but each time they realized we were not human, and we were able to drive them away."

Diana felt excitement building. "How did you do that?"

Aleph held out his hands, palms up. After a moment, the veins below the skin began to pulse and glow with silver light. A spark shot out of his left ring finger.

Gus met Diana's eyes. "Perfect."

This wasn't the best idea Kali had ever had. She didn't think it was the worst, either, but of course, she wouldn't know that for sure until it either succeeded or she found herself hacked to death with Viking axes.

Up on a hill at the north end of Manhattan was a branch of the Metropolitan Museum of Art called the Cloisters. The building, situated in the middle of a park and composed of old monastic structures, had an aura of history and strength, and it commanded a striking view of the river and the landscape below.

So perhaps it was an unsurprising choice for the camp of the Norse gods.

Thor says it reminds them of Valhalla, Quetzie relayed. *Ooooonly this is much, muuuuch smaller. And the roof is not made of golden warriors' shields. And the walls are not made of spears. And there aren't six hundred and foooorty dooooors. But otherwise, fairly similar.*

Kali sent her thought to Quetzie: *Could you be a little less conspicuous?* She could clearly see the neoquetzal "surreptitiously" flapping away on the other side of the bank of trees. She and Thor were rolling up the vast expanse of the West Side Highway in his chariot, pulled behind the galloping hindquarters of his two slavering goats. Quetzie had informed them that the goats' names, translated, meant "Toothgnasher" and "Toothgrinder," which didn't make them any cuddlier.

I am being inconspicuous! Quetzie protested. *They'll never see me coming! I swoooop in like the wind, invisible as air, heroic ahoy!*

Kali rolled her eyes and Thor grinned. She hoped including Quetzie in this plan was a good idea, but she couldn't think of any other way to get Tigre up to the Cloisters as fast as she and Thor were traveling. At least she had left Miracle safely back at the apartment. The less the gods knew about her, the better.

Kali hated the idea of leaving the actual theft of the pouch to Tigre, but she knew she could provide a much better distraction as she fought Thor. At least they'd be evenly matched; Tigre would have been crushed with one accidental swing of Thor's hammer. Not that she'd explained it to Tigre that way, of course.

To Kali's relief, Quetzie dropped out of sight as they approached the ramp to the Cloisters. Thor flicked the reins to send the goats surging forward, and they soon pulled up in front of the museum with a rolling peal of thunder from his chariot wheels.

"Wow," Kali said, jumping out. "I've never been here before." *I bet Mom and the girls would love it. Don't think about that now.*

Thor descended behind her, flinging the reins back in the chariot and giving the closest goat a firm pat on the back. With a huffy snort, the goats trotted off down a side road, where Kali could see a short figure waiting to unharness them.

Thor rumbled something, gesturing at the front door of the Cloisters. Kali stepped forward and realized someone was standing in the shadows just inside the door. She recognized the shape of the hat and cloak. It was Odin, king of the Norse gods.

"Shiva's little destruction goddess," Odin grumbled. "I can't say I'm pleased to see you. I don't suppose you have any idea where my ravens are?" His single eye, piercingly blue, was fixed on her with an unpleasantly knowing gaze. However, Kali had the feeling this was his normal expression, calculated to make you feel as if he knew all about you, whether or not it was true.

She stared into his face without flinching. "Haven't seen them. Gee, I hope they're okay." This was a favorite trick of hers; since the statement was clearly half a lie, it made it harder for her interrogator to figure out if the other half was, too. She gave Odin a toothy smile.

Odin's eyebrows lowered. "Then perhaps you can tell me what you're doing here."

"You might want to ask Thor," Kali said. "I think we're going to fight, but my Norwegian isn't so great."

"Swedish," Odin harrumphed. He barked a question at Thor, who responded with large gestures and animated expressions that made Kali very nervous. She couldn't even speak his language, and she could still tell that he wasn't telling the whole truth.

Luckily, Odin seemed to believe his avatar. He actually looked pleased, although in a sinister, violent way.

"You *are* here to battle!" he said in a delighted voice. "It's about time. I'd better kick everyone and make sure they're awake, then. What about the judges? Shouldn't we summon them?"

"It's going to be a long fight, I presume," Kali said.

"You can call them when it looks like someone is finally winning."

Odin grinned wolfishly. "A long fight—well, we shall see."

Thor winked at Kali and they followed Odin into the dimly lit stone lobby. Kali felt like she was entering a church. She tested her sixth sense and felt Shiva watching her, but she knew he wouldn't manifest now, even to stop her from fighting Thor. He knew he was in too much trouble, and that there was nothing he could say that she would listen to.

"I've requested that we fight outside," Kali said, "and Thor seemed to agree, although he could just as easily have been saying 'Why yes, the sky is blue, how remarkable.' You know, it's hard to tell."

Odin spoke to Thor, and Thor nodded, pointing to a hallway. They argued for a moment, then headed in that direction, both of them still grumbling. Kali guessed that Odin had suggested one of the interior courtyards, but Thor, as they had planned, was leading them to an herb garden that was open to the river on one side.

As they came into the courtyard, Kali strolled ahead to the wall overlooking a hillside that swept down to the river. From here, she could look across and see an untouched wilderness in New Jersey, a block of land bought specifically so it would stay undeveloped and provide a view from the Cloisters. Kali leaned on the wall, looking out, and then, as casually as she could, she glanced down.

You call that hiding? she thought.

Well, there's not a lot of fooooooooliage for us to work with,

Quetzie protested. *Just keep them away from the wall.*

Sure, Kali thought, this time to herself. *No problem.* Tigre lifted his hand in a nervous salute and then ducked as Quetzie tried to back farther into the trees below the wall. It was still hard to miss the shimmer of her feathers and the enormous beak sticking out of the leaves.

Thooooor's right behind you. He says to duck, Quetzie relayed, and Kali spun and dropped to her knees as his hammer whooshed through the air over her head. She launched herself forward from there, tackling his legs and bringing him to the ground with an enormous *oof.*

The Norse gods were starting to line the arches around the courtyard, leaning against the columns and shouting "THOR!" and other, less intelligible things. As Kali rolled away, grabbing a couple of rocks from the ground, she scanned the crowd for Frey.

There he was. The tall blond god shook his hair back from his head and grinned with perfect white teeth as he spotted her looking at him. Kali threw the rocks at Thor, timing their explosions to happen near his face, but not so near that any fragments would hit him. He roared with convincing pain and charged toward her, but she stamped her foot and the bricks below him erupted like miniature volcanoes, sending him hopping and dancing away again.

Thor reached the safety of a flower bed and whirled his hammer over his head, bringing it crashing into the stone wall beside him. A bolt of lightning shot out from the impact, and Kali barely had time to dodge. The gods behind her were not so lucky, and from the shouting, she guessed a couple of them had gotten singed.

Okay, Quetzie, she projected, *tell Tigre that Frey is standing about twelve feet from the overlook wall, inside the garden, on the right if you're looking in from out there. He's sitting on a ledge between two small columns, against a wall. And the pouch is on his belt. You can bring Tigre on up anytime now.*

She set fire to the tangled weeds around Thor's feet but made sure that it was a slow-moving fire, so he'd have time to dart to the next flower bed without getting his boots burned. In response, he tried the hammer and lightning trick again, but this time she knew it was coming and was across the garden by the time it glanced harmlessly off an archway.

Tigre wants to knoooooow how he's supposed to get to Frey without being noooooooticed.

Are you serious? Kali said, ducking another hammer swing and ramming her shoulder into Thor's chest. *That's his whole job. We're doing our part, distracting everyone. All he has to do is grab the stupid pouch and run. OOF.* She tumbled sideways into a small tree as Thor flung her off. *Tell Tigre if he would like to come up here and get smashed into trees and flagstones in my place, be my guest.*

Quetzie didn't respond, and Kali concentrated on hurling more exploding rocks and bricks at Thor. For fun, she made some of them fly past him and shatter in the midst of the gods. She spotted Frey's sister whisking her feathered cloak out of the way of another lightning bolt. Odin stood at the entrance to the garden, his arms folded and his face hidden below the brim of his hat. Occasionally, he lifted his gaze to the sky, as if looking for his ravens. Next to him was the hulking shape of one of his wolves.

Then, finally, Kali spotted the top of Tigre's head rising

over the wall in the corner where a tree mostly obstructed the view. His hands grabbed the stone edge and he hoisted himself up and over, dropping low to the ground.

Kali glanced around, but the eyes of the gods were fixed on her and Thor. She dove for Thor's midsection, and as they stumbled to the ground, she wrapped her arms around his hammer and tried to wrest it from his grasp. Thor bellowed something that sounded genuinely ferocious, and they were soon rolling across the bricks, tugging on the hammer with all their might. Kali could tell that he had more brute physical strength, but she had better leverage, because she was clinging to the gigantic head of the hammer.

Thor is yelling that the hammer is his and youuuuu can't have it, Quetzie relayed.

I kind of gathered that on my own, Kali informed her.

He's noooot pleased. That's his magical hammer.

I'm not really going to take it! Kali said, exasperated. Didn't anyone but her remember the plan? Or that they were on a mission here?

Suddenly, a growl reverberated around the courtyard, so deep and rumbling that the stones vibrated and leaves were shaken from the trees. It sent such a chill down Kali's back that she actually paused for a moment, long enough for Thor to yank the hammer free with an indignant expression.

"INTRUDER!" Odin bellowed. He pointed a long, thin finger straight at Tigre, who was creeping along the wall inches away from Frey. Tigre froze, petrified, and the other gods began shouting at once. Most of it was in languages Kali didn't know, but a few English words stood out.

"INTRUDER!"

"KILL HIM!"

"THROW HIM FROM THE WALL!"

"Oh, for crying out loud," Kali muttered. She scrambled to her feet and sprinted across the courtyard. Frey was still in the act of turning to Tigre, a surprised and amused look on his face, when Kali ran up, seized the blue pouch, and yanked it free from his belt. She shoved Tigre and they ran pell-mell toward the wall.

Quetzie! Kali shouted in her mind. *You better be there!*

As the gods' footsteps pounded behind them, she and Tigre swung onto the top of the wall and then, without pausing, leaped into space.

The wind whooshed past her face and she closed her eyes, wondering if she could survive the fall, if she was as strong as she felt inside, and then her legs connected with something. When Kali opened her eyes, she saw the neoquetzal flailing sideways as she slid along one wing and Tigre struggled to find a handhold on Quetzie's back.

Kali shot out her free hand and grabbed a fistful of feathers, stopping her slide just before the neoquetzal overbalanced and dropped her.

OW, Quetzie objected.

Thank you, Quetzie, Kali thought fervently. *You really saved us.* The neoquetzal unfurled her tail in a pleased spiral and beat her wings to carry them upward.

Clinging to slippery green feathers, precariously balanced, Kali and Tigre glanced backward at the courtyard of the Cloisters, which was growing smaller below them. It looked like a beehive swarming with activity. They could see the sun reflecting off weapons throughout the crowd. Thor stood at the center, gesturing.

Let's hope Thor can convince them, Kali thought, clutching the pouch to her chest. It felt too light and flimsy to be their one great chance. *Let's hope they let him come after the ship alone. I'm not looking forward to fighting off a horde of angry Viking gods.*

But as they rose into the sky, she could see Frey harnessing a large glowing animal into a chariot, and she felt as if she could still sense Odin's freezing gaze on them all the way south.

Gus felt ill. He felt like giant fire sprites were dancing a polka in his intestines. He felt like he needed to be holding a spear, but Diana didn't want to attract the crystal hunters' attention before they needed to. He couldn't understand how she could be eating a granola bar so calmly.

"They're just standing there," he whispered.

"They don't know what we're up to," Diana murmured.

"I'm not sure I do, either," Anna said.

"We're waiting," Diana said. "Something will happen soon."

The three of them were seated on a bench in a waterfront park at the very southern tip of Manhattan. From here, there was a clear view out into the ocean; as Kali had pointed out, they wouldn't have to sail down the river and along Long Island if they left from here. Something about the view—the expanse of water, dented with white-topped waves—gave Gus a weird thrill, like the world was suddenly open to them. He could feel Oro stirring inside him, as if the Polynesian god was pleased by the sight of the sea.

But the ocean wasn't free to them, not yet. All along the shore, arranged at even intervals, were crystal hunters, the kind that looked like human-sized praying mantis hybrids. Their eyes glowed with neon intensity, and they all seemed to be staring at the avatars.

On the plus side, they were ignoring Aleph and Bet. The two boys were running fearlessly along the wall at the edge of the water, behind the crystal hunters. Gus couldn't believe their balance. They looked like they were just playing, but in reality they were "assessing the crystal hunters" and "devising a stratagem," as Bet put it.

"I feel horrible about this," Diana said. "I wish we could have helped Aleph and Bet before asking them to do this for us. It seems so dangerous."

"They'll be fine," Gus said. "And they couldn't do what we need them to if they were human already."

"But we haven't even talked to Shiva yet," Diana said.

"I think Kali's right about that," Anna chimed in. "He might figure out what's going on. Better to leave it to the last minute, when he'll hopefully do anything to try to keep her here."

"But what if he won't do it?"

"Say no to Kali?" Gus said. "Would you? Especially when she's already so furious with him?"

Diana sighed and glanced up again. She was pretty sure there was someone on top of the nearest apartment building, watching them. Her instinct said Shiva, but she wasn't sure why.

Suddenly all the crystal hunters' heads snapped up in perfect unison. Their line extended as far along the waterfront as Gus could see.

"Uh-oh," Diana said. "It's starting."

"What is?" Anna said.

"The gods know something's up," Gus said. "They're activating the crystal hunters." He touched Diana's shoulder and a spark leaped between them. "The protection is still in place, though. Maybe they'll forget to remove it."

"I wouldn't count on that," Diana said.

All along the river, crystal hunters were starting to march. From the north they marched south; from the south, they marched north, closing in on the spot where Diana, Gus, and Anna sat. But still the crystal hunters didn't approach the avatars; they stayed in an orderly formation, lined up along the water.

"What are they doing?" Anna said.

"They're closing ranks," Gus answered. "Concentrating their forces here. They're assuming we're working with Kali and Tigre and intend to leave with them."

Diana looked up at the sky, but there was no sign yet of Quetzie. Suddenly she felt a strange twisting feeling right under the surface of her skin. Was it the protection being removed? Gus rubbed his arms, and she guessed he was feeling it, too.

"Okay," she said. "Time for our part." She stood up and casually tossed her granola bar wrapper into the nearest garbage can. All the crystal hunters, now standing shoulder-to-shoulder, seemed to tense, a ripple of energy flowing down the line.

Behind them, Aleph and Bet paused in their game, still balanced on the wall. They'd seen Diana's signal; Gus hoped they'd really be able to do what they'd described. He stood up and took Diana's hand, which tightened around his. Her hand was warm, and he realized with a jolt of both fear and happiness that there was no electric shock. At last they could touch each other again—but the crystal hunters would be able to hurt them now.

Aleph and Bet raised their hands, now glowing with the silver light. An eerie cry came from the north end of the line, as if they'd been spotted, but before the hunters could move, Aleph and Bet plunged their hands into the necks of the nearest creatures.

Those four crystal hunters shrieked angrily as the silver light shot through their bodies, colliding with the purple veins of electricity. As the light got brighter, Gus could see the openings at the backs of their necks where the boys had plugged in their hands. And then the purple glow started to fade, and the silver raced through, obliterating the last of it. As it reached the hunters' shoulders, it jumped to the next hunter and did the same thing there, and then the next, and then the next. Like a flame tearing through a row of paper dolls, the silver glow spread down the line faster and faster in each direction, disappearing off into the distance.

And then the four in the center dropped to their knees and collapsed facedown on the pavement. And then the ones on either side fell, and then the next.

Diana ran forward and caught Aleph, who was starting to sway dangerously. He closed his eyes and toppled off

the wall, knocking Diana down among the wreckage of
the hunters.

Bet jumped down next to them, his face twisted in
dismay.

"Is he all right?" Bet said. "I told him to moderate his
output! Mine is automatically regulated—I can't release
energy faster than it's coming in from the sun. But Aleph
has to keep track of it himself, and he can be so impul-
sive. Aleph!" Bet shook his brother's wrist. "Aleph, reboot!
The sun is right up there; just recharge. I know you can.
Concentrate! Aleph!"

"Here," Gus said, folding his jacket and sliding it over
so Diana could rest Aleph's head on it instead of on the
ground. The smaller boy was limp and still. With his
synthetic-feeling skin, he seemed suddenly like a large
doll, nothing more.

"Hang on, Aleph," Diana said. "Help is coming. We're
going to make you human now, so stay with us."

"If we can," Anna added. Seeing Diana's expression,
she said, "Sorry—misguided honesty. Ereka moment."
She smiled apologetically.

"Shiva!" Gus yelled. "Shiva, I know you're watching us!"

There was a loud *pop* and all at once the three-eyed
Indian god was standing next to him.

"Only because watching Kali was making me nervous," Shiva said. "And there's no need to shout."

"Is Kali coming?" Diana asked anxiously.

"She'll be here in two and a half minutes," Shiva said,
"if she doesn't fall off that ridiculous bird first. You're all
making a very foolish mistake, by the way."

"Of course you think so," Gus said. "But it's not your freedom and your choices and your family that's being held hostage."

"Kali is my family," Shiva said. "But I won't try to stop her. She's already so angry with me."

"There is something you can do," Diana said. "It won't make her forgive you, but she'd appreciate it—we'd all appreciate it."

Shiva looked down at Bet, who was crouched beside Aleph, holding his brother's wrists.

"This isn't really what my powers are for," he said with a frown.

"So what?" Gus said. "Fighting Norse and Egyptian and Greek gods isn't what Kali's powers were supposed to be for, either."

Shiva sighed. "All right. If it will help her love me again." He rubbed his forehead, touching the area around his third eye, and then knelt, placing one hand on Bet's head and the other on Aleph's chest.

"I am the life force," he murmured. "I destroy, but I also create."

Gus blinked. He could see two more ghostly arms extending from Shiva's torso: one holding a drum, the other a curl of fire. The fire swirled up and up and around and soon encircled Shiva in a dim orange light. The circle of flames passed through Aleph and Bet, but neither of them seemed to feel it. Bet's eyes stared into Shiva's, his expression blank.

A huge flutter of wings sounded above them. Gus looked up in time to see Quetzie hurtle past, coming to an ungraceful landing in the water with an enormous splash.

Kali surfaced first, floundering in the water and letting off a volley of curses before Tigre's head bobbed up.

"Quetzie!" Tigre protested. "The water's f-f-freezing!" He started swimming for the rocks below the wall.

"And I can't—" Kali's next few expletives were muffled by a wave crashing over her head. "—AMMIT!" she was shouting as she came up again for air.

"I think she's saying she can't swim," Diana said, standing and taking a step toward the wall.

"I can swim," Gus said. "I'm a good swimmer. I'll go." He was already kicking off his shoes. Farther along the waterfront he'd seen some stairs that led down to the ocean.

"Quetzie, help Kali!" Diana called. "Tigre!"

I'm trying, the neoquetzal answered, *but she's very slippery.* Quetzie thrust her wing at Kali, but that wound up creating another wave, which sent the Indian avatar under again. Absorbed in swimming for shore, Tigre hadn't noticed Kali struggling.

Gus made it down to the rocks just as Tigre pulled himself onto them, shivering. The rocks were jagged and slimy underfoot, buttressing the wall at a steep incline. Gus realized that they were lucky the waves were small here; if they were more forceful, Tigre would probably have been battered against the rough edges.

Kali had finally managed to grab a handful of Quetzie's feathers, and the neoquetzal was trying to tow her to the wall. It looked to Gus like they'd have better luck if Kali could use both her hands, but she seemed to be clutching something in one.

"Is that the ship?" Gus asked Tigre. *"Skid-bad-whatsit?"*

Tigre nodded. His teeth were chattering too hard for

him to speak, but he started back toward the water to help Kali.

"I got it," Gus said. "Stay here."

He lowered himself into the water, letting out a gasp. It was really cold, and a lot murkier than the ocean he and Andrew had often swum in. Trying not to think about what was down there, Gus shoved himself off and swam over to Kali with strong, even strokes.

"I h-h-hate water," Kali sputtered. "St-st-stupid swimming. St-stupid BIRD."

Hey, Quetzie said. *If I'd tried to land on land, I would proooooobably have whapped you into a tree up there. Is that what youuuuu wanted?*

"I can take the pouch," Gus said. "That might help."

Kali shook her head. He wondered if she didn't trust him. He certainly hadn't trusted her—he still wasn't completely sure what to think of her. Wary distance seemed fair for both of them.

So he helped support her against Quetzie until they were close to the rocks, and then he towed her over to one that was flat enough for her to lie on.

"I can't believe you don't know how to swim," he said as she gasped for breath. "You seem so tough."

She glared at him. "I *am* tough. But I live in New York. No sane, normal person ever needs to go swimming here."

"Hey, guys," Diana called from above. Her voice was so full of excitement that Gus could guess what had happened. "Shiva did it! It worked!"

Aleph and Bet appeared on either side of her, leaning over and waving with enormous grins. They didn't look any different to Gus, but Diana tousled Aleph's hair and the kid waggled his hands—no silver glow.

Shiva poked his head over on the other side of Bet. "Kali?"

"I'm not speaking to you!" she yelled.

"As long as you're okay," he said. "Which you seem to be."

Kali snorted and sat up, wringing out her hair, which had come loose from its usual ponytail and hung in a dark wet curtain down her back. Gus saw a small smile cross Shiva's face, like he knew he was at least on the path back to forgiveness.

"Is Anna up there?" Tigre called.

"Right here," she called back. "I'm glad you're all right." Tigre grinned, despite the shivers still wracking his body.

A roll of thunder shook the sky, and Kali shot Tigre a suspicious look.

"Not me," he said with a shrug.

"Sounds like Thor," Gus said, standing and shading his eyes. Sure enough, the thunder god's goat-drawn chariot was rumbling down from the clouds. As it came closer, Gus saw that Thor had stopped to pick up Miracle. He wondered if Kali had told Thor to do that.

Kali untied the strings of the ice blue pouch and pulled out a tiny folded square about the size of a Post-it note.

"That's it?" Gus said. "That's what's going to get us all out of here?"

"Are you an expert dwarf engineer?" Kali said in a perfect imitation of the judges. "Then don't question the mastery of the expert dwarf engineers." She started unfolding it, peeling each layer back carefully but quickly. As it got to be the size of a large cat, Kali leaned forward and rested it on the water, still opening up the sides. Gus stood back as it got larger . . . and larger . . . and larger. . . .

Suddenly, when it was about as big as a car, the folds started flipping out on their own. Kali let go and stood back.

Thor says it'll do the rest on its ooooooown, Quetzie informed them. *Once it is tall enough, it will drop a ramp to the land so you can enter the ship. And then, at the very end, the sails will unfuuuuurl, and it will take off for its destination, so everyone must be ooooooon board by then.*

"Thanks," Kali said. "Come on, we have to get back up to the top of the wall."

She scrambled away across the rocks, muttering angrily as the sharp edges caught at her pants and grazed her knees. Gus and Tigre followed. Gus kept looking back to watch the ship unfolding; it was the strangest, most mar-velous thing he'd ever seen.

"Are we taking Aleph and Bet and Miracle with us?" Gus asked as they all reached the level pavement of the park. Anna was waiting at the top of the stairs, and she threw her arms around Tigre in a giant hug.

"Why not?" Kali said. "The ship is big enough to hold a whole Norse pantheon. I think it can fit three extra kids. Speak of the devil," she said as Miracle ran up to them. Thor was getting out of his chariot behind her. Kali scooped the smaller girl up and whirled her around. Kali seemed a lot more cheerful now that she wasn't drowning, Gus thought. In fact, she seemed downright happy, like their plan had really succeeded. He wasn't going to relax until they were on that boat, though.

"We're going for a trip," Kali said to Miracle. "Come see." She tugged the girl over to the wall and pointed at *Skidbladnir*, still unfolding in the water below. "It's turning into a ship that'll take us far far away from here."

"But I can't go with you," Miracle said. "I have to stay and take care of my people."

"The subway dwellers?" Kali said. "I'm sure they'll be okay."

Miracle shook her head. "Thank you, Kali, but without General Pepper, they need me even more. I've helped you, and that's the important thing. Maybe I've fulfilled my destiny." She smiled.

"How do you know we won't need you again?" Kali said, resting her hand on Miracle's smooth, pale head.

"Well, come back if you do," Miracle said cheekily. "But I know that the people here need me more."

"Aleph, Bet, this is Miracle," Diana said, coming up with the two boys. Now that he was closer, Gus could see small differences: more animation in their faces and eyes, a fluidity to their movements that he hadn't realized was missing before. "And these are my other friends—Kali, Tigre, Thor." Thor grinned at the sound of his name.

"We almost met," Kali said, nodding at the boys. Aleph looked bashful.

"Aleph and Bet want to stay, too," Diana said. "They want to stay at the museum."

"Now that we're real, we want to try to make our own art," Bet said.

"And then hang it in the museum!" Aleph said. "So we'll be just like Monet and Rodin and Hokusai!"

Kali's brow furrowed. "But . . . I'm not sure it's safe here."

"Sure it is," Bet said. "We wiped out a lot of crystal hunters today."

"And you scared off the flying ones," Miracle said.

"What if they come back after we're gone?" Kali asked.

"Don't worry," Miracle said. "I've survived this long. We can take care of ourselves."

Gus wondered if that was true. Miracle had been outside the subways for only a couple of days; what did she really know about surviving in the world? And he could guess what Kali was most worried about: If the gods were angry at the avatars' escape, what would stop them from taking their revenge on these three kids?

Kali gazed at the ship, which was now tall enough to be seen over the wall. A railing started to fold up into place along its side, and then, at the front, a ramp levered out from the deck and started unfolding toward them. Masts were already starting to sprout like trees in a fast-forwarded nature documentary.

With a sigh, Kali shoved her hair back from her face.

"I'll stay here," she said.

"What?" Diana and Tigre said at the same time.

"I'll stay with the kids," Kali said. "Someone should be here to protect them. You guys get on the ship and go."

"No way," Tigre said. "You're our— We don't— You're the one with all the ideas! We don't even know where we're going."

"Where *are* we going?" Anna asked.

Kali grinned. "Well, they can't stop us now, so okay. Africa."

"Africa?" Anna said. "Seriously?" She looked less than thrilled, but Gus was having trouble following the logic, too.

"Think, people. Remember what the gods said—they made an agreement with the African gods to leave each other alone. Africa's off in its own world, pretty much, and these gods can't get to it, or they'd be breaking the agreement. So they can't follow us there, they can't watch us there, and we'll be able to figure out our next step without being spied on." She paused, twisting a cord of wet hair. "I mean, you will."

"That's what I'm talking about," Tigre said. "How are we supposed to do that without you?"

"Hey, you're smart," Anna said, squeezing his hand. "And you'll still have me."

"I know," Tigre said. "But Kali—I mean—"

Anna looked hurt, and Gus figured he should jump in.

"On the other hand, she would be able to protect the kids better than any of us," he pointed out. "She's strong enough to do that, which—no offense—at least Tigre's not, Anna's not, and I'm not. Diana maybe, but—"

"It doesn't matter," said a deep, rumbling voice. "None of you is going anywhere."

"Oh crap," Kali muttered.

Gods began to appear along the pavement, many of them stepping over the crystal hunters with disgusted looks. It reminded Gus of the scene in Central Park just a few days ago, when they had all appeared in the first place. But now he knew Diana wouldn't go anywhere with them. He wouldn't be separated from her again. As if reading his mind, Diana reached out and took his hand, and he felt warmth spread through him.

It seemed like there were fewer gods this time, though. None of the Egyptian gods bothered to make an appearance, except for Maat, who was standing with the other judges and looking grumpy. Next to her was Ganesh, but apart from him, Gus didn't see any gods that looked Indian, except for Shiva, who was already standing on the outskirts, just watching. There were a few new gods who looked like Anna, though. Apparently the Sumerians weren't hiding anymore.

Tigre's gods were represented by Tlaloc, whose eyes were bulging even more than usual.

"WHAT IS THIS FOOLISHNESS?" the Aztec storm god bellowed. "PUNY AVATAR, I SEE NO PATH TO VICTORY THIS WAY!"

"For any of you," Zeus said coldly. "You get on that ship, and we can't promise what will happen next."

"Sounds great," Tigre said. "Maybe we'll get to make our own decisions, then."

There was a clunking sound behind them. Gus glanced over his shoulder and saw the end of the ship's ramp landing on top of the wall.

"We'd love to stay and chat," said Kali, "since last time was so fascinating, but my friends have to board now, or the ship will leave without them."

"That's *my* ship!" Frey shouted, rolling up in a giant chariot. The creature pulling it—the one Kali had seen from the air—was an enormous boar with glowing golden bristles all down its back. "I demand that you return it immediately!"

"Or what?" Gus said. "You'll kill us? That sounds like cheating to me. Sounds like it would disqualify your avatar."

Frey's face turned bright red. He didn't look quite so handsome this way. "Thor!" he yelled, and then said something in Swedish.

He's oooooordering Thor to retrieve Skidbladnir *for him,* Quetzie announced.

Thanks, Quetzie, Gus projected.

Thor began shouting back.

Thor doesn't like the fact that they lied to him, Quetzie translated. *They never toooold him that you were all moooortal now. He thought if he defeated you, you'd all go back to being gods, and the world would return to the way it was.*

"Yeah, maybe lying to your avatar isn't such a good idea," Gus heard Kali mutter.

Thooooor is saying something to me, toooooo, Quetzie said. *He says he wants to stay with Miracle and the other two. He says Miracle is like his little sister from his mortal life. And that Kali should get on the ship instead. That he'll stay and hoooooooold off the other gods while you run on board.*

Kali looked sharply at Thor, but the Norse avatar didn't look back at her. He was still engaged in a shouting match with Frey.

Kali oooooobjects. She says it isn't safe for Thor, either. He says at least Frey definitely won't kill him. She says she's stronger than he is and can prooooootect them better. He's laughing at her, and I think that's pretty funny myself.

Kali scowled.

Kali says she doooooesn't need any comments from the

peanut gallery. Is that me? Am I the peanut gallery? Does that mean I get peanuts?

"Are you okay?" Gus heard Tigre say. He turned and realized that Tigre was talking to Anna, who had dropped his hand.

"I don't want to go to Africa," Anna said in a strained voice. "I think we should all stay here. Tigre, if you cared about me, you'd agree."

Gus pretended he wasn't listening, feeling awkward about eavesdropping. At his side, he felt Diana tense, and knew she was hearing the conversation, too.

"But why?" Tigre asked. "I mean, of course I care, but we already decided—Anna, what's wrong?"

"*You* decided," she snapped. "Or rather, Kali did, and you followed her, like you always follow people."

"Hey," Tigre said.

"Because she's powerful, because she's strong, because she's decisive and for some idiot reason you trust her."

"Anna, you're beginning to sound like Ereka," Tigre protested.

Anna laughed. "You mean my sister?" she said. "My decoy? My partner?"

The realization hit Gus seconds too late. He spun toward Diana, trying to pull her away, but he'd barely moved when Anna plunged the knife into her stomach.

Surprise. That was all he could see on Diana's face. Her eyes were wide, green, like a much wilder ocean than this one. She didn't look scared. She didn't look like she felt the pain of a blade slicing through her skin. She just looked surprised, as if her coffee had turned out to be lemonade instead.

There was a lot of shouting going on. Diana's hands were on Gus's shoulders. She was sliding slowly to the ground.

"Judges!" Anna shouted. "Witness this battle! I have defeated this avatar fair and square and I demand the powers of *both* goddesses inside her!"

Gus put his arms under Diana's elbows and tried to hold her upright. He thought he was talking, but he couldn't tell what he was saying. He kept hearing "all right, all right," but he knew that nothing was all right or could be all right as long as there was so much blood spilling out of Diana.

"Anna," he heard Tigre say, and all his confusion, his disbelief, his grief was in that one word.

"My name is Inanna," Anna said. "If you'd done even a tenth as much research on me as you did on your precious Kali, you'd know that I'm not just a goddess of love. I'm a goddess of war, too, Tigre. I am blazingly powerful. My city was the greatest place on earth, and I defeated everyone I battled. I was the goddess of love long before this poor imitation came along. And now I demand her powers."

"Not until she's fully dead," said another voice—Athena's. It was sad, firm, resigned.

"She's not," Gus whispered. "She's not dead."

"Then step aside, you cow-eyed mistake," Anna snapped, "and let me finish this. Or I'll kill you both together."

Gus slid his hands up Diana's arms to pull her closer. That last option sounded fine to him.

But suddenly, Diana's body was yanked from his arms. He stumbled forward, reaching for her, and saw that it was

Kali, not Anna, who had pulled Diana away and was now lifting her into her arms. Everything suddenly sped up.

Anna shoved Gus aside, but before she could get to Kali and Diana, Thor stepped in her way.

"Gus!" Kali said. "Tigre! Snap out of it! Let's go!" She was already moving, climbing onto the ship's ramp as fast as she could, weighed down by Diana. Gus followed without thinking, leaping onto the wooden boards. He could feel the vibrations of Tigre behind him, and he wondered how they could get away without being chased by Anna or the gods. But when he turned to look down, he saw the massive back of Thor standing at the bottom of the ramp, arms folded menacingly.

"NO!" Anna screamed, pounding on Thor's chest. "She's mine! She's my kill! Kali, don't you dare steal her and her powers from me!"

Gus jumped down onto the deck of the ship. Above him, sails were whooshing into place all along the masts. Tigre landed next to him, and they both turned to push the ramp off the edge of the ship. It wobbled, then fell, crashing onto the rocks below. The last sail billowed into place, and *Skidbladnir* eased away from the shore, picking up speed as it caught the wind.

Kali put Diana's limp body down in the first room she came to. It was palatial, with an enormous wooden bed already outfitted with crisp white sheets. The nice thing about magical ships, according to Thor, was that they came fully furnished and stocked with food and water. If nothing else, at least they'd have plenty to eat for the next couple of days.

"Too bad, Frey," Kali muttered as she saw Diana's blood spread across the pale linens. The former pop star was nearly as white as the sheets. Kali tore off a pillowcase and pressed it to the wound.

Gus stumbled in the door behind her. "Oh my God," he said as he saw Diana. "We have to call Apollo. We have to—"

"He can't get here," Kali said. "No one else can get on this ship while it's moving. That's part of its power; that's why we'll be able to make it to Africa."

"Then why did you bring her here?" Gus cried. "Apollo could have saved her."

"Not before Anna killed her," Kali said, shaking her head. "Where's Tigre?"

"Up on deck," Gus said, kneeling beside Diana's bed and replacing Kali's hands on the bloodstained pillowcase with his own.

Kali found Tigre slumped against the railing, his arms wrapped around his knees.

"I trusted her," Tigre said as Kali came up to him. "I thought she—I thought she at least liked me."

"Maybe she did," Kali said, "but this is war."

"Why would she do this now?" Tigre asked. "We were about to escape. She could have come with us, stayed on our side."

"She was on her own side," Kali said. "She knew that once we got to Africa, none of the judges would be able to witness any battles. It was her last chance to kill Diana and still get her powers. She must have felt especially threatened by her."

Cheer up, Tigre, came Quetzie's voice from above. *You*

still have me! The most beauuuuuuutiful friend ever!

Kali looked up at the neoquetzal. Quetzie's ruby red underbelly gleamed in the sunshine, and her long tail streamed out behind her like an elegant kite. Back toward New York, the sun was dipping lower in the sky. Kali couldn't believe she'd woken up this morning intending to kill Diana herself. Victory had been within her grasp, and now instead she was on a magical Viking ship en route to Africa, along with the two lamest avatars, plus one with her life force bleeding slowly out of her.

Thor said good-bye, Quetzie said. *He said if you find a way hoooome, come get him. He misses his family, toooooo.*

And Miracle had a message for you, Kali. She said youuuu wanted to know what "Dad" looooooooooked like. She says whenever he appeared in her visions, he was either a dark-haired man or a large dog.

A large dog? Kali thought.

That's what she toooooooooooooooooold me.

Kali frowned at the western horizon. Something more urgent was happening.

"Tigre," she said. "I think you need to calm down."

"I am calm," he said. "I mean, I'm not freaking out. I guess I should be, but I just . . . I can't believe this is happening. It's too— Why?"

She pointed toward the setting sun. Tigre pulled himself up and looked.

Dark storm clouds were massing, piling higher and higher, starting to block out the sun. Lightning flashed in the depths of the storm, and even from this distance they could hear the rumble of thunder.

"Uh-oh," Tigre said. "That's not me. I swear."

Kali leaned over the railing. The sea below them was turning a murky, ominous brownish green, and the waves were smashing into the planks with greater and greater force.

"Could be Poseidon," she said. "Or Tlaloc, or whichever Mesopotamian weather god Anna is working with. Or all of them together."

"Anna," Tigre said quietly. "How could she do this to us?"

"Okay, Tigre," Kali said, grabbing his elbow. "Time to snap out of it. You said you worked in a doctor's office in Santiago, right?"

"No!" Tigre resisted as she dragged him belowdecks. "No, he was a veterinarian! I don't know anything!"

"You know more than we do," Kali said, throwing him into the room where Gus and Diana were. Gus had tossed aside the first blood-soaked pillowcase and was using a second to apply pressure. "Do what you can."

"I'll help," Gus said.

"No, I will," Kali said. "You're going to go keep this boat afloat."

"Me?" Gus said. "Why would I—"

"You're a Polynesian god, aren't you?" she said. "They're all seafaring people. Try to contact the god in your head, see if he has any useful advice."

Darkness fell suddenly. The three of them lost their balance as the ship tipped dangerously to one side. Diana moaned softly, then dropped deeper into unconsciousness.

"Move!" Kali snapped. Watching Gus dart out the door, Kali took a deep breath.

It was going to be a rough journey.

So off they go, full of hope and fear and confusion and human frailty.

Off they go to Africa, where their gods can't follow.

But I can.

See you there.

... to be continued in Book Three:
KINGDOM OF TWILIGHT